THE GIRL WHO SLEPT WITH GOD

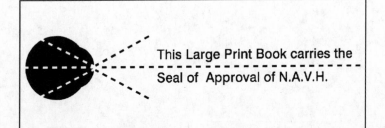

This Large Print Book carries the
Seal of Approval of N.A.V.H.

THE GIRL WHO SLEPT WITH GOD

VAL BRELINSKI

THORNDIKE PRESS
A part of Gale, Cengage Learning

GALE
CENGAGE Learning·

Farmington Hills, Mich • San Francisco • New York • Waterville, Maine
Meriden, Conn • Mason, Ohio • Chicago

GALE
CENGAGE Learning®

Copyright © 2015 by Valerie Brelinski.
Thorndike Press, a part of Gale, Cengage Learning.

Thorndike Press® Large Print Core.
The text of this Large Print edition is unabridged.
Other aspects of the book may vary from the original edition.
Set in 16 pt. Plantin.

LIBRARY OF CONGRESS CATALOGING-IN-PUBLICATION DATA

Brelinski, Val.
  The girl who slept with God / by Val Brelinski.
    pages cm. — (Thorndike Press large print core)
    ISBN 978-1-4104-8497-0 (hardcover) — ISBN 1-4104-8497-1 (hardcover)
    1. Sisters—Fiction. 2. Pregnant teenagers—Fiction. 3. Evangelicalism—Fiction. 4. Idaho—Fiction. 5. Domestic fiction. 6. Large type books. I. Title.
PS3602.R447G57 2015
813'.6—dc23   2015029718

Published in 2015 by arrangement with Viking, an imprint of Penguin Publishing Group, a division of Penguin Random House LLC

Printed in Mexico
1 2 3 4 5 6 7 19 18 17 16 15

To my mother and father

To fall in love is to create a religion that has a fallible God.

Jorge Luis Borges

On the last day of August in 1970, and a month shy of her fourteenth birthday, Jory's father drove his two daughters out to an abandoned house and left them there.

The trip had not taken long. Her father piloted the car with resolute determination toward the very edge of town. He drove past the railroad tracks and the fish hatchery and the rodeo grounds, past the sugar beet factory and the slaughterhouse and the meat-packing plant; all the while Jory stared out the window in a silent fury. Next to her in the Buick's backseat, Grace was practically unconscious. She lay slumped over with her head resting accidentally on Jory's shoulder, her drool dampening the upper portion of Jory's T-shirt. Jory gave her sister a shove and then turned toward the window. Black Cat Lane and Chicken Dinner Road and Floating Feather rolled past — long, twisty lanes sided with fields of sugar beets and alfalfa and corn. Jory watched a lone mallard drop and skid like a bomber onto an irrigation ditch while three goats perched king of the hill–style on a salvaged roof a farmer had put out for them. Her father continued on past several vast silagey-smelling feedlots, and then the fields grew even larger and the scenery more sparse and the houses less frequent, and finally he turned down a narrow unpaved lane that Jory had never seen before. Then he stopped the car and opened the door. Jory refused to look up at the strange house where she and her sister were now to live. She sat in the backseat with her hands between her knees until her father pulled her forcibly out of the car and set her on her feet in the dirt.

The house of their exile was ancient and dilapidated, its white siding weather warped, its roof's shingles curling and covered with moss. And below the sharp peak of the house's second story, an enormous diamond-shaped window stared out from its gable like the jack of diamond's lonely eye. But it wasn't the condition of the house that mattered, Jory knew, as much as its location. The house was safely hidden away on a back acre of Idaho farmland, far from any schools or churches or stores or neighborhoods. And it was this isolation for which Jory's father had paid. Privacy was of the utmost importance now, he had said. Or perhaps more correctly, the word he was looking for was *secrecy.*

Her father unwedged the few taped-together boxes from the Buick's trunk. One at a time, he carried them up the house's peeling green steps and deposited them onto the living room floor. Jory stood holding the screen door open and taking occasional, unwilling peeks at the dim interior of the house. A brown couch sagged dead-cat-like against one wall. The portion of the floor she could see from the doorway was made of sloping hardwood, and was partly covered by a gray flowered rug that must have been bride-beautiful at some point a very long time ago. Jory heard the car door slam. After a second, her sister came wandering up the porch steps. Grace leaned against the door frame for a moment and then wobbled toward the couch, where she proceeded to lie down on her side, her face buried against one of the sofa's armrests.

"I think that about does it." Her father wiped his hands down the front of his khaki pants. "Yup," he said, gazing about the room. "There you are."

Jory gave him a hard, bright look. "Here we are."

He searched for something in his pockets. He whistled "Red River Valley" and patted down his shirtfront, and then his pants pockets. "Ah!" He held up a small silver key. "You'll be needing this." He smiled and handed it to her.

Without looking at the key, Jory tossed it onto the top of one of the unopened boxes.

"Hey, now," her father said in his calmest voice. "You don't want to lose that." After walking over to the cardboard box and retrieving the key, he handed it to her once more, this time pressing it into her palm and closing her fingers firmly around it.

"Don't you have another one?" She inspected his face.

"Well, Mom and I will keep an extra, of course." He shrugged. "Just in case."

"Just in case?"

"Yes, and don't forget, there's milk and things that need to go in the fridge. Also, the front door may stick a little when you first try to open it, so you'll have to shove hard and jiggle the handle up and down." He demonstrated and then paused, waiting for a look of recognition that Jory refused to give. "Okay, well, I'll be back to check on you in a day or two. I think Grace's correspondence course books should be here by then, so I'll bring them along." He studied the ceiling the way he always did when he needed hope or inspiration. "You might want to get Grace into bed. The doctor gave her a little something to calm her down. A shot or a pill or something."

"I noticed."

"You know," he said, ignoring her tone and marching on, "you've got just about everything here." He cast a proprietary glance around the room. "I think you girls are all set. Really. I think that about does it."

She stood and stared at him. His smile seemed sewn in place.

"Dad."

He stepped toward her and then pulled her head tight against his chest. For a moment she listened to his huge heart's muffled thumping. Then she could feel him sigh. He stepped back and put his hands on either side of her face. Bending down, he pressed his lips against a spot in the middle of her forehead. "JoryAnne," he whispered, and then touched the spot firmly with the tip of his finger, as if sealing the kiss into place.

She had a sudden impulse to slap him.

Jory sat on one of the boxes with her back to the door, and as her father pulled the Buick out onto the roadway she could smell the dust that drifted up in the wake of his leaving. For a moment she remained like this, and then with a start she jumped up and scrambled toward the house's stairway, leaping up the steps to the second-floor landing and its diamond-shaped window. Breathless, she hung on to the window's angled frame and peered out. The glass was slightly wavy and thick, but she could see everything below: the sway of a giant willow, the branches of a plum tree set to shaking by old men crows already drunk on its rotting fruit, the steady trajectory of her father's green Buick disappearing down the graveled country road. She watched, unmoving, until the last of the car's comet tail of dust evaporated into the late afternoon air. Then she sank down onto her knees on the hardwood floor. This high perch made her feel removed and above, as far away as banished maidens locked in smoothed-stone towers. Forever gazing down, they waited for nothing, for knights who were already dead and wouldn't be coming.

That first night she refused to sleep in either of the two iron-framed beds. She didn't unpack any of the boxes either. As it grew dark, she covered Grace with a red plaid blanket and then moved out onto the back porch and sat on its wooden floor with a wedding quilt she'd found on one of the beds wrapped around her. *I John 4:7 — Beloved, let us love one another,* the quilt admonished in embroidered script, courtesy of Laveeta Lamar Hicks. *John 15:13 — Greater love hath no man,* proclaimed Eleanor Genevieve Doerksen. *Let love be your greatest aim . . . For God so loved the world . . . Love never fails.*

"Fuck you. And you. And you." Jory twisted the quilt around to its other side. Here there were no Bible sayings, only endless twining circles — wedding rings stitched carefully in pink and gold thread. She ran her hand over the puckered material. How many days and nights did it take to sew something like this? And did each woman do her own portion separately, or did they gather over a long sewing table in someone's living room and talk as they worked? And why did they do it anyway? Look where it

15

had ended up. They were all dead, the quilt-makers and the bride, and their painstakingly stitched words meant nothing . . . nothing.

She pulled the quilt tighter around her shoulders. Something about the way she was sitting, hunched and small, reminded her of how once when she was little, to spite her mother, she had hidden beneath a table in the back corner of the public library. She had watched from behind the table's great carved wooden leg as her mother stood in line, checked out her books, and then calmly set off for the drugstore with Jory's two sisters in tow. Jory had come out from her hiding place then, smacking her head hard on the table edge in her hurry, just in time to see the three of them walking past the glass doors of the library and on down the sidewalk, her little sister occasionally stooping to scratch at something on her knee.

Jory was quite sure that she had forgotten that incident completely. She glared up at the sky and the points of the stars blurred together. She cried then, a few big, splintered sobs, and pounded at the porch's floorboards with her bare heels over and over until finally, wondrously, it hurt enough to stop. She rocked back and forth hugging her knees, holding her bruised feet carefully off the floor while her chest seized, her lungs catching at frayed threads of air. She wiped her nose on a corner of the quilt, and then held still listening. The night air hummed with the same happy insects. A farm or two away a dog barked, and then barked again. She was still here. Nothing had changed. What had she expected? She tipped slowly over onto her side, clutching the quilt, and let her face slide against the cool of the painted wood porch. *God is love,* she thought. *For God so loved the world.*

The sunlight slanted through the screen of the porch, warming her face and bringing the gradual knowledge that she was somewhere strange and that her neck was now very sore. She sat up slowly. Several parts of her body ached from a night on the wood floor. Her feet in particular, and the backs of her heels. She stepped over the heap of quilt and marched into the house, letting the screen door whap shut behind her. Inside the doorway, though, she stopped and stood.

In the morning light, the kitchen looked as if someone had cut its angles out with left-handed scissors, and it smelled like cat food and old bleach, or damp, many-eyed potatoes. Jory walked slowly from the wide double sink to the prehistoric gas stove, and then to the linoleum-topped kitchen table. She was supposed to live here in this place, in this peculiar old house that smelled like someone else's cast-off life. She could feel herself breathing in an irregular way, as if she had to concentrate in order to make her lungs expand and relax.

She walked into the living room. Grace was lying on the dead cat couch still wearing her tennis shoes and snoring softly beneath the plaid blanket. The unopened boxes squatted in a circle around them. One of the boxes had a large paper sack on top that was leaking something pink and white. A large blossom-colored pool had formed around the bag and was now dripping down the side of the box. Cherry vanilla. He'd always bought it for her when she was sick or sad. Once, when Jory had to have stitches, he brought the whole carton into her bedroom wrapped in a dishtowel and fed her one spoonful after another while he explained how scar tissue formed. How even the stars healed themselves. He had been wearing a tie with small green ducks on it.

Jory found one of her tennis shoes under the couch and the other near the front door. She crammed them onto her feet without untying the laces. After one glance back at her sister, she fled out the door and down the painted steps, the backs of her bruised heels burning like fire.

The road that led away from the house was lined with cottonwood trees, and little bits of the fluff blew all around her and clung to her hair as she strode fast and faster past weedy patches and fields of corn and late summer wheat. She passed a barn that had faded to an unidentifiable color. A large spotted dog lay panting in a strip of shade beneath the barn's overhang. The dog inspected her; it raised its wedge-shaped head and blinked slowly, but did not get up. Jory kept walking. Once, she turned around to look behind her, and still, even at this distance, she could see the house's diamond-shaped window winking at her in the late morning sun.

She hadn't noticed the heat. The blood now hummed in her head as she marched along, kicking up spits of loose gravel. The flat string of road ran on ahead for as far as she could see, shimmering and wavering a little at its farthest point. Jory made a half-strangled noise deep in her throat and sat down hard next to the edge of the road. A drain ditch bristling with cattails rushed foamily past her feet.

The wind began to blow in short, dry little gusts that she could feel in the sweaty sections of her hair. A large crow sailed past and then landed clumsily on the thick stalk of a cattail. The bird maneuvered briefly, attempting to vary its grip in hopes of a stronger foothold, but quickly gave up and flapped on. Jory stood and peered toward the road. A rounded truck the color of curdled milk was coming toward her. She stared as it passed her, and then suddenly with a bump and a sigh it pulled off onto the road's steep shoulder and came to a stop. She could hear a crow squawking insistently somewhere overhead. The truck reversed gears and backed up slowly to the spot where she was standing. AL'S FROZEN ICE CREAM TREATS, the truck's passenger side read. TASTY AND DELICIOUS! The man inside was already leaning across the seat to open the door. "Miss your bus?" he said, smiling. The truck's front seat was high above her and she had to grab at the crease-hardened hand he offered down. With a powerful pull he hoisted her firmly up onto the cab's slick vinyl seat.

"Well, hello there," he said. He raked his blue-tattooed fingers through his ponytailed

hair and made no move toward going anywhere.

Jory stared out through the windshield at
the road she had just come down, and then
behind her at the tiny diamond-windowed
house nearly hidden in the trees. She could
feel the back of her throat suddenly swelling
hot and tight with tears. "Where have you
been?" she whispered. "Where *were* you?"

"Well," he said, "in between selling delicious ice cream treats, I've been busy scour-
ing the landscape for *you.*" He rested his
elbow on the seatback and with one finger
pushed a stray strand of her hair behind her
ear. For a second, neither of them moved.
Then he reached out and pulled all of her
past the gearshift and onto his lap. She sat
sideways across his hard legs and leaned her
head against his shirt, breathing in his smell.
It was the same as always — engine grease
and cigarette smoke and something unidentifiable that she always thought of as burned
sugar. She closed her eyes. Through his
chest she could hear him humming a song
she didn't know. He held her carefully with
one arm and she could feel his muscles
tense as he put the truck into gear and then
steered them back out onto the road. He
flicked the switch on the loudspeaker and
as the truck jounced along music played

21

above her like a carnival tune from a faraway fair, a tinkling gypsy music as strange as a blue tattoo. It followed them like a long holiday all the way down the road to wherever it was they were going.

■ ■ ■ ■

PART ONE:
THE HOUSE ON
NINTH AVENUE

■ ■ ■ ■

CHAPTER ONE

It was like this.

There was to be no mixed bathing, no circuses or bowling alleys or pool halls, no card playing (except Uno), no dancing or movie watching, no makeup or pierced ears or flashy jewelry or immodest dress of any kind. Men were to have short hair and women long and Joy was spelled Jesus and Others and then You. Some things were so taboo that no mention was even necessary: alcohol, premarital relations, and swearing. *Gosh* and *gee* and *Jiminy Christmas* were out, as were *fart* and *butt.* Sundays were for Sunday School and Junior Church and Bible Quizzing, not for working or going to the grocery store. It all sounded funny when she said it out loud, but really it wasn't.

Jory had tried explaining this to several incredulous listeners when they were all in sixth grade at Eisenhower Elementary, and now she was glad to be going to Arco Christian Academy, where everyone already knew and understood and there was no need to discuss any of it over sloppy joes and fruit betty surprise. It had made her feel tired and squinty eyed to have to repeat why her mother wore her father's Phi Beta Kappa key on a chain around her neck instead of wearing a diamond wedding ring, and why they had a bomb shelter in their garage instead of a car, and a ham radio antenna where the TV antenna should be, why they ate lentil loaf nearly every night and kept a refrigerator in the backyard full of nothing but apples, and why she and her sisters had all skipped first grade. There were way too many things to explain and no words for half of it. And for quite a while, when she was younger, she hadn't known she would have to.

Her father was just her father, people had always called him Doctor, he had always gone to Harvard and discovered new moons and ridden his old black bike to teach each day and run around their backyard twenty times each night still wearing his work shoes. And her mother was just her mother who didn't work and didn't drive and didn't go anywhere or talk to anyone except at church and at the library, where she went twice a week to check out as many books as they would allow her and to place orders for new ones they hadn't had the foresight to order themselves. This was just the way it was, the way they were and had been and would be forever. Like Polaris, the polestar that always pointed north, so were the five of them together: her father and mother and Grace and then Jory and Frances. The Quanbecks. No matter where Jory went or how she turned or where she was standing in the world, there they still were, unmoving, as the rest of the stars and planets whizzed past under the watchful gaze of God's bright eye.

"I see you Jory!" Frances's face was smashed against the back screen door. She licked the metal screen and then made a face. "*Yick*. It tastes like burned pennies. Come in and do Spanish with us."

Jory held very still and said nothing.

"Come on. Grace made Spanish milk and Spanish oatmeal and Spanish bread and we have Spanish money to buy them with." Frances disappeared for a moment, and reappeared holding up a colored bill that she flattened against the screen. "See?"

"Go on, Jory. You can help your sister for once." Esther Quanbeck rinsed her daughters' white Keds off with the irrigation hose, squirting each one clean with a blast of water that made the shoes jump and flip across the yard. "Jory," she said, a little louder this time, "for the love of Pete, go on."

"I'm tired of being the Mexican heathen woman. I already got baptized and bought groceries. Twice."

Her mother straightened up. "Jory," she said, "if you felt seriously about something, Grace would indulge *you*. Besides, you're not doing anything important anyway." Her mother turned and went back to the shoes, pinning them down with her bare long-nailed toe as she sprayed.

Jory let the back door slam shut behind her. Inside the garage — what *used* to be the garage — was the raised platform of the bomb shelter's ton-heavy door, an upright piano painted white that her mother had won at a church raffle for checking out the most missionary books, a large chalkboard, and several old-style wooden school desks, their metal legs all welded together in a row. Resting against the wall and strewn across the cement floor were Grace's ten-speed bike, a pogo stick, three Hula-Hoops, a box of dress-up clothes, an old baby stroller, a hamster cage with Jory's pet rat Ratfink inside, and several messy stacks of *Sky and*

Planet, Christianity Today, and *Der Spiegel.*
Frances was already seated in one of the school desks. "Sit by me," Frances whispered, as if they really were in school, patting the wooden lid of the desk behind her. Jory slid into the desk and glared toward the front wall, where Grace was writing *"el pan"* in her careful up-and-down printing on the blackboard. With her back to them, Grace seemed like a tall dark-haired stranger — someone both regal and authoritative — not like anyone related to Jory at all.

Unlike Grace's coffee-colored crop of hair, Jory's was a golden blond, lighter on top and darker underneath. "Like winter wheat waving," her mother had once said. Jory cherished this phrase since it was one of the few favorable things her mother had ever said about Jory's appearance. Her eyes were not a deep brown like her mother's. Frances had inherited those. Jory's were the same mild sea blue as her father's, while seventeen-year-old Grace seemed to have received an eye color from some far-distant relative — an uncle or cousin with eyes the color of steely gray marbles that seemed capable of sending out X-rays or purest radiation.

Grace turned and beamed at both of them. *"Buen día y recepción a la sala de* clase española," she said. "Now, who can tell me what this is?" Grace held up the empty milk carton their mother had rinsed out and saved from the garbage for this very purpose. "¿Cuál es éste?"

Frances waved her hand wildly. "Two percent!" she shrieked.

Grace's smile wavered only slightly. "Jory, how about you? ¿Qué es?"

"La leche," Jory muttered, slumping low in her seat.

"Excellente." Grace placed the cardboard carton onto Jory's desk. It wobbled emptily for a second and then tipped over. Before she could right it, a thin trickle of whitish liquid ran across Jory's desk and onto the floor. "Oh, shoot," said Grace.

"No problemo," said Jory, scrubbing at the wetness with her bare foot.

"Hey, that was Spanish," said Frances, turning around to view the drippage.

Grace smiled. "Pretty close, Frances. And because you knew that, you get to go and get the paper towels."

"Good grief — I'm not a complete moron, you know." Frances stood up and marched inside.

Grace began to line up the other cans and cartons and boxes of foodstuffs on their card table. The week before, Grace had borrowed their father's label maker and had carefully printed out a Spanish label for every box of spaghetti and powdered milk and can of chili and Campbell's soup and Chicken of the Sea tuna. Even the pieces of fruit their mother had let Grace "borrow" were labeled with their new Spanish names. Each *manzanita* and *limón* had a sticky red label carefully applied to its skin. Jory picked up the can of Del Monte fruit cocktail. "What's the word for *marshmallow*?"

Grace glanced up from her organizing. A tiny knot formed between her dark eyebrows. "How strange," she said. "I'm not sure." She stood still, thinking. "Maybe it's *la mechoca*. Oh," she said, after a second, "I don't know it."

Frances slammed the door between the laundry room and the garage. "Here," she said, thrusting the roll of paper towels at Jory.

"You probably won't need to know it anyway." Jory wiped at the sticky spot on her desk. "It's probably *el marsh-a-mellow* or something."

"No. I'm sure there's a word for it. There's a word for everything." Grace stood perfectly still, her hand resting on a can of stewed tomatoes. "I have to go look it up."

31

She turned and opened the kitchen door, letting it fall shut behind her.

"Where'd she go?" Frances plunked down onto the piano stool and began twirling herself around.

Jory said nothing. She gazed down at the can of fruit cocktail she had in her hand and then felt underneath the edge of its label with her fingernail. She peeled back the corner of the label. With one quick flick the can became nameless. Or nameless in Spanish anyway. Jory picked up another can.

"Grace is going to kill you," said Frances, who had stopped her twirling to watch.

"Me vale mierda." Jory pulled off the can's label and tossed it onto the garage floor.

"I know what that means," said Frances.

"Good for you, *idiota,* " said Jory. She wondered how long it would take Grace to notice that her hard work was being undermined — that her freakish obsession with becoming the world's youngest evangelist was being sabotaged by a member of her own supposedly loyal camp.

Tonight the sky was covered by clouds, a long gray bank of them that spread thick and low against the Owyhees and seemed to weigh the air down so that when Jory breathed her head felt heavy as if she were balancing books on it, which of course she wasn't. *A Girl of the Limberlost* was lying open on her lap to page forty-two, and she was sitting in her lawn chair in the front yard just like everyone else: her mother and father and Grace and Frances — they each had a lawn chair and a book. This is what all five of them did every night after dinner, except when it rained — then they sat indoors.

"Oh, my, will you look at that — just like ducks in a row — little to big." Mrs. Reisenstein stood just outside their curb with Mr. Reisenstein, who was holding their ancient cocker spaniel, Penny, by a leash. They were both smiling.

Mr. Reisenstein shaded his eyes with one hand. "You Quanbecks sure are a reading bunch, aren't you?" His grin widened expansively. "Must be something mighty interesting in all those books to keep you at it night after night."

Jory didn't need to look up to see her mother's fierce, tight-lipped smile.

"Actually, Len and Patsy" — Grace pulled her sandaled feet out from under her and advanced with an enthusiastic spring toward their neighbors — "I've been reading a fascinating book called *Your God Is Too*

33

Small, by J. B. Phillips. Maybe you've heard of it."

Grace called them Len and Patsy! Jory could not look up, she could not. She held her breath and stared unblinking at the toes of her tennis shoes.

"It attempts to answer some of the fundamental questions that people have raised over the centuries about Christ and our relationship to Him. Something I'm sure you, like I, have thought long and hard about."

Jory dared to peek at Grace out of the corner of her eye. Grace's head was tilted slightly to one side, and she smiled as she waited. The Reisensteins were still standing at the curb, although Mrs. Reisenstein now had her hand tightly around her husband's upper arm.

"Well, we were just heading to Albertsons for some ice cream, actually." Mr. Reisenstein cleared his throat. He gave Penny's leash a hopeful jingle.

Jory's father stood up and moved over next to Grace. "We're glad you stopped by," he said. He smiled his slow smile and then held his hand up in a wave as the Reisensteins walked quickly away, dragging their dog behind them.

"*Really,* Grace." Their mother shook her

head, and no one said anything for a minute or two.

Grace sat back down in her chair and pulled the hems of her pedal pushers carefully over her knees. "I felt compelled to witness."

"That's perfectly fine." Their father moved his chair closer to Grace's and sat down in it with a sigh. "That's a wonderful impulse."

"They're Jewish, Oren." Their mother closed her eyes and leaned back in her lawn chair.

"They're German," said their father. "Reisensteins . . . Rolling Stones."

"Rolling Stones?" said Jory.

"They're German-Jewish," said their mother.

"What's *Jewish*?" Frances glanced from one parent to the other. "What is it? You mean like Jesus-Jewish?"

"Sort of," their mother said.

"Not just sort of," said Grace, sitting up. "They're Jewish *exactly* like Jesus. The Jews were God's chosen people, Franny, and even though Jesus was one of them, the Jews chose not to accept his messiahship. They think that Jesus was an impostor."

"You mean the Reisensteins are going to hell?" Frances's eyes grew wide.

"Yes," said Grace. "I'm afraid they are."

35

"Oh, for Pete's sake," said their mother.

"Well," said their father, "I don't know about you girls, but all that talk about ice cream has made me hungry." He tried smiling.

No one smiled back.

"Is an impostor like a magician?"

Jory could hear the Tribletts' Pekingese from down the block beginning to bark at something. It barked over and over on a one-note scale at perfectly timed intervals until suddenly a door slammed and someone yelled, "Shut up, goddammit!" and then everything was quiet again. The Quanbecks all gazed down at their books.

Jory continued to sit very still, silently turning pages without looking at them until her mother asked if someone would please turn the porch light on before they all went completely blind.

That night, as Jory lay in bed waiting to fall asleep, she listened to the sound of her father pounding around the oval-shaped track he was slowly wearing into their backyard. *Pound . . . pound . . . POUND.* She could hear him coming closer, running toward her window, and then suddenly past, as he curved by the plum tree and around the irrigation ditch and on toward the swing set. Their backyard was a quarter of an acre wide, and her father ran twenty times around the whole thing each night after he got home from his teaching job at Northwestern Bible College.

Jory flopped over on her mattress trying to find a softer, more comfortable spot. For someone who viewed the body merely as a temporary shelter for the soul, her father seemed to care a great deal about keeping his in good shape, whereas her mother cared not one iota. While her father did his twenty laps around the backyard, her mother lay on the couch reading historical biographies of Queen Victoria and Eleanor Roosevelt and filching Hershey's Kisses out from between the couch cushions (which is where she kept them to "soften"). Jory was only vaguely embarrassed by her father's running — although she was grateful he waited until dark to engage in this activity — but lately nearly everything about her mother's body filled Jory with a certain alarm. It was so frighteningly female, with its overabundant breasts and hips, and its thighs and calves and upper arms seemingly made of floppy doll rubber. And when her mother wore culottes or skorts, which she frequently did in the summer, Jory couldn't help thinking that her mother's knees and thighs resembled two Beluga whales threaded with undersea veins running tight and blue beneath their milky fat.

Jory was aware that it was only her own response that had shifted. Nothing about her mother was any different than it had ever been: her heart-shaped face with its dramatic widow's peak and slightly pinched features that seemed to expect, if not invite, disappointment, her permanently chapped lips that lent her mouth a pinkish rosy tint and made her appear to be wearing lipstick even though she hardly ever was. The few times Jory had seen old photographs of her mother she had been shocked to discover a lithe and coquettish girl seated provocatively on the car hood of a '49 Packard, her hair a mass of golden brown curls and her tightish pants rolled up above her knees. In another photo, this same slim girl was laughing as she stood on tiptoe in a boat being rowed by a grinning young man in a navy uniform. In these pictures, her mother appeared far more confident and charming than Jory currently was, or ever might be.

"That was before I met your father," her mother had said, sighing and sliding the black-and-white photographs back into the album. "And before I joined the church." Jory had also seen her parents' wedding photos, though, and she knew that her mother still looked young and almost beautiful even then. It made Jory both angry and dismayed to think that her and her sisters' introduction into the world had effected this transformation in their mother. But she knew it was so.

Her father was rounding the patio now, she could tell, running past the irrigation siphon and the clothesline, where their Keds still hung, strung up by their knotted laces. The sad, disheartening thing that seemed to have damaged or broken her mother appeared not to have touched her father at all. Jory supposed it was one of those mysterious, usually unspoken things that came with being a capital-*W* woman. The obliquely shaming filmstrips from sixth grade. The machines in public restrooms that dispensed tubelike objects for a quarter. The hot water bottles that hung like red rubber nooses from the showerhead. The blood and the pads and the tubes and the fetuses and uteruses and the embryos, all fat and sloppy and squishy and liquidy. All of it inside and unknown and fascinating and horrifying in equal measure. Her father and all other men remained blithely outside of these objects and events and acted as if this were by choice: laughing and joking and shooting guns and shoving each other around. *Women's stuff! Ha ha ha!*

And yet, and *yet,* she also longed to be as beautiful and lovely as the teeny-footed geisha on her grandmother's paper fan, or the coconut-shell-wearing girl on the Tahitian vanilla bottle. She wanted to have people (men and boys, in particular) be awestruck and speechless at the sight of her feminine beauty. She wanted to be powerful, but with a power she could control. She didn't even know what that *meant.*

Her father was still running his circuit around the yard, his endless striding growing ever closer and then slowly away. She wondered, not for the first time, what she would do without the sound of his rhythmic footfalls to drag her eyelids down, how she would ever be able to fall asleep without the accompaniment of his running to carry her safely there.

This morning, Jory had seen her sister's breast. It was quite pointed and completely purposeful looking — as if something inside of it were working very hard to get out. Plus, there were the bumps — larger than gooseflesh and kind of blistery looking all the way around her sister's red-pink nipple. Jory stood next to Grace's bed and said the word again in her head. Nipple. Nipple. *Nipple.* It made her feel nauseated and thrilled at the same time.

"Mom said to bring you these," Jory said, laying a pile of folded T-shirts on Grace's bedspread and keeping her eyes down so that Grace wouldn't think she'd been peeping at her. "Sorry I didn't knock."

"That's all right." Grace didn't seem that embarrassed. She pulled her thick swimsuit straps up over each shoulder and smoothed down the slightly drooping pleated skirt that she had sewn onto the bottom of it. She did a half turn in front of Jory. "Does this look all right — I mean, does it look modest enough?" She peered dubiously down at her bottom half.

Jory thought the bathing suit looked like something a spinster aunt from the 1920s would wear. Or maybe a grandmother during the Great Depression, if she suddenly had a yen to go swimming. Jory wouldn't be caught dead wearing that suit. "It looks fine," she said.

Grace pushed her hair behind her ears and then bent and snapped open the locks on her suitcase. Grace wore her hair in a totally unstylish boy cut: a dark close-cropped cap of side-parted hair with longish bangs meant to partially obscure the large rose-

41

colored birthmark on her forehead. The doctors had tried to remove the mark when Grace was three, but it hadn't worked and their father had been worried about the level of radiation anyway. Grace was awkwardly shy about the mark and often dipped her head down when she was talking to people, although if anyone directly mentioned the birthmark, she blinked and acted as if she had no idea what they were talking about. It was confusing and somewhat contradictory, as was nearly everything connected with Grace.

Jory sat down on the bed next to the open blue suitcase. "How do you know how much stuff to take?"

"They give you a list." Grace was pulling things out of her dresser drawers and carrying them over to the suitcase: a white leather Bible, a can of Aqua Net hair spray, pairs and pairs of day-of-the-week panties, six knee-length dresses, a Spanish dictionary, rubber thongs, some mosquito repellent, a bottle of Wind Song perfume, a *Tips for Teens in Troubled Times* daily devotional reader, three unopened packages of run-proof nylons, and a garter belt. Grace was going to Mexico on a mission. Even though she was only seventeen, their church had picked her because of her extraordinary fervor and because she wanted to go. Jory's mother had initially had a fit — a silent fit that involved her lying in the bedroom with the door shut for two days — but she had relented in the end because their father thought it would be a wonderful learning experience for Grace and because, he said, you should never, ever stand in God's way.

Jory thought it also had something to do with the fact that her parents were scared to death of Grace. Especially *lately.* Lately, for some unknown reason, Grace had become an even more exaggerated version of her already odd and intense and intractable self. Grace had always been tall and straight with very serious gray eyes and black winglike eyebrows and had played the piano in front of the whole church with no sheet music and no mistakes, but suddenly last spring she had stood up during the middle of Sunday evening service and testified that she was now sanctified and had rededicated her life to Christ and to His Kingdom, and then she had worked all summer long as a youth minister and turned around and put the paycheck Pastor Ron gave her directly into the offering plate when it was passed to her during early service. Jory still remembered the look on her mother's face when she saw Grace's three-hundred-dollar check lying in the collection plate. *Come Ye Apart,* it said on the purple-and-gold satin banner that hung above the choir loft at the front of the church. Even so, Jory knew her parents were worried that Grace had come a little too far apart. But how could they complain? What would they say? That their oldest daughter was just too selfless and holy and Christlike? Sometimes Jory wanted to ask Grace things. To look into her cool, pond-bottom gray eyes and ask her if she, Jory, had imagined that moment in church, that tiny second when Jory could swear she had seen Grace smile just as the collection plate reached their mother's outstretched hand.

"Aren't you scared?" Jory asked as Grace folded a lilac-sprigged nightgown on top of everything, tucking its lacy bottom edge into a corner of the suitcase.

"Of what?" Grace closed the lid on the suitcase and fastened the latch with two quick clicks.

"I don't know . . . being gone, I guess." Jory drew her knees up and tucked her chin between them. "Being that far away."

Grace gazed at her and smiled. It was the same brilliant smile she gave to all the visitors in church as she handed them each a *Welcome Friends* sticker, and to Ruby and

44

Pearl, the retarded twins in Vacation Bible School, and to Richard Richardson, the hugely fat-bottomed choir director each time she told him, no, she was very flattered and honored, but no, she wasn't allowed to date until she was eighteen. "You don't think that God was scared when He came down to earth as a man, do you?" Grace asked.

Jory stared at her sister's fathomless gray eyes. *No,* she thought. *I bet he was petrified.*

Tonight was Grace's good-bye dinner. In the kitchen, there was a large chocolate cake with pink frosting that read *We Love You, Grace* in smeary letters. Jory had spent most of the afternoon making the cake while her mother was in the bedroom crying. At one point during the afternoon, her mother had come out and blown her nose and then picked up the frosting tube and written *Don't Go, Grace* in large, shaky white letters. Right before dinner Jory had blended the letters back into the frosting and started again.

Now the five of them sat in their usual places around the maplewood table. Her father was squashing his lentil loaf into a paste and forking it into his mouth in the happy fashion he did every night. He

45

glanced up at Jory and smiled. Jory looked back down at her plate and began cutting her loaf into smaller and smaller pieces. She moved these pieces around to brand-new locations on her plate. Once, in fifth grade, her Sunday School teacher had invited all the girls in her class to spend the night. After they had gotten done splashing around in Mrs. Jewel's freezing blue swimming pool, Mrs. Jewel had made them dinner: spicy cooked hamburger and cheese with shredded lettuce and tomato chunks in some kind of hard envelope-like shells. "What *are* these?" Jory had asked Mrs. Jewel, still shivering slightly under her beach towel. "They're wonderful." "You mean the tacos?" Mrs. Jewel had said, opening her eyes wide and laughing. Jory had laughed quickly too, and said no, no, she was just joking — she loved tacos, they were her favorite. Now she stirred her canned peas with her fork. She knew that her family and their habits were beyond strange. Even in fifth grade it had been apparent that her parents were of a different breed than the rest of the citizens of Arco. The Quanbecks didn't even pass unnoticed in their own evangelical church, which was full to the brim with odd conservative folks of every stripe and shade. Jory hadn't realized the full extent of their strangeness when she was younger, but with each passing year the exotic nature of her family was becoming more noticeable. And more horrifying. And it wasn't just the food that they ate or didn't eat, or the old battered car that they drove (which had been given to her father from the college in lieu of a paycheck), or the endless book reading, or even the plain and modest hand-me-down clothes that each of the Quanbeck daughters wore in turn. It was the fact that her parents acted as if this were the better, more superior way. As if it were not only vital, but practically holy to never watch TV or buy anything new or show any interest in what was modern or current or popular or fun. And it was being these very things — modern and current and popular and fun — that Jory most wished for and aspired to in life. And this was a problem.

"I'm going to take baton twirling with Deedee Newman," Frances announced suddenly.

"So," said Jory.

"It costs fifteen dollars and it's at the high school gym." Frances stared unblinkingly at Jory. "It's all summer." Now Frances turned toward their mother. "Dad said I could."

Jory's mother seemed to be saying something with her napkin. She creased and re-creased one edge of it. "Baton twirling, Oren?" she said in a strange voice. "Isn't that the type of thing cheerleaders and Miss America contestants do?"

Jory's father stopped chewing. He picked up his glass of milk and then seemed to think better of it. He cleared his throat. "Well, it seems to me that they're just little girls, Esther. Does it really matter if a few little girls march around in a gym pretending to twirl batons? I don't think baton twirling is technically a form of dancing."

Her mother wadded up the creased napkin and threw it at Jory's father. It hit him softly in the tie and then fell onto his plate. He sat perfectly still, looking at their mother in disbelief.

Grace held her fork and knife suspended above her plate. "Would it be possible to borrow your Spanish Bible commentary, Dad? Pastor Ron says that yours is probably quite a bit more comprehensive than mine."

Jory's father turned his head toward Grace and opened his mouth slightly just as their mother stood up and grabbed Jory's plate. "Jory, if you're not going to eat that, why don't you give it to Frances? I can't stand it when you leave perfectly good food just lying there." With two quick swipes, she scraped its contents noisily onto Frances's clean plate.

Frances surveyed her newly filled plate and took several deep breaths. "I do too get to take baton," she wailed. "I already picked one out and it has silver and gold streamers and I have four dollars of allowance left." She gulped frantically.

"Frances." Grace leaned forward. "Pastor Ron says that at least half of the children in Guanajuato are severely malnourished. Think how lucky you are. Those children have probably never even seen lentil loaf."

Jory's mother knit her dark eyebrows together. "Was that some kind of a joke?"

"We have cake!" Jory jumped up and glanced from person to person. "We have cake," she said again, a little more softly.

"I like cake," her father said.

"Oh, by all means," her mother said, rubbing at her temples with both hands. "Bring on the cake."

Now there were only four lawn chairs and four books and once a week an airmail letter covered with stamps of bright birds with yellow-and-green tails. The letters weighed nothing when Jory held them in her hand. Inside the paper was crinkle thin and lavender colored and covered with Grace's firm, straight up-and-down printing. The church in Guanajuato was going up on schedule. Grace was learning to make bricks. The villagers were very grateful for the box of clothes and old *Reader's Digest*s and the powdered milk. On a bus ride to Lake Chapala, Grace had seen an old woman carrying a chicken in her purse and once the chicken got out and another old woman grabbed the chicken and put it in *her* purse and then there was a fight — a big fight.

"Oh," Jory's mother said, her lips crumpling at the corners. She brought the letter closer to her face and squinted a little as if she might have read it wrong.

"A chicken!" Frances screeched. "How did she fit a chicken in her purse?"

"*Shh,* Frances. Their purses are probably different than ours — more like big mesh bags or something." Her mother waved her hand as if waving away all purses everywhere. "*Any*way," their mother said, lifting the letter up again. "She says the church group visited a coffee plantation, and then they went to the *mercado,* where everyone bought bananas and mangoes, which were delicious, and really nothing at all like American fruit. Oh!" she said, dropping the letter back into her lap. "Don't they need to wash the fruit? Oren! Don't they?"

Their father put down his magazine. "I'm sure they did, Esther. Grace is a very smart girl." He smiled and tried to pat their mother's hand, but she was peering at the letter again, and he patted the metal armrest of her lawn chair instead.

Their mother sighed and shook out the lavender paper and continued reading: " 'There are men everywhere here. They line the streets and alleys. None of them seem to have jobs. They stare at me and make comments and hissing noises through their teeth. Pastor Ron says it is probably because I'm so tall. That they've probably just never seen a girl as tall as me before.' " Their mother's voice died suddenly away and she jerkily refolded the lavender sheets and stuffed them back into the envelope, but she hadn't done a very good folding job and now the letter didn't seem to fit anymore.

Frances squinted at her mother. "Shouldn't she have said 'I'?"

"Shut up, Frances." Jory stood up out of her lawn chair and grabbed her little sister's hand. "C'mon, I think I hear the ice cream man."

"Ow! You're hurting my arm." Frances glared reproachfully at Jory. "I don't hear anything."

Jory said nothing but held tight to Frances's strong little hand and pulled her down the sidewalk. She stopped after about a block and a half. "Listen," she said.

"Oh." Frances's face softened. "How did you hear him?"

"I don't know." Jory shrugged. "I just always do."

The truck's tinkly carnival music reminded Jory of things just barely hidden, like Easter eggs and sparklers the second before they catch and light. The two of them stood together watching the small white truck approaching in tiny increments, its tinny music growing ever louder. Finally it swerved over to the curb and stopped next to them. The man inside stared down at them expectantly as the music ground to a halt. "That's not Al," said Frances loudly.

"It's okay." Jory walked staunchly toward the open door of the truck. "She'll have the Chocolate Swirl and I'll take a cherry Push Up." Jory blinked a couple of times in quick succession and then took the smallest of steps backward.

"Hm-*mm,*" said the man sitting in the driver's seat. He leaned his elbow on the steering wheel and rested his chin in his hand. His long red hair was tied back with an old black shoestring. "They're made with whipped lard, you know."

"What?" Jory practically whispered. Was he talking to her?

"Whipped lard. Not even real lard, actually." He grinned, revealing a silver tooth somewhere in the back of his mouth. "Fake lard. Now that's worth thirty-five cents of babysitting money."

"I don't babysit." Jory could feel a rush of blood flooding her neck and face.

"Why not?"

"I — I'm not very maternal."

"Me either." The ice cream man frowned at her. "Who's this, then?"

"My little sister." Jory tried to bring Frances around in front of her, but Frances was having none of it.

"Well, Sister Sue," the ice cream man said, opening the lid on his silver freezer and pulling out a chocolate-covered ice cream bar, "here's your bit of sheer deliciousness, or as delicious as you can get using ice milk." He stepped down one of the truck's steps and held the paper-covered treat out to Frances. Frances was clutching the back of Jory's shorts and would not let go, so Jory took the ice cream for her. "And," he said, reaching back into the freezer again, "one cherry Push Up for the lady with daisies in her eyes." He held the ice cream bar in front of

53

his chest. Jory noted the hand holding the ice cream. There were tiny red hairs on each of his knuckles and some kind of blue tattoos between two of his fingers. She reached into her pocket again and pulled out the quarters. "Nah," he said and gave his head a shake. "These are definitely on the house." Jory had to take the ice cream. She reached for it and felt his fingers, rough and warm, still holding the wooden stick. "Well," the ice cream man said, and moved up into the driver's seat, "back to work." He nodded at Jory. "Look out. Those melt quick."

Jory watched as the truck lurched away from the curb and then tootled on down the street.

"Who *was* that?" Frances asked, her ice cream sloping toward the sidewalk. "Do you know him, Jory?"

"I'm not sure," she said slowly, not sure which question she was answering.

CHAPTER TWO

Early the next morning, even before it got hot, the lady from the tall stucco house on the corner came to ask if Grace could babysit, and of course Grace was in Mexico and had been for a month, so now, amazingly enough, Jory had a job. A real job that paid a dollar twenty-five an hour, even though Jory wasn't very maternal.

Mrs. Hewett was beautiful like Linda Evans on *The Big Valley,* but with higher heels and still higher hair. Her husband was a private detective. Jory's mother always said she couldn't imagine what on earth there was to detect in Arco, Idaho.

Now, at the suggestion of Jory's new job, her mother was shaking her head. "She smokes," she said. "And that skirt!" She made the strange clucking noise in the back of her throat that stood for all manner of verbal disapproval. "I don't *think* so."

"I'll be good. I'll do a good job. I can witness." This last was a final effort on Jory's part. A trump card that should be pulled out only in emergency situations.

Her mother lifted one eyebrow. "That would be the day," she said. "At the very least, though, I expect you to be a good example over there. A good Christian example, Jory."

Monday afternoon found Jory at the Hewetts', dutifully poking Barbie and Ken into their coral-colored Corvette and arguing with Dinah, Mrs. Hewett's three-year-old daughter, about which doll would drive.

"Barbie doesn't drive," Dinah was insisting. "And Skipper's the baby."

"Skipper is nobody's baby. She's like some cousin or orphan or something. I mean, look at her hat."

"I don't like you." Dinah chugged over and climbed up into a high-backed chair at the far end of the living room.

"What a coincidence." Jory rewound her ponytail and then pulled a piece of gum out of her shorts pocket. She began to unwrap it and then stopped. She held the piece of gum out. "Want some?"

Dinah climbed warily down from the chair. She hummed a little as she dragged Skipper's dog along on its side by its little

56

leash, then sat down on the floor to unwrap the gum. "Skipper can too go."

"Only if she's in the trunk." Jory rolled the Corvette along the sculptured carpet. "They're probably gonna make out. You know, kiss and stuff. Strictly grown-up beeswax."

Dinah frowned.

Jory stopped the car and folded her legs under, Indian-style. "You do know how to kiss, don't you?" She rolled her eyes and sighed dramatically. "Look, I'll show you. Come over here."

Still clutching the plastic dalmatian, Dinah inched closer to Jory.

"Stick out your lips a little. Like this. And close your eyes." Jory leaned forward and touched Dinah's lips with her own. They were smoother and different than she'd imagined. It was like kissing a fat flower come to life. Jory sat back. "Now this time you kiss me."

Dinah rested one small hand on Jory's shoulder and pressed her face up next to Jory's. She smelled like baby shampoo and graham crackers. Jory felt a small worm twist sweetly somewhere in her stomach. Dinah carefully put her mouth on Jory's and Jory pressed down a little, turning her head slowly from side to side.

"See, that's how they do it on TV." Jory smiled and pushed her bangs back. "Doesn't your mom ever kiss you like that?"

"No. Jory, I want some Quik."

"Doesn't she kiss your dad like that? I bet they do when you're asleep."

"Why can't Pinky come in?"

"Because he pees all over everything, that's why. C'mon, after your Quik you're supposed to take a nap."

Jory opened the door a little and peeked in to see if Dinah was really asleep or only pretending. She could hear the clock's soft tick and Dinah sighing a tiny bit every once in a while. She took off her Keds and padded quietly over the thick carpet.

In the Hewetts' bedroom the shades were down; only amber-colored light filtered through and lay in slanted bands across the floor. The bed was huge and covered by a shiny deep purple bedspread. Jory sat down on the edge of it and felt the smoothness under her bare legs. She ran her hand along the satiny bedspread and then over the knobs of the dresser beside it. In the top drawer were panties and bras and complicated-looking garter belts. Jory pinched the rubber stocking nibs in and out of their metal clips. Mrs. H had day-of-the-week panties exactly like hers! *Saturday* stitched in red on black nylon — obviously the most sinful day. Her *Monday* and *Tuesday* panties had faint stains in the crotch, though. Not blood, which Jory knew about in theory, but something else. She glanced back at the bedroom door and then quickly pulled her tank top off over her head. She tried on each bra in turn. The black lace one that had no straps at all but still stayed up, and the shiny red bra that had rubbery push-up pads that snapped in and out. She examined herself in the round vanity mirror. Her new nipples seemed very small and pale peeking out of the dark blue lace. She turned to the side to see. The mirror was low and she couldn't see her head at all, only the bra and the bare skin below. She touched one of her nipples for a second and watched it pinch together at the tip. An internal string of some sort tugged tight between her nipple and her navel and Jory quickly unhooked the bra and crammed her tank top back on. She folded the bras back into the drawer, skipping entirely over the slips and nylons, with only a quick glance at the Summer's Eve boxes and can of Gentle Spring Hygiene Spray.

The bottom two drawers evidently belonged to the detective. Boring black and brown socks in neat rolls, white jockey shorts (gross and huge!), and tons of pitted-out undershirts. And under the undershirts were magazines. Jory sat down on the floor and held one in her lap. She turned each page, a weight settling inside her that was heavy and fluttery at the same time. Miss February cupped her own impossible breasts as if testing them for ripeness. Some of the women did this to their bottoms or the inside of their thighs as well. Miss August appeared to be in pain or possibly praying. A tiny cartoon woman wearing only gloves winked as she rode a rocketlike lipstick toward a long-tongued moon.

After closely inspecting all of them, Jory felt like the time she'd gone swimming in her cousins' pool with an ear infection. Her head and chest were tight and buzzing and she had a strong desire to run her fingertips over and into the pictures — the women were so smooth and swollen, and oddly more real than anything she had ever seen. Women like this actually lived somewhere and knew that men were turning the pages slowly and then faster to look and look and look at them. They wanted men to be looking at them. Didn't they? Jory stood up and began shakily stuffing the magazines back into the drawer. She couldn't remember what order they had been in, which month had been on top. It probably didn't matter. Within seconds, she had refolded the undershirts and tried to smooth away any footprints she might have left in the carpet, then closed the bedroom door with a soft click.

Virgil Vail stood on the platform playing "Fill My Cup, Lord" on his trumpet while the elders passed the collection plates from row to row. Rhonda Russell snickered and nudged Jory, showing how she was missing two front teeth on top, even though she was nearly fourteen. The dentist said it was just too bad and a fluke, but Jory thought that, even without her front teeth, her best friend possessed the allure of a gypsy. She had slanted cat eyes and black bangs that hung down to her eyelashes and knew all the lyrics to "Cherry Hill Park" and everything else that was necessary to know. Everything that Jory had no thought of knowing. Rhonda had even gotten Andre, of Andre's Hair Salon, to pierce her ears. Jory was filled with unbelievable envy. Jory's family was so strange, and Rhonda's whole life was so *cool.* Even Rhonda's *parents* were cool. Even though her father was a Christian music minister, he let Rhonda and her sisters watch TV and drink Coke and straighten their hair. A few times Rhonda's mom had even driven Rhonda and Jory to Super Thrift, where they had spent the better part of several afternoons deeply ensconced behind the makeup counter, carefully testing all the lipsticks for just the proper shade of frostiness. Jory had swiveled the beautiful pinky-white crayons up and down, inhaling their diaper rash ointment smell and picturing a tube's gold chunkiness sliding oh so neatly into her imaginary fringed leather purse.

As Virgil Vail and his trumpet stepped down from the platform, Brother Elmore stood up from his chair and moved briskly toward the pulpit. "Tonight we have a special treat," he said, rubbing his hands and grinning broadly at the Wednesday night crowd. "Our church's very own science scholar, Dr. Oren Quanbeck, is going to speak to us. You all know who he is, so I don't even have to offer up his ten-page résumé." Brother Elmore grinned again.

Rhonda turned to Jory and widened her cat eyes. "It's your *dad,*" she whispered.

"I know," said Jory. She squinched her toes together inside her shoes.

"His distinguished record speaks for itself," Brother Elmore continued. "And even if we don't all understand everything he says" — Brother Elmore paused to let a murmur of laughter run through the congregation — "we know we will be the better for hearing it. So, as it says in Matthew 11:15, *He that hath ears to hear, let him hear.*" Brother Elmore smiled once more and stepped away from the pulpit.

Jory stared fixedly at the wooden floor beneath the pew. She refused to lift her eyes toward the front of the church, where her father, in his good brown sports jacket and striped tie, was shuffling some three-by-five-inch note cards against the wooden top of the pulpit. She had heard him practicing this speech down in the bomb shelter earlier that afternoon and she knew exactly how it went. Even so, it gave her a strange feeling in her stomach to listen to that voice and those words coming out of the pulpit microphone. It seemed as if he were speaking into her ear alone, but through an enormous tunnel of some kind that filled all the available space in the church with his particular and achingly familiar voice. She peeped out from under her lids at the people sitting in the pews close by. They were all staring straight ahead, intent — listening to her father. Jory felt naked. And nervous. And fearfully, fearfully proud. The three things her father always made her feel.

Her father set his note cards down and paused for a moment. "There wasn't a lot of excitement on my father's farm in Kansas," he said, "just mainly work, but I found that in the summer evenings I could go into my mother's vegetable garden and lie down and look up at the stars, and it was a wonderland. It was also, I guess," her father continued, "a form of escapism. I was captivated by the notions of infinite space, of how the planets moved and what the stars were made of. From the age of six or seven I can remember wondering about these things." Jory knew the part that was coming next; she could feel herself anticipating the words as if she had made them up herself. How by the age of twelve her father had made a radio out of chicken wire and an old vacuum tube, and at fourteen he had built his own telescope. It was then, he said, that he'd had his first glimpse of the real magnitude and mystery of the heavens and man's tiny, ridiculous place in it.

It was that same year that his mother became ill, very ill. The doctors in town said tuberculosis, then rheumatic fever. His mother grew so thin he could see her ribs beneath her dress. She lay in bed, her breath only the smallest movement of the bedcovers. He did his chores and then tried to learn how to cook so his father would have something to eat when he came in from the cornfields. On Palm Sunday, his mother asked his father to bring the elders to their house after church. He could still remember the sight of the eight men in black suits and dusty farmers' hats walking single file up their dirt driveway. He peeked in from the doorway as the men took their places around his mother's bedside and prayed, the mingled rise and fall of their voices sounding like the hum of his father's bee boxes in springtime. As they prayed, one of the men brought a small brown bottle of oil out of his pocket and placed several drops of it on his mother's forehead, rubbing it in with his callused thumb. They moved closer to his mother then, leaning across the bed to each place their two hands on some part of her body. As he watched, he felt a sudden, hot jolt run through his throat and down his legs — he could remember the feeling still — as if he'd been plugged into a socket, as if it were his body they were touching instead of hers. Later that day, his mother sent him out to the barn to find his father, who had been pretending to trim some of the horses' hooves while the elders were there. When they came inside, she was sitting up in bed, her hair combed and braided, and she told his father that she wanted some peach cobbler. Made with the sweet white Elbertas from the back end of the orchard. She smiled. He and his father spent the rest of the evening picking peaches in the dark.

"I knew that my mother had been healed, and that it was a miracle," he was saying now over the congregation. He cleared his throat and readjusted his reading glasses, pushing them farther up onto the bridge of his nose.

"I am a scientist now myself," he said, "and perhaps ironically, one of the very things that continues to convince me of the existence of God *is* the so-called 'inexplicable.' Consider the essential mystery of the birth of the cosmos. The recipe that was required for its creation is mind-boggling in both its complexity and precision." Jory's father spread out his hands as if to indicate the immense difficulty of the explanation he was about to give. "For example, the strength of the attractive nuclear forces in our universe is so peculiarly precise that, were it even slightly different, hydrogen would be a rare element, stars like the sun could not exist, and the emergence of life would have been impossible. Had the nuclear forces been weaker, on the other hand, hydrogen would not burn and there would be no heavy elements, and again, we would not have a universe hospitable to creatures like us. The universe, moreover, is constructed on such a scale that stars in a typical galaxy are twenty million million miles apart; were the distances between stars just two million million miles, life could not have survived on our planet."

Jory cringed slightly at the mention of all these million-millions. It reminded her of math class and she was worried that other people were being reminded too. Sermons should have only very simple equations with small numbers in them. People couldn't remember the huge sums. Grace had told her this.

"Consider too the careful positioning of our very own earth," her father was saying, oblivious to Jory's or anyone else's mathematical dismay. "In order for any planet to produce life — complex life, such as ours did — it has to lie within what we astronomers euphemistically call the 'Goldilocks Zone': a distance from its star that is not too hot, not too cold, but just right. It is only in this zone that a planet would be close enough to the star to have liquid water, yet not so close that its oceans would boil away, and not so far that its oceans would freeze.

"But how exactly did all this careful exactness and minute precision come about? you may ask. How did this perfect recipe for creation occur? Was the universe with its life-giving laws and perfectly spaced galaxies a marvelous fluke, a random accident, a precipitous bit of happenstance?" Jory's father leaned forward. "I am convinced that the enormous complexity of the cosmos together with the marvelous harmony of reality bear witness to the plausibility of a creator. Can I prove this theory? No. Can I prove the opposite? No. Nor can any other scientist. For all of science's brave claims to the contrary, the birth of the universe still remains a mystery — an unexplainable miracle. Much like the healing of a physical body. Or the splendor of the night sky above a Kansas farm. Or an old man and a young boy picking peaches in the dark."

Jory's father stood holding the wooden sides of the lectern. "Many Christians seem to fear that the end result of scientific inquiry is an inevitable loss of faith. I find this notion somewhat confusing since my lifelong study has only reaffirmed my belief that a mighty hand is at work in the wonders of the world. We must remember" — Jory's father's voice seemed to be shaking its finger slightly — "the ability to question and search for answers is a God-given one. We were made by Him to think and to wonder and, yes, sometimes even to doubt. But the natural world is always there as a reminder of the glory and majesty and the mystery of its Maker. Even Job on his ash heap gazed around him and wondered where the light came from and how the hail was formed. We should do no less. May God bless you," her father said. "And keep you." He turned from the pulpit and walked back to the empty chair behind him.

"Your dad's so smart," said Rhonda. She twirled a lank piece of black hair between her fingers. "Does he like peaches or what?"

Brother Elmore stood at the podium, smiling. "Thank you so much, Brother Quanbeck, for those truly inspiring words of wisdom." He held up the night's bulletin. "Now don't forget," he said. "After the service there will be a potluck in Franklin Hall to celebrate the Jewels' return from Papua, New Guinea. They are only here on a short sabbatical, so I know you'll all want to come and greet them — if not with a holy kiss, then at least a friendly handshake."

Jory and Rhonda were waiting for Brent Sandoval to request "Sit Down, I Think I

Love You" for Rhonda. They listened to Rhonda's transistor radio clear till ten o'clock, but they couldn't really tell because there were lots of L.'s, and even two L.R.'s, but none of them were from B.S. "I don't like him anyway." Rhonda was bent over in her nightgown, polishing her toenails. "He's like half Indian or something."

"Why doesn't he go with Stormy Aguilar, then?"

"Maybe they're from warring tribes or something." Rhonda ran her tongue over her toothless spot and they screamed with laughter and ran out into the living room even though they had their shortie pajamas on.

"Girls. Really." Rhonda's mother glanced up mildly from the white nurse's uniform she was hemming. "How's your sister doing, Jory? Isn't she in Puerto Rico now?"

"She's in Mexico." Jory sat down breathlessly in one of the Russells' orange plastic chairs. "She'll be back in a few weeks."

"That's right. Well, I hope she isn't drinking the water." Mrs. Russell tossed the white dress onto the seat of a rocking chair. "Oh, my," she said, stretching her freckled arms above her head and bending from side to side until her back made a sudden popping sound. "You know, you wouldn't catch any of my four heading off on a mission. Not unless it was to Bermuda and there were nothing but good-looking boys there."

"Oh, *Ma.*" Rhonda gave her mother a look of disgust and then fell backward onto the couch.

Jory gazed around her. This was where she wanted to live. If only the Russells would agree, she could call her parents and tell them that this was where she would be staying from now on. She could sleep on their ratty orange couch and eat their tater tots and wear all of Rhonda's clothes. The air here was filled with some kind of greasy warmness — like fried hamburger left overnight in a pan. The whole house was messy and sloppy and unfolded. You could eat cereal out of the box. There *was* cereal! And no one seemed to care one whit about particle physics or whether sanctification was a secondary act of grace or if lentils were the best-known source of protein and vitamin B.

Sometime later that night, Jory tried to tell Rhonda about the detective's magazines, about how the naked women had practically emerged and sprung forth from the pictures, but Rhonda just peered at her sideways and said, "You are seriously a homo," and went back to playing the bot-

71

tom hand of "Heart and Soul" on their rickety old piano.

Jory bumped Grace's ten-speed up into a slot in the bike rack in front of Super Thrift. She unhooked her beaded change purse from around the handlebars and counted the folded bills that were packed tightly inside. She zipped it up again and slipped the coin purse into the back pocket of her cutoffs. The automatic door whooshed open and she walked into the Listerine coolness of the store, heading straight for aisle C. She stopped in front of the display case. It was still there. The Budding Beauty by Maidenform in a 30AA. Lightly padded for extra shaping with crisscross straps for gentle support and elastic stretch cups to allow for change in the still-growing teen. The girl on the front of the box smiled tanly in her half slip and bra.

Jory held the box next to her stomach and floated toward the makeup and jewelry section. If the lipstick was still $3.99, she would definitely have enough left over for a bottle of Love's Fresh Lemon Cologne. Anyway, Rhonda Russell wore Love's Baby Soft Cologne, so it wouldn't be like copying. What if she got some of that Sun In stuff you sprayed on your hair to make it blonder?

Her mother would *kill* her — she said bleached hair was cheap with a capital *C*, for tramps with a capital *T*.

Jory picked up a pair of silver hoop earrings with tiny stars suspended from the center. She held them next to one ear and then the other, moving the display mirror so she could see. Her mother had said no pierced ears ever — it was in the church manual. Jory sighed and put the earrings back on the display counter and then turned and headed for the lipstick case. She would have to decide between Icicle Frost and Petal Pale. What a choice. She pulled one tube out of the display case and then the other. The goldy caps slid off with the most satisfying little suctioned pops. Twisting the waxy sticks up, she rubbed a tiny bit of each of the pointed tips onto her wrist. They both appeared sufficiently silvery — maybe Icicle Frost was a little bit more glossy, though. She felt a thrill run through her. At home she would put on her bra and a little bit of the lipstick and her white T-shirt with the lace inset and before her mother could say anything she would ride Grace's bike over to Kurtz Park to see if Rhonda was there. Her head seemed to open like a window, and she walked as fast as she could toward the front of the store. A very small man with a blue short-sleeved shirt and large armpit stains suddenly stood in front of her. He took a step closer and squeezed her elbow. Hard.

"Come on," he said. Jory could think of nothing except the smell of Sen-Sen on his breath. The little man walked her and her bra box quickly down the garden supply aisle and toward the back of the store. Jory could feel a kind of fistlike burning in her chest. "What's wrong? I don't understand what's going on," she said. He walked her through a set of swinging doors and then suddenly they were inside a little room marked EMPLOYEES ONLY.

"Have a seat," he said and sat down himself at a desk and began writing something on a pink notepad. Jory sat on a metal chair across from another man, this one wearing a tie.

"Give me that," the tie man said. Jory glanced down in surprise at the box and handed it to him. He immediately wrenched open the top of the box and pulled out the folded bra. He rooted around in its creases for a minute, shook it once, and then dumped it onto the desk, where it lay, its small white cups pointing stiffly toward the ceiling. He grabbed the golden lipstick tube from her and plunked it down next to the bra.

The man with the tie pointed a pen at her. "Stand up and empty your pockets."

Jory stood and started fishing around in the front of her shorts as though expecting to find something. "But I don't have anything." She shoved her hands into her back pockets. "Wait. I've got my change purse." She held it out almost triumphantly.

"How much money is in there? Never mind." He grabbed the purse, unzipped it, and started making a pile of bills next to the bra. "Over thirty bucks. So what'd you need to steal earrings for if you got thirty bucks?" He leaned back in the swivel chair and twisted the cap on his pen back and forth expectantly.

"What? What do you mean? I didn't. I mean, I didn't take them. I tried some on sort of, but I didn't take them." She thought she was starting to cry, but instead felt herself give a strange little laugh. "I've never taken anything in my life." In desperation, she tried to force him to meet her eyes. "I swear. I haven't."

"Where are they, down your shirt?"

"Okay, Al." The small man in the blue shirt turned around from the desk and his writing. "We'll have to get one of the gals from up front in here for that."

"What? Oh, yeah. Well, get Janet or Velma or whoever."

The blue-shirted man pushed himself out of his metal desk chair and disappeared out the door.

Jory stared at a poster, right over the tie man's head, of a man throwing a Frisbee to a dog. Underneath the dog it read: A HEALTHY EMPLOYEE IS A HAPPY EMPLOYEE. A time clock thwacked loudly at the minute change. She could feel her heart beating in her throat like the time the dentist gave her too much Novocain.

"Why not hand them over? They're worth what — three, four bucks? So your parents will ground you and you won't be welcome here anymore. Big deal." He sat slowly forward in the squeaky leather chair and began digging a hole in the desktop with a pushpin. He paused in his digging and fished a cigarette out of his shirt pocket. "You smoke?"

"I don't have them," Jory whispered. *"Please."* Her chest was pumping now like she'd just crested the hill to their house on her bike. "You're completely wrong." She said it louder.

"I got one of these ear staples, see? This doctor my wife sent me to was some kind

76

of thera-hypnotist or whatever. Said every time I get the urge to smoke I'm supposed to twist this little deely bobber here and think pleasant thoughts." He lit up and inhaled deeply. "I'm still twisting."

The door opened and a fuzzy blond woman in an orange work smock stood suspiciously in the doorway. She glared at the tie man. "My till ain't counted."

"Ed'll stay at your register."

"I'm on break in ten."

"Alma, all you have to do is . . . you know, whatever." The tie man shrugged helplessly and then coughed once and eased out of his chair. He pulled on the end of his tie and then punched Jory lightly on the shoulder on his way out the door. "You kids behave yourselves. Alma, you write up the report when you're done. I've got markups."

The blond woman seemed slightly blurred, like someone had taken an eraser to her outer edges. She wore a silver ring on every finger, even her thumbs. "Honey." She breathed audibly and crossed her arms. "I don't want to do this, but you're gonna have to take off all your things."

"No. *NO.* I didn't do anything." Jory could feel something flattening and then spinning in the back of her head, flattening and spinning. She was back in grade school on the crowded rushing playground listening to the other kids' voices sounding sharp like the side of a penny and then flat like the face. "I mean, I've, I've got this skin disease. Like some kind of ringworm thing and" — her eyes darted wildly around the little room — "it's getting worse. It's completely contagious."

"I'm sorry, hon." The woman lowered her faint cloud of hair and shook it back and forth slowly. "They told me I have to check everywhere. So if you just stand there, I'll take a quick look-see. Okay?" She turned her smudgy eyes back up to meet Jory's and reached a silvered hand toward the front of Jory's blouse. Jory shrank back against the tie man's desk. The blond woman frowned. "I know how you feel, doll, but it's either me or some policeman."

Jory couldn't seem to think; she kept watching the woman's coral-colored lips puckering and pinching. Her lipstick seemed to have nothing to do with her lips. It was a separate thing altogether. *So you just hold still and I'll do all the work,* it was saying. Jory stared down and saw the woman's shiny fingers undoing the buttons on her sailor blouse. The shirt was open now and Jory could feel the woman running her sharp little hands up both sides of her ribs, up and down her back, and then around in front and over her cold-tightened breasts. "No earrings here," she could hear the woman saying. "Don't you wear a bra, hon? You're almost grown enough. Now turn around and hold your arms out to the side, okay?" The woman turned Jory around to face the desk, sliding her hands underneath the waistband of Jory's shorts, unsnapping and unzipping. Jory shut her eyes and kept them shut. Her cutoffs were down around her feet. "We'll leave these underthings on." The woman spoke quietly, as if to reassure herself. "I can just feel around and see enough this way, I think." Her hands were quick and darting like some kind of firm little fish nosing out food from every hidden bit of coral. Jory's eyes suddenly opened all on their own. The wall was beige, she told herself, a mushroom beige or a sort of light taupe or maybe golden brown, and something had once been tacked to the wall in four places, a bulletin board maybe, or a large picture, and now there were faint lines left, a lighter spot and four holes, one in each corner. They weren't big enough to be nail holes, they must have used thumb tacks or pushpins, or needles, or . . . she didn't know — *she didn't know.* "I used to have these," the fish lady was saying, her words coming out all strangled and mixed up with her breathing. "Day-of-the-week panties — that's right, I had them too. I remember now. And Tuesday was always blue."

Out in the parking lot, Jory ran toward the bike stand and pulled the ten-speed up and out of its slot with one huge jerk of her arms. She jumped on and pedaled toward the curb, nearly hitting the small white ice cream truck that was pulling in. The man in the driver's seat yelled, "Hey, wait!" and slammed on his brakes, but she didn't stop and once she was on the street and riding like mad she forgot to think about the man and his red-haired fingers, his tiny blue tattoos. The bike's wheels made an incredible whizzing sound as she pumped and pushed the pedals around and around. Her tendons in her knees burned and the bushes and trees flew by and the houses' colors melted together like old crayons left in the sun. She could feel the wind pulling her hair back tight against her head; the rubber band had worked free long ago. She kept her lips pressed close together, her teeth fitted firmly, one against the other. She breathed carefully through her nose, counting only the number of times she blinked, the number of blocks left to go, the number of houses until hers.

No one was at the dinner table even though the places were still set with milk in the glasses and a cold square of lentil loaf on each plate. Jory walked quickly through the house, running her hand along the corners and edges of each thing she passed. Table. Chair. Kitchen counter. Oven. Toaster. Light switch. Wallpaper with the green roosters on it. Her father was always home from teaching by now. "Dad?" she called. "Dad?" She found them down in the bomb shelter. Her father had his headset on and was listening to a shortwave message from Pastor Ron in Guanajuato. Grace hadn't been feeling well and the elders thought it best if maybe she left Mexico a few days early, although Grace herself had made it clear that she didn't want to go. No, they didn't think it was anything serious, only some intestinal disturbance — the water perhaps, or the aftereffects from her typhoid shot maybe. Jory watched her father nodding his head as he wrote this information down on the back of one of his QSL cards. *Typhoid?* he had written in his clear, firm printing, and underneath that, *Cholera? Hepatitis?* He drew circles around each one as he listened. Jory's mother made a little noise and left the room, brushing past Jory without even looking at her. Frances was sitting underneath her father's homemade desk sorting some shiny round metal slugs into piles. "Look, Jory." She held up a handful for inspection. "We're rich!"

Jory knocked a small knock on her mother's bedroom door, and then pushed the door open as quietly as she could. Her mother was lying on the bed with her apron still on and a wet washcloth over her eyes. Jory leaned against the door's edge and watched her mother breathing.

"They're going to fly Grace home tomorrow," Jory said. It felt very strange to be looking at her mother while her mother couldn't see her. Her mother could always see her. Always. Even with her eyes closed, her mother could see her. "Grace is going to be okay. She is. Dad says so." Jory didn't know why she was whispering. She moved over to the bed and sat on its corner. She smoothed the yellow rose design on the quilt over and over with the palm of her hand. "Mom?" she said. *"Mom?"*

Her mother lay perfectly still on the bed, giving no sign of having heard anything at all.

■ ■ ■ ■

Later, Jory lay in her own bed and listened to her father pounding around the backyard. He had already done his twenty times; she had counted. She got out of bed and kneeled next to the window. Even though it was dark, she could see his outline moving slowly past the fence and beyond. After twenty-five times, she gave up counting. Her eyes had adjusted now and she could see a tiny bit of light glinting off the silver pen he still had in his shirt pocket. She pressed her hand against the window screen so she could see even better, and peered upward. The moon was nearly full and she was sure that if it weren't so very bright she could see the stars that were bound to be up there. What did the stars look like to someone in Mexico? What did they look like to someone in jail for supposedly shoplifting? She wanted to ask her father when he came jogging past, but as he finally pounded right next to her window, she saw the expression on his face lit up by the moon and she let him go by. As he moved farther from her, the noise of his running melted away, and she heard something like carnival music in the distance, a tinkling kind of gypsy music as faint as a blue tattoo, growing slowly closer and closer to where she knelt waiting in her window.

CHAPTER THREE

Jory and Frances weren't allowed to go. Their father was going to go pick Grace up from the airport and drive her straight to the doctor's all by himself. Their mother wasn't going because she was still lying on her bed with a wet washcloth over her eyes, the shades pulled down, and the bedroom door shut. And Jory and Frances weren't going because, as much as their father would love to have both of his favorite girls along, as much as he'd love to have their company, it was going to be a longish trip with nothing much to see or do in the way of fun. It would just be a lot of bag carrying and boring medical stuff, and they'd be glad they'd stayed home. They would. But he would be sure to tell Grace they loved her and they could see her as soon as Dr. Henry gave her a clean bill of health. As their father told them this, he glanced occasionally at the three-by-five card on which he had made notes, and then kissed the top of Frances's head and told Jory again to call Mrs. Mangum at the church office if she had any problems, any at all, and not to bother Mom because she needed to rest. And then he was gone.

It was hot outside, but there was nothing else to do, so they sat on the curb with their bare feet in the gutter and shot stones at the streetlight with Jory's slingshot.

"Hey, watch, Fran." Jory lowered her sights and took careful aim at one of Mr. Garmendia's cats. "Take that, Afro Cat."

"Don't!" Frances shrieked and swatted hard at Jory's arm.

Jory turned and pointed the slingshot at Frances's face and pulled the rubber band back as far as it would go. "You are so stupid sometimes."

Frances stared at the slingshot. "Mom will kill you if you shoot me."

Jory turned away from Frances and watched the furry black tomcat pick its careful way through the weeds that bloomed wildly in the empty lot across the street. She sent a rock sailing toward the portion of its backside she could still see. "Mom can't kill me if she won't ever get out of bed."

"She'll get up. She's not supposed to yet because of her sick headache."

"Oh, yeah, right — her *headache.*" Jory aimed at the rear wheel of Mr. Garmendia's old blue Plymouth. The rock made a wonderful pinging, denting sound as it hit and then ricocheted off the car's metal hubcap. Her mother's headaches coincided unsurprisingly with anxiety-producing events or any activity she strongly disapproved of. And they always involved closed doors and wet washrags and blue pills of some sort.

Frances swirled her big toe through the muddy trickle of water that ran down the gutter. "Dad says that animals have their own special kind of heaven — a different place or section or something — but why would they?" Frances shaded her eyes with her hand. "Jory, what's typhoid?" She squinted against the noontime brightness. "What is it?"

"It's something Grace doesn't have." Jory tied and then retied the knots in the slingshot's rubber band.

"Is she going to die?"

"Yes, and so are you — when you're ninety-two." Jory made a lunge for Frances, grabbing her around the waist and tickling her underneath the ribs where she was the most susceptible. "Ninety, ninety-one,

87

ninety-two!"

Frances screamed, tossing her head back and forth — she was terribly ticklish. Suddenly she gasped and wrenched Jory's hands away. "Wait — stop it, Jory, stop it — listen!" Frances jumped up and pointed down past the end of their block, where the little white truck could be seen coming around the corner. "I heard him before you did!"

The truck inched toward them incrementally. It swerved a little and seemed about to stop every few feet even though there was no one on the street but them — its loopy music winding up and back down again like the tail on a broken, tree-caught kite.

Today he had a hat on. Jory could see it through the windshield of the truck: a weird brownish-looking hat like the kind newsboys in old TV shows wore. His red hair crinkled out from the sides and back of it.

"Well, Mother Mary," the ice cream man said. He had pulled the truck to a stop right by their feet and was leaning out from the driver's seat. "And here's Sister Susan too." He grinned broadly, revealing a set of beautifully white teeth. "What'll it be today, madams?"

"I'm not Sister Susan," Frances said, staring at a spot near her toes, but Jory glanced directly up into his face. "We won't be buying anything today," Jory said, still looking at where tiny red whiskers were sprouting all along the bottom portion of his cheeks and jaw.

"Why not? Not hungry?"

"No," Frances said, standing up. "We don't have any money. Our dad went off to the airport and didn't give us any."

"Hey, okay. Well, how about two of the house specials on the house? We're having a sale, you know — anything red and carcinogenic." He lifted his hat and turned it around, front to back. "That is, anything technically cherry or strawberry flavored is so marked down that it could for practical purposes be considered, um, actually free." He stood up and bent partially out of sight, his large red-haired hands lifting and reaching inside the silver freezer's door.

Frances had moved closer to the doorway of the truck without Jory noticing. "Our sister is dying," she said, and took the Good Humor bar the ice cream man held out to her.

"No, she's not." Jory stood up, but she couldn't figure out where her hands should go now. "She's not."

"Okay." The red-haired man squinted his eyes at something off in the distance. "Say, do either of you ladies know anyplace nice to take a swim? The kind of place where dogs can go too and nobody squawks much?"

"Like the lake?" Frances broke off a piece of the ice cream's cherry coating with her fingers and placed it flat side down on her tongue. "Do you have a dog?"

"I used to. Where's the lake?"

Jory was standing next to Frances now. She stared up into the truck's interior, quickly memorizing the clear green beads hanging in a loop around the truck's rearview mirror, the transistor radio that sat on the dash in a black leather case, his blue-striped shirt with ROGER embroidered in red above one pocket. "Don't you live here . . . Roger?" She could feel something in her rib cage tightening and burning a little. She closed her eyes. Maybe he hadn't heard her.

"Ha!" He hit the spot where the name tag was with the flat of his hand. "Roger! Wouldn't that be something? Roger Mylander. *My land, Roger!*" This last he said in some high, squeaky lady's voice.

Jory took a step back. "I know Roger Mylander," she said. She now dared to look at the ice cream man's yellow-brown eyes. They had tiny crinkles at the corners that made him look like he spent a lot of time smiling. Or else squinting. "He sells houses for Reddish Realty."

"He goes to our church." Frances had squatted back down on the curb in order to eat the ice cream bar with greater ease.

The ice cream man sat down too. He got down from the driver's seat and perched on the truck's metal step and held his hands out in front of him. He spread his fingers wide, as if examining the backs of them for dirt or scars. For an instant, Jory could see the small blue tattoos between his fingers. They looked like fish tails or maybe tiny hooks. "Where do y'all go to church?" he said.

"Garden of Gethsemane Church of the Nazarene." Frances reeled off this information proudly.

Jory glanced away, pretending a sudden interest in something on the Reisensteins' front porch. Her shame at having to discuss their churchgoing with him was like a live thing — a small wriggling worm that left a red-hot trail as it climbed higher up her throat and face.

"Bible-thumpers, hm?" he said, looking at Jory for a long moment. "I'm not from around here, so I don't have the foggiest notion where the lake is. What do you think?

Could one of you draw me a map, maybe?" He pulled a small paper napkin out of his shirt pocket and after fumbling around in all of his pants pockets he finally produced a pen. He handed them both to Jory, and she held them out in front of her as if she'd never had any contact with either before.

"I'm not very good at drawing directions." She wrinkled her nose. "I could probably tell you how to get there, though."

"Hey," he said and slapped himself in the forehead like the man in the V8 commercial. "I've got a better idea. Why don't you two ride along with me, and you can show me how to get there?"

"I don't know." Jory had no idea what to say — was he serious? "It's pretty far from here."

"Really? Shoot." He took his hat off and turned it around and around in his hands. He looked different without it — younger and a little forlorn — like the dog that used to live in the alley behind Albertsons. "That's too damn bad. It's so hot, you know — I was really looking forward to some swimming."

"Well, there's the canal. The Elijah drain ditch. It's a lot closer." She knew that she was moving deliberately down a road her

92

mother had told her never, ever, *ever* to go on.

"Hey, great! And y'all have to come too." He stood up and put his hat back on, and then he held his hand out to Jory.

She reached up and took it.

The water in the canal was freezing cold. Frances wisely sat on the grassy bank, making dandelion chains and eating another cherry Push Up. Jory, however, did not want to look like a baby, so she had waded out until the water reached her waist, and there she stood, feeling the current pull and tug at her legs.

"C'mon in," the ice cream man yelled at her from the middle of the canal. He was stroking furiously against the current, going nowhere. "Wow!" he shouted. "This is incredible!" He ducked under the water and then came up in a different spot, his red hair all dark and slicked to his head like an otter's.

Jory had no idea what she was doing here. The whole thing was like some really strange dream that was sweeping her along and would end with her living someone else's life way across town somewhere. He used bad language and she had seen several silver beer cans rolling around in the back of the ice cream truck. Plus, he was out there in the water in a pair of blue cutoffs. Only a pair of cutoffs, no shirt or anything. Her father always wore a T-shirt when they went swimming. He said it kept him from getting sunburned. Jory had never seen a man with his shirt off before, except for maybe once or twice when old Mr. Garmendia was mowing his lawn. The ice cream man had slightly curly red hair on his chest. It traveled in a V down to the top of the blue cutoffs, and he had two terribly pink nipples that reminded her of raspberries. And whenever he came up on shore, like he was doing now, his wet shorts dragged down and exposed some small, rounded, muscly place above each of his hip bones.

"Hey," he said, plowing toward her through the shallow water. He stood up next to her and gave his head a shake, squeezing at his hair to get the water out. "Don't you want to come in? It's not that cold when you get used to it, plus the water's pretty clear. You can see almost to the bottom."

"No, that's okay." Jory held her arms tight to her chest. "I'm really not that good of a swimmer."

"Well, you know what? How lucky for you, because I just happen to be a certified swimming instructor." He flexed his arms and struck a muscle man's pose. "Junior life-guard, third class. So here we go, tadpole, time for your first lesson." He tried to take her hand, but Jory pulled back from him, her feet sliding a little on the canal's muddy bottom. "Okay, okay," he said in a quiet voice, "don't panic. I won't let anything happen to you — we'll take it nice and easy. What's your real name, blue eyes?"

"It's Jory. *J-o-r-y.*" She took another step away from him in the water.

"Well, alrighty then. How do you do?" He bowed and held out his wet hand. "I'm Grip."

"Grip?" She examined his face to see if he was teasing her.

"Yup, and I have a brother named Early. My mother was a strong believer in going with her first impressions. She told fortunes too." He had his arm around her waist now and was walking her slowly toward the deeper part of the canal. "She thought intuition was the thing. 'Always trust that stone in your gut,' she would say. 'It will never steer you wrong if you pay attention to which way it's twisting — sharp or smooth, sharp or smooth.' " The water was up to Jory's chin, but Grip was holding her tightly with both of his arms. She tried to turn around to look at the shore, to see if

Frances was okay, but he whispered, "Sharp or smooth," and then in one quick movement he lifted her up and took a big breath of air and they were floating. They were in the middle of the canal, where the water went down, down, black, blackest, and he was floating on his back and she was floating on top of him, his arms still wrapped around the waist portion of her wet cutoffs. The water barely lapped over her stomach as they moved with the current. She let her head lie back on his chest, watching the clouds in the sky move past, and the tiny holes where the stars were sleeping, each with one eye open. She could feel his legs under hers warm and wet and him moving his feet a little bit, but everything was so gentle that it was as if he and she weren't really moving at all, as if the sky was the thing sailing past all slow and easy, as if they were merely resting on the water. "Hold your breath," he said in her ear, "and keep holding it." And then he had slipped out from under her and she was alone in the water, floating like before, only slightly heavier now, her legs hanging free in the cool of the water, the darkness below her still pulling her smoothly along on its current, until suddenly, just like that, her body twitched in recognition of its untethered-ness, its terrible precarious freedom in this deep volume of water, and she jerked and thrashed and fell. She had taken in only a mouthful or two of water when he got her. He held her up and kept treading water until she quit choking. "Put your arms around my neck," he said, so she did. He turned around in her arms until he was facing away from her and then he began swimming. "Let your legs hang free behind you," he said as he pushed his arms through the water. She rode on his back to the shore.

Grip gave Jory a striped Indian blanket to hold around her in case she felt cold. He showed Frances how to move the gearshift when he put in the clutch, and then he changed gears about a million times so Frances could shift over and over. "Like that?" she would say. "Like that?" as they lurched down the road. Jory sat on the metal floor of the truck, her back leaning against a huge cardboard box of paper napkins. Grip had turned the transistor radio on, but Jory could still hear Frances happily babbling away above the song about making love in the green grass behind the stadium. Jory took her comb out of her back pocket and tried to rake through her wet rat's nest of hair. She couldn't swim and she'd nearly drowned and she probably looked horrible and like a complete baby. Her shorts and shirt were damp and clinging to her braless front, she had goose bumps everywhere, and she couldn't think of anything to say. She just sat there doing and saying absolutely nothing like some sort of idiot child. Rhonda Russell would have been doing and saying plenty.

"Hey, you doing all right back there?" Grip had turned around in his seat to look at her.

She nodded and tried to smile, but her mouth wouldn't seem to work properly. For some stupid reason she could feel her throat getting tight with tears. When he turned back around, she took the pointed end of her comb and stuck it through the side of the cardboard box. Hard.

Back on Ninth Avenue, everything appeared unchanged. Jory had almost expected to see the house in flames or her mother standing in the driveway in her bathrobe surrounded by police cars and revolving lights. But, evidently, no one had even noticed that they'd been gone. Frances had already hopped out of the truck and was running toward the backyard, where Afro Cat could be seen lying in a patch of late afternoon sun. Jory folded up the Indian blanket and put it on top of the cardboard box. She walked as casually as she could past the driver's seat. Grip grabbed at her back pocket as she tried to step out the truck's door. "So, when's our next swimming lesson?" he said, tugging gently on the fabric of her shorts.

She still couldn't think of anything to say, but now it didn't seem to matter. She couldn't bear looking at him, but she smiled down at the truck's metal floor, and after a moment he let go of her pocket. She didn't turn around to watch him drive away either — she kept walking toward the house, waiting for the sweet twinge that would start in the small of her back, the happy eye in her spine she knew would open wide when the truck's tinkly music began to play.

Before Jory even woke up, she could hear the hum of her parents' voices. They were talking in the kitchen in low, fast tones. Jory got up quietly so she wouldn't wake Frances and put on a pair of shorts and her *Spy vs. Spy* T-shirt. She walked nonchalantly into the kitchen and opened the refrigerator. Her parents were no longer talking. "You're up," Jory said, looking only at the plastic milk jug.

"Yes," her mother said. "Of course."

"How'd you sleep?" her father asked as he always did.

"Fine," she answered as she always did. "Where's Grace?"

Her father took a small bite of toast. "Do you want some juice?" he said. He picked up the carton and held it up toward her. "There's just enough left."

Jory's mother fastened and unfastened the top button on her bathrobe. "Grace is out back."

"She is?" Jory turned and set the milk jug down on the counter with a thump. "Is she okay?"

"Grace is fine," her father said firmly and began buttering another piece of toast. "She's a little tired and worn-out from the trip and Dr. Henry's going to take another look at her next week and maybe run a couple tests, but, you know, she's going to be just fine. Absolutely fine."

Jory's mother glanced at her husband and then got up and went to the sink, where she stood looking out the window at something.

Grace was lying on the chaise lounge in the very middle of the backyard with an old green bedspread pulled over her. She was facing the sun and her eyes were closed.

Her hair was longer than Jory had ever seen it. Jory felt suddenly shy, as if she'd never met her sister before. "Aren't you hot?" she said, and then blushed. It was a stupid thing to say to someone you hadn't seen in nearly three months.

"No. Not really." Grace's voice was very quiet and sort of far away. She seemed completely unsurprised to be discussing this with Jory. "It's just that it was so hot in Mexico that now I feel cold everywhere else." Grace said this without opening her eyes.

"Are you sick?"

"I don't know. I don't think so. Everything looks kind of strange, but maybe I'd just never noticed it before."

"Is that why you have your eyes closed?" Jory bent closer to the chaise lounge, as if Grace might not be able to hear either.

"Like the streets. Have the streets always been this wide? They seem incredibly wide. And clean. Everything is so big and so clean and empty."

"You could come look at my and Frances's room." Jory smiled even though Grace couldn't see her.

"Things smell strange, too. The house, our house, it smells like . . . classical music. Like Rachmaninoff or maybe Albinoni." Grace

101

laughed a short laugh that was almost a bark. "Dad says I probably just have culture shock. He says it happens all the time, but usually the other way around. That when you get to a foreign country, you feel like this, not when you come back home."

Jory watched a tear ooze out from under one of Grace's closed lids and slide partway down her cheek. She had never seen Grace cry. Or if she had, she didn't remember it. "Do you want me to go get Mom?" she whispered.

"No." Grace wiped at her face with the hem of the green blanket. "No, I'm okay. Really. So," she said, smiling crookedly at Jory with her eyes still closed, "tell me everything that happened while I was gone."

Jory thought faintly, briefly of attempting this. "There's nothing to tell," she said finally. "I got a babysitting job with the Hewetts."

Grace pulled the bedspread up even higher, until it covered her chin and mouth. "That's wonderful, Jory," she said in her new, faraway voice. "What a perfect chance for you to witness."

Tonight their church was having a welcome-back service for Grace. The other mission workers were still in Mexico for another

102

week, but Grace was going to share her slides from Mexico and give a talk about the ministry work they had done there. Their mother did not think this was a good idea. She said Grace needed to take it easy and rest. That the last thing Grace needed to be doing was to be giving speeches. Their father said nothing. Now Jory and Rhonda Russell were sitting in the pew behind Jory's mother and Frances, and Frances kept turning around to stare at them. "She's so cute," Rhonda whispered generously. Jory poked Frances's hand with one of the tiny gold pencils they kept in the hymnal holders. "Turn around," Jory hissed. Frances squealed and her mother turned and gave Jory a look.

Jory's father stood in the middle of the red-carpeted aisle helping Grace set up the slide projector, while Brother Elmore took a long-poled hook and — *swooosh* — pulled the big white screen down until it covered even the empty wooden cross at the very front of the church. Someone, somewhere, turned down the lights and everyone got quiet. Jory loved this part of church — the light dimming on darkish Sunday evenings. It felt like all the world was enclosed and breathing in this one room. You could suddenly feel the people next to you, the quiet

103

coughing and leg crossing and the smell of breath mints and perfume and unfamiliar shoes moving against the hardwood floor. In the darkness now she could hear Grace, but not see her. "Mexico is a land of many colors," Grace's disembodied voice was saying. "A place of plenty and a place of want." The slide projector clicked loudly and the screen was filled with a picture of a tiny boy with huge black eyes. The boy was wearing only a pair of bright red plastic sandals and he was holding a fly-encrusted chicken bone. *Click-chunk* went the projector. "We came to offer help and aid and to bring a message of new life to the people of this beautiful country. A message of eternal life for those whose earthly lives may not be filled with joy." On the screen, a woman with no discernible teeth smiled broadly as she held up some kind of hairy-looking fruit. *Click-chunk.* "A better way for those who live in darkness — a light by which to see." Two old men looked up from their work. The chicken whose throat they had just slit hung upside down, its blood draining and pooling onto the men's bare feet. Jory could feel her mother's spine stiffening in the pew in front of her. "Gross!" Rhonda whispered hotly into Jory's ear. *Click-chunk.* "We came to bring the love of Christ to

104

people who, people who . . ." Grace's voice faltered. The cone of light that spun out from the slide projector whirled with dust motes and gave off a smell of burning plastic. On the screen a million tiny houses clustered on top of each other against a brown hillside, while in the foreground a bone-thin dog scuttled past. Jory squinted into the darkness, but could see only the outline of Grace's head and, behind her, their father, bent over the projector. Grace began again, but now it was as if she were breathing or dreaming while she spoke, as if she were in a huge, soft rush to get it all out. "It was strange," she said in this new voice. "The people keep their dogs on the roofs here — they bark all night, but they hardly ever jump down — and every morning the people all sweep the sidewalks and the balconies with long-bristled brooms and lemon water — sometimes the people below get wet, but they always laugh, and little boys carry newspapers, and huge net bags filled with bananas and oranges, and big blocks of ice, all on their bicycles." On the screen a group of large white people in short-sleeved shirts stood next to the beginnings of a concrete foundation. *Future Sight of the Guanajuato Church of the Nazarene,* a handwritten sign proclaimed. The large people smiled through their sunburns. "White-uniformed guards stand in front of the more beautiful buildings and they carry rifles and whistle long, complicated tunes, and there are pigeons everywhere — there was one that slept outside my hotel window and made a smoker's cough sort of noise all night long until I could hardly sleep, and old women sell long slabs of sticky brown candy in the *mercado* that have flies crawling all over them, but no one seems to mind." Jory's father seemed to be having trouble with the projector. The slides came faster and faster and then stopped altogether on a picture of a brightly colored plaster saint with no nose. "The garbage men wear cowbells on their belts so people will know they're coming and bring out their garbage and the houses and buildings are orange and pink and gold and lime green like rainbow sherbet and every night everyone goes to the plaza to look at and talk to everyone else and at sundown the bells ring and it's time for Mass — inside the church is like the inside of those Easter eggs with peepholes cut in them, gold and robin's egg blue — they keep the hands and hair of Saint Beatrice, the twelve-year-old virgin martyr, in a glass coffin there." Grace took a big breath. "Once I saw a man carrying a pink Barbie purse, its strap was broken and inside was nothing but dog food."

Jory sat very still and stared straight ahead, even though she could feel Rhonda Russell looking at her sideways out of the corners of her slanted eyes. Someone had turned the lights back on and Jory's father was talking quietly to Grace and holding her by the arm. Grace smiled shakily at him and then pulled out of his grasp and headed toward the platform at the front of the church. Brother Elmore was standing and trying to smile as Grace climbed the stairs and approached the podium, but Grace brushed right past him and gripped the wooden pulpit with both hands. She stood straight and tall as she always did and Jory could tell that her mother was beginning to cry in the pew in front of her. Grace continued to stand there saying nothing, just looking out over the audience. All the people in the congregation seemed to be holding their breath.

At last Grace leaned a little toward the microphone. "When I was exactly seven years old," she said, "I listened to Hazel and Harmon Schmelzenbach speak in a Sunday night service just like this one. They showed us slides from Swaziland, Africa, of muddy rivers and huge snakes and red-painted natives holding spears in front of grass huts, and I knew right then that I was being called by God to be a foreign missionary. I knew, even though I was only seven years old, that God had sought me out, and that I had been chosen for this very purpose, and that everything in my life should be lived toward that end. I had to wait almost ten more years before I could go on a mission of my own. But I spent that time studying and praying and fasting and planning for the day that I, too, would be able to say, 'Here am I, Lord, send me,' and then come back to my home church bearing witness of the work that I had done in countries that had never heard the good news of the Gospel."

Grace stopped for a moment, pushing her hair back with her hands, her birthmark partly visible. Even from where she was sitting, Jory could see the faint line of sweat that dotted her sister's hairline. "And tonight," Grace said, her voice shaking, "tonight is that night." She regripped the pulpit and seemed to sway a little on her feet. Jory noticed that her father had slowly been approaching the platform the whole time Grace was speaking, and he was now climbing the carpeted steps up to his daughter. "But the work the Lord has done in me has just begun," said Grace with a radiant smile. "His plans for me are greater than I had even anticipated." Her father had now reached Grace and was stretching his hand out toward her arm. Without turning her head, Grace swatted her father's hand away. *"Behold the handmaid of the Lord,"* Grace said, *"may it be done unto me according to thy word."* Grace took two steps around her father and walked down the platform stairs and all the way up the red-carpeted church aisle and out the back door. Everyone in the pews listened as the church's heavy oak door thudded shut behind her.

"Where'd Grace go?" Frances stood up on the seat of the pew and turned toward the back of the church. "Where are your teeth, Rhonda?" she said loudly, peering down at both of them.

Brother Elmore was giving a signal to the organist and then waving his hands at the congregation. "Let's all stand. Page one fourteen in your hymnals, folks — 'We'll Girdle the Globe with Salvation' — page one hundred and fourteen. The first, second, and final verse."

CHAPTER FOUR

In August, the air would bake all day, getting hotter and hotter each afternoon until finally sometime around eight or nine at night the sky would turn a purple-blue and licks of heat lightning would dart and flicker silently at the edge of the horizon, like silver snake tongues trying to catch a smell of the evening. Jory loved the air then; it felt thick and smelled like new dirt, the kind that violets and mossy things grow in, so she didn't even mind so much the stars being gone. At this time of day, she liked to walk barefoot on the sidewalk that was still warm from the sun. Even if you came out at midnight, it wouldn't have cooled off. From where she was tightrope walking along the curb, she could see Mrs. Hewett sitting on her front step smoking. The end of the cigarette glowed large and then went out. Even though she'd never seen one, Jory imagined that this is what a firefly must look like — like a lonely cigarette smoked by a ghost. She said these last words over in her head and then softly out loud.

"Jory," Mrs. Hewett said.

Jory made her way through the grass to the Hewetts' front porch and stood a few feet away from Mrs. Hewett's long tanned legs. She watched the red tip of Mrs. H's cigarette glowing in the darkness. Smoking was an abomination in the sight of the Lord. It destroyed healthy lung tissue and healthy lives. And it looked so cool.

"I still haven't paid you for last week." Mrs. Hewett flicked expertly at her cigarette and a BB of ash flew onto the cement. "Let me go get my checkbook."

"No, it's okay. I can just get it on Monday."

"If you're sure." Mrs. Hewett took a long puff. "Say, did your father have any luck finding someone to go to Mexico? Jack would have done it, but I said no, I didn't want him gone that long. I feel too lonely here with just Dinah and me. This is *not* the most exciting town in the world." She dropped the cigarette into her can of Tab and it went out with a hiss. "But I'm sure he'll find somebody. Maybe he should even try the cops down there, although I hear they're not much better than the crooks."

111

She laughed briefly. "Maybe they *are* the crooks."

Jory tried to smile. "I better go, I guess."

"Oh, sure. Um, Jory —" Mrs. Hewett took out her pack of Kools and began tapping it against her thigh. "I'm really sorry about whatever happened to Grace. Whoever the guy is." Mrs. Hewett slid another cigarette out and held it between her fingers. She gazed off at the night sky. "You know, if it doesn't cool off soon, I may just have to kill myself."

Jory walked back down the sidewalk to her house. The porch light was on and small white moths fluttered and circled endlessly above the evergreen bushes. The sky was completely dark now and the purply clouds had moved away. A sliver of a fingernail moon hung over their backyard, but the rest of the sky was as blank as cloth.

Inside, her mother was washing dishes and her father was sitting at the kitchen table peeling apples with his old Swiss Army knife. Jory slid into one of the chairs next to him. He held out a slice of apple to her on the blade of his knife, but she shook her head.

"They're still good," he said. "Not like the ones you get at the store. Those are mere imitations of apples. Not even reasonable

112

facsimiles." He smiled.

"I was talking to Mrs. Hewett."

"Um-hm." Her father picked up another apple and made a neat nick at its top.

"She thinks someone did something to Grace in Mexico. A man, I mean." Jory could feel her face and neck getting hot. This was not the way she talked to her father. This was not what they talked about.

Her father had a perfect curl of red apple skin hanging off the end of his knife. He set the apple down on the table, curl and all. He glanced up at Jory's mother. "So much for confidentiality," he said. He took a long breath and then let it out again. "Jory, there are some things in life that are, well, private. Personal things that don't necessarily benefit from a public discussion."

Jory said nothing.

"Not every topic demands a public airing."

"I'm not public. I mean, *the* public."

"No," her father said after a moment, "maybe not. But do you really feel it's imperative that we talk about this right now? At this very second?"

Jory waited. Out of the corner of her eye she could see that her mother had turned off the faucet and was standing next to the sink with her hands in the dishwater.

Her father folded his hands together in front of him. "I'm working very hard here, Jory, to keep things on an even keel."

Jory picked up her father's knife and gouged a small hole in the green linoleum tabletop. "Even the neighbors know more than I do."

"That's enough, Jory." Her mother dropped a large handful of silverware onto the counter.

No one said anything more, and after a while her father recaptured his knife and went back to peeling apples and her mother began rinsing the dishes. Jory stood up then and walked down the hall to her room. Grace's bedroom door was shut and Frances was already asleep in the bed across from hers. Jory lay down on her bed on her back and closed her eyes. If she were at Rhonda's right now, they'd be watching *The Avengers* on TV or drawing breasts and mustaches on her troll dolls. Or maybe they'd get out her (hidden and illicit) Ouija board to find out which boys from school they would marry. Jory sat up. She could hear that jingly carnival music playing somewhere off in the distance. She couldn't tell, though, if it was coming nearer or drifting farther away. The window at the foot of her bed was already open because of the heat, but the screen was not. She pulled and jiggled the little buttons at the base of the mesh screen, but nothing happened. She thought she could hear the music becoming the slightest bit more faint. With both hands she pushed hard right in the middle of the screen until it made a small popping sound and fell out of its moorings and onto the grass below. Jory pushed the wooden window frame up as far as it would go and stuck one leg through until it touched the ground below. She pulled her other leg after it.

Outside she could hear the music more clearly. She walked down the street until she could see the white dot of a truck several blocks ahead of her, and then she began to run. She ran quietly down Ninth Avenue, her feet barely tapping the ground. There were no cars and she ran smooth and steady down the middle of the road, the warm air flattening her T-shirt against her chest. It was like swimming through perfect water, the outside temperature the same as her insides. Like she had no skin. As she loped past, she could see people inside their houses watching television or sitting in the lamplight at kitchen tables. It was as if she were a ghost drifting by — she could see them but they couldn't seem to see her. She had read a book in school like that: a man who died revisits his home and floats quietly past the places and people he has known without them ever sensing his presence. It was a sad book, Jory remembered. Sad, but wonderful.

The ice cream truck was much closer. In fact it was now stopped under a streetlight next to the grassy lot the kids called God's Park because of a drunk old man who used to hand out Bible tracts there for money. She slowed to a walk and tried to breathe normally. He was lying near the truck in a patch of tall grass with his arms crossed behind his head. She walked over and stood next to his lower legs. "Hi," she said, panting only slightly.

He leaned up onto his elbows. "Well, hey there." He peered behind her. "Where's your little chaperone?" His hair was in several braids that stood out at various angles from his head.

"In bed."

He cocked his head at her. "It's pretty dark out here for a lovely young lady such as yourself."

"Well," she said, sitting down in the grass, "I guess I'll just have to chance it." She plucked out a long weed and began peeling back its layers of green skin. She smiled

116

slightly, amazed at her own daring.

"How about a Swirl Top? A Push Up? An Old Milwaukee?" He stood up and went over to the truck, disappearing inside. After a moment, his head reappeared. "Here," he said, and tossed a shiny can in her direction. She tried to catch it, but it fell at her feet and rolled a few inches away. "Better not open it for a minute," he said, coming around the side of the truck. "Pretty explosive stuff."

He sat down next to her and took a long swig, and she watched his Adam's apple bob up and down the length of his throat. He picked up the other beer and opened it and passed her the can.

She held the beer in her hand. It was ice cold, and a bitter metal smell wafted up from the triangular opening. Her mother would cry if she could see her doing this. "I'm not really thirsty," she said, and put the can on the ground between them.

He shrugged. "More for me," he said, and lay back down in the flattened grass.

Jory leaned cautiously back into the grass next to him. The sky was huge and dark. She could hear crickets in the weeds nearby, and maybe even a frog or two. "My big sister went to Mexico and now there's something wrong with her," she said.

"What do you mean? Is she sick?"

"I don't know. No. Not exactly. But she says things smell different, and she stays in her room and cries all the time under a blanket, and my dad tried to hire a detective to go to Mexico and look for some man, but he won't talk about it." Jory sighed. "And my mom is furious at everyone."

"Wow," he said. "How old is your sister?"

"She's seventeen. She turns eighteen in December."

They lay there and the crickets scratched and chirped as soft and as near as Jory had ever heard them.

He pointed up. "Have you ever noticed how when the clouds move in the sky at night, it looks like the stars are moving and the clouds are holding still. You know what I mean?"

"She's pregnant, isn't she?"

"And sometimes when the clouds move especially fast, when they're really zooming along, it's like the whole world, the whole curved earth you're lying on, is holding still while the sky above is flying, and all you can do is just hang on."

He had reached out his hand and was holding hers. Not too tight, just loosely as if it were almost accidental, as if it were a thing that they had fallen into, like rain falling easy and gentle out of the sky. The sky. It was dark as a purple-black plum but pierced here and there by tiny fingerlings of light. A few brave stars that had poked right through the rough cloth that held the world together. An entire, perfectly spaced constellation. A whole family of stars, with not one star missing.

CHAPTER FIVE

The air in the house on Ninth Avenue took on a strange, musty smell. A cramped, closeted smell that reminded Jory of the nursing home her grandfather had lived in for a month before he died. Each day when Jory came home from babysitting she would open their front door and the odor would strike her anew — it was a smell of things stored in boxes, dusty and sour, of roots and things growing underground — the smell of a place where people are deliberately staying in one spot. Where people are moving as little as possible.

Their father was gone. No one had said why, but he was now in Mexico. He had kissed Jory good-bye early one morning when she was still in bed. "Be very good, and take care of Frances," he'd said, smoothing back her sleep-wrinkled hair. "And don't cause your mother any problems. All right?" She had nodded. Her father had stood up and the mattress felt suddenly light and insubstantial as a cloud, as untethered and free floating as a leaf dropped into a stream. *"Wait,"* she'd said, sitting up in bed, but he had already picked up his suitcase and was closing the front door.

Their mother had taken to living in her bedroom with the shades drawn, and Grace was spending nearly all day in hers. Some new and unspoken contract had been devised by which Grace and their mother agreed never to deliberately intersect: a wordless schedule that allowed for only one of them to be outside of their bedroom at a time. This was mostly not a problem since their mother left hers only to use the bathroom or to take more of her headache pills with a glass of milk.

Yesterday, though, Jory had been standing in the hallway when her mother came back from the kitchen at the exact same time that Grace opened her bedroom door. "Oh," Grace had murmured. "Sorry." She lowered her eyes. Her mother said nothing. For a moment the three of them stood in the hall looking at the floor. "Maybe you should be," their mother said, her voice so low Jory couldn't quite be sure she had heard it. Their mother turned then and went into her room and shut the door. Jory continued standing in the hallway. Grace made a coughing sound and padded down the hall into the bathroom.

Grace wore the same outfit day after day: a knee-length green skirt that had been the bottom portion of her Pathfinders uniform and an old white button-down shirt of their father's. She rolled up the sleeves, but the rest of it, the front of it, was huge and hung down almost to her knees. It didn't matter what she was doing, that's what she wore, although these days she didn't seem to be doing much.

Jory understood that it was her job not to ask any questions, but to keep Frances occupied and out of the way until whatever it was that was happening to her family had finished happening. It was a state of emergency, but one that revealed itself through suspended animation: the four females drifting slowly past each other in the house like apologetic ghosts. Each day someone was in her bedroom crying, except for Jory, who had nothing to cry about. They didn't go to church or anywhere. Their mother finally sent Jory to the grocery store for plastic plates and cups and silverware because she said she wasn't washing dishes. She wasn't cooking either, and they were going to have to fend for themselves for once in their lives, which meant Rice Krispies for breakfast and hot dogs for lunch and dinner. Jory made Kool-Aid popsicles for Frances and Grace, who said the smell of hot dogs made her sick. No one said anything about buying school shoes, or about the fact that school started in nine days.

At night, it was almost the worst. Everyone went to bed early, even their mother, who spent most of the day lying on her bed anyway. Jory would toss and turn, flipping from one side of the sheet to the other, trying to find a cool spot. She could hear the scritching of the nighttime insects and car tires kicking up gravel on the road, and far, far away the faintest sound of tinkly carnival music. It didn't matter, though. She couldn't leave. Her father would never forgive her if she slipped out and left the others alone. Although what her presence in the house would do to prevent anything, she didn't know. And what could possibly happen that hadn't already? As the night grew on, she could see the beams from car headlights shifting shapes on her ceiling. They moved across the ceiling like searchlights, looking and looking.

And then her father came back. He drove

their green Buick home from the airport and parked in his usual spot in their driveway. Jory watched from inside the front window, as if she weren't allowed to go outside and greet him. "Well, hello," he said, and set his old black suitcase down on the hardwood floor.

"Hello," Jory said, and hugged him hard around the waist — something she hadn't done since she was little.

"Where is everyone?" Her father gazed around the living room as if the brown couch and upholstered rocker and birchwood coffee table were all new to him.

"Oh, you know." Jory shrugged and they looked at each other.

Her father walked toward his bedroom and Jory trailed behind. He stopped in front of the closed bedroom door and then knocked once, something Jory had never seen him do before, ever. Nothing happened, so he turned the door handle and went in. Before the door shut behind him, Jory caught a glimpse of her mother lying on the bed in her faded blue bathrobe, a wet washrag across her eyes.

Jory went into her bedroom and opened her closet door and squeezed inside. She parted blouses and skirts and sat down underneath them on the closet floor. The closet wall was the same as her parents' bedroom wall. She had occasionally done this before, listened in on her parents' private conversations, but only when they had been about her, when she had been in trouble and needed to know the extent of her disgrace and punishment. This was different — this was about someone else. She put her ear against the wall and listened. Her father was telling her mother how much he had missed her and that he had come back as soon as he could. Jory knew he would be rubbing her mother's foot as he said this, stroking her instep in the way that she said helped her headaches. What happened? her mother asked in a voice that meant, *Dispense with the niceties.* Who was it? she asked. Where is he? Well, her father said, that's the problem. There doesn't seem to be anyone. What do you mean, there isn't anyone? Jory could tell her mother was sitting up now, the washrag cast aside. There has to be someone. Some person . . . some *man* is responsible for this. Completely and utterly responsible. And that *man* should be in jail! Jory could hear the bedsprings give a sudden sharp creak. It's criminal, Oren, and I just can't stand it. I mean it, I can't. I agree, I agree, her father said, but if she won't tell us who it was, how are we to know? Pastor Ron has no clue — no one there does. They never saw her with anyone. They never knew that she was out alone, ever. I searched high and low. I talked to everyone, even the police. No one seems to know anything about it. Her father's voice dropped in pitch. I lost my temper more than once. So? *So?* her mother said. You should have done a lot more than lose your temper. There was a pause, and Jory held perfectly still. I just don't know what to do, Esther. Her father sounded tired. I'm at a loss here, he said. Her mother was crying now, in a bitter, broken way that seemed to contain within it a large element of blame. No one said anything for a long moment, which meant no doubt that her father was now rubbing her mother's back. Jory lifted her head until her face was covered by the scratchy material of Frances's winter coat. She breathed in the smell of wool and dust and forgotten pennies in pockets: the smell of Frances and of their closet — of this house, this home.

That night at dinner, the five of them sat around the maple table in the way they always had, as if nothing had happened, as if they had just imagined the past three weeks and their strange in-house vacation.

Their father fixed his gaze on each of them in turn and smiled. "Here are my three lovely daughters," he said.

"Here we are," said Jory.

Their mother was rubbing her temples with both hands.

"Well," said their father. "What are we all doing after dinner? Frances, what do you have planned for the evening?"

"I'm riding my bike," said Frances.

"Very good, very good," said their father. "Jory, what about you?"

Jory shrugged. "I don't know. Reading, I guess."

"All right. How about you two ladies?" Their father smiled brightly at Grace and their mother. "How does a walk down to Albertsons for some ice cream sound to you two?"

Grace pushed her mashed potatoes from one side of her plate to the other. "I'm afraid ice cream makes me sick."

"That's *it*!" Their mother threw her napkin onto the table and screeched her chair back from the table. She stood looking at all of them. "I can't do this. I can't!" She turned and looked at Grace. "Just tell me who it was, Grace. Just tell me who it was so we can do something. Who was it, *who was it, WHO WAS IT*?"

"Esther." Their father stretched his hand out toward their mother, but she stepped out of his reach. "Esther," he said again.

"It was an angel," said Grace, looking up for the first time. "An angel with dark hair."

No one said anything.

Frances switched her gaze from her mother to Grace. "Angels have yellow hair," she said. "Like curled taffy."

Their mother sank back down in her chair.

"He said that you wouldn't understand." Grace's eyes seemed to come alive for the first time since she'd been home. "He said I shouldn't tell anyone because no one would believe it. No one ever believes — Jesus, John the Baptist, Elizabeth, Mary — no one ever believed them at first, did they? Even Jesus's own parents didn't recognize him. There's no point in discussing this because you couldn't possibly understand what has happened to me — it's beyond your ability to comprehend." Grace leaned forward, the skin of her face ablaze as if radiating some kind of internal heat. Jory had never seen her look like this, except for the time years ago when she had come home from Junior Church and said that now she was saved.

"Grace." Their father's voice was quiet. "We very much want to understand."

Their mother had her eyes closed tight

and her hand over her mouth.

"Help us to understand this," her father said in the same quiet voice. Jory recognized it as the voice he used on dogs he wasn't sure wouldn't bite.

Grace folded her hands and rested them on the table. "I didn't ask for this," she said. "It was given to me. It was a thing that was given to me alone, and I alone am to bear it."

Their mother made a soft gasping noise behind her hand.

Grace seemed not to notice their mother. She smoothed the tablecloth where it wasn't lying flat. "I said yes to Jesus long ago, so how could I possibly say no now?" She looked up. "Aren't we always supposed to say yes to God? Dad?"

"Well," said her father. He picked up his fork and put it down again. He cleared his throat. "Yes, of course, we should say yes to God. But first we have to be sure that it is indeed God who is making the request." He spoke quite slowly and seemed to be considering each of the words before he let them out of his mouth. "Wouldn't God always have our best interests at heart?"

Grace leaned forward. "Did it seem like He had Abraham's best interests at heart when He asked him to sacrifice Isaac? Or how about Jesus? Do you think it seemed like God always had *His* best interests at heart?"

"This isn't a theological discussion." Their mother raised her voice. "You are having . . . a . . . baby. And it isn't *God's.*"

Frances put her glass of milk back down. "Grace is having a baby?" Her entire face lit up. "Is it a girl?"

"None of you have any idea what you are saying." Grace's voice was shaking. "I knew it would be like this. I never even wanted to come home from Mexico. At least there I felt good about my calling, about what I've been called to do. Here, I'm surrounded by people whose minds are too small to accept anything other than what the newspaper or the television or, excuse me, the science books tell them."

"What?" their mother said.

"Grace," their father said.

"You went to Mexico to spy on me." Grace's mouth grew tight. "You went to see what I had been up to, but what you didn't realize is that you wouldn't find anything because what you were looking for is from man, and what you see in front of you is from God." For a moment Grace seemed about to say something more. Instead, she closed her mouth, pushed her chair back,

130

stood up, and walked out of the room.

Their mother had both of her hands over her eyes as if to blind herself to the situation. She shook her head back and forth. "No," she said. "No, no, *no*. This isn't happening."

"Now let's stay calm." Their father ran his hand through his hair. "Let's just stay calm and *think* for a minute."

Their mother made a horrible, animal-like sound deep in her chest and sank back down in her chair. She seemed to slowly deflate and grow small, her shoulders rounding and hunching forward until her head was hanging just above her plate of uneaten food. She began to sob in an unguarded way that Jory had never heard before.

Their father's eyes shifted around the table. His glance fell on Jory. "You two go outside and play. Now."

"Mom," said Jory.

Her father gave her a look. "I mean it, Jory. Just do what I tell you to."

Jory got up from the table. "For Pete's sake," she said. *"For Pete's sake."* Even now, it was the worst thing she was allowed to say.

Outside, it was almost dark. The days were

131

already starting to get shorter. Jory and Frances sat on the curb and gazed out into the street. "But how can Grace have a baby?" Frances whispered, squinting up at Jory. "She's not married."

"Just be quiet, Frances." Jory picked up a bottle cap and twisted it back and forth between her fingers. The bottle cap read IT HASTA BE SHASTA. Jory tried to spin the bottle cap off her fingers the way she had seen the boys at school do. It skidded off her finger and fell into the gutter.

"Where will it live?"

"With us, I guess." This was a new thought to Jory. An actual baby that took up space and needed things. She had lain in her bed at night and thought about how the baby had gotten there — she had thought about that quite a bit — but she had never thought about what would happen after.

"I want it to sleep with me." Frances turned and put her hand on Jory's thigh. "Can it?"

"Don't be stupid," said Jory. Across the street, a light winked on above the porch at Mr. Garmendia's house. Soon he would come out and take his nightly stroll around the neighborhood, his three cats trailing single file behind him. "Maybe she'll give it up for adoption." As soon as she said this thought, Jory realized it was a possibility.

"No," said Frances mildly. "We'll keep it."

Mr. Garmendia opened his front door and made the soft clucking sound he used to call his cats. Two of them scurried out from under the bridal wreath bush. The third sauntered slowly up from behind the garage.

"An angel's baby," Jory said. She ran her bare feet across the thin layer of dirt in the gutter. It was soft and slightly warm even though the sun had already gone down.

"Look," said Frances, pointing up. "It's the first star."

"I know," said Jory. "I saw it."

"Make a wish."

"No." Jory squinched the dirt between her toes. "You make one."

Frances gazed upward and began, *"Star bright, star light, first star I see tonight, I wish I may, I wish I might, have this wish I wish tonight."* Frances closed her eyes and moved her lips silently. "There," she said, opening her eyes.

"What'd you wish?" Jory took a twig and made a large swirling letter *G* in the dirt.

"I can't tell you or it won't come true."

Jory nodded.

"But I'll give you a clue — it's about Grace," Frances leaned closer and whispered. "It's about the color of the baby's hair."

Jory sat on the curb long after Frances had fallen asleep in the grass. No one seemed to remember that they were even out here. Her father had been running around the backyard for quite some time now. Inside the house it was dark. She watched the moths as they fluttered around the cone of light that swirled below the corner streetlamp. The moths flitted up to the bulb as near as they dared and then dashed or fell away, scorched or filled with incandescent joy, Jory couldn't tell which. A lawn mower droned on somewhere down the block. Who would be mowing their lawn in the dark? Someone was riding a bicycle down the street toward her; she could see its faint outlines and hear tiny pieces of gravel pinging out from under the bike tires as it came on. The bicycle moved closer and then stopped right at her feet. She looked up and, even in the darkness, she knew him.

"Hey," he said.

"Hey," she said, her face filling warm with blood.

He got off the bike and leaned it against their largest evergreen. "Nice night," he said. He sat down on the curb next to her.

She could smell the odor that he gave off: burned sugar and cigarette smoke and something sharp, like pepper. "The forecast said something about rain, but I don't think so." He rubbed at his eyes with his knuckles and then stretched his legs out in front of him. "What's new?" he said.

"My sister's having a baby," she said.

He tilted his head. "I kind of thought that was old news."

"It's God's baby."

"Wow," he said. "That *is* new." Grip whistled softly through his teeth. "What do your parents have to say about that?"

"They're having a nervous breakdown."

"I suppose so, I suppose so." He pulled a crumpled cigarette out of his shirt pocket and began bending it back and forth. "You know, my mother used to think she could communicate with angels. Or hear them or something."

Jory wondered what had happened to his mother, and then realized she wasn't sure she wanted to know. She watched as pieces of tobacco dropped onto Grip's pant leg. "Where's your ice cream truck?"

"Home. I think the clutch is going out, but I'm too lazy to do anything about it. Hey," he said suddenly, "want to go for a ride?" He made pedaling motions with his hands. "Around and around?" He tilted his head at her. "C'mon," he said, "it's a beautiful night."

Jory sat sideways on the front of the bike's metal crossbar while he pedaled and steered and leaned around her shoulder looking for cars. They rode all the way down Ninth Avenue, veering around parked cars and cats and potholes. They rode faster, whizzing past people in bathrobes watering their lawns or putting out their garbage cans. The night air blew her hair back behind her and he kept having to spit wayward strands of it out of his mouth. Jory felt like laughing and screaming at the same time. Did you ever see *Butch Cassidy and the Sundance Kid*? he yelled into her ear. Is it a movie? she asked. Yep, he said. Then I didn't, she said. That's too bad, he said. You're Katharine Ross and I'm Paul Newman, stealing Robert Redford's girlfriend away for a little two-wheel rendezvous. He pedaled furiously up the long incline of Deer Flat Hill, standing up on the pedals and leaning forward and making the bike wobble. She screamed and clutched his arm and then they reached the top, and then just as suddenly they were flying downhill. Jory was all feeling. The rush of the wind past her ears and the black road forever unzipping beneath the bicycle's wheel left almost no room for thought. If she died like this, she would just have to die. We have to slow down now, he yelled, but not too quick or we'll wreck. He turned the handlebars and they began to loop crazily from one side of the road to the other. Now it felt more like swimming than flying. The bottom of the hill was coming up, she knew. There was a stop sign at the very bottom. We'll have to run it, he said. Hang on. But she already was. There was nothing more to hang on to. They flew past the stop sign and through the cross street. He had just started to brake when they hit the patch of gravel. She knew then that they were in trouble, but there was nothing to be done. The bike tilted and skidded sideways in a way that no bike should, the back tire sliding clear around toward the front. Jory flew off the bike, sliding flat and hard against the graveled pavement, her palms and hip burning like fire.

She could hear Grip swearing now in the dark, and the sound of a bicycle tire spinning all on its own in the air. "Where are you?" he said. *"Shit."*

She stood up from the ground and tried to examine her hands, but it was too dark and she couldn't tell what was blood and what was just shadow. "I'm here," she said.

He helped her up and dusted off her shorts. He examined her hands and hip and made a sharp whistling sound through his teeth. The bike too looked ruined, its front wheel now oddly bent and misshapen. They left the bike where it was and started walking. After a half mile or so, he saw her limping, and he had her jump up onto his back so he could carry her piggyback-style. "Hey," he said as they bumped along with her feet banging clumsily into his thighs. "I'm sorry. I'm a complete idiot and a jerk. If you hate me for the rest of your life, I'll understand."

"So much for Paul Newman," she said, and kicked her heels against his legs a little.

He turned his face toward hers with a look of surprise and then kissed her quickly on the nose. "You are all right," he said. *All right.*

She closed her eyes and rested her chin on his shoulder and smiled the rest of the way home.

Her father was sitting on the front step. The porch light was on and he had his pocket-knife out and was peeling the bark off a willow branch. She had seen him a block away and had made Grip stop and let her walk on by herself. "Hi, Dad," she said, holding her hands casually behind her.

"Where've you been?" He said this without raising his head from the careful notches he was cutting.

"Out," she said. She sat down gingerly next to him. "Just taking a walk."

"Taking a walk at ten thirty at night — is this the type of thing you've gotten used to doing while I was away?" He cleaned the last bit of bark from the very end of the branch, then folded the blade back into the knife handle. "Is this your typical nighttime activity?"

"No," she said.

"Good," he said. He stood up and stretched. "Let's see that it stays that way. We've got enough to worry about already." He held the screen door open for her. "Right?"

"Right," she said.

As she passed by him through the open door, he put his hand on her shoulder. "I'm counting on you, Jory." He gave her shoulder a squeeze and then stood unmoving on the porch step.

"Aren't you coming in?"

"No," he said. "I think I'm going to stay up and watch the sky for a bit. Vega is especially bright tonight."

She latched the screen door and stared at

him from behind the mesh. "What does that mean?"

He sat down on the top step. "Nothing," he said, and pulled his knife out of his pocket. "It just means that August is through. Summer is over. It will be a fall sky from now on."

Jory watched him wipe both sides of the knife blade on his pant leg. "Good night, Dad," she said.

"Good night." Her father picked up the willow branch again and turned it over in his hands. "By the way," he said, his back turned toward her, "don't leave your sister sleeping in the front yard like that ever again." He cut a small notch in the base of the branch. "She's just little. You have to watch out for her."

Jory stood behind the screen door. "I do," she said. "Usually."

"*Usually* is a scary word." Her father took the end of the knife and slit the branch in two, all the way up. "When a scientist says 'usually,' you know it's time to get out the protective eye gear." He turned and caught her eye. "That sounded almost like a joke, didn't it? It wasn't meant to."

"I know," said Jory.

"Good," her father said, nodding but not smiling. "Good."

That whole week their father stayed home from work — a thing he had done only once before, when Frances had given him the chicken pox. He spent most of his time doing mysterious errands in the car. Driving somewhere and doing something that no one was allowed to do with him. Sometimes, late at night, Jory could hear him talking on the phone. On Thursday, their father drove Grace to the doctor — a doctor clear up in Blackfoot this time — where she was going to be observed overnight. Grace said she wasn't scared to see a psychiatrist — "a *Christian* psychiatrist," their father kept clarifying — but Jory had seen how tightly she was holding on to her overnight bag. The next day, their mother stayed in her room and Frances was sent next door to the Hewetts' — a thing rarer still than the chicken pox. Jory spent the afternoon lying on her bed and trying to read *They Came to a River* while not picking at the huge scab on the side of her hip. Finally, after she had drifted off to sleep without meaning to, her father came in and sat at the foot of her bed. Even though she was asleep, she could feel his weight where it was holding the quilt tight against her feet. She opened her eyes and saw him looking at her the way he did when he was nervous, when he was going to tell her she was grounded, or how love between a man and a woman was a powerful chemical force and should be taken very seriously, as seriously as a chemist would if he were nitrating glycerol.

"Well," he said.

Jory sat up and waited.

He appeared to scrutinize his hands as they rested on top of her white bedspread. He bent and unbent his fingers.

As a father, he said, he had not done everything he should. He realized that now. He had been busy, too busy, and perhaps not very observant; he had taken his good fortune in his family for granted, and now, well, now certain things had happened because of it. At least partly because of it. No, not just partly — he amended — he was as much to blame as anyone. He ran his hands through his hair. Children depended on their fathers to protect them. Even when they didn't realize it, Frances, Jory, and Grace, even Mom, they were all counting on him to protect them from things that could harm them. It sounded simplistic and maybe even archaic, but sometimes, he had discovered lately, the truth was both. He shook his head. He couldn't change what had already happened. He couldn't do anything about the things that were already done. As much as he might want to, he couldn't fix those things. He took a deep breath and let it out through his nose. But he could do something about right now, and right now Mom needed some rest and Grace needed some time and some privacy from prying eyes and wagging tongues, and Jory needed to help him make sure they both got these things. It was going to require a certain amount of sacrifice and compromise, and maybe even a little discomfort for a while. But he knew he could count on Jory to do her part. He knew she wanted what was best for her sister and her mother, that she understood how important it was that they all got through this difficult time in one piece. She just needed to trust that he had all their best interests at heart. He glanced up at Jory. That might not have been the best choice of words, but she knew what he meant. She was just going to have to trust him.

"Dad?" said Jory.

"Mom and Frances will be staying here at home with me, and you and Grace will be temporarily staying in a very nice little house I found for you out at the north end of Arco."

Jory sat completely still underneath her quilt. "What?" she said. Her voice came out in a small squeak.

"It will only be for a while. Just until things have calmed down some. And then you can both come home. But for now I think it's vital that Mom get the rest she needs and for Grace to have some time to herself to think things through. And you can be there to keep her company and make sure that she's doing all right." He patted her leg through her quilt. "I'll be checking in on you every little bit, bringing you groceries and necessities — things like that. Oh, and I've got correspondence course materials ordered for Grace, and she can complete her class work that way — she'll get her diploma through the mail. I looked it up, it's just as valid as a regular diploma. I don't think any colleges will object — although I might have to do a little more research on that." Her father rushed on. "Plus, there's a wonderful woman who lives in the main house in front of yours, Mrs." — he pulled a white note card out of his shirt pocket — "Kleinfelter. That's it. She'll check in on you too, just to make sure that you're getting along all right." He tried to smile. "Just think — no parents to tell you what to do every minute. You two girls on your own. It'll be like having a slumber party." Her father glanced at the note card. He folded it in half and then in fourths. He re-creased the note card's edges with his thumbnail. "A slumber party," he said again.

"Grace isn't going to *school*?"

He shook his head. "I think it would be better if she didn't."

"Where is this place — this house?" Jory could feel her voice getting higher, her throat filling with a burning knot of something. "Does the Academy bus run clear out to the country? How will I get to school?"

"You know, I was thinking about that, and I realized that there's a perfectly good school right out on the edge of town — Schism High. The building's a little bit on the old side, but I'm sure the teachers and the kids are just fine."

"*Schism?* Where all the goat ropers go?" Jory felt the first tears spilling over and dropping down the side of her nose. "No," she said. "No, Dad."

"Jory," said her father, "don't make this hard." He moved up on the bed next to her. He put his arm around her shoulder and squeezed her tightly against him. "You're my big girl," he said into her hair.

"I'm not," she said. "And I'm not going. Make Grace go live there by herself." She pushed herself away from him. "I won't go," she said. She glared at him and swiped at her eyes with the back of her hand.

"I'm sorry," he said. "Please try to understand. I have to do what's best. I have to think of everyone."

She stood up and threw the quilt back onto the bed. She kicked at the bottom drawer of her dresser. "You can't make me," she said.

"The groceries and your winter clothes are already in the trunk of the car."

Jory turned and stood in front of him, her heart beating hard in her throat. What desperate thing could she say or do to make him reconsider? "I stole a pair of earrings," she said.

He reached up from where he was sitting and took hold of one of her hands and then the other. "I know," he said. "Where's your suitcase?"

■ ■ ■ ■

Part Two:
The New World

■ ■ ■ ■

CHAPTER SIX

Jory gave Grip a final wave and watched as the ice cream truck pulled out of the long dirt driveway. Then she sighed and started up the steps of Henry Kleinfelter's diamond-windowed house.

Inside, Grace had woken from her drug-induced stupor and was now sitting up on the dead cat couch, wearing her old green Pathfinders skirt and their father's long-sleeved shirt. She was drinking cherry vanilla ice cream through a straw. "Do you want some?" she asked, stirring it around in her blue metal glass. "I put the rest in a bowl in the freezer."

"I thought ice cream made you sick."

"It does, sort of. But I'm so hungry." Grace's voice was faraway and dreamy. She took another sip. "Where've you been?"

"Nowhere." Jory sat down in a greenish chair. She felt no need to explain her absence. She didn't want to explain Grip and his ice cream truck either. She ran her fingers over the dark wooden scrolls carved into the chair's armrests. The grooves in the wood were perfectly finger-size, smooth and almost warm, as if they'd been pressed into place instead of carved.

"That psychiatrist gave me some kind of shot." Grace laughed a strange soft laugh that made it sound as if she had something thick lining her throat. "He and Dad both seemed to think I needed tranquilizing for some reason."

Jory peeped up at Grace. "What's it like? Being tranquilized, I mean."

"I don't know," Grace said. She yawned and then shivered. "It's strange. It's kind of like having the flu, except you don't feel sick. Like when you lie on your bed in the afternoon and watch the sun move in inches up your bedspread. You know? It's like I'm seeing and hearing stuff but it's all kind of muffled. Or like I'm watching myself from a little ways away." She shrugged. "I can't describe it."

"What are we supposed to do here all the time?" Jory gazed around the room. "There isn't even a radio or a TV or anything."

"We're supposed to come to our senses. That's what we're supposed to do."

Jory tried to keep her voice light. "Well,

maybe you could hurry up and do that, then."

Grace gave Jory a sad look.

Jory stood up. "We're stuck here now. *I'm* stuck here."

"Well, I'm not crazy," Grace said. "And I didn't steal any earrings either."

Jory stared at Grace. "Dad told you?"

Grace said nothing, instead she stared at the floor with a sudden intensity.

Jory shook her head. "I never stole anything. Not earrings or anything else! The man at Super Thrift just thought I did. Thinks I did."

Someone was knocking on the front door.

Grace didn't move, she didn't even seem to blink, so Jory walked to the door and stood on her tiptoes to look out the three paned windows at the top. A thin, tallish woman with a knot of hair the color of old bones was standing on the stoop. "It's her," Jory whispered, and opened the door.

The old woman attempted a smile. "Hello," she said, looking Jory up and down. "You must be the younger one. I'm Hilda Kleinfelter. Your neighbor. Well, more like your landlord actually. No, wait, you bought the house, didn't you? Well, I rented the house out that last time, so I keep thinking you're paying rent. Hmph." She shook her head. "Well, I am your neighbor." She didn't hold out her hand, although Jory kept expecting her to. In fact, she kept her arms tightly folded across her chest. She was wearing a faded housedress, blue with small purple flowers on it, and thin ankle socks with what appeared to be men's brown work shoes.

"Well, oh, um," said Jory, "would you like to come in?" The old woman moved with surprising quickness into the front room. "This is my sister Grace," Jory said, pointing to Grace, who had not risen from the couch. Mrs. Kleinfelter nodded and murmured something and gazed about her. "You've got some unpacking, I see," she said, a note of slight irritation entering her voice. "I *always* hated the unpacking. Never minded the moving, just the unpacking. Well," she said, continuing her surveillance of the room.

"We just got here," said Jory.

"Um-hm, um-hm. I don't know if you know this or not, but this was my brother Henry's house. I lived up front with Dix, and Henry lived out back here by himself. For forty-eight years. Yes." She shook her head up and down. "We had quite the farm — apple and cherry orchards, seed corn by the acre, quite the place. Things had to be

152

scaled back considerably, though, once Dix went on."

Jory had no idea what response was called for and glanced quickly at Grace, who merely sat and smiled peaceably. "It's very nice," Jory said finally.

"Oh, it's all right, I guess." Mrs. Kleinfelter rubbed the toe of her shoe across the faded roses in the rug. "Mmph," she said, and seemed to decide something. "Well, I'm gone," she said, and started toward the door. "You girls take care of yourselves. Your father seemed to think you needed some taking care of, but I can see you're all grown up. I wouldn't know the first thing about it anyhow. I told him I'd look in on you and I will, but that's it. As I said, I wouldn't know the first thing about it." Mrs. Kleinfelter turned the door handle and moved down the front steps.

"Good-bye," said Jory, but Mrs. Kleinfelter was already some ways across the yard.

"There goes our neighbor," said Grace sleepily. "She never minded the moving, just the unpacking."

Jory shut the door and sat down in the brown chair again. "Who *doesn't* mind the unpacking?"

Grace stretched her arms above her head. "Frances," she said. "She thinks it's like opening presents. Remember that time at the motel up in McCall? She opened her suitcase and said, 'Look, here's my shoes!' like she'd thought she was never going to see them again."

"That's right!" Jory said. "But she wouldn't use the toilet until Mom took the 'seat belt' off." Jory laughed. "And Mom made the devil's food cake to bring with us, but it was so red it looked purple and I said it was possessed by the devil and Mom said that wasn't funny and threw the whole cake in the motel trash can," Jory said. "And then she made me go sit in the car and I got to spend the night in the backseat."

"Not the whole night," said Grace.

"Maybe not the entire night," Jory admitted. Sometime after it got dark Grace had sneaked out of the motel room with a blanket and pillow for Jory. A fact that made their father feel so terrible that he had come out too and brought both his daughters back inside, where their mother and little sister appeared to have slept soundly through the whole incident.

Grace seemed to be thinking about something. "Once when I went with Dad to Missoula and it was Valentine's Day, I was mad because he wouldn't let me go to the accreditation meeting with him, so I sat in the motel room and cut out all these hearts and cupid shapes from the motel phone book and taped them to the walls and windows."

"Did he make you sleep in the car?"

Grace stretched out on the couch. She rested her head on one of the armrests and closed her eyes. "No, but he made me take the cut-up phone book to the motel manager and tell him what I'd done."

"Eeek," said Jory.

Grace pulled her hands up under her chin. Her voice was drowsy and slow, almost like an old record winding down. "The time we went to Pacific Lutheran I got so sick that Dad had to take me to their school nurse, and when we were walking out of her office, I fainted, but Dad didn't stop, he just kept walking out to the car. The nurse had to go out and get him and bring him back in. I was still lying on the office floor. The floor had big green and white squares of tile. I remember waking up with my cheek pressed against one of the green ones."

"He *left you* there?"

"Well . . . not exactly. Not really. I don't know what it was. He claimed he just hadn't noticed. But it was almost like he'd been embarrassed or ashamed or something that I'd passed out like that."

"Why did Dad always take us on those

155

accreditation trips anyway? It's not like there was anything for us to do there. All we ever got to do was sit around in motel rooms and student center lounges."

"It was supposed to give Mom a break," said Grace. "You know. Just like now."

This silenced Jory.

Grace turned over on the couch. "Oh," she said, and sighed. "I just feel so tired. It's like I'm being pulled underwater by a big hand that never lets go. Just when I think I'll stand up and go do something, this smooth, watery feeling comes over me and all I want to do is lie down."

"It's okay," said Jory.

"No, it's not," said Grace. "I promise I'll get up in a little while." She yawned again.

Jory sat in the brown chair and watched dust motes playing up and down in the air above Grace's head. The sunlight slanted in through the small window above the couch, turning Grace's dark hair a glowing shade of chestnut red. It reminded Jory of the Shetland pony they had always ridden at their grandfather's cabin. The pony's name was Shorty, he had a reddish brown and white coat, and he was *mean*. Whenever Grace would get up her nerve to finally get on him, he would head to the nearest low-hanging tree branch and walk directly under it, scraping Grace off onto the ground. Jory was smaller — and, according to her father, braver — and whenever Shorty tried this trick with her, she simply flattened herself to Shorty's back and held on.

Jory watched Grace sleeping with her hands tucked under her chin. Her father was wrong, she thought. It hadn't been a matter of bravery. It was just that Jory, even more than Grace, feared falling. And that wasn't all. On vaccination day at Eisenhower Elementary, Jory and her second-grade classmates had had to line up in the long wood-paneled hallway with their sleeves rolled up high. At the front of the line waited two nurses, each with a hypodermic needle carefully hidden behind her back. Smallpox and diphtheria. Jory counted and recounted the number of children in line in front of her. She licked her lips. Just then the sixth graders from the top floor came down the stairs, their bare arms already bedecked with round Band-Aids — small, flesh-colored badges of bravery. They filed past and, as they did, Grace stepped out from her place in line and took Jory's hand. For a moment the two sisters were locked together — Grace's warm hand gripping hers — and then Grace was pulled back into line and pushed along. Even afterward, Jory could still feel the pressure of Grace's fingers as the line in front of her grew shorter and shorter.

Her older sister had always gone first, and she always made sure that Jory could safely follow. Even when the following was going to be frightening.

Grace got up and washed all the dishes that they'd brought and the ones already in the cupboards, while Jory hung up her clothes and made up both of the upstairs beds with some sheets and blankets that she found in the hall closet. The sheets were white and soft as an old T-shirt, but they smelled mildewed and the blankets were like something you'd find in a teepee or a cabin: gray and scratchy, with red and black stripes in a zigzag pattern. She sat on her bed and tested the mattress spring. The metal coils beneath made a zinging sound each time she bounced. The tub in the bathroom was like one she had seen in an old John Wayne movie on TV, long and white with a cloth curtain on wire rings that pulled all the way around it like an oval drape.

"A real claw-foot tub," Grace said, wiping her hands on a dishtowel.

"Look at this soap." Jory pulled out a bar of grainy brownish stuff from the brass soap holder. "It is soap, isn't it?"

Grace pulled the shower curtain all the way back and stepped into the tub. She sat down in it and leaned her head back against the porcelain rim. "Look, I can stretch all the way out. It must be six feet long." She draped her arms across either edge of the bathtub and then let her hands hang down almost to the floor. "I'm Bathsheba," she said, "and I'm *bathe*-ing." Grace turned her head toward Jory. "You, however, don't look anything like David."

Jory sat down on the black-and-white tile next to the tub. Grace was still acting very strange. Her voice sounded like it belonged to someone else. Someone on a TV show or in a play. Jory ran her hand across one of the tub's feet. Across the eagle claw part that held a smooth white ball. "Grace," she said, "I feel weird. I don't feel good."

"You'll get used to it," said Grace.

"What if I don't?" Jory rested her head on the tub's rim. "What if they have to put me on tranquilizers?"

Grace laughed, a low drowsy sound. "Well, then, I guess you'll be just like me," she said. "And Mom."

Jory lifted her head. "Mom's taking tranquilizers?"

Grace ran her bare toes over the tub's

rusty faucet.

"No way," Jory said. "Dad says medication like that is a sin. That it interferes with God's ability to speak with you." Jory peered at Grace's face more closely. "He would never let Mom take pills. It's against church rules."

"She told him it was either that or she was leaving."

"Leaving?"

"She said they'd have to send her to Blackfoot if he didn't get her something."

Jory was struck dumb by the thought of her mother threatening to be taken to the insane asylum.

"This tub is just like Aunt Annette's," Grace said in her new drifty voice. "I remember it from the time we went to San Diego."

"We never went to California."

"You weren't born yet. But I remember that Mom and Dad went off somewhere — to some observatory, I think — and Aunt Annette gave me a bath. There was a white whale that had shampoo in it. She took off its tail and pink shampoo came out. And afterward she cut my hair — she trimmed it with little nail scissors — and she put my cut-off hair in the toilet and flushed it all down and then she said, 'Now don't tell your mom — it'll just be between us girls, okay? It'll be our little secret.' And then she gave me some black cherry pop." Grace had begun to cry soundlessly. She leaned forward and large solitary tears dropped slowly off the end of her nose.

Jory tried looking at the bathroom's peeling wallpaper, at the strange washbasin with the crooked wooden medicine cabinet hanging above it, the egg-shaped globe of a light fixture that hung down on a chain like the hall lights in her old elementary school. "Don't cry," she said.

"I'm not," said Grace, taking the tail ends of her shirt and wiping her eyes. Grace lifted her chin. "It was just like I said. He told me not to tell anyone because no one would believe it. He said I was chosen for a very special purpose and had been born for this very reason. And that God wanted it that way. That he wanted me." Grace gripped either side of the tub and pushed herself up. "Out of all the women in the world, he wanted *me*," she said.

"Okay," said Jory. "All right."

Grace stood up and stepped out of the tub. She walked unsteadily down the hall to the bedroom. Then she went inside and closed the door behind her.

Jory sat on the floor. Late afternoon light

filtered through the bathroom window and fell in warm bands across her face and neck. She thought about what Frances would be doing right now. Was she wondering where Jory was — had she even noticed that she was gone? This was her second night away from home, and tomorrow was the first day of school and her very first day of high school. At a school she'd never been to before. Jory leaned her head against the wall and felt its paint flake off against her cheek like the scales of some enormous molting reptile. How had her life become something so strange to her? So foreign and unrecognizable and terrifying? She wanted to cry, but she knew she wouldn't, in part because there was no one there to comfort her if she did.

CHAPTER SEVEN

Her father showed up before Jory even had a chance to pick out her clothes. Jory peeked down the stairs and watched as he marched briskly about the living room picking up stray sweaters and shoes, unpacking boxes of books and winter coats. "We better get a move on," he called up the stairs. She could hear him talking to Grace, who was in the kitchen eating cereal.

Jory had been up before it got light. She couldn't sleep. By the time she had made it down the stairs her father was standing in the front room holding a white paper grocery sack. "Mom sent you this," he said, holding the bag out. Jory was so glad to see her father, so achingly glad to smell the clean, familiar smell he brought in with him, that she wanted to hit him. As she stood there looking at him in his brown suit and tie, a sudden shudder ran through her head as if she really had. She blinked hard and then took the bag and ran back upstairs. She sat down on her bed holding the sack against her chest. After a moment she unfolded the sack's top; inside were two pumpkin cream cheese muffins that her mother had not made, that her father had obviously bought at Albertsons on his way here. She pulled the paper wrapper off the bottom of one and took a bite. It was wonderful — still warm from the bakery's oven and full of velvety cream cheese. She put the muffin back in the bag and folded it shut. She stood up and moved past the iron-framed bed and opened the window next to it. She tossed the bag out the window, watching it land on a dry patch of grass after bouncing off a rounded fuel oil tank on the back side of the house. She shut the window and went to the closet, where she pulled her yellow skirt off its hanger and then rummaged through Henry Kleinfelter's bureau drawer until she found her striped sweater. She had no idea what people wore to Schism. She had no idea what they said or thought or did after school or if they all drove cars or rode wild ponies or what. Even though Arco Christian Academy was considered by public school kids to be too square and religious and uncool to be believed, the kids at ACA always made terrible fun of the kids who went to Schism, but if they ever saw any of them at a store downtown, they quickly looked the other way. And walked the other way. Some boy on Schism's football team had supposedly killed another boy after a game — just because Schism lost.

Jory had a sudden thought. She ran into Grace's room and slid open her top drawer. Inside were panties and socks and nylons and several white bras. Jory took the bra that looked the smallest and ran back to her bedroom and closed her door. She took off her sweater and put the bra on, hooking it up as quickly as she could. In the mirror above the bureau she viewed the results. The cups of the bra pointed emptily away from her chest like small, collapsing pyramids. She ran back to her sister's room once more. A nylon in each cup helped. Somewhat. Jory walked downstairs with inordinate care and casualness.

Her father was now sitting at the breakfast table with Grace, tracing a pattern on the tabletop with his fork. Grace was looking at her own hands, which were folded in her lap. Neither of them was saying anything.

Jory hugged her schoolbag to her chest.

"There she is," her father said, smiling and pushing back from the table with a great deal of enthusiasm. "Grace tells me that you two are getting along just fine here."

Jory glanced at Grace, who was now gazing out the window. Neither of them spoke.

"Well," he said, sighing, "I suppose we'd better get this show on the road." Her father pulled his car keys out of his pocket. "Grace, want to come along for the ride?"

"Really?" said Grace. "Aren't you worried that someone might see me?" She stared steadily at her father. "I'm not tranquilized anymore. I might do something rash."

Her father stood silently in the kitchen. "The first day of high school," he said finally, turning toward Jory. He shook his head. "That's a pretty big day. I should have brought the camera."

"That's okay, Dad." Jory peered down at her knee socks and old mary janes. When she'd picked these shoes out last year, they had seemed just right, brown suede with a black button on the strap and nicely chunky heels. Now she wasn't so sure.

"Well, here we go," her father said, placing a firm hand on her back and leading her to the door.

Schism High School was located at the very northern edge of Arco, near the border of the neighboring town of Rimrock. Her father kept up a steady stream of talk as they drove past acreages and farms, sugar beets and alfalfa, pumpkins and newly harvested mint. Jory watched out the window as men in coveralls adjusted mesh baseball caps and walked slowly toward outbuildings and barns and pickups, happy dogs wagging at their heels. Jory imagined the women inside the houses — the women were always inside — making breakfast with the TV on, ham and eggs or maybe pancakes. On Jory's and her sisters' birthdays, they got pancakes for breakfast, apple pancakes with Granny Smiths sliced thin and tart in the batter. Jory didn't suppose that her mother would be making her any pancakes this year.

The road outside became more narrow and then finally unpaved. The farmhouses grew smaller and more dingy and then gave way to long fields of alfalfa and corn and finally to scrub brush and weeds and lone cottonwood trees. They bounced along the dirt road in silence, her father finally having run out of things to say. The road curved over a brown hill, then turned left past a small grocery store called the Day 'N' Nite and then, much too soon, they were there. Jory gazed out the car window at the two-story cement block buildings that made up the school. The main building had been painted a bright yellow gold reminiscent in Jory's mind of egg yolks and Donald Duck's feet. SCHISM HIGH SCHOOL, it read in brown block letters above the double glass doors. HOME OF THE SCHISM SKULLCATS. *"Skullcats?"* Jory turned her eyes toward her father's. "Dad," she said, "please. Please don't make me go."

"Look," he said, turning and laying a large hand on top of her cold one. "If it's really that bad, we'll figure something else out. But today I need you to try it. Just try it for me. Okay?" He squeezed both of her hands in his and then opened the car door and stepped out.

Jory watched as other cars pulled into the dirt parking lot, a horrible tight, sick feeling in her stomach. They were mostly muscle cars, Firebirds and Camaros and GTOs painted in bright metallic colors, with an expectedly large number of pickup trucks as well. Students were already gathering into groups, slamming car doors and yelling happy insults at each other and pulling cigarettes and tins of chewing tobacco out of back pockets. Jory's head felt full of something thick and humming. She held her schoolbag close and got out of the car without looking around her. She kept her head down as she and her father walked up the wide cement steps and through the front door of the school.

The air inside was a revelation: warm and fluorescent and awash in smells of warm sauerkraut and floor polish and old linoleum. The upstairs hall was a hive of activity: teachers and students all rushing past, their talking a buzz of mostly indecipherable words. Jory tried to memorize which way she and her father were going and what door was what, but there were too many — too many smells and sights and too much information. She was already lost. Her father was explaining to a frazzled-looking woman behind a tall wood-paneled counter that Jory was a new student and that he would be bringing all her records tomorrow or the next day, but that for now she just needed to sit in on classes and get a class schedule and a locker — things like that. Her father was wearing his professor clothes and using his professor voice and the woman was smiling and pulling out forms from beneath the wooden counter. Jory tried to take deep breaths and she suddenly realized how very, very hungry she was and how very long it would be until lunch. "Dad," she said. "Dad." She pulled on his coat sleeve. "I need some lunch money."

"Oh, and what bus route will she need to take to get home?" Her father had borrowed a pen and was filling in one of the forms. "We . . . *she* lives on . . . Deer Flat Road — the north end."

Jory turned and watched more students jostling each other as they clattered up and down the hall stairs. The girls were all wearing pants, jeans mainly, tight, low-hanging, leather-belted Levis that had denim inserts sewn in the bottom part of the legs so that they flared out over the wearer's shoes. And colorful snug-fitting T-shirts and leather vests and wide-collared suede jackets. Their hair was nearly always long and straight and parted in the middle and two of the girls that walked past her now were wearing fringed moccasins (!) with tiny bells attached to the laces. They jingled and laughed as they passed, flipping their sheaths of dark hair behind their shoulders. They wore peace sign earrings and black eyeliner and carried notebooks covered in stickers that said KEEP ON TRUCKIN' and THE LIZARD KING LIVES and I WAS A DRAFT DODGER IN THE WAR ON DRUGS. None of them were wearing skirts. Or mary janes.

"Dad," Jory said again. *"Dad."* But her father was now discussing the merits of physics I versus earth science. "To my mind," he was saying, "it makes much more sense to have them take physics their freshman year and chemistry their sophomore year and save the biological sciences for the very end." The woman behind the counter listened and smiled even though students were lining up behind Jory. "They need that grounding in the cellular sciences before they try to tackle the larger physical concepts. Little to big, atoms before molecules and so on, you know?" The woman behind the counter seemed to know.

By sixth period, Jory was beyond feeling. She had given up the notion of looking for bright spots — a philosophy she had clung to during first period — and was now merely interested in survival. It mattered not one bit that she had had to eat lunch by herself or that the only person who had talked to her all day was a boy in cowboy boots who had asked her if she was a foreign exchange student. She was living for the moment when she could board the bus home — every bit of her being was intent on that goal.

Mr. DeNovia, the earth science teacher, was explaining to them how geodes formed. Jory had her new spiral notebook out; at the top she had written *Rocks: Our Friends* and underlined it twice. "Geodes begin as bubbles in volcanic rock," Mr. DeNovia was saying in his oddly effeminate voice, "or as animal burrows, tree roots, or mud balls in sedimentary rock." *Mud balls,* Jory wrote down. How could such a hairy man have such a high voice? she wondered. Mr. De-Novia produced a sliced-open geode from a cardboard box on his desk and held it up. He gave it to the girl at the head of one of the three classroom tables and told her to examine it and pass it on. He continued with his lecture: "Over time, the outer shell of the spherical shape hardens, and water containing silica precipitation forms on the inside walls of the hollow cavity within the geode." *Hard,* Jory wrote, and then put *gets* in parentheses. The boy seated next to her at the table handed her the geode. "We always called 'em thunder eggs," he whispered, and then stared straight ahead.

Jory was too surprised to say anything.

"I don't know why."

Jory looked sideways at the boy. His hair was the color of dirty straw and it was short and stuck up from his head in odd little tufts. He had on an old flannel shirt with a torn pocket. The pocket had a sucker stick falling out of it.

"I think thunder eggs are different,"

whispered Jory.

"I don't think so," he whispered back.

"Excuse me," said Mr. DeNovia. "Is there something you two would like to share with the class?"

"Not really," said the boy, scooting a little lower in his chair.

Jory held perfectly still.

"Crap," the boy said very quietly.

Crap, Jory wrote down on her paper, and then scratched it out.

When the bell rang, Jory stuffed her books and papers into her schoolbag and walked quickly out of the classroom. She bypassed the row of lockers and continued down the hall — she had no idea what her locker combination was and no intention of ever coming back to find out. She only wanted to get outside. To get up the stairs and outside and then home. *Home.* That's how she thought of the diamond-shaped-window house now, right this very minute. Streams of students were heading in all directions, laughing and yelling and latching on to each other as if they hadn't seen each other in months. Two long-haired girls in front of her shrieked as they wrapped their arms around each other's necks. "What's the word?" screeched the first one. "Thunderbird!" shouted the second girl. "What's the price?" the first one continued. "Forty twice!" the second girl exclaimed, and then tripped and dragged the other one down with her and they collapsed onto the floor in a giggling heap. The boy who had sat next to her in earth science jogged Jory with his elbow. "Wow," he said. "Way too much zigzag."

"Yeah," Jory said, although she had no idea if this was true, or what this assessment meant exactly. They veered around the two girls, who were still lying on the floor laughing.

"Hey," he said. "Here. You dropped this." He held out a crumpled nylon by its toe.

For a moment Jory didn't remember. And then in a rush she could feel the blood flooding her neck and her face. "That's not mine," she said, walking faster, her eyes on the ground ahead of her.

"Huh? I was right behind you when you dropped it."

She shook her head.

"Okay," he said. He wadded up the nylon and shot it, overhand, toward a garbage can. It fell short. "Shit," he said. "Hey, where are you from," he asked, running to catch up with her. "You seem kind of like you're from somewhere else."

174

"I'm from here," she said. "Around here."

"Did you go to Rimrock last year? I never saw you there."

"No," Jory said. "I went . . . somewhere else." There. She had confirmed it. She was a freak from somewhere else.

"So, what do you think of Jism?"

"What?"

"Jism High." The boy gave Jory a close look, then shook his head slightly. "Never mind," he said.

They had come up the stairs and were now outside in the dust and glare of the parking lot. Jory felt as if several days had gone by since she had first stood there this morning. "Where are the buses?" she asked him, squinting and turning. "Do you know?"

"Sure," he said. "Over there." He pointed back toward the gym. "You ride the bus?"

Jory was too tired to care whether or not riding the bus was the worst, most uncool thing to admit to. She nodded.

"Yeah, well, okay then. Catch ya later." The boy waved and jogged off toward a pickup truck that another boy was already backing out of the parking lot. "Hey, hang on, dickhead!" he yelled as he grabbed on to the tailgate and jumped into the bed of the still-moving truck.

Jory walked toward the gym. She had no idea which bus was hers. There were four buses parked in a row beneath the gym's overhang, but no drivers in them. Small groups of kids shoved each other onto and off of the buses. Jory waited in line and then climbed the steps of the closest bus. She peered inside. "Which bus is this?" she asked a large girl sitting in the front seat. The girl stared at Jory and smiled hugely. A boy with black hair combed completely down over his forehead in long greasy bangs leaned forward. "It's Number 2," he said. He pointed a thumb in the large girl's direction. "She's a retard. She don't never say nothin'." He sat back down in his seat.

Jory stepped down out of the bus. Her neck and shoulders were terribly sore, as if she had been lifting heavy books onto shelves or swimming across a large lake. She glanced across the parking lot. Students were piling into cars and pulling out of the parking lot as if escaping a burning building, tires screeching and engines roaring, all of them in an apparent rush to get out first. Maybe she could ask the woman in the front office which bus she was supposed to get on.

As quickly as she could, Jory made her way back into the school building and up the stairs. She walked down one long hall after another looking for the secretary's office, feeling her armpits becoming slicker with each step. Finally, as if by magic, she turned left and there it was, where it had been all along. She opened the office door and saw the reassuring wood-paneled counter. The woman from that morning, though, was nowhere to be seen. Instead, a hunched balding man in striped overalls pushed a mop in incremental motions across the beige linoleum floor. "Uh, sir," Jory said, "is the secretary here?"

"Nope," the man said. He plunged the rag end of the mop into a yellow bucket. "Someone had a little *ax-i-dee-dent* in here." He inclined his head toward the door. "Took 'em down to the nurse's." The man pulled the mop out of the bucket and plopped it onto the floor again.

"Do you know which bus — I mean, do you know if any of the buses out there go to Deer Flat Road?" Jory licked her lips and willed the man to look up again.

"Those buses go every which way," he said. He rested the mop against the high counter and turned to look out the window. "And that seems to be where they're heading right about now."

Jory stood on her tiptoes. Through the

window she could see the buses, one after the other pulling out of the parking lot, leaving a great cloud of dust in their wake.

Jory left the office and walked down the front stairs. She pushed the heavy glass door open again. There was no one to ask, no one to call: her father was at work, her mother couldn't drive, Grace didn't have a car. Maybe she should just start walking, maybe she would remember the way back once she got down the road a ways. She gazed across the flat expanse of the nearly empty parking lot. Out of the corner of her eye, she spotted a miraculous thing: there, turning into the school's far drive, was the ice cream truck. She took a few hesitant steps toward it and then began to run.

"It was awful," she said as she put her book bag down by her feet. "So awful you can't believe it."

Grip turned toward her and made a sympathetic face. "Even the kids?"

She shook her head.

"Do they wear boots and spurs?" He downshifted, cresting the small brown hill and turning left next to the Day 'N' Nite.

"Yes. So do the teachers."

"Right on. Sounds like my kind of school."

Skullcats," Jory said, making claws with

her hands. *"GRRRRRHhh."* She pulled her knees up to her chest and tucked her skirt under on each side. "I'm never going back."

"Ah, c'mon."

"I'm not."

"It couldn't have been that terrible."

"I'm not kidding — you think it's a joke, but I can't go back there. I know I made it sound funny, but it wasn't like that. The kids all smoke and the girls look like they're twenty-five . . . I can't explain it." Jory shrugged helplessly and hugged her knees even tighter. "And it was like my dad didn't even *notice.*" Jory glared at him, then abruptly began to cry.

"Hey," he said. *"Hey."* He steered the truck toward the side of the road and braked and then turned off the engine. "It's not so bad," he said again. He moved his legs around until he was turned completely toward her. "I like cowgirls."

"I don't," she said, sniffling, but also thrilling at his concentrated attention. "I like Indians."

"Well, okay. So you'll wear moccasins."

"I only have stupid-looking mary janes." She held up an offending foot for his inspection. "And my parents hate me."

"Nah. *My* parents hate *me.*" He made a mock grimace. "Your parents hate me —

everybody's parents hate me. But nobody," he said, looking at her, "hates you."

"Why do your parents hate you?"

He shrugged. "No reason in particular, I guess. I'm just not exactly who they were hoping for."

"Who were they hoping for?"

"Oh, I don't know. One of those kids on *Flipper* maybe — all blond and tan and self-sufficient, pulling in the fishing nets while looking out to sea and saying, 'Gosh, we better hurry, it looks like rain.' Something like that."

Grip clicked on the radio and they listened in silence as a sweet-voiced man crooned: *"The face in the moon — that's you, that's you. The face in the moon, that's you."* "All righty, then," said Grip abruptly. He started the truck's engine and pulled back out onto the roadway. "Time to get you home, Miss Schoolgirl."

"I know you think I'm a baby." A note of bitterness and self-pity crept into Jory's voice. "You'd probably think Schism was perfectly fine. You'd just stomp right in with your boots and your long hair and be the fun cool guy."

"Are you nuts?" Grip shifted gears and stared with concentration at the road in front of them. "I spent most of high school

180

in lockdown. I was cool and fun all right."

Jory turned her face back toward his. "Lockdown?"

"Yeah, you know. Juvie. Juvenile detention."

"Why were you in there?"

"Because I was a troublemaker and a stupid punk."

"You were?"

"Yeah." Grip steered the truck up the last little hill before Deer Flat Road.

"What does that mean? What did you do to be a punk?"

For a long moment he said nothing. Then he glanced at her and said, "The usual. Breaking and entering, fighting, drunk and disorderly — that kind of thing."

"Oh," she said, not knowing what expression to put on her face, her tongue suddenly feeling awkward in her mouth.

"The usual," he said again.

"The usual," she said. "Well, I guess that's not so bad, right?" She picked her book bag off the truck's metal floor and began to fish aimlessly about in it. She poked her hand into one pocket after another, not looking at him.

"See," he said. "That's who I am."

She pulled a pen out of her book bag and clicked its top button in and out. "No, it isn't — that isn't who you are."

"Yes, it is," he said. "And way more be-sides."

He looked at her, and for the second time she noticed that his eyes were not a normal brown, like most brown-eyed people, but a yellow-brown more like an animal, like a sad-eyed, brown-eyed dog.

"You're wonderful," she said. "You're a wonderful person."

"You don't know squat," he said, and pulled to a stop in the dirt road in front of Mrs. Kleinfelter's house.

Jory sat in the truck, unmoving.

"Go on," he said. The truck's engine was still running. "You'd better get."

Jory's eyes stung as she picked up her book bag and jumped out of the truck. She stood in the dip in the road next to the truck, waiting for him to lean out the window and take back what he'd said, to say something that would change things, make it all seem funny, the way he always did.

He pulled away from the curb without even waving, without looking back.

Jory stood in the road until the ice cream truck disappeared down the street. He had never said anything like that to her before. She threw her book bag down and watched as it tipped over in the dirt and spilled out several pencils and her English I reader. Jory left her bag in the road and walked up the cement path to the old woman's house, her head ringing with every single event of this horrible day. She climbed the steps and knocked on the front door. Then she rang the bell, pushing in the old-fashioned round button and listening to its flat insistent buzzing going off inside the house. After a moment, Jory rattled the door handle and then opened the door and stepped inside. "Hello," she called. "Mrs. Kleinfelter?" The house was silent and smelled faintly of ramen noodles. Jory could not believe she was doing this. She had never gone inside anyone's house without being invited, and she had no idea why she was doing this now, but it felt thrilling, both shameful and intimate, like watching someone undress from behind a closet door, a thing she *had* done once when she spent the night at Rhonda's and they had spied on her sister, who was trying to bleach her pubic hair with Jolen mustache bleach.

Jory stood quietly breathing in the living room, looking at the curlicued cuckoo clock and the long blue couch that had lace doilies covering its back and arms, the matching blue plaid armchairs, and the old-fashioned television in its wide wooden console. The floor was hardwood like their own house, but there were braided oval rugs in shades of lilac and green and yellow put down here and there, and a bookcase filled not with books but with small painted figurines: gilded swans, Chinamen pulling rickshaws, grand ladies in pink-frilled ball gowns with poodle dogs on tiny gold chains. Glossy black panthers slinking along and ballerinas poised on one opalescent toe. Jory picked up each figurine in turn. They were made of ceramic and weighed next to nothing and felt smooth and cool to the touch. Their surfaces had all been painted and then had some kind of shiny glaze put on them. All the figures, even the animals, had individual expressions of joy or exertion or anger painted onto their minute faces. Tiny paintbrush strokes that slanted eyes into envy and curled lips into hunger or haughtiness. Each one had a hole cut deliberately into the bottom to keep it from exploding in the kiln. When her father had brought her a Hummel figure back from Germany, he had explained the firing process to her. Jory stuck her little finger into the hole in the base of the ballerina. She was wiggling the ballerina back and forth on her finger as Mrs. Kleinfelter walked into the room. "Oh, merciful *heavens,*" Mrs. Kleinfelter said, pressing a hand to her chest and taking a step backward. "You nearly scared me to death."

"I'm so sorry," Jory said, trying to take the ballerina off her finger and put it back on the bookshelf without attracting any attention.

Mrs. Kleinfelter sank down into an armchair. She fanned herself with a gardening glove that she had been carrying. "Oh, my goodness," she said.

"I was just coming over to ask if I could use your phone, because ours isn't connected yet and I thought I heard you say to come in, but I guess I must have misheard because I guess you were outside or something." Jory gestured frantically and moved closer to the front door. "So, I'm really sorry I scared you."

"Yes, indeed," Mrs. Kleinfelter said, still breathing heavily. "Yes, indeed. You shouldn't go frightening old people like that. I'm lucky I didn't have a stroke. *You're* lucky I didn't have a stroke. What would you have done then? I'd like to know. Me down on the floor with my eyes rolled back." Mrs. Kleinfelter shook her head. "Do you know any lifesaving techniques? Are you a registered nurse? No? Then you'd better not go wandering into old people's houses and scaring the living daylights out of them." Mrs. Kleinfelter closed her eyes. "Go on, then. The phone's in the kitchen."

"Oh, no, that's okay. I shouldn't bother you any more," Jory said.

"You've bothered me this much, you might as well go a little further."

Jory stepped carefully past Mrs. Kleinfelter and into the next room. An old rotary dial phone just like the one in her and Grace's house hung on the yellow wall beneath a picture of a man sleeping next to a haystack. Jory leaned over an ancient-looking stove and picked up the phone's receiver. She dialed the first number that came to her head.

"Hello," her mother said. *"Hello?"*

Jory listened to her mother breathe for a second more and then she hung up the phone.

She walked back out into the living room. "No one was home," she said to Mrs. Kleinfelter. "But thanks anyway. And I'm really sorry." She stepped past the armchair where Mrs. Kleinfelter was still sitting and put her hand on the front door knob.

"I made those myself," Mrs. Kleinfelter said. "I used to think I might do some real kind of painting once upon a time."

186

"The figurines? They're beautiful," Jory said, moving back over to the bookshelf. She picked up the panther and ran her finger along his sleek head. "How did you get the eyes to look like that? Like green jewels?"

"Um-hm. You know in that poem — what is it, you know the one, we used to have to memorize it in school — where the panther sneaks down and snatches up the girl, except he's really a highwayman or a sultan or something powerful like that? Yes, well, his eyes are like green fire. That's what I was trying for anyway. You mix a little ground mica in with the paint. That's what does it. I used it on the toe shoes, too." Mrs. Kleinfelter eased herself out of the chair and walked over next to Jory. She picked up the ballerina and handed it to her. "When I was a little girl I wanted to be a dancer. Can you imagine?" Mrs. Kleinfelter gave a soft snort through her nose. "Well," she said. "I guess there's no harm in dreaming, is there?"

"I wish I knew how to paint."

"There's nothing to it." Mrs. Kleinfelter shrugged dismissively. "This kind, anyway. All it takes is patience mainly."

Jory placed the ballerina back next to the swan. "I can draw," she said. "My mother taught me. When I was little, she used to let me sit on her lap and she would help me hold the pencil and guide it over the paper until I could do it on my own — until I could draw the flower petals and the leaf veins all by myself." Jory put her hands in the front pocket of her sweater. "I'd forgotten that," she said.

"Sometimes I think I've forgotten practically everything I ever knew," Mrs. Kleinfelter said. "They always tell you that if it's important, you'll remember it." Mrs. Kleinfelter waved her hand. "Good, bad, you forget most of it sooner or later."

"I wish I were old," Jory said, and then felt instantly foolish.

Mrs. Kleinfelter made a chuckling sound way back in her throat. "Oh, no, you don't," she said. "No one does."

"I kind of do."

"That's only because you're not old yet. I'm seventy-one," she said. "Which is better than seventy-two, I guess."

Jory stared at Mrs. Kleinfelter. At her old men's work shoes and her bony arms with the blue veins running practically at the skin's surface. She wanted to bury her head in Mrs. Kleinfelter's flat bosom. "I'll be fourteen," she said. "Next week."

Mrs. Kleinfelter nodded. "Now *that's* an

age. I was engaged to my cousin when I was fourteen. Parley Pearson. I had loved him since I was ten and he was twelve. We didn't tell anyone we were engaged, of course, but we were, just the same. He gave me a ring braided out of horsehair that he'd stolen out of his mother's jewelry box. We thought we'd get married when I turned sixteen. Lots of girls did back then, you know. But a couple months later, he got a girl from Graham County pregnant, and that was that." Mrs. Kleinfelter moved the Chinaman's rickshaw back and forth on the top of the bookshelf. "I guess I remember a few things after all."

"What happened then?" Jory ignored the voice in her head that said she was being too nosy. "When did you meet your husband?"

"Oh, I ran off with Dix the first chance I got. I was still mad about Parley, really, and I wanted to show him I could do the same. So I did." Mrs. Kleinfelter laughed. "Guess I proved my point, didn't I?"

"Did you have any kids? I mean, do you have any kids?"

Mrs. Kleinfelter seemed to be arranging something invisible and bothersome in her hair. "Children?" she said in a strange voice. Her hand fell from her hair. With an abrupt movement she took the ballerina from Jory's hand and set it firmly back on the bookshelf. "What is your name?" She cocked her head at Jory. "I suppose it seems a little rude to be asking only now, doesn't it?"

"It's Jory," Jory said.

"*Jory.* That's kind of pretty. Although it sounds a little like a boy's name, too."

"Yes," Jory said.

"Mine's Hilda. Which I despise, but I've given up the idea of changing it at this late date, so you might as well call me that."

"All right," said Jory, blushing at the thought of calling her this.

"Where's your sister? I haven't seen much of her lately."

"She's inside, probably. She's not feeling very well."

"Your father didn't explain to me why it is that you two are living out here, and I suppose it's none of my business, so I won't ask."

"We're having some family problems," said Jory. She turned the panther a centimeter to the left, and then back again.

"Well, that's pretty much the way with families, in my experience."

"I don't know," said Jory. "I only know mine."

"Most of them are pretty much the same, I think. Good and bad mixed together in a small bag. Or a small house. Although maybe your house was bigger than mine."

"No," said Jory. "I don't think so."

Mrs. Kleinfelter glanced up at the cuckoo clock and then made a sudden move toward the television console. She leaned down and turned a large knob on the front of the TV until it clicked. She sat down in one of the blue plaid chairs. "It's time for my show," she said.

Art Fleming appeared on the screen along with three *Jeopardy!* contestants. Jory and Mrs. Kleinfelter watched in silence.

"The sound is turned down," said Jory.

"I know," said Mrs. Kleinfelter. She continued to stare at the screen.

One of the contestants, a young man with a crew cut and black glasses, won fifty dollars in the category of "Potent Potables." Jory watched Mrs. Kleinfelter watching the television. "Don't you want to hear the answers?"

"Not really," said Mrs. Kleinfelter. "I kind of like pretending I'm getting them all right."

"Oh," said Jory. "Okay." She moved toward the front door. "Well, I better get going. I'll see you later, I guess."

"Tell your sister I hope she gets better," Mrs. Kleinfelter said without turning around. "I'd send her something, some soup or something, but I don't have any."

"That's okay," said Jory. "Soup probably makes her sick."

"Is Antarctica the same thing as the South Pole?"

"It's a part of Antarctica. It's the southern-most point."

Mrs. Kleinfelter nodded. "See now? That boob said something else, didn't he? He's going to lose, you can just tell." She leaned forward. "Australia! *What is Australia!*" She grinned and leaned back. "I'm better at this than you might think."

They watched the next question come up.

"Asia," said Jory.

"What about Africa?"

"I think it's smaller," said Jory, sitting down too.

Outside, the sun was already heading down toward the west side of the Owyhees. Jory watched two crows light in the maple tree in Mrs. Kleinfelter's front yard. The crows were so heavy that the branches they were on dragged downward. Each time they stepped sideways, the branches bounced up and down. The crows didn't seem to like this trampoline effect and one at a time they lifted heavily off and flew on. Jory walked out into the road and picked up her book bag. She brushed the dirt off as best she could. For some reason, she left the pencils lying there.

Tall, dried-out hollyhocks leaned and drooped against the side of Mrs. Kleinfelter's house. Jory plucked off one of the dying flower's blooms. When they were little, their mother had shown her and Grace how to turn them upside down so that they could be made into dolls, their blossoms forming lacily ruffled skirts. Jory walked along the path worn into the grass that ran between the front house and the back, dragging her book bag behind her. Grace was sitting on the steps in front of the diamond-windowed house. She was wearing a pair of men's patched denim overalls over an old white T-shirt and her bare feet looked long and pale. She was digging her bare toes in the dirt. "Where on earth have you been?" she asked. She held a hand up over her eyes.

"Remember hollyhock dolls?" Jory held out the wilted blossom. "And how Frances called them hoopy skirts?"

"Dad called from work to see if you got home okay and you weren't here. He's really worried."

"I bet." Jory began pulling off the flower's silky pink petals, one at a time.

"What happened?" Grace squinted up at her. "Did you miss the bus?"

"Yes, I missed the bus. I missed all four of them. But it doesn't matter because I'm not going to school there. Ever." Jory dropped the denuded stem onto the ground. "It's a horrible place, and I won't go back and Dad can't make me." Jory sat down in the grass. "I don't see why I can't go to Arco Christian. It's not like *I'm* pregnant."

Grace sat up and hugged her knees to her chest. "That's right," she said. "You're not."

Jory smoothed her hand back and forth across the nap of the grass. "Sorry," she said, though she could hear that her voice didn't really sound very sorry at all.

Grace looked up. "I know it doesn't seem fair. That you have to live out here too, along with me."

Jory said nothing. She knew she should feel grateful that Grace was saying this, but instead it was as if Grace's words validated all of Jory's feelings of being persecuted unjustly. A hot flicker of self-righteousness rose up inside her. "Dad and Mom stuck me out here to keep an eye on *you*. Because they think you're nuts. Did you know that?

They think you're completely insane. *That's* why we're living out here — because they don't want anyone else to know that you're crazy. And *pregnant.*" Jory could feel her heart speeding up to keep pace with the flight of furious thoughts in her head. The day's events and their effects were finally spilling out in a bright, bitter stream. "And because they're too ashamed to have anyone know that this is what happened to their daughter. Their wonderful, holy, Christlike daughter."

Grace's face grew very pale, but her eyes seemed to take on more light. She pushed her hair back, revealing the now pinkening edge of her birthmark. "No one thinks that I am crazy," she said slowly, enunciating each word as if she thought Jory had suddenly gone deaf. "Not Mom or Dad or even that . . . psychiatrist they made me go to."

Jory said nothing, but she refused to look away from her sister's face.

"They're just scared, that's all."

"Yes," said Jory, "of *you.*"

"That's always the way it is with people when they first encounter an act of God." Grace sounded as if she might be explaining this to herself. "Even Moses didn't recognize the burning bush, and Jacob thought he was wrestling with a man, not

195

an angel."

"Oh, Grace — this isn't the Bible. It's just Arco."

Grace ran her hands down the thigh portion of her overalls. "I've prayed and prayed, and God has told me that He will open their eyes to the truth when it's time, and that for now I'll just have to be patient. And have faith. *Beloved, think it not strange concerning the fiery trial which is to try you, as though some strange thing happened unto you. But rejoice, inasmuch as ye are partakers of Christ's sufferings; that, when his glory shall be revealed, ye may be glad also with exceeding joy.*"

Jory bent down and picked up her book bag and hefted its strap onto her shoulder. " 'Glad with exceeding joy.' " She shook her head at Grace. "Is that really how you feel?"

"Yes," Grace said, and then paused. "Sometimes."

"Not always?"

"Not all the time. But maybe it's not supposed to be that kind of rejoicing. Maybe it's more of a solemn gladness."

"You sound like Dad."

Grace looked surprised. "Really?"

"It wasn't a compliment."

The sun had crept down and was beginning to hide itself behind the tallest of the

196

mountains. What was left of the light poured across the Kleinfelters' yard in concentrated beams, turning the branches and leaves and tips of everything a luminous golden red, as if the outside edges of each had suddenly caught fire. She was reminded of those gilded capital letters that monks outlined in scarlet and gold in old illuminated manuscripts. Jory stood on the porch and stared out across the smallish stretch of grass that separated the two houses from each other. "Who do you love?" she asked suddenly.

Grace glanced up at Jory from her seated perch on the bottom step. "Well, God, of course, and you and Mom and Dad and Frances." She was silent for a second. "That's about it, I guess, in terms of real love."

"Who do you love most?"

Grace rubbed her bare foot through a patch of weeds below the step. "I don't know. I try to love God with all my heart."

"I don't."

"Jory!"

"I don't. I love someone else instead."

"Don't say that."

"It's true. I never loved God that much to begin with and now there's not enough room left over for him anyway."

Grace stood up and dusted off the seat of

Henry Kleinfelter's overalls and then she leaned against the wooden porch railing. Her voice, when she spoke, was so quiet that Jory could just barely make out the words. "Dad didn't really say I was crazy, did he?"

Jory pulled the rubber band off of one of her braids, giving it a sharp yank. She rolled the rubber band into a ball and threw it out into the yard. "Even if he did, it doesn't matter, since he already thinks you're some kind of saint or something."

"Not anymore, he doesn't."

"Well, whose fault is that?"

Grace gave her sister a look of pained forbearance. "You don't understand anything."

"Right," said Jory. "It's all too mysterious and wonderful for someone like me to comprehend."

Grace allowed a second or two to pass. "You know, I think Dad just moved us out here because he was worried he'd lose his job. That the people at the college wouldn't understand."

"Which they wouldn't, of course. Since the whole thing is completely insane."

"That would make sense, though," Grace mused on obliviously. "Since he has to support all of us on his teaching salary."

"Didn't you hear anything I said?" Jory

shook her head. "He just doesn't want anyone in town or at church or anywhere to know you're pregnant because it would ruin his own perfect reputation."

"That's a terrible thing to say," Grace said quietly.

"It's true, though," said Jory. "How could he be a church elder or academic dean at Northwestern Bible College with you sticking out to there?" Jory curved her hands out in front of her.

The two sisters stood looking at each other. The early evening air was taking on a sweet coolness and somewhere high above them in a maple tree a flicker gave a wistful one-note call.

"You've just had a long day," Grace said finally, soothingly — although Jory couldn't tell quite who it was she was trying to soothe. Whom. *Whom* she was trying to soothe. "And you're feeling cross. You always say things you don't mean when you're cross." Grace gave Jory one of her most radiant and patient smiles. "I'm sorry, Jory. I know all of this is really hard for you."

Jory studied her sister, knowing this was the exact moment at which she, too, could and should apologize. "I'm starving," she said. "What are we having for dinner?"

Grace tried to blink back her disappointment. "Whatever we want," she said, her smile dimming just slightly. "Imagine that."

Jory opened the double-doored cupboard that hung directly over the sink. Their father's feelings of guilt could be read in the amazing grocery purchases he had made: Nestlé's Strawberry Quik, Mystic Mint cookies, Peter Pan peanut butter, Lay's barbecue potato chips. Forbidden food full of sugar and chemicals and carcinogenic dye. The good stuff.

Neither Jory nor Grace could cook. They could clean and iron and sew — these they had all learned in Caravans, in Indian Maidens and Pathfinders on Wednesday nights at church, earning diamond-shaped badges to put across their green sashes — but their mother had always done the cooking because their father liked things "a certain way": unflavored, unsweetened, with the peel still on and the vitamins and minerals still intact. Plain and healthy and raw was the way their father liked his food. No salt or sugar, and only legumes and nuts for protein. Spices like garlic and pepper and onions made his scalp tingle. As did pop. Once, at a party in high school, he frequently liked to recall, he had been given a Coca-Cola (he always shook his head at this point) and the scalp tingling had lasted for

200

days. The body was a temple. An untingling temple. "Animals have the right idea," he would say, munching down another Jonathan apple, core and seeds and all. "At least when it comes to food," their mother would amend.

Jory watched as Grace bent and tried to light the stove burner with a match. They both jumped back when it caught with a *whoomp* of blue flame. "Whoa," Grace said, blowing on the match. "I have no idea what I'm doing here."

"You're doing fine," Jory said, and handed her the black skillet. She peeled the bacon strips apart from each other and dropped them one at a time into the pan, where they began to sputter and pop.

"How do you know when they're done?" Grace poked at a piece of the bacon with a fork.

"When they turn nearly black," Jory said. "They have to crinkle up like old snakes." She could feel herself getting slightly giddy at the prospect. At the two of them here in this house choosing and preparing their own food. Alone. All by themselves. It reminded her of when they were little and they had made a secret fort on Grace's bed with blankets and the yardstick. The light underneath the blanket was the warmest yellow imaginable. They had turned their desk chairs upside down on their desks too, and then sat between the legs, pretending they were using the pivoting feet on the chair legs to copilot a plane soaring over the high Himalayas and the vast African savanna. But they were low on gas, and one after the other the plane's engines began to sputter and choke and die. Finally they were forced to parachute out above the dark and deadly Amazon, where enormous snakes and jungle cats slithered and roamed. Jory shivered even in remembrance. When had they stopped doing that? How long ago had that been?

Grace attempted to turn the spattering slices from one side to the other. "Ouch. *Ouch!* Forget it. They can just cook on this one side." Grace wiped her burned hand across the bib of her overalls.

"No! They have to be turned. I watched Rhonda's dad do it and he flipped them over. They won't be done right."

"Then *you* flip them." Grace held the fork out toward Jory, who was backing away. "Ah! Very brave," she said, and went back to poking at the bacon.

"You have to put them on a paper towel when they're done." Jory reached into the refrigerator and pulled out a head of lettuce. *Their* head of lettuce. And here on the windowsill were *their* tomatoes. And on the counter was *their* applesauce . . . sweetened applesauce with sugar in it. They were going to drink pop with dinner. Shasta grape pop. Jory put the head of lettuce under the faucet and turned on the water. "How do I get the water out?"

"I don't know. You pat it or something. With a dishtowel."

"We don't have any dishtowels."

"Use a napkin."

"*Pat* is a weird word." Jory turned and held the dripping head of lettuce in front of her, a soggy napkin underneath.

"Here. Come here." Grace reached out for the lettuce. She rolled it up and down against the front of her overalls. "See? Drier already."

"Very sanitary," Jory said.

Grace took the head of lettuce and tucked it carefully underneath the waistband of her overalls. She gazed down at the results.

"Wow," said Jory.

Grace continued to stare solemnly down at her abdomen.

The front door opened and shut. *"Knock-knock,"* their father called out from the living room. "Anyone home?"

Grace slid the head of lettuce out of her

overalls and put it on the counter. She turned and began forking the bacon out of the pan and onto a plate.

"We're in here," Jory answered, feeling a surprising stab of disappointment.

Their father ducked slightly as he walked beneath the curved entryway into the kitchen. "Well, here you are," he said, "safe and sound. I was beginning to worry."

"Nothing to worry about," said Jory. "I made it home okay." She turned and began tearing leaves of the lettuce into smaller pieces and putting them in a yellow bowl that she lifted down from one of the cupboards.

"What happened to your bus?"

"Nothing," Jory said quickly. "What do you think of our dinner?"

"It certainly smells . . . *bacony.*" Their father put the books he was carrying onto the kitchen table. He leaned over the frying pan and peered at the remaining pieces of bacon. "Well," he said, "look at you two. You're cooking dinner." He straightened back up and gazed around the kitchen, blinking, as if it were too bright. "Think of that."

"What did you think we'd do?" asked Grace, not looking up from her work.

"I meant," he said, "that I'm *proud* of you.

That I'm proud of the way you're fending for yourselves."

"Really?" said Grace. She continued in her careful slicing of a tomato.

Jory brought the jar of applesauce over to the table and sat down. "Why don't you eat with us, Dad?"

"Oh, no — that's a sweet offer, but your mother will be expecting me to eat when I get back." He sat down at the other end of the table and began curling the edge of a place mat between his fingers.

"How's Frances?" Jory stared straight ahead at her father.

"She's fine. First day of school. She loves her teacher but doesn't like the other kids. Plus, she says she's bored — she's tired of reading about elephants that wear pants. The usual."

"I'm not going back to Schism, Dad." Jory continued to stare at him.

"Well." Her father moved the place mat forward and backward on the table. "We can talk about that."

"I'm not going to go there."

"Well," he said again, "we need to think about what's best here. The law says you have to go to school until you're sixteen, so that part's not open to debate. Schism is close by and it's a perfectly decent school.

205

Its curriculum is a little outdated, that's true, but it seems to be covering the bases fairly well academically."

Jory shook her head.

"The kids may not be quite what you're used to."

Grace sat down and handed Jory a sandwich. Jory looked at it, then set it down on her plate. "I want to go back to Arco Christian."

Her father took a deep breath and let it out through his nose. "I realize that. But we've already discussed why that might not be the best idea right now."

"I wouldn't talk to anyone about anything, if that's what you're worried about." Jory glanced at Grace and then back at her father. "I wouldn't say a word."

"I'm sure you wouldn't mean to." He readjusted the place mat, aligning its edges with the table's. "But that's not the whole reason."

"You're punishing me, aren't you? I can't go back to my school because of the earrings, right?"

"No. No. That's not true. Mom and I have forgiven you for that. It's just, well, we think it might be good for you to have some time away from things — to rethink your situation a bit. Reappraise the way you want to live your life."

Grace put her sandwich down. "That sounds a lot like punishment, don't you think?"

Jory gave Grace a fleeting look of amazement. She sat up in her chair. "The kids all smoke and swear, Dad. Aren't you worried about what kind of influence that will be on me? Don't you care if I start to smoke? Or drink?"

Her father leaned forward and spread his hands out flat against the tabletop. "I don't think you will, Jory. I'm fairly certain of the things we've taught you."

"Fairly certain?"

"Fairly certain."

"I just won't go, then." Jory pushed back from the table. She stood up and leaned against her chair. "The truant officer will have to come and get me."

"All right," her father said slowly.

"All right," said Jory. She turned and walked through the living room and out the front door.

Outside it was dark and cool, with a hint of what real fall would bring. Jory sat in the porch swing next to her book bag. She pushed off against the porch's wooden flooring with her feet and swung back and forth in the darkness. A light was on in Mrs. Kleinfelter's house. Jory wondered if she was still in the living room watching a silent television. She wondered what Mrs. Kleinfelter was having for dinner. What was it like to live all by yourself, with absolutely no one there? No one to talk to or cry with or even to touch, ever? Jory pulled her sweater sleeves down until they covered her hands. She listened to the swing's chains groaning where they had been screwed into the wooden slats in the porch's ceiling.

Her father opened the front door and came outside. He stood on the door's threshold, looking out into the evening. He put his hands in his pockets. "Just try it for a semester," he said. "One semester."

"One month," Jory said.

"Three months."

"One."

Her father laughed. "Two months," he said. "And that's my final offer."

Jory pushed off again with her feet.

"You're going to be okay," he said. "We're all going to be okay."

"Right," Jory said. She continued to let the swing take her back and forth.

"Come on," he said. "Walk with me out to the car."

Jory got out of the swing and they started

down the steps together. They walked past the shadowy bridal wreath bush and the hollyhocks and the plum tree. "What do you think of your neighbor," her father asked as they passed Mrs. Kleinfelter's house.

"I like her," Jory said.

"Good," her father said. "She seemed nice when I spoke to her." Jory's father stepped over the curb and walked out into the road. He stood next to the driver's side of the Buick, and then he opened the car door. "We miss you at home," he said.

Jory looked into her father's eyes, which were the exact same color as her own. "You could take us back, then."

As they stood next to the car, a truck came quickly down the road toward them. They watched its headlights coming closer. It pulled to a stop next to the Buick and even in the dusky light Jory could read the hand-painted lettering on its side. Grip leaned out the truck's window. He looked first at Jory and then at her father. "Do either of y'all two know how to get to Lone Star Road from here? I seem to be lost." He smiled in an open-faced way that made Jory's heart thrum.

Jory's father moved closer to the truck. "Lone Star's at least a couple miles in the opposite direction," her father said, pointing. "Back that way," he said, "to the north."

"I must be all turned around." Grip shook his head. "I never was any good at directions. Not much good at apologies either." He waved and pulled the truck back out into the street.

Jory and her father watched the truck's taillights dwindling away. "Not the brightest fellow," said her father. "He's still going the wrong direction. Maybe he's been drinking."

"Maybe," said Jory, and squeezed her hands together tightly inside her sweater sleeves. She jumped up on her toes and quickly kissed her father's cheek. "Bye, Dad."

"Well, good-bye to you too," he said, and kissed her back.

Grace was already doing the dishes. Jory's bowl of applesauce and her sandwich sat on the table. "It's not warm anymore, but it's probably still good," said Grace, turning around.

Jory sat down and picked up the sandwich. She suddenly felt incredibly hungry. "We could get a TV," she said.

Grace rinsed out a glass. "Pastor Ron says that television is a mind-numbing diversion," she said. "And that it encourages violence and immorality."

Jory rolled her eyes. "Oh, really? Well, who was it that used to sneak out of her bedroom to see Barnabas Collins every day at four o'clock sharp?"

"What?" Grace turned and faced Jory, her face and birthmark distinctly rosy colored. "I did not. I was just keeping you and Frances company."

"You were completely in love with him. Him and his wolf-head cane and his sexy fangs." Jory made a vampire face and raised her fingers up into claws. "You thought he was devastatingly handsome." Jory was making most of this up, but Grace, for some reason, blushed even more furiously.

"Anyway," said Grace, turning back around and intently scrubbing at a dish, "we don't have any money, so we couldn't get one even if we wanted to."

"Maybe I could steal one. I'm supposed to be pretty good at that."

Grace shook her head.

Jory spooned up some applesauce and stirred it around in her bowl. "We're reading *Lord of the Flies* in English I. It wasn't allowed at ACA. It's a banned book or something. Maybe I should call Mom up and tell her I'm reading banned books."

"I'd rather read anything than do my trig-

211

onometry."

"Yeah, but you don't really have to do it. It's all just correspondence stuff."

Grace scoffed. "Just correspondence stuff? I have to send all my homework off and have it graded the minute I'm done with it. It's just as hard as regular school, but without any of the good parts."

"What good parts?"

Grace turned off the water and turned around. She leaned against the sink. "You know," she said, and shrugged helplessly.

"You mean like football games when it's cold and they have a bonfire afterward and the Pep Club sells popcorn and apple cider and cinnamon doughnuts? And then everybody gets thrown in the ditch? And the hayride last year with the squirt guns? Remember when Mr. Vanderwoode let them turn his barn into a spook house, and Lydia Quenzer was too scared to go inside but Brian dragged her in anyway and she cried and her mom had to come get her? And then the time Donna Hazen jumped on the trampoline in her dress on the field trip and so we didn't get to go into the Kuna Caves after all."

Grace moved over to the table and sat down in the chair next to Jory's. "I always loved chapel days and when the choir sang

and we lit candles. It felt real. And holy."
Grace smiled. "And the Noontime Bible
Study. I felt like I was able to do some
genuine witnessing with the other kids then.
That I helped strengthen their daily walks
with Christ."

Jory said nothing. Noontime Bible Study
— one of Grace's proudest achievements —
had been popular only with the weirdest of
the weird: the loners and the bed wetters
and the acne-ridden of Arco Christian. Only
those kids who would have been relegated
to the farthest tables in the lunchroom will-
ingly attended Noontime Bible Study.
Ruthann Hoagterp, who wore dresses down
to her freckled calves, and sad, silent,
already balding Clarence Muldoon were
two of its longtime members. Jory had even
heard through the junior high grapevine that
Art Tolman had told Grace she should start
a club called HAHA — Hicks and Homos
Association — and that he had left a note
in the school's suggestion box to that effect.
Even at ACA — where it was genuinely difficult to seem odd or unusual — Grace had
made a career of being the most sincere and
determinedly devout girl the school had
ever known. Jory had had to work very, very
hard to keep Grace's reputation as an
eternally smiling goody-goody from rubbing

off on her own. It was a shameful fact, but several times early in her tenure at Arco Christian Jory had tried to pretend that she didn't know who Grace was. Later, she had resorted to claiming her older sister was adopted, as if this might explain away Grace's extreme moral rectitude and apparent lack of self-awareness. Worse yet, when other students would give Jory a half-admiring, half-appalled look and ask whether her sister was "always like that," Jory would be forced to admit that, yes, she was. She was always like that.

"And Valentine's Day, when the Service Club took pink carnations around to each of the classrooms and gave them to people from their secret admirers." Grace was still reminiscing.

"And you got one from Darryl Hofstetter." Jory made a gagging noise. " 'Dear Grace, I like your face, it's smooth and pink and soft as lace, your friend, Darryl Hofstetter.' Remember how he used to sit behind you on the bus each day?" Jory shivered with disgust.

"Oh, he wasn't so bad. He was actually kind of sweet."

"Sweet? You could smell him clear at the front of the bus. Everyone had to open their windows."

"That's mean, Jory. He lived all alone way out on that farm with only his great-grandfather. He didn't know any better."

"He smelled like sour milk! Like wet clothes left all night in a washing machine."

"Jesus never cared what people looked like or what they smelled like."

"That's 'cause he never smelled Darryl Hofstetter."

Grace threw the dishtowel at Jory and Jory flinched and laughed, catching the towel as it dropped toward the floor.

"But seriously," said Grace. "Our bodies don't have to be everything. They're only part of us."

"Yeah," said Jory. "But that's the part of you that has us living out here, you know."

Grace seemed to be thinking about something. She gave Jory a crooked smile. "Things smell so weird to me now, and food tastes sort of different too. Even oatmeal tastes strange. Like it almost has meat in it or something."

Jory made a face. "Meat?"

"And I can't hold my stomach in anymore." Grace looked down at her midsection. "It's like my stomach muscles just won't do anything."

"Yuck," said Jory. "Do you still feel sick?"

"Sometimes when I first wake up I feel

like I'm going to gag or throw up, but instead I just sneeze."

"Wow," said Jory.

"I know," said Grace. She laughed and then so did Jory. They laughed and laughed with Grace holding one hand on her stomach. It was a familiar moment, Jory realized — the two of them giggling together — it was just happening in an unfamiliar place and for a very unfamiliar reason. Their laughter died away slowly and they sat silently at the table.

"Are you scared?" Jory asked.

"Yes," said Grace. She sounded surprised to be saying this. "Sometimes I feel like I'm completely alone."

Jory was struck.

"And I miss Frances," Grace said, as if trying to soften the blow of what she had just said.

Jory nodded. "Me too. What if she forgets us?"

"She won't. She never would."

"She might." Jory listened to the loud tick of the kitchen clock. "It's my birthday next Sunday." She studied her folded hands, examining the way her fingers folded over each other. *Here's the church, here's the steeple, open the doors, and see all the peo-*

ple. "What if they won't even come and see me?"

Grace stood up and walked over to the sink. She turned her back to Jory and immersed her hands in the dishwater again. "Well, then I guess we'll just have our own party," she said, picking up another dish to wash. "All by ourselves."

CHAPTER EIGHT

Jory and Grace had spent the last hour trying to find an outfit remotely acceptable for Jory's second day at school.

"What you have on your body doesn't really matter," Grace said, giving up on her search for something that would approximate a pair of bell-bottomed jeans. "It's how you act and what you say that's important."

"Oh, right, here we go again," Jory said and rolled her eyes.

"It's true," Grace insisted. "It's only your spirit that matters."

Jory held up a light blue sweater against her chest.

"Well, I want my spirit to look really cool," she said, and gave the hopeless blue sweater a fling. She was now wearing a pair of brown wool pants that were too small for Grace and a white thermal undershirt–type shirt she had found in the basement in an old box of clothes. It smelled a little strange, like apples left out too long, but Jory thought it looked sort of neat. Or close to neat. She had also borrowed Grace's black dress boots, but even with two pairs of socks they were a little big, and Jory kept curling her toes inside of them. She felt almost as if she were wearing a costume. As if she were in a play, pretending to be the girl going to school.

Jory jogged down the hill to the bus stop and stood next to an old elm tree at the edge of a large sugar beet field. She waited as nonchalantly as possible, eyeing the few passing cars, hoping that the next vehicle she heard would be her bus. The school had called early this morning telling her where to wait for Bus 17. Why, when there were only four buses, was hers Number 17? Jory chewed at the end of the wool scarf that Grace had lent her.

At ACA, all the girls were required to wear dresses with sleeves and modest necklines and skirts that came down to the middle of the knee. If your dress or skirt length was questionable, if there was any question about it being shorter than knee length, Mr. Mordhorst made you kneel on the floor of his office so that he could measure it with the yellow tape measure he carried in his pocket. Jory had never had this horror happen to her, but Rhonda Russell had had to kneel on Mr. Mordhorst's carpet several times already. Pants were strictly forbidden, except during PE class or on field trips to the Bruneau Sand Dunes or the Craters of the Moon, when the girls were allowed to wear culottes or skorts (if they were knee length). Makeup and jewelry were frowned upon. The boys had to wear collared shirts and dress pants. No T-shirts or blue jeans. Last year, Jory had asked Mrs. Mordhorst if black jeans were permissible and had gotten a demerit for it. "Bad attitude," Mrs. Mordhorst had written on the form she sent home to Jory's parents. "This sort of sarcasm is unattractive in a young Christian girl." On chapel days the girls wore dress-up dresses and nylons and the boys wore ties. Jory had never sat in a school desk while wearing pants. She had never sat in a school *bus* while wearing pants. She tied and retied the knot in her scarf. Earlier, Grace had come into Jory's room when Jory had been sitting on the bed in her wool pants and Grace's bra as she tried on clothes. Grace had glanced at Jory and then away, saying nothing. Jory had blushed hotly, but she hadn't taken the bra off.

Jory's stomach hurt. She hadn't been able

to eat breakfast this morning either. During fourth grade, the awful year of Mrs. Hickerson, Jory's stomach had hurt every day and she had been forced to give up breakfast entirely. Each morning she stood in front of her father and begged him to tie her dress's sash tighter. It still felt loose; couldn't he tie it tighter? "I'm getting blisters," he said, laughing, but he retied it anyway, resting his large hand on her head before letting her go. One afternoon, after a particularly bad round of Math Slap, Jory sat down at her desk after her turn at the board and vomited across her notebook. A little bit of it splashed against the shoes of Ginny Price, the girl who sat in the desk next to hers. Ginny had jumped up and shrieked as Mrs. Hickerson marched down the aisle and stood next to Jory's desk. "The nurse's," she said. "And hurry up." Jory lay on the narrow cot in the nurse's office until the end of the day. When it was time to go home, she stood up, but her stomach hurt so badly that she began to cry. The nurse, who was actually Robbie Shannon's mother and only volunteering for the day, went and got the principal. Mr. Steinbroner insisted on driving Jory home in his large black Lincoln. Jory sunk deep into the leather of the front passenger seat, saying nothing as the

221

tears plopped heavily onto the skirt of her dress. Mr. Steinbroner, too, was utterly silent except to ask finally where to turn and which house was hers.

At home, her mother had had to come out to the car and speak to Mr. Steinbroner and listen to his admonitions about getting Jory to a doctor right away. "For heaven's sake, Jory," her mother said, once she got her inside the house. Her mother turned Jory around and pulled the knot out of her dress's sash with one quick jerk. Jory felt immediately better. Her mother shook her head. "Your dress was just tied too tight." She frowned. "What on earth is wrong with you?"

"Nothing," said Jory. But they both knew better.

That same night, as she lay in bed, her father had sat next to her and told her about the time he had to switch from a one-room schoolhouse in Kansas to a big public high school in Colorado and how he came home from the first day with a sick headache that kept him out of school for the next three days. He had rubbed Jory's back as he told her this and said he was sorry she was so much like him. Jory liked the back rub, but even in fourth grade she knew her father was wrong — she was nothing like him.

Grace was like their father. Brave and good and holy. Jory was more like their mother: moody and angry and afraid. Which was why she and her mother fought and fought. Jory had heard her mother tell her father this earlier that night, from where she sat inside her closet. "I recognize her tendencies," her mother said in a low voice. "You'd think you'd have more patience, then," her father said. Jory could hear her mother sigh. "That's not apparently how it works."

Once, later that same year, her mother had found Jory sitting on her bedroom floor poking the inside of her mouth with a straight pin. "Jory, what on earth are you doing?" her mother asked.

"Nothing," said Jory, hiding the pin underneath her leg.

"Why are you sticking that pin in your mouth? Answer me."

Jory ran the pin down the inside of her knee sock. "I have to go to the dentist tomorrow," she said.

"So?"

"I wanted to see what it felt like. Getting a shot."

Her mother dropped the stack of folded laundry onto Jory's bed. She stood up and put her hands on her hips. "A coward dies a thousand deaths," she said, "a brave man, only one." She turned and walked out of the bedroom.

Jory still knew that quote by heart. *A thousand deaths,* she said to herself now as she peered down the road, nervously looking for the bus. *A thousand and one. A thousand and two.* Something that looked suspiciously like an old yellow school bus rounded the far corner and chugged ever closer to where Jory was standing — her stomach aching as if encircled by a knotted sash tied tight beneath her heart.

Jory ate lunch by herself. Grace had made her a peanut butter sandwich that Jory kept in her locker until the lunch bell rang and then she took it and her baggie of potato chips outside onto the grassy patch of lawn between the main building and the gym. She sat down next to a scraggly evergreen bush and peeled the plastic wrap away from her sandwich. She took a bite and chewed dryly. All around her were groups of kids, laughing and yelling and touching each other and doing very little eating. If this were her *real* school, she thought, the one she went to all the time, she would be doing her best to find some group to fit into, but since she had only a few more weeks to go — well, it didn't matter if she was unpopular, it didn't matter if she remained a complete outsider, a freak, a loner, an exchange student from somewhere else.

Her stomach hurt.

She left the rest of her last potato chips in the baggie and put it inside the brown paper bag Grace had given her. She glanced around at the endless reconfiguring of the various groups of students. Several boys wearing cowboy boots and tight Wranglers with large belt buckles swooped and ran and slapped each other and yelled as if playing some complicated game. Another group of slightly older looking students with longer, shaggier hair and sloppier patched and un-hemmed Levis stood in a tight circle under-neath the gym's overhang, a distinct haze hanging over their carefully hunched heads. One girl with beautiful long black hair broke away suddenly from this pack and ran shrieking and jumping onto the back of a boy wearing an old plaid shirt and an army jacket. The girl leaned over his shoulder and told him something that made him laugh and tip backward. The dark-haired girl then screamed and hung on to the boy's back and they both fell to the ground. The kids behind them jumped out of the way, and someone said, "Way to go, *spaz*." Jory recognized the boy on the ground as the one who had spoken to her in yesterday's earth science class. She had never seen the girl before. The two of them lay on the ground, still laughing. "God, get up, you freaks," said a blond-haired girl wearing a patchwork denim miniskirt. "Mullinix will think you're stoned and come out here." Mr. Mullinix was the principal. Jory had met him this morning when she'd gone into the office to get her locker combination. He was a falsely smiling man with a face like several potatoes lumped together. He seemed completely harmless to Jory, but she knew sometimes those were the worst kind. Mr. Pemberton, at church, was like that. He had an innocuous gray beard and a cheerful round face, but he was always coming up behind the Junior Church girls and rubbing their necks and telling them they felt tight — did they need a back rub? He had good hands, he said, flexing his fingers. Were they sure? They were always sure, but it didn't make any difference. Once Jory was standing outside the women's restroom talking to Olivia Pemberton when Mr. Pemberton came up behind and began massaging the back of Jory's neck. "Oh, Dad," Olivia said, her face turning bright red. "What?" he said, rubbing and kneading steadily. "Jory doesn't mind." Jory had smiled gamely. She

226

was a chicken and a coward. It was true.

An errant Frisbee thwacked against Jory's upper arm and dropped to the grass next to her. She picked the blue disk up and a girl in a Doors T-shirt loped over and held out her hand and then ran off again. This wordless interchange made Jory feel like someone visiting from another planet. She didn't belong anywhere: not with any of the groups here, not with the goat ropers or the popular athletic kids or especially with the long-haired cool kids. She was a freak destined to always lurk on the fringes of everything. The lunch bell rang and the students all groaned and with great deliberation began putting their cigarettes out and their trash in the trash can, or at least aiming it in that direction. In a straggling, swearing swarm they began heading back toward the main building. Jory stood up, her legs stiff from sitting on the ground for so long.

"Hey," the boy from earth science said, slowing his pace to match hers. "I didn't see you."

"I saw you," Jory said.

"Oh," he said and laughed. "You mean back there? We were just fooling around. Jude gets a little carried away sometimes."

"Jude?"

"Judith Mullinix. Jude. The girl with the

dark hair."

"What, is she related to Mr. Mullinix?"

"She's his daughter." He laughed. "How'd you like that — having the principal be your dad?"

"I can sort of imagine it."

"Really? Not me." He opened the school building's front door and they walked inside, heading downstairs toward the earth science room. "My dad's a crop duster. He'd rather be dead than be cooped up indoors. He hardly ever comes in our house, except to eat dinner. Sometimes my mom puts his plate of food on the back porch step, just to be funny."

"Are you sure she's being funny?"

He stared at her. Jory noticed that his eyes were a dark gray-blue and that his lashes were long. Longer than hers. "Maybe she's mad," Jory said.

"She doesn't seem like it."

"Moms are weird."

"Girls are weird." He grinned at her, and then seemed to get suddenly shy. He turned away and let her walk into the earth science room by herself. Jory tried not to look at anyone as she made her way to her desk.

Right as the tardy bell rang, he rushed into the room and plopped down in the seat next to hers. They sat next to each other in silence as Mr. DeNovia handed out the attendance sheet and told them to get out some paper to take notes on. She watched as he wrote his name down on the attendance sheet and then handed it to her. *Laird Albright.* Jory signed her own name and handed it on to the girl sitting next to her. Jory leaned slightly in Laird's direction. Mr. DeNovia was busy drawing a picture of a subduction zone on the chalkboard.

"I knew a guy whose name was Phil Albright," she whispered. "His dad was a missionary and he got eaten by Peruvian cannibals." She widened her eyes and made what she hoped was a funny face.

Laird didn't glance up from the notes he was making. "Yeah," he said. "That was my uncle."

Jory leaned quickly back. She stared at the chalkboard where Mr. DeNovia was coloring in the oceanic crust with a piece of blue chalk. "Really?" she whispered.

He shrugged. "It was a long time ago. I don't even remember him."

"Your uncle was a *missionary*?"

Mr. DeNovia turned with the chalk still in his hand and faced the class. "Am I going to have to separate you two?"

The girl next to Jory gave a soft snort.

"When a continent runs into a piece of

seafloor," Mr. DeNovia said, knocking the point of his chalk against the chalkboard, "it's like a Mack truck running into a Volkswagen. Not very pretty." The end of Mr. DeNovia's chalk broke off and fell to the floor.

A boy in the back of the class gave a brief guffaw.

Mr. DeNovia bent over and retrieved the chalk. He stood up and smiled ruefully at this lone evidence of class participation. "But at least there's a clear winner in this wreck," he said, wiping chalk dust down the front of his pants. "And the seafloor basalt ends up in pretty much the same position as the VW: under the truck — or continent, as the case may be. This may seem like a drag for the basalt, but remember, it isn't all that happy on the surface anyway."

"A drag for the basalt?" Laird whispered the words out of the side of his mouth.

Jory smiled surreptitiously.

"This gives it the heat it needs to remelt and complete the differentiation process which was so rudely interrupted at the spreading ridge. And when it cools, guess what forms?" Mr. DeNovia glanced around the room. He picked up the attendance sheet. "Mr. Frankamp?"

A black-haired boy sitting to the left of

Jory frowned. "I don't know, man," he said. He jabbed his pen point into the wooden tabletop and made a drilling motion with it. "But you make rocks sound like they're people or something. Like they're all happy and sad and shit. Whoops." He grinned at the boy next to him, who punched him in the arm. "I mean, sad and *stuff*."

"Thank you for that clarification." Mr. DeNovia continued on as the class snickered. "The materials that make up the earth's form may not be living in the way that we, as humans, think of as *living*, but their processes, just like ours, are ones of progression and change. They are in a state of flux, just like plants and animals and, yes, human beings." Mr. DeNovia squinted slightly and began waving his hands. "Expansion, movement, changes in temperature and size and shape. Acting upon other elements and being acted upon. I'd call that living, wouldn't you?" He quit waving and stood quietly at the front of the room for a moment, looking at the backs of his hands. Then he walked over to his teacher's desk and sat down. "Why don't you go ahead and begin reading in your textbooks. Chapter Four, I think it is. Let's just skip over One and Two. You people obviously are already well acquainted with the earth's crust." He opened his desk drawer, peered inside, and promptly shut it again. "You've been outside. You've seen it."

As Jory reached into her book bag, she felt a sudden pang. Today was the first day of PE. Just thinking about it made her feel sick. Jory glanced around the classroom at the other girls. None of them seemed like they were worrying about it. One girl behind her had even fallen asleep. Jory clenched her toes inside Grace's boots and made a soft involuntary groaning sound.

"What's wrong?" Laird whispered.

"Nothing," she said. "I guess I don't feel so good."

"Girl stuff?"

Jory gave him a blank look.

The girl sitting to the left of Jory leaned forward. "He wants to know if you're on the rag." The girl was wearing a beaded choker with a tiny elephant hanging from the middle of it. "Guys always like to think you're on the rag every minute."

"I'm not," whispered Jory, feeling her face turning red.

"Well, if you are," said the girl, "go see the nurse. She'll give you a Darvon."

"No *way*," said Laird.

"Yup," said the girl, nodding. She glanced over at Mr. DeNovia, who was busily packing papers into his bag. "She has Valium too."

"No stinking way." Laird leaned even farther over the table. "You're full of shit."

The choker girl had begun digging in her suede purse. "Check it out," she said, unwrinkling a Kleenex and pulling a tiny yellow pill out of the middle of it. She put the pill on the table for inspection.

Laird leaned past Jory and picked up the pill. "Hm," he said, turning it over and looking at it closely. He licked the pill once and then put it in his pants pocket.

"Hey, you freak," the girl whispered. "Give that back." She laughed and tried to reach across the table.

"Dream on," said Laird, leaning back and laughing.

"*All right,* table three," Mr. DeNovia said. "That's probably enough fun for this period."

Jory sat silently thinking. The nurse. Why hadn't she thought of the nurse? She could go to the nurse! Jory put her pencil between the pages of *The Earth and Its Wonders* and told herself, no, do not be stupid. If she allowed the idea about the nurse to take root much longer, she would find herself missing PE and being driven home by Mr. Mullinix. She was squinching her toes together in her boots and trying to will herself into bravery when the classroom door opened. The students all turned their heads at this exciting event.

"Who's that?" Laird peered intently at the man standing just outside the doorway.

"It's my father," Jory whispered, as surprised by this as anyone else.

Jory and her father stood out in the hallway. Jory kept her arms folded tight across her chest and her eyes deliberately trained on the floor. She could hear the quiet sounds coming from inside the open door of the earth science classroom — students sighing and turning pages in their books, someone coughing and then scooting the wooden legs of their chair back. Jory listened to the large corridor clock's muted ticking. "You can't just come to school like this, Dad," she whispered.

"Well, honey," her father said in his normal tone of voice, which seemed suddenly to Jory unbearably loud and capable of carrying all the way down the hall. "Grace called me at work and said you'd forgotten your PE clothes. I left my meeting with the admissions committee just to get them for you." He handed her the large brown Albertsons bag that contained her sweatpants and tennis shoes. "I thought you'd be pretty glad to see me."

Jory held the bag down by her side, as if it were full of something that smelled. "I guess you can go now," she whispered, her chest a tight knot of bad feelings.

"Okay." Her father brought his lips together and gazed off toward the bank of pale green lockers. "All right. I'll do that. I'll get back to my own school." He took a step toward the stairs, but then stopped. He reached out and put his hand on her upper arm. "Are you doing fine? Is everyone here treating you kindly?"

Jory looked up at her father, incredulous.

"I'll take that as a yes." Her father patted her arm. "Okay, then."

"Dad."

He raised his eyebrows.

"Never mind."

"What? What is it?"

"It's nothing."

They stood in the hall looking at each other.

"I don't feel so good."

"What do you mean?"

"I don't know." Jory closed her eyes. "I don't feel okay. Something's wrong with me."

"Like what?" He stepped closer and studied her face.

"Like something bad."

"You'll have to be a bit more specific."

"I think I need to go home." Jory swallowed and gripped the bag of clothes tight.

"Are you sick?"

"Um-hm."

"Do you have a fever?" Her father tried to put a hand on her forehead, but she stepped back.

"No, it's not like that," she whispered. "It's girl stuff."

Her father blinked. "Oh," he said. "Well, all right. Hm. Let's see. I guess we'll have to tell someone. The secretary or someone."

"She's upstairs." Jory turned away from him. "I'll go wait in the car."

Her father nodded.

"I have to get my books first."

Jory stepped toward the open classroom door. Inside, everyone looked up as she walked quickly toward her end of the table. She gathered up her papers and books and began sliding them into her book bag.

"Hey, what's up?" Laird whispered as he watched her progress. "Where're you going?"

"Miss Quanbeck, are you planning on leaving us?" Mr. DeNovia stood in front of her.

"I have to go home," Jory said, not pausing in her packing. "A family emergency."

"Oh, dear," Mr. DeNovia said. "Nothing too serious, I hope."

All around the classroom the students lifted their heads and stopped whatever they were doing and were happily listening to this exchange. The girl with the elephant choker smiled at Jory, a strange, almost winking smile. "I have an emergency too," she said, loudly, and stretched her arms above her head. "A boredom emergency."

"That's too bad, Sylvia." Mr. DeNovia checked his watch. "Since we've still got a good twenty minutes of study time left."

"Bleh." The girl named Sylvia stuck out her tongue at Mr. DeNovia's back. She leaned past Jory and whispered to Laird, "I could really use that thing you've got in your pocket."

"That's what they all say." Laird grinned and then turned toward Jory. "What happened? Is somebody dead?"

Jory scooped up her pen and slung her book bag strap over her shoulder. "I wish," she said.

It was hot in the car. Jory's back stuck to the Buick's vinyl seat as she and her father drove along in silence. Jory watched the farmhouses slide by. She had ridden back and forth past this terrain enough that some part of her head had already memorized the landscape. The small, neatly kept green farmhouse and then the slightly more ostentatious redbrick one, the twinned metal grain silos overlooking the corral with the Appaloosa and the horse racing barrels, then the grayish house with its sagging, broken-toothed shutters and the rusty tractor peeking up from the weeds of the side yard. Cottonwoods, willows, elms, and then rows of cypress trees for windbreak. She could narrow her eyes and have all of it click past like so many train cars. She slumped lower in the seat. She was missing PE. The relief she felt churned bitterly in the lowest part of her stomach. She bit her inner cheek until a tiny thrill of pain forced her to stop. "I hate you," she said under her breath. It wasn't quite apparent who she was speaking to. Her tongue sought out the bitten spot in her cheek again. Her father drove on, his eyes on the road ahead.

Jory and her father stood outside the car. "Thanks for bringing my stuff," Jory said quietly.

"Of course," her father said, and gave her arm a final squeeze. "See you at home," he said, and then almost visibly winced. "I'll see you later," he said.

"Will you be coming over on Sunday?" Jory picked up her bag of PE clothes and held it to her chest.

"Sunday?"

"For my birthday?"

Her father seemed to be thinking about this, as if it required a great deal of study. "Well, of course we will," he said at last.

"All of you?"

"All of us." Her father nodded firmly. "We will *all* be over," he said. "On Sunday. For your thirteenth birthday." He ran his hands down the front of his pant legs. "That's a very special day."

Jory deliberately bit down on the already raw spot in her cheek. "It's my *fourteenth.*" She ran up the driveway and up the porch steps without looking back. Her father evidently was still standing next to the car, going nowhere.

"What are you doing home?" Grace held a hand above her eyes, shading them from the sun. She peered up at Jory from where she was seated on the front step of the porch, an open copy of *Teen Guideposts* on her lap.

"I'm not home," Jory said, brushing past her. "And neither are you."

"What?" Grace turned around to watch Jory mount the top stair.

Jory opened the front door and went inside. She threw her book bag and the Albertsons bag onto the couch. Then she ran up the stairs and went into the bathroom and sat down on the closed toilet lid. She put her chin in her hands and closed her eyes. She rubbed her feet across the small squares of tile. Outside, she could hear the muffled sounds of her father's calm voice talking to her sister, and then there was the sound of a car engine starting up. Jory could hear her sister coming up the stairs.

Grace knocked quietly on the bathroom door. "Jory," she said.

"What?" said Jory, after a long moment.

"Are you okay?"

Jory waited another few seconds and then stood up and unlocked the door. She stood in the doorway and faced her sister. Grace had a strange new expression on her face, one of pity mixed with a sort of radiant undisguised love. Jory felt sick. Grace folded her hands in front of her. "Dad says that you — well, that you're not feeling very good."

Jory looked down at the swirled knots of wood in the hallway's floor. "Yeah, so," she said. She traced one of the swirls with her toe.

"Do you have anything . . . anything to use?"

Jory felt her face heating up. She shook her head.

Grace's voice grew even more quiet. "Is this your first time?"

Jory said nothing. Her tongue sought out the bitten spot on the inside of her cheek.

Grace leaned shyly in toward Jory, her face still shining with the new expression. "God's made you into a woman now," she whispered.

Jory bit down on the raised spot in her cheek and tasted the metally tang of her own blood.

"You know," Grace was still whispering as if they were at the library or in church, "I don't have pads or anything for you to use since I'm not — well, since I don't need anything now."

"That's okay."

"Well, no, obviously it's not." Grace made a little humming sound in the back of her throat. "Oh," she said suddenly. "I think maybe I'll go talk to Mrs. Kleinfelter."

"Don't do that." Jory gave Grace a pleading look.

"It's all right." Grace put her hand on

241

Jory's arm. "Don't be embarrassed. All women help each other with this. We all understand. I'll go see if Mrs. Kleinfelter is home. I'll be right back." Grace gave Jory another shy smile and then turned and headed down the stairs.

Jory slid down the wall and sat down on the bathroom floor. She was beginning to feel quite well acquainted with the small black-and-white tiles. Things seemed to be slipping past her control. Things that used to seem solid and firmly in place had now become liquidy, all slippery and impossible to grasp — like those slidey, shape-shifting puddles of mercury that escaped from the glass thermometer she had dropped when she was little. Because her mother would have had a fit if she'd known that Jory had broken their thermometer, Jory had tried and tried to scoop up the silver blobs, but it was like trying to pick up something only slightly thicker than water. She had finally resorted to half scooting the liquid rolling balls of silver under their old brown couch, where they probably still were, for all she knew. She leaned her back against the claw-foot tub and felt her heart beating like the steady, apparently unstoppable thing that it was. So many things had happened that she never would have dreamed could take place, and yet here she was still breathing and eating food and carrying on like none of it had changed anything. What would it take to make her body stop — anyone's body stop — doing the things it did every day? Could your parents send you away and could your sister go nuts, could you lie stupid lies and steal things and maybe even kill someone, and yet nothing would happen to you? What about hell? What about punishment? Maybe that *was* the punishment — maybe Grace and the angel baby and the banishment to Henry's house was the punishment for the things Jory had done before. Maybe this was how God got back at you — maybe you didn't have to wait for hell. Maybe it came to you, like a large, messily wrapped and half-expected package in the mail. Jory knew her father would be disgusted by this pseudo-theology. God didn't send packages. He didn't need to. God just let you get in trouble all by yourself. And then he let you pay for your mistakes all by yourself too.

Jory slowly unbent her legs and then stood up and peered out the bathroom window. Down below she could see Mrs. Kleinfelter slowly backing an ancient brown Ford truck out of her barn and into their driveway. Jory didn't even know Mrs. Kleinfelter had a car. Grace was standing on their porch watching

Mrs. K's incremental progress. Obviously a conversation had taken place.

Jory sighed and turned from the window and went down the stairs and out the front door to meet her fate.

"That's awfully kind of you," Grace was saying as she squinted at Mrs. Kleinfelter.

"Oh, it's nothing. I have a couple things of my own I need to get there." Mrs. Kleinfelter waved any thoughts of imposition away.

"Only if it's no trouble." Grace turned to Jory with a bright look. "Guess what? Mrs. Kleinfelter's going downtown."

"Um-hm," said Jory, in as noncommittal a way as she could muster.

Mrs. Kleinfelter stood next to the pickup rooting around in something that looked like the kind of mailbag a pony express rider would have used.

"Is that your purse?" Jory asked. "How cool."

"Oh," said Mrs. Kleinfelter, looking down at the bag as if for the first time. "It's an old army satchel of my husband's. I think he carried photos in it." She lifted the flap on the bag up and down. "I'm not a very pursey sort of person."

"Me either," said Jory.

"All right, then," said Grace. She smiled

encouragingly at the two of them. "We'll see you two in a little bit."

Inside the truck it was very warm and smelled of dust and closed windows and Doublemint gum. Jory ran her hand over the car seat's upholstery. It was stiffly scratchy.

"Horsehair," said Mrs. Kleinfelter and put the truck in reverse. She craned her neck and peered behind her as she backed out of the driveway and onto the main road. She inched her cautious way out onto the minimal traffic of the back roads of Arco. They passed the sugar beet factory and then a sign advertising the college. "Is that where your father works?"

She nodded. "He teaches astronomy."

"Oh, the *stars.*" Mrs. Kleinfelter said this as if she were saying the word *God.*

"The planets and moons and all that stuff." Jory rolled the window down an inch or two and felt the wind blow through the sweaty pieces of her hair.

"I can't picture what that must be like — to know all those things about the sky and everything up there. All those things that are *beyond* us. Your father must be an awful smart man."

"Yes," Jory said. "He knows everything."

The two of them rode along in silence for a while. Mrs. Kleinfelter drove on into the town, past the Toot 'N' Tell and the Red Steer and Wretha's Beauty Salon. She made two more careful turns and then pulled the truck into a parking lot. Jory stared up at the sign at the front of the store: SUPER THRIFT. She felt her heart beat faster.

"Well, here we are." Mrs. Kleinfelter turned off the truck's ignition and turned to Jory. "Are you ready?"

Jory sat unmoving in the passenger seat. "Is there another drugstore we could go to?" she said.

"Well, there's a Penny Wise somewhere over on the north side. It's clear across town, though." Mrs. Kleinfelter squinted in at Jory. "Why? Is there something wrong?"

"Oh," said Jory, in the same small voice, her usual creativity deserting her. "I don't know . . . I'm just not sure I know where anything is in there."

Mrs. Kleinfelter shifted her bag from one shoulder to the other. She cleared her throat and then lowered her voice. "Well, I think I can probably help you find whatever you need."

Jory's face and neck grew hot. This was her own fault. Her own fault. Her own fault. She opened the truck's door and stepped out into the brilliant sunshine of Idaho on a late September afternoon. Her heart hammered on, oblivious, healthy and strong, as she walked across the parking lot and through the familiar front door of Super Thrift Drug.

Inside, the smell was exactly the same as before: the new plastic of wading pools and Hula-Hoops mixed with Listerine. The air was artificially cool and somewhere over or underneath it all Glen Campbell was sadly insisting that the Wichita lineman was still on the line. Jory tried to look everywhere and nowhere at once. Mrs. Kleinfelter was walking down one aisle after another with a quickness that made it difficult for Jory to stay safely glued to her shoulder. Mrs. Kleinfelter came to a sudden stop at the pharmacy counter.

"Hello, Phil," she said to the red-faced man behind the counter. She pushed her brown pill bottle across the counter. "Just my usual."

"Sure thing, Mrs. K." The red-faced man tried to smile at Jory, but Jory refused to make eye contact with him; instead, she tried to slouch nonchalantly behind Mrs. Kleinfelter while still glancing all around her. She saw several customers milling about and a female employee she didn't recognize. Maybe the store had changed hands. Maybe all the old employees had quit and moved away. Maybe they had all died and gone directly to hell.

"I don't know why they insist on always keeping it fifty degrees in here." Mrs. Kleinfelter craned her head around as if to locate the offending thermostat, or the "they" who were in charge of it. "It's not as if they're storing meat."

Jory smiled grimly.

"I haven't turned the air on in my house in ages. It's actually just a swamp cooler. Henry insisted that real air conditioners gave him sinus infections." Mrs. Kleinfelter picked a pair of reading glasses off a circular display stand and tried them on. She bent down and inspected herself in the display's tiny mirror. "Oh, dear," she said.

The red-faced pharmacist slid the window on his glass enclosure open and leaned out. "All righty, then," he said. "Here you go." He handed a little white bag to Mrs. Kleinfelter, who was busy poking the reading glasses back into their slot. "Say, is this a granddaughter?" He smiled in Jory's direction, revealing a row of teeth squarely curved and yellow as those of a horse.

"Oh, my, no," said Mrs. Kleinfelter. She

took hold of Jory's arm. "This is my neighbor girl, Jory."

"Well, she's just as pretty as you, so you can understand my mistake." The pharmacist winked.

"Oh, Phil." Mrs. Kleinfelter shook her finger at him and put the white bag in her purse. She turned around and began walking back through the store aisles in the same brisk fashion as before. "Why do men always think they need to remind you that they're men?" she muttered. She shook her head and Jory trailed in her wake, trying to look casual, invisible.

Mrs. Kleinfelter marched down one aisle and then another. Finally she stopped next to the large display of mysterious feminine products. Jory had scrutinized this amazing array surreptitiously many times in the past, but today she had no interest in theorizing what you did exactly with the multitudinous pads, creams, sprays, wipes, nozzled bottles, etc. that all promised discretion, secrecy, and security.

"These feel pretty much like diapers, if you ask me, but they do the trick." Mrs. Kleinfelter's voice seemed unnecessarily loud. She handed a bulky rose-colored box to Jory. The woman on the front of the box was standing in a field of flowers and gazing

249

peacefully out at nothing. She held a daisy in her languid hand. *Modess,* the box read in swirling script, . . . *because.*

Mrs. Kleinfelter now handed Jory a much smaller, flatter box. "That's the belt," she said. "It looks more complicated than it actually is." Mrs. Kleinfelter shook her head. "You won't believe it, but in my day we had to wash our secreties out by hand. That's what we called them: secreties. Unmentionables were your underwear."

Jory cast a quick glance up and down the aisle. A blond woman with two small children in her cart wheeled around the corner and stopped next to them and stared at the display. She sighed loudly and then suddenly swatted the older child on the head with her wallet. "Dammit, Darren," she bellowed at the child, who was clinging to the side of the cart with an air of desperation. "Sit your ass right back down, now!" A man wearing a plaid fishing hat picked something off the shelf a little to the left of them and then walked away, whistling tonelessly and giving them and the blond woman a wide berth.

"I'm not sure about those Tampax. I know they're a modern thing and all . . ." Mrs. Kleinfelter was reading the back of yet another type of box.

"That's probably plenty," Jory whispered. "I think we can go now. Really."

"Hm," said Mrs. Kleinfelter. "We just never used these in my day."

"It's all right," Jory said, and tugged faintly on Mrs. Kleinfelter's coat sleeve.

"Jory!"

Jory whirled around to see Rhonda Russell leaping up the aisle toward her. "What are you *doing*?" Rhonda was saying. "Where have you *been*?" Rhonda flung her arms around Jory's neck. *"Everyone thinks you're dead,"* she shrieked happily.

"I'm not," Jory said, glancing behind Rhonda.

"Oh, my gosh, Mark Pilkington said he saw you and Grace waiting tables out at the Red Eye in Homedale and I told him he was insane." Rhonda looked Jory up and down. "Why aren't you in school? Why aren't you at church?"

"You got cheerleader," Jory said, taking in Rhonda's pleated navy-and-silver skirt and fitted sweater with the tiny silver-helmeted man on the front. " 'Arco Christian Academy Crusaders,' " Jory read out solemnly.

"ACK-ACK!" Rhonda squawked. "Isn't it hilarious?" Rhonda twirled around in the aisle and watched her own skirt unfurl like an umbrella. "You won't believe it — Mr.

251

M is making us hand out tracts to the other cheerleaders during halftime. We're supposed to do our Hello Cheer and then give each of them a 'Four Spiritual Laws' booklet. It's so embarrassing I could die. I mean literally *die*. I hate our shoes too — look at them — they look like orthopedic shoes for eighty-year-olds. Oh . . . sorry." Rhonda stared at Mrs. Kleinfelter, who was staring back at her. Rhonda leaned closer to Jory. "Is that your grandma?" she whispered.

"No," said Jory. "You got your new teeth in."

"Yeah, my dad got his janitor job back and my mom said if he didn't pay for them I would never find a husband or ever leave home, so he forked it over." Rhonda grinned deliberately and then ran her tongue across her front teeth. "They still feel weird. Paul Farwell made me kiss him the day I came back from the dentist."

"Gross," said Jory.

"I know," said Rhonda, sticking out her tongue. "He asked me to the Halloween party and everything." Rhonda grabbed Jory's wrist and tried to pull her farther down the aisle, away from Mrs. Kleinfelter. "Whenever I called your house, your mom said you were sick." Rhonda peered at Jory with her slanty-cornered eyes. "Why aren't you at school?"

"Oh," said Jory. "Well." She lowered her voice. "I'm going to Schism."

"What?" Rhonda gripped Jory's arm more tightly. *"Schism?* No, you're *not!"*

Jory nodded.

"Get out!"

"Yeah, my dad thinks — I don't know — that I — that Grace and I — need . . . more of a chance to witness to unbelievers. Or something." Jory tried to shrug.

"Schism!" Rhonda's mouth with its brand-new teeth hung slightly open. "How completely grody!" She was silent for a moment. "Are there any cute guys there?"

Jory glanced up and down the aisle. "Just a sec," she said. Jory walked back to Mrs. Kleinfelter. "I'm going to go outside and talk to my friend for a minute, if that's okay."

"Oh, all right," said Mrs. Kleinfelter. She glanced at Rhonda, who waved. "Here," Mrs. Kleinfelter said, holding her hand out for the box of Modess and the sanitary napkin belt. "I'll pay for these and meet you out at the car."

At the thought of getting out of the store, an immense weight lifted off of Jory. Super Thrift and its cantilevered roof sailed gently up and away into the upper hemisphere, like the cycloned house in *The Wizard of Oz* in reverse, an enormous drugstore-shaped balloon disappearing into the nothingness of the sky. "Let's go," she said to Rhonda, peering behind her and grabbing Rhonda's hand and pulling her down the feminine products aisle and past the shampoo/conditioner/hair coloring/hairnet aisle.

"You have to come to the Halloween party," Rhonda said. "You could even stay over." She squeezed Jory's arm. "There's gonna be a haunted house and everything. Oh, hey — look!" Rhonda picked a red paisley bandanna off a rack of farm clothing and began tying it, gypsy-style, around her head. "We could go as hippies."

"Or pirates." Jory gazed longingly up at the store's front entrance.

Rhonda stopped and squatted down so she could see the bandanna's effect in a display mirror. "Hippie pirates," she said, smoothing the sides of her hair. *"Sweet."*

"Oh, no," whispered Jory. "No, no, no."

"Seriously, look at this," said Rhonda. "It's so perfect."

"Miss." The man with the pit stains stood in front of Jory and Rhonda. "You know you're not supposed to be here." His arms were crossed and he looked exactly the way Jory remembered him: short and balding,

254

with hair in the front that was like the fuzz on a baby duck. "I'm going to have to ask you to leave now," he said.

"What?" Rhonda looked blankly at the man. "Why? I need to buy this bandanna first."

"You'll need to go, unless you'd like me to call the police."

"Let's go." Jory tugged at Rhonda. "C'mon."

"What?" Rhonda looked dazedly at the man. "I was just trying it on."

A few customers had started to glance over at the three of them.

"Let's go, girls." The armpit man grabbed at Rhonda's arm.

"This is in*sane.*" Rhonda shook her arm out of the man's grip and widened her eyes. "Is there a law against trying things on?"

"No, there's a law against shoplifting." The man recrossed his arms.

"Excuse me," said Mrs. Kleinfelter. She had come up beside them, holding the large box of Modess in front of her. "Is there a problem here?"

"Yes!" Rhonda turned to Mrs. Kleinfelter. "He thinks I'm — I don't know — shoplifting or something, just because I tried on this bandanna." Rhonda's voice rose up in pitch. "I was going to buy it. I didn't walk out with it or anything."

"Sir," said Mrs. Kleinfelter, "I think you must have made a mistake."

"It's no mistake," said the man. He pointed at Jory. "This girl here is a shoplifter and a thief and has been banned from our store. Her parents were notified and a report was filed over two months ago. I can show you all the paperwork if you want."

Rhonda and Mrs. Kleinfelter looked at Jory. Jory looked back at them, and then at the floor.

"Well," said Mrs. Kleinfelter. She cleared her throat. "I have to say that whatever happened, however many months ago, is no reason for any kind of rudeness or *man*handling now, and — and . . . I will personally never be coming back to this store, and I will be telling all of my friends to never come to this store, and I will be saying the same to anyone I speak to, so —" She thrust the box of Modess into the man's arms, along with the sanitary belt and the smaller box of Tampax. "I'll just leave these with you because I certainly don't want to be accused of shoplifting." She turned to Jory. "I think we're done here," she said.

Mrs. Kleinfelter began walking toward the front of the store. Rhonda and Jory followed behind her. They walked past the racks of bandannas and cowboy hats and folded overalls, past the shoppers who had been silently observing this interchange. "Wow," whispered Rhonda, and gazed at Jory, her eyes huge.

"It's not what you think," said Jory.

"I don't know what I think," Rhonda said. "Except . . . *wow.*"

They walked through the *whoosh* of the automatic door and out into the parking lot.

The three of them stood outside blinking in the afternoon sunlight.

"Well, holy cow," Rhonda said, in a reverent voice.

"Do you need a ride home?" Mrs. Kleinfelter shaded her eyes with her hand.

"I rode my bike here," Rhonda said, apparently just remembering. She walked across the sidewalk and pulled a blue tenspeed out of the bike rack and swung her leg over the bike's bar. "I guess I'll see you later," she said to Jory.

"I guess," said Jory. She watched as Rhonda pedaled shakily out of the parking lot, her cheerleader skirt billowing out behind her.

"I think she forgot something," said Mrs. Kleinfelter, pointing to her own head.

Rhonda was already halfway down the

block. Even at this distance, the red bandanna stood out like a small warning flag. A bright little beacon bobbing up and down, up and down as she pedaled steadily away from them.

In the pickup truck, Mrs. Kleinfelter turned on the radio and they listened in silence as a man sang twangingly about trailers that were for sale or rent. As they drove, Jory kept her face turned toward the passenger window and tried not to have any thoughts. Even so, she kept having sharp little flashes of the armpit man pointing at her and saying, *This girl here, this girl, this girl,* as if it were a kind of sentence being handed down. *This* girl.

They were halfway back to the house, to Henry's house, when Mrs. Kleinfelter suddenly sat up straight. "Oh, no, we didn't buy you your things!" She snapped off the radio and gave a sigh. "I got distracted."

"It's all right," said Jory.

"We could try the Penny Wise, or maybe the Albertsons on Seventeenth. Let's do that. I can turn around here and head back toward Seventeenth. It's not that far."

"It doesn't matter," said Jory. "I don't need them."

"I know you're feeling bad or guilty or

258

whatever, but that doesn't mean you have to be a martyr. Certain things can't be stopped or ignored, no matter how bad you feel." Mrs. Kleinfelter slowed the truck and made a wide U-turn in the middle of the street.

Jory closed her eyes for a second and then opened them again. "I don't need any pads or Tampax or anything because I'm not having my period. I've never even had my period."

Mrs. Kleinfelter drove another block and then pulled over next to a small house with a large German shepherd chained in the front yard. Jory could see the dog's tail wagging forlornly against the dirt-packed lawn. Mrs. Kleinfelter turned off the ignition and sat staring at the steering wheel.

"I didn't want to go to PE," said Jory. "I know it sounds dumb and I can't really explain it, but one thing sort of led to another, and now I'm supposedly having my period."

"I see," said Mrs. Kleinfelter, still gazing forward.

"I can't explain it," Jory said again. "I just keep saying things to get out of doing things and then it just gets worse and worse." Jory could feel hot tears building up behind her eyes. "I'm a horrible person. I am. I'm the worst person, and I'm a complete chicken too."

Mrs. Kleinfelter finally turned her gaze on Jory. "Well, it must take a certain amount of bravery to steal things."

Jory made a sound that was a half laugh, a crying laugh. "That's the funny part," she said. "I didn't even take anything. They must have told my parents I did, but I didn't, and my mom and dad didn't even ask me — they just believed *them*. They believed the armpit man, and a man you've never seen, the earlobe guy, the man with the tie with little flags on it. My parents believed them over me!" Jory began to cry in big, ragged, choking gasps that sounded horrible, even to her. "And a woman took my clothes off," she gasped out. "A woman with red hair and lots of silver rings. She took my clothes off and no one even cared." Jory put her head on the dashboard and cried. Then she leaned back in the seat and howled and cried with both her arms covering her face. She could hardly breathe.

Mrs. Kleinfelter dug around in her pony express bag and pulled out a bedraggled-looking Kleenex. She handed it to Jory.

Jory tried to wipe her face. She scrubbed at her eyes with the Kleenex and took a few huge breaths. She blew her nose loudly, and then gasped a few more times. Her chest kept heaving in a weird way she couldn't control.

"It'll get better in a minute or two."

Jory nodded. She tried to flatten out the Kleenex against her leg.

"Does this have something to do with why your parents moved you all the way out to Henry's house?"

"No." Jory gasped, her lungs still stutter-stepping. "Not really. Well, maybe that's part of it. But it's mainly because Grace thinks she's having an angel baby, and they don't want anyone to know. They don't want anyone to know that she's crazy and that she's pregnant. And, I guess, that I'm a shoplifter — they probably don't want anyone to know that either."

Mrs. Kleinfelter ran her hand across the base of the steering wheel. "She's pregnant," she said.

Jory nodded. "She said God came to her and gave her this baby somehow, and now my parents have flipped completely out."

"Well, yes," Mrs. Kleinfelter said. "I suppose so."

Jory suddenly realized that she had just done the thing she wasn't supposed to do. She had now told Mrs. Kleinfelter everything about their family, and before that, she had told Grip. Who wasn't she going to tell?

Mrs. Kleinfelter made a sad, disapproving noise with her tongue.

Jory felt sickly, sharply guilty. And traitorous. "I guess it's not so bad," she said. "I mean, my dad just wants what's best for us." She pulled and straightened the Kleenex into several pieces. "He's just trying to do what he thinks is best for everyone. For all of us."

"Yes." Mrs. Kleinfelter nodded slightly. "That's a hard thing to know sometimes — what's best, I mean."

"Yeah," said Jory softly. It came out more like a sigh than an actual word.

"I really hardly know what to say. I can't think of a single phrase that seems appropriate here." She smiled briefly and then frowned again. "Maybe, 'This too shall pass.' " Mrs. Kleinfelter turned and put her arm across the seat of the car, then patted Jory on the shoulder, three short pats, so light that Jory could barely feel them.

"Okay. Well, then." Mrs. Kleinfelter sat back up and turned the truck's engine on. "I guess if we don't need anything from any drugstores, we should just be heading on home." She put the truck in first gear. "How does that sound to you?"

Jory nodded.

Jory watched the houses and driveways and fences go by. She felt horrible in a way that wasn't entirely bad. Her eyes hurt and her nose was plugged, but she felt a certain amount of relief, as if she had been purged of a dreadful thing that had been housed inside her body. It was like throwing up — the worst part was beforehand and the best part was afterward, although no part of it was very good.

"I don't understand." Grace was standing at the front door talking to Mrs. Kleinfelter in a low voice. "Why didn't Jory buy anything?"

Jory could hear them talking even though she was in the kitchen, mainly because she was holding her breath and listening as hard as she could.

"Well," Mrs. Kleinfelter said, "Jory doesn't seem to need anything after all."

There was a small space during which no one said anything.

"I don't understand," Grace said again. Jory could picture the expression on Grace's face as clearly as if she were in the living room with her.

"You should talk to Jory," Mrs. Kleinfelter said. "And, Grace, I would be as kind as possible about it if I were you."

From behind the kitchen door, Jory blushed.

"Well, I certainly will." Grace sounded somewhat indignant at the idea of her not being kind, and Jory's face continued to burn. There was a moment of silence. "Well," said Grace, "thank you for doing this favor for us."

Mrs. Kleinfelter gave some sort of muffled response and Jory heard the front door shut. She scampered over to the refrigerator, pulled open its door, and tried to look interested in its contents.

Grace sat down at the kitchen table. "I'm sure you heard all that."

Jory stood holding a box of raisins.

"So?" said Grace, her eyebrows raised.

"I don't think raisins need to be refrigerated," Jory said.

Grace said nothing.

"I'm just not having my period after all." Jory said this into the refrigerator. She put a jar of mayonnaise farther back on the metal shelf and picked up and examined a can of sliced peaches. "I thought I was, but I guess I wasn't."

Grace remained silent.

"That happens sometimes, doesn't it?" Jory turned and watched Grace tracing her

fingernail along a crack in the table's linoleum.

"Jory," Grace said. "Lying is a sin."

Jory held the can of peaches tight to her chest.

Grace sighed. *"A false witness shall not be unpunished, and he that speaketh lies shall perish."*

Jory stared at her sister. "So I'm going to die because I said I was having my period? What about you?" Her voice rose uncontrollably. "What about *your* lying?" With a solid *thunk,* Jory put the can of peaches down on the kitchen counter and walked across the room and then out the back door. The screen door gave an awful screech and then slapped firmly shut behind her. Jory walked through the backyard, past the clothesline and the desiccated tiger lilies and the propane tank. She bent down and scooted under the curved wooden arch of the grape arbor and crawled along until she was completely enclosed by its leafy greenness. The smell in here was intoxicating: rich and sourly purple, just like the grapes that were almost ready to be picked. Jory squatted on the moist ground and looked at the tendriled vines surrounding her. A curly bug inched its way across the thickness of a stem. Underneath the arbor, it was completely quiet and shaded — a whole other world that existed and moved slowly and incrementally on while no one was noticing or caring. If only she could stay right here. In sixth grade she and most of the rest of the class had passed around a semi-forbidden book about a boy who got lost in the woods for a month after summer camp. The cover of the book showed two widened eyes peering out of a dense web of green branches. Jory had read the book at least twice, its scariness completely counter-manded by another feeling — a sweetly gut-twisting feeling almost as lush and illicit as the one produced by the magazine pictures she had found in the detective's underwear drawer. To be completely alone and on your own in the forest, to do exactly as you pleased, to swim and sun with no clothes on, to know your parents were sick with grief and worry . . . Each of her classmates had read the book in turn, handing it off wordlessly to the next reader in line. Jory scraped a clump of mud off her shoe. She could hear the back door open and shut, the screen door's spring stretching and then pulling tight again. She held perfectly still. She could hear Grace moving slowly through the grass. She waited. Grace, too, seemed to be waiting. Jory had a sudden

266

memory of the time that she and Grace had decided to run away from home. Their mother had caught Grace taking photographs of Jory kissing their next-door neighbor boy, Kenny, with her new camera. Grace had just gotten the camera for her tenth birthday and wanted to practice taking photos and thought Jory and Kenny made likely subjects. The three of them had gone out behind the garbage cans where they wouldn't be disturbed and then Grace had had them pose: holding hands, smiling at each other, and finally kissing. Their mother had come out then with a bag of trash and had just lifted a metal lid off one of the trash bins when she spied the three of them crouched and motionless between the cans and the backyard fence. Jory could still remember the look on her mother's face and the round, shieldlike lid she held aloft in one hand. Kenny had been sent home and Jory and Grace to their separate bedrooms. Later, their father came home from work and gave them each a lecture on the proper use of photography and then he had confiscated the roll of film. That night Grace had crept into Jory's room with her blue suitcase. Jory had put her own pajamas and her *Wizard of Oz* book inside and they walked past their parents, who were reading in the living room, and out through the kitchen and through the back door. They had gotten all the way to the middle of the alley when Grace decided the suitcase was too heavy and they sat down in the dirt. They decided they would wait until the next evening to run away.

Beneath the grape arbor, Jory held her breath and listened to her sister now softly calling her name. After a minute or two, Jory stood up and parted the branches and came out into the yard. Grace looked at her sister standing there in the dusky light and without saying anything the two of them walked back inside the house, letting the door fall shut behind them.

CHAPTER NINE

After fifth period, Jory walked her bag of clothing over to the gym. She had no idea where exactly they were supposed to meet — in the locker room? By the bleachers? The printed class schedule just read, *GYM.* Jory opened the heavy metal door and stepped inside. The inside of the gymnasium was large and dim and smelled like floor varnish and stale popcorn and armpits. Boys in shorts and tennis shoes ran and dribbled basketballs up and down the hardwood floor, the rubber soles of their shoes making agonized squeaks and squawks as they pivoted and leaped and ran. The soaring height of the gym's ceiling made each sound echo as hollowly as if the gym were gigantic, the size of some immense frightening palace where matters of national importance were decided. The somewhat sinister-edged metal bleachers had been pulled out only on the left side of the gym, and at the far end, behind one of the backboards and between the two huge scoreboards, was a stage of sorts covered by heavy maroon curtains. An outline of an enormous fanged and snarling feline had been painted in gold across the middle of the curtain. *Skullcat Country!* was printed in flowing gold script beneath the cat's head. Jory shivered and tightened her grip on her bag of clothes. She was going to do this. She *was*.

Jory saw a girl sitting on the first row of bleachers and walked toward her as casually as she could. "Hey. Hi," she said, then cleared her throat. "Do you know where freshman PE meets?"

"Boys or girls?" said the black-haired girl who Jory suddenly recognized as Laird's friend from lunchtime.

"Girls," Jory said before she could think.

"You sure?" The dark-haired girl, the principal's daughter, rolled her black eyes and tried to stifle her laughter.

Jory walked past the dark-haired girl, her face burning. She passed a drinking fountain and walked down a short flight of cement stairs as an unforgettable smell of damp towels and wet windowless concrete and floral-scented aerosol deodorant rose up to greet her. This was the girls' locker room. Inside it, girls walked back and forth between the small mesh cages that now held their school clothes and towels and Wella Balsam and Lemon Up shampoo. Some girls sat on wooden benches talking and laughing as they pulled on their T-shirts and bent to tie their tennis shoes. Jory sat down in an empty space on the long bench and began taking off Grace's boots. She felt sick.

A very tall girl sitting next to her held her bare feet out in front of her. "Lookit. My toes are practically webbed," the girl said to her friend, who was standing in front of Jory in a bright red bra and panties.

"Shut up," the friend said. "At least they don't look like old peanuts, like mine."

The tall girl squawked with laughter. "Your toes look like an old *penis*?"

Jory looked at the red-bra girl, who was now pulling on a pair of cutoff jean shorts. The girl had an amazing line of dark hair that began at her navel and ran downward. Jory scootched out of her pants and quickly replaced them with the pair of gray sweatpants from the Albertsons bag.

"You're supposed to wear shorts," the tall girl said, looking at Jory.

"Oh," said Jory, blushing again. "I didn't know."

"It probably doesn't matter," said the girl with the red bra. "Miss Smith won't give a shit as long as you show up and run around and stuff."

"What kind of thing are we going to be doing today?" Jory asked, nervously pulling off her sweater and pulling on her T-shirt in two swift motions.

"I don't know," said the red-bra girl. "Something stupid."

"Yeah," said the tall girl. "Something stupid with balls."

"Sounds like Stuart," said a third girl, who stood up on the other side of Jory.

"You liar," said the tall girl. "You think he looks just like Tom Jones."

"What's new, pussycat? Whoa-o-oh-oh," sang the red-bra girl into her fist.

"Eat shit, Luanne," said the third girl, who flipped her long brown hair up into a ponytail. She examined the results in the mirror that ran directly above the length of the bench.

"Eat it yourself," said the tall girl. "I know you went to the submarine races with him."

"You made out with Stuart Stossel?" The girl in the red bra had a look of horror on her face.

The girl with the ponytail threw her hairbrush at the tall girl. It hit her on the side of the head and bounced off onto the locker room floor. The locker room grew

272

suddenly quiet, except for the tall girl, who was swearing, and one very thin girl, who leaned against the wall of mesh lockers, giggling.

"All right, ladies." A highly freckled woman in a stiffly pleated navy skirt walked over to the bench and held up a clipboard. She turned a page and ran her index finger down it. "Who's here? Everyone that needs to be? Great." The woman smiled and revealed some smallish white teeth with a prominent gap between the front two. "All of you, upstairs," she said. "Now."

They were doing the Presidential Fitness Test. John F. Kennedy still wanted them all to be fit Americans, even though he was dead. There were five stations and five fitness skills to perform: sit-ups, push-ups, pull-ups, rope climbing, and running. Jory stood in line with the other girls who were waiting to do sit-ups. Miss Smith would blow her whistle and one girl would do as many sit-ups as she could in the time allowed, while another girl held her feet. Jory was paired with the red-bra girl. "Do you want to go first or what?" The red bra-girl stood with her hand on her hip.

"No," said Jory. "You can go first."

"Gee, thanks," said the girl. She sighed

and looked behind her, apparently hoping to see something more interesting than freshman girls doing exercises. "What's your name?"

"Jory," said Jory. "What's yours?"

The girl sighed again. "It's Rhea," she said. "As in diarrhea, and yeah, I've already heard it. Come on. We're up."

Rhea lay down on the floor with her hands behind her head and Jory kneeled by her feet and held her ankles. "God," said Rhea. "I fucking hate sit-ups."

Miss Smith blew her whistle and Rhea lurched upward. Jory felt the tension of Rhea's whole body underneath her hands. It was strangely intimate. Rhea was wearing a pair of boys' red-and-white-striped sports socks and they slid up and down beneath Jory's hands each time Rhea wrenched herself up and back. Jory moved her grip higher onto Rhea's bare knees; she could feel the hairs on Rhea's legs and the slip of lotion and sweat. "Twelve," said Jory. "Keep going." She felt a sudden surge of competitive thrill, as if the two of them were striving toward a goal. As if they needed to beat the others. "Sixteen. Seventeen. Eighteen." Miss Smith's whistle blew. Rhea lay flat on the floor.

"Switch," yelled Miss Smith.

Jory scooted over onto the floor and Rhea kneeled below her, her forehead gleaming with sweat. "Don't try too hard," Rhea said.

"What?" said Jory, leaning up on her elbows and squinting at Rhea.

"If you do good now, you get a bad grade at the end." She gripped Jory's ankles. "It's how much you improve that matters. Or some bullshit like that." Rhea took a hand off Jory's leg and wiped at her face.

The whistle blew.

"One," said Rhea, loudly, even though Jory had not even lain down or begun.

Jory flopped onto the hard floor and then wrenched herself upward.

"Four," said Rhea.

"Cut it out," said Jory, and fell back onto the floor, her neck quivering with the effort.

"Thirteen," said Rhea.

Jory's heart was racing. She tightened her stomach muscles and pulled and heaved, over and over.

"Sixty-two," said Rhea, taking her hand off to wave at a basketball boy who was walking past. "Hey, Lewis," she said. "You going to Frankamp's after school?"

Jory could feel something like laughter coming up in her stomach. She closed her eyes and pulled and heaved some more.

The whistle blew.

"Seven," said Rhea as Miss Smith paused next to them with her clipboard.

"What?" said Jory, sitting up as fast as she could. "I did way more than that!"

Miss Smith had already moved on to the next couple.

"You'll thank me later," said Rhea, who stood up and was swiping at the back of her shorts. "Did you see that guy, Lewis?"

Jory stood up. "I did at least eleven," Jory said. She could hear the whininess in her own voice.

"He's got a Band-Aid box full of dope. He keeps it in his locker."

"So what?" said Jory. She couldn't believe that Miss Smith now thought she could do only seven sit-ups.

"Well, geez, you're loads of fun," said Rhea. She pulled up her socks and headed toward the chin-up bar.

Jory trailed slowly behind her.

The principal's daughter was the one holding the clipboard next to the pull-up bar.

"Who put you in charge?" Rhea eyed the black-haired girl.

"I forgot my PE clothes," said Jude, smiling. "So Miss Smith asked me to help her out."

"Oh, sure," said Rhea. "Very convenient."

Jory watched as a short, bone-thin girl from her Spanish class tried unsuccessfully to pull her chin up and over the bar. The girl hung straight down from the bar by her arms for several seconds and then dropped to the floor.

"You can't pass PE if you don't do the fitness test." Rhea pushed back the cuticle on her thumbnail.

"Oooh, I'm really worried." Jude wrote 0 next to the skinny girl's name and then looked at Jory. "Your turn," she said.

Jory felt her stomach tighten. It didn't matter if she couldn't do this. It was better, in fact, if she didn't. That's what Rhea had said. Jory walked over to the lowest of the three bars. She reached up with one hand and then the other. She pulled upward. It took forever for her eyes to come even with the metal bar. *"Jesus,"* said the dark-haired girl, "just forget it." Jory pulled and pulled. Hard. "One," someone said quietly. "Two," the same voice said. "Three." It was Rhea. "Four." Jory's arms were quivering. She could feel herself making a terrible, teeth-baring face. "Come on," said Rhea. "One more." Jory felt as if her arm muscles might be actually tearing. She lifted her chin. It was almost up to the bar. Almost. She hung there, quivering, not moving up or down.

"Drop," someone said. It was the principal's daughter. "Drop," she said again. "You're done." Jory pulled a fraction of an inch more. *"Five,"* Rhea crowed. Jory dropped to the ground. She held her hands up toward her face. She couldn't uncurl her fingers.

"That last one doesn't count."

"Don't be such a dick, Jude." Rhea tried to grab the clipboard.

Jude stepped away from Rhea. "What does it matter? Nobody wants to do well on the first try anyway." She wrote the number 4 next to Jory's name. "There," she said.

Rhea shook her head.

"It's okay," said Jory. And for some reason, it was. Jory flexed her fingers. They felt marvelously sore.

Jory and Rhea ran laps around the gym. They puffed and pumped their arms back and forth, their tennis shoes slapping echoes against the gym walls. "We're the only two left," Rhea said as they curved past the bleachers. She grinned at Jory. At some point during the Presidential Fitness Test, they had decided to do well. They had now run everyone else off the floor.

"Why aren't you in any of my classes?" Jory asked.

"I am. I'm in world history and speech,

you idiot."

"What?" Jory laughed. "I never saw you."

"Yes, you did. You just didn't notice. You were too busy being a stuck-up snob." Rhea wiped the arm of her T-shirt across her face. "C'mon. Let's stop now. I feel sick."

"Just one more," said Jory. She was filled with a kind of airy feeling, as if her stomach and head had been scooped hollow and pumped full of helium. She felt suddenly sure she could run forever.

"That's fourteen laps, girls," said Miss Smith as they ran past. "Let's call it good."

"Everyone else is taking showers," said Rhea. "Come on, Jory."

"Just one more," said Jory. "One more time around."

"You're insane," said Rhea, chugging next to her.

They ran around the bleachers on the other side, under the backboard and past the stage, and then Jory veered to the right, jogging past the drinking fountain. They pounded down the cement steps and into the locker room. "Fucking *A,*" said Rhea, flopping down on the wooden bench. "We're track stars."

"You're idiots," said a blond girl who was now combing through her wet hair.

Rhea stretched out full length on the

bench. "I think I'm going to barf," she said.

Jory smiled and untied her shoes.

All around them girls sprayed Arrid Extra Dry and Love's Baby Soft and applied Yardley lip gloss in the mirror. They stuffed clothes into the mesh lockers and clomped back upstairs again, their ponytails swinging.

Jory waited till the stair climbing died away; then she took off her sweatpants and T-shirt and ran her towel over her sweaty legs and chest.

Rhea turned over on the wooden bench and groaned. "You think I'm kidding about the puking," she said, "but I'm not."

Miss Smith and Jude clattered down the stairs and into the locker room. "Nice work, girls," said Miss Smith, looking at Jory and Rhea. She handed her clipboard to Jude. "Okay, read off the numbers and copy them into the grade book. When you're done, bring the grade book and the leftover towels back to my classroom."

"Miss Smith? When is Jude going to take the Presidential Fitness Test?"

"That's a good question, Rhea." Miss Smith looked up at Jude.

"Maybe you should have her demonstrate for the rest of the class on Thursday." Rhea turned to Jory. "Jory here was saying she

280

needed some tips on chin-ups."

Miss Smith nodded. "Not a bad idea," she said. "You girls better hurry if you want to be dressed before the bell rings." She turned and slapped back up the concrete steps in her shower room thongs. The gym door slammed in the distance.

"Thanks a whole lot, Durham," said Jude.

"Anytime," said Rhea cheerfully.

Jory looked down at the floor and pulled on her corduroy pants. She turned toward the far wall and held her towel around her shoulders while she tried to slip on Grace's bra.

"So modest," said Jude as she leaned against the bank of clothes lockers.

"Just like me," said Rhea, deliberately pulling her T-shirt off over her head and stepping boldly out of her cutoffs.

"We've all seen your fur line already," Jude said. "God — haven't you heard of electrolysis?"

Rhea stood in the middle of the room in her red bra and panties. "In Europe none of the women shave their legs *or* their pits," she said.

"That's because they're all dykes or lesbians," said Jude.

"Aren't all dykes lesbians?" Jory said, and then instantly regretted this remark.

Jude let out a laugh and stared at Jory with a certain amount of surprise.

"I just meant logically speaking." Jory wrenched her head through the top of her sweater. She pulled it down around her waist and began tugging her boots on.

"Besides," Jude said, turning pointedly to Rhea, "it's not your pits I'm talking about. And this isn't Europe, either, in case you haven't noticed."

"What?" said Rhea. "Arco isn't in Europe? I want my money back."

Jory peeked up at Rhea. Her body was tan and muscular, like a boy's almost, except for the breasts that overflowed from the red bra. Jory was amazed at the way they hung there suspended in space like things half solid and inverted. She grabbed her book bag. "I'm gonna miss the bus," said Jory.

"You ride the bus?" said Jude.

Jory blushed. Riding the bus was obviously the worst form of social suicide.

Rhea still stood straddle legged in her underwear. "Hell, *yeah,* she rides the bus. She *rides* the bus. She rides *the* bus. She rides the *bus. She rides the bus!*"

"Wow," said Jude. "That was weird. And really unattractive."

"I'm going," said Jory.

"So long," said Jude, smiling and shaking

her head.

Jory glanced back at Rhea. "See you tomorrow," she said.

"You bet, track star." Rhea smiled and crossed her arms. *"Hasta mañana."*

"Four miles," Jory said, taking a long swig of milk. "Can you believe it?"

"That's pretty amazing." Grace sat at the kitchen table with a stack of books and their father's slide rule. She was still wearing Henry Kleinfelter's overalls. "I've never run that far in my life."

"Me either!" Jory put the milk carton back in the refrigerator and gave the door a happy slam. "Maybe I should go out for track."

"May*be.*"

"I'm just kidding, of course. I'm not staying there. In a few weeks I'm going back to ACA." Jory sat down at the table across from Grace.

"I know."

"Dad said I could."

"Um-hm."

"He did."

There was a quiet knock at the front door.

"Dad doesn't knock," said Grace.

"I'll go," said Jory.

Through the glass in the door she could

see Grip standing on their doormat and smiling. He was holding a rectangular package in his hands. His hair was in a kind of bun on the top of his head.

Jory's heart thrilled piercingly. There had been a part of her that feared she might never see him again. She didn't care about anything he had previously done, or said, or said that he'd done. She put her hand on the doorknob.

"Who is *that*?" said Grace, who had come out from the kitchen and was now standing behind Jory.

"Oh, um," said Jory in a small voice. "Well . . ."

"Jory, for Pete's sake," Grace said, reaching around Jory and opening the door. "Hello," she said, smiling her best work-and-witness smile at Grip. "Can we help you?"

"Oh, hey." Grip switched his gaze from one sister to the other. Jory could feel the skin on her neck getting hot. "Well, say, I have something for Jory here," he said. He held the box out. "A sort of back-to-school present, I guess. But I could come some other time. Later or tomorrow or something." He half grinned. "Y'all are probably in the middle of dinner, aren't you?"

Grace gave Jory a wordless look. Jory

stared at the floor. Grace opened the door a bit wider. "You're not a schoolteacher of Jory's, are you?" Puzzlement still flickered across her face.

"Now *that* would be something," he said, stepping into their living room.

"This is Grip," Jory said finally, her voice sounding as if she'd never used it before. "And this is my sister Grace."

Grace shook Grip's hand. "Grip?"

"It's my cross to bear." He put the box down on the coffee table. "A mother with a warped sense of humor."

"So, how do you two know each other?" Grace folded her hands in front of her.

"Grace." Jory whispered.

"Just curious," said Grace.

"Well, lemme see. Jory was in my employ this summer." Grip cleared his throat. "She was my assistant and right-hand man during the months of June and July. I guess you must have been in Mexico during that time."

"Grip tried to teach me how to swim," said Jory. Suddenly this statement seemed like less of a good idea.

"Really?" said Grace, glancing from one of them to the other, as if trying to determine something without actually having to ask.

Grip shrugged and smiled again.

"Well," said Grace slowly. "You're welcome to eat with us if you'd like. *Grip.*" She turned and then walked out of the living room and into the kitchen.

"Shoot," Grip said, moving a step closer to Jory. "Is this not a good idea?"

"I don't know," said Jory. She found herself whispering for some reason she couldn't explain. "It's just so strange. I never imagined the two of you meeting."

"I didn't think about her answering the door." Grip shrugged. "You know," he said, glancing toward the kitchen, "she doesn't look so crazy."

"She's not, exactly."

"Hey," he said, and leaned over the coffee table. "Here. Come on, open 'er up." He handed the box to Jory. It was wrapped in newspaper with a white paper napkin swan on top. "Origami," he said. "I'm a master."

Jory sat down on the dead cat couch and held the box. "It jingles," she said. "Is it for Christmas?" She peered up at him, suddenly shy. With great carefulness she pried at the tape at one end and then on the other. The newspaper came off in a sheet and fell to the floor. She lifted the lid on the box. Inside were moccasins. Brown suede fringed moccasins with tiny silver bells attached to the laces. They were the palest shade of mocha brown and soft to the touch, like the ears of a fawn Jory had once touched at the Boise petting zoo. *"Oh,"* she said. For some strange reason, she felt tears gathering in the back of her throat. She held the shoes in her lap.

"I don't know if they're your size," he said. "They look pretty close, though." He picked one up. "Try them on."

She bent down and pulled off Grace's old boots. She slipped her feet into one of the moccasins, and then the other. They were the tiniest bit big, but she could wear thicker socks. Thicker socks would make them nearly perfect. "Thank you," she whispered.

Grip smiled. "Those girls at Schism won't know what hit 'em."

"Ha," said Jory, wiping at her eyes. "They think I'm a complete and total weirdo."

"Nah," he said. "They're just jealous."

"I don't think so." Jory gazed in wonder at her feet. She didn't recognize them. She took a step and listened to the silvery sounds the bells made. *Pocahontas,* she thought. *Sacagawea. Tiger Lily.* "Thank you," she said again.

Grip nodded. "I guess this was my lame-ass attempt at an apology."

"Oh, hey — that's okay. I shouldn't have

bugged you about that juvenile detention stuff anyway." She tried to shrug and make her face look as unbothered as possible.

They both glanced down at the floor and neither said anything for a moment.

"Guess what?" she said finally, turning her eyes up toward his. "It's my birthday."

"Really? You're kidding."

"On Sunday," Jory said.

"Well, what do you know," he said, shaking his head. "Nineteen, right?"

Jory smiled.

Grace walked into the living room holding a can opener. "What's that jingling noise?" she asked.

"My shoes," Jory said. She held her left foot out toward Grace. "Grip got them for me." She smiled at Grip. "For my birthday."

Jory could feel Grace taking Grip in, seeing him as if for the first time. His hair, the blue tattoos, the slightly spotted brown work shirt. "Well," she said. "They're very pretty."

"They're even the right size," Jory said.

"What do you two think — beef stew or chili?" Grace pulled her eyes away from Grip and smiled faintly at Jory.

"Oh, wow," said Grip. "I should have said something. I don't really eat meat."

"What?"

"I'm a vegetarian."

"A vegetarian?" Grace stood still holding the can opener.

"Yeah, I know it's a pain in the ass. But you know, I can make my own stuff, if you'll let me. I do it all the time no matter where I am."

"Dad's a vegetarian," Jory said.

"No, he's not." Grace frowned.

"Well, he might as well be."

"Hey," Grip said. "How about you let me take a peek in your kitchen and see what I can rustle up?"

"Oh," Grace said. "Well . . . okay, I guess." She turned away.

"Come on, Indian Maiden, you can help me." Grip tilted his head in the direction of the kitchen.

Jory followed behind him, listening to the snowy sound of her shoes as she walked.

The three of them sat at the kitchen table beneath the hanging light. A salad with lettuce and canned lentils and red beans and other exotic-looking ingredients Jory and Grace had been keeping at the very back of the cupboard now filled a large blue bowl.

"I'd like to pray first," Grace said. "If that's all right with you."

"Oh, sure," said Grip. "Y'all do whatever you'd like. Whatever you normally do."

"That's what we normally do," said Grace.

"Not always," said Jory.

"Nearly always," said Grace. "And if not in literal speech, then in spirit."

Grip's eyebrows scrunched together in thought. "Does that mean that you're thinking a prayer in your head, or that you're just kind of meditating on something like Buddhists do?"

Grace leaned forward in a way Jory was very familiar with. She gazed at Grip without blinking. "What it means is that even if you aren't speaking the words out loud, you are still communing with God. You are actively trying to listen to the still, small voice of the Holy Spirit so that you can praise and thank Him even more fully."

"You know —" Grip nodded his head. "That's so weird that we're talking about this 'cause just last week I read this article in some magazine — *Psychology Today,* maybe — and it said that when you're really praying, it's like you're in an alpha mind state." Grip picked out a piece of lettuce from the salad bowl and popped it in his mouth. "That praying or chanting can produce a state of optimal creativity or something. There was a photo of this old black woman who makes crazy quilts like spiders on acid after she prays — all these wild purple and blue and red stars and comets and stuff all stitched together." Grip shook his head. "It was incredible."

Grace resettled her napkin on her lap. "That's quite fascinating. Although I'm not really sure that making strange quilts is what prayer is all about."

"Oh, well, sure." Grip lifted a slice of cucumber out of the bowl and began crunching loudly. "Just goes to show you the power of prayer, is all." He smiled.

Jory reached for a piece of bread.

"Although," Grace said, "there seems to be less and less point in saying grace now."

Jory let the piece of bread drop back onto the plate. "Sorry," she said.

"Me too," said Grip. "Hey —" He reached out for Jory's hand and then Grace's. "C'mon, you go right ahead and pray."

"Well," said Grace, "all right." She looked down at the table, at their newly linked hands, and Jory could see Grace's cheeks flushing a light shade of pink, the way they did when she was mad or embarrassed or suddenly pleased. Grace closed her eyes and then cleared her throat. *"We thank thee, Lord, for this our food, for life and health and all things good. May manna to our souls be given: the bread of life sent down from heaven. These favors we ask in Christ's* name. Amen."

"Amen," said Grip loudly. He smiled at Jory and gave her hand a squeeze before letting it go. "That's a sweet prayer — is that what you folks pray at every meal?"

"Yes," said Grace. "It's the prayer we learned when we were little." She blushed again, turning her birthmark an even redder shade. "I don't know why I keep repeating it. It's childish."

"Nah. Things like that can be comforting." Grip spooned some salad onto Jory's plate. "You have to at least try it now — I worked hard on this." He scooped up some more. "Grace?"

"Okay. All right."

Grip arranged the salad on Grace's plate. "Is that enough? How about just a little more?"

"Oh, no — that's plenty."

"C'mon — don't tell me you didn't have stranger stuff than this in Mexico."

Grace didn't bother looking at her plate; instead, she turned to Jory. "You know, I thought you said you were babysitting this summer."

"I was," Jory said, stirring the food on her plate.

"But in between times, she was a big help with my sales and my deliveries." Grip nodded. "She's highly efficient." He gave Jory a wink.

"Your sales? What do you sell?"

Grip drank down the last of his iced tea. He wiped the back of his hand across his mouth. "Oh, you know, the essentials — frozen dairy treats and such."

Grace lifted a forkful of salad toward her mouth. She chewed for a moment and then swallowed. "You're the ice cream man," she said. It wasn't a question.

"Yup." Grip smiled. "Guilty as charged. Although I'm trying to remain open to other, less glamorous career possibilities."

A sound came from the living room — a soft knocking quickly followed by the front door opening and shutting. "Hello," a female voice called faintly.

"Who's that?" Grace turned around in her chair.

"Oh," said Jory, her fork in midair. "That's Hilda."

"Who?" said Grace.

Mrs. Kleinfelter now stood hesitantly in the kitchen doorway, peeping at the three of them. "I'm sorry to be interrupting your suppertime," she said. "I was just hoping Jory might come help me fix my television set. My show's on and I feel strange if I can't see it." She twisted her hands together as she spoke.

"You know how to fix TVs?" Grace sounded more than surprised by this new information.

"Well," Jory said, "no."

"How about your young man here?" Mrs. Kleinfelter turned toward Grip. "Do you know anything about old RCAs?"

Grip put his napkin on the table and pushed his chair back and stood up. "Is it the sound or the picture?"

"The picture. I don't give a hoot about the sound. I just want to see Art Fleming and the questions." She had already started back toward the living room and Grip was following her. "Is that your truck out front in the drive?" she was saying. "It's parked a little close to my mums." The front door shut with a bang.

Grace scooted her chair back and then stood up from the table and walked toward the cupboards. She took out a glass and then turned around. "Just how old *is* he, Jory? Twenty-five? *Thirty?* I can't believe Mom and Dad actually let you work for him."

"Well, they did," Jory lied bravely.

"And why is he bringing you presents? What do you think Dad would say if he knew that man was coming out here to see you?"

"His name is Grip, remember?" Jory stared down at her plate, at the strange half-eaten salad. "And he's my friend. And now that I have to go to Schism, he's my only friend. So I guess I'm not supposed to have friends anymore? Or birthday presents?"

"Oh, Jory."

"Grip is the only person that really cares about me."

"That is so not true."

"Yes, it is," said Jory. "He understands me."

"He doesn't even know you."

"That's what you think."

With a ringing sound, Grace set the drinking glass on the counter. "What's that supposed to mean?"

"Nothing. It doesn't mean anything."

Grace sat back down in her chair. "Jory. Have you done something?"

"Have *I* done something?" Jory looked at Grace.

Each of them sat silently, as if contemplating the feasibility of continuing the track of this conversation.

The front door opened and shut again. Grip walked through the living room and kitchen doorway and then stood next to the table. "Blown tube," he said, frowning. "Too bad, too. I think she'll have to go to a repair shop to get one. Those old cathode tubes are nearly impossible to come by now." He scratched at his head. "I was thinking maybe we could entertain her for a little bit. She seems kinda lost without her show. So I hope it's okay — I invited her back here."

"Well, of course," Grace said, only her eyes registering her feelings about this entire turn of events. "The more the merrier."

Mrs. Kleinfelter sat at the table looking faintly shamed and childlike. She kept re-arranging her silverware.

"Grip is a vegetarian," Grace told her. "Which explains our slightly unusual dinner menu."

"Oh, I'm hardly ever hungry this time of night anyway." Mrs. Kleinfelter moved her fork slightly to the left. "I'll just try some of this good-looking bread, if you don't mind."

Grace passed Mrs. Kleinfelter the bread and then handed her the butter dish. "Right before you got here, Grip was talking to us about the power of prayer."

"Really?" Mrs. Kleinfelter continued to examine her plate. "Well, what do you know."

"Do you attend church?" Grace poured

some iced tea into Mrs. Kleinfelter's glass.

"Oh, Dix and I used to go over to First Congregational every once in a while, but I'm pretty much out of the habit now."

"At Garden of Gethsemane we have early morning and evening services on Sundays, and midweek services on Wednesday nights too."

"Well, that's certainly a lot of services. Is that where you girls go? This Garden of . . . Gethsemene?"

"We haven't gotten to go as much as we would like to lately." Grace set the iced tea pitcher down. She took a shallow breath. "I've been having my own sort of personal services here at home, and, you know, if you'd like to join me, I'd be very happy to have you come." She turned to Grip. "Oh, and you too, of course."

Mrs. Kleinfelter straightened her silverware again. "That's a very lovely invitation," she said.

"Sunday morning, hm?" Grip stopped eating. "What time are we talking?"

Grace turned toward Grip with a certain amount of amazement. "Nine thirty," she said. "But maybe that's too early for you."

"Oh, no," he said. "I may not look like it, but I'm an early riser." He grinned at Jory and Mrs. Kleinfelter in turn. "How about some dessert, ladies? Anybody here like ice cream?"

They sat in the living room and ate their ice cream bars. "This is very nice," said Mrs. Kleinfelter, with a hint of surprise in her voice. "I haven't sat in Henry's house like this for quite some time."

Grip was kneeling down next to an old wooden cabinet in the corner of the room. He opened a drawer and pulled out a record album. "These are old seventy-eights," he said. "*Really* old ones."

"That's a victrola of sorts," said Mrs. Kleinfelter, licking at her butterscotch Push Up. "Although I don't know if it still works."

Grip stood up and lifted the top lid on the wooden cabinet and gave a low whistle. "Would you look at that."

Jory came over and peered inside. She had seen something like it once in the Boise Historical Museum, along with a Teletype machine, several Indian scalps, and a stuffed two-headed calf.

Grip was blowing dust off the record and placing it carefully on the victrola's spindle.

"You have to wind it up first," said Mrs. Kleinfelter.

Grip flipped a small switch, wound the victrola's crank quite a few times, and then placed the needle carefully down on the record. A soft hush of staticky popping and hissing issued forth. Jory turned and grinned at Grace and Mrs. Kleinfelter. Suddenly a sound like an old-timey carnival filled the room. Grip opened both of the cabinet drawers down below and the strange dance hall music got even louder.

"Oh, my," said Mrs. Kleinfelter. She placed her ice cream bar down on its wrapper on the coffee table. "Oh, my. That's — oh, who is that — what is her name? . . . Annette Hanshaw! Henry's favorite singer. I think he had a little crush on her."

The tinkly sweet-sad music sounded like it was coming from far away or deep down in a well somewhere. Or maybe as if the woman singing down in the well was holding a coffee can over her mouth. She was saying that her blackbirds were bluebirds now, while kazoos or ukuleles or fiddles or something played along at a superfast tempo. As if love could only be expressed in double time. "I've never heard anything like it," said Jory.

"It's the thirties," said Grip, turning another record over in his hands. "Or maybe the forties?"

Mrs. Kleinfelter stood up and walked over to the victrola. "Henry loved this music," she said. She shook her head as if to clear away this thought. "He was a little sappy that way."

"Oh, come on." Grip took hold of both Mrs. Kleinfelter's hands and made her sway slightly back and forth with him in time to the music.

Jory grinned shyly and then glanced at Grace, who was sitting stock-still on the couch.

Grip and Mrs. Kleinfelter were now slowly circling the living room, doing some kind of improvised dance steps that they both seemed to mysteriously know. Mrs. Kleinfelter was smiling but still shaking her head, even as she moved her feet in their brown work shoes with ease.

On the record, the whip-poor-will on the hill was telling the girl in the well that it was true, her blackbirds were bluebirds now. Days of gladness had come, days of sadness were done, and yes, her blackbirds were *bluuuue*-birds now.

Grip was saying something in Mrs. Kleinfelter's ear. He dipped her down toward the floor and she gasped and said, "Oh, my," then reached her hand back to keep her hair in place. Grip pulled her gently upright and they both laughed as if sharing a joke only the two of them understood.

"Okay, Grace," Grip said breathlessly after setting Mrs. Kleinfelter on her feet, "your turn."

Grace gave Grip a strange, lopsided smile. "No, thank you," she said. "Dancing is a sin."

"Oh, dear," said Mrs. Kleinfelter, still rearranging her hair.

The record crackled to an end and then hummed silently, still turning on the spindle.

"Jory?" Grip turned and held out his hand.

Jory did not look in Grace's direction. "That's okay," she said. "I guess not."

"Well, that is too, too bad," said Grip, smiling and mock wiping his forehead, "because I was just getting warmed up."

Jory looked down at her shoes, at the fawn-colored moccasins that he had given her. She scuffed one shoe slightly against the floor and listened to the silver bell tinkle. "Maybe another time, though." She said this so quietly that only he could hear.

Grip smiled and bent down and pulled another record out of the victrola's bottom cabinet. He looked at its sleeve and read the title. " 'I've Got Something in My Eye'?"

"Oh, that's a good one," said Mrs. Kleinfelter. *I've got something in my eye and it's you, you, you.*" She glanced over at Grace on the couch. "At least I think that's how it goes."

"I *love* music." Grace stood up and smoothed Henry's shirt down over her abdomen. "I've played the piano since I was five. I've been the church choir director. I just don't think that God approves of men and women dancing together . . . for obvious reasons." Grace picked up the sticky ice cream wrappers that Jory and Mrs. Kleinfelter had left lying on the coffee table. She held these gingerly between her fingertips and walked out of the living room and into the kitchen.

Jory could hear Grace opening and shutting the kitchen cupboards and putting dishes in the sink.

"Well." Mrs. Kleinfelter shifted her gaze from Jory to Grip. "I think I'd better be getting on home." She moved quickly toward the front door.

Jory followed Mrs. Kleinfelter and leaned against the door frame. "I never got to say thank you for yesterday. I meant to, but I forgot."

"No need for that." Mrs. Kleinfelter stepped out onto the porch and down the steps. She waved her hand without turning around and then was swallowed up by the darkness of the unlit space that separated their two houses. Jory could see her bone-colored hair moving just faintly through the autumn night.

"I guess that's my cue." Grip stood behind Jory. "Hey — seriously. I'm really sorry if I caused any trouble." He made a mock grimace that turned into a yawn, and then linked his hands and stretched his arms above his head. "Wanna walk me out to my truck?"

Jory peeked back toward the kitchen. "Okay," she said.

The night grass was wet and Jory stopped and took her moccasins off, carefully setting them back on the porch. They walked through the grass and down the dirt drive-way and stopped next to the ice cream truck. Grip's shirtfront glowed a dull green in the bit of light shed by a slivered moon. "That's a waxing crescent," said Jory.

"A what?" Grip reached into the truck's interior, rummaged around for a moment, and then surreptitiously pulled out a can of Old Milwaukee. He quickly popped the top and took a long swig. "Your sister doesn't have binoculars, does she?" He grinned and wiped his mouth with the back of his hand. "What were you saying?"

Jory shrugged. "Nothing. Just dumb stuff

my dad taught me."

"Like what?" He took another long drink.

"Oh, you know, just that if the left side of the moon is dark, then the light part is growing bigger, so that's *waxing,* and if the right side of the moon is dark, then the light part is shrinking, and that's *waning.*"

"Hm," said Grip. He gazed up at the moon. "So wait — if I can see the right side of the moon, like now, it means the moon's gonna get bigger, and if I can see the left side, it's getting smaller. Right?"

"Right." Jory smiled.

"I never thought about this before, but I guess we always only see that one side of the moon, don't we? The side with the sad old guy's face."

"We don't really even know what the other side looks like, the dark side. It's there, but we don't ever see it."

"Just like some people." Grip waggled his eyebrows and then lowered the pitch of his voice. "With their dark sides all safely hidden away."

Jory stared into his browny-gold eyes trying to judge the level of his seriousness. With Grip it was often hard to tell when he was joking and when he wasn't.

"You'll have to teach me some more of this stuff. This astronomy stuff," he said.

"The sun and the moon and the stars."

"And the planets," said Jory. "And the constellations and the galaxies and solar flares and white dwarves and red giants and black holes."

"Wow," said Grip. "Sounds like it's getting pretty crowded up there." He climbed up onto the truck's driver's seat, and then leaned down and planted a kiss on the top of Jory's head. On her hair, where her middle part was. "See you later, stargazer."

As soon as he put the truck in reverse, she peeked up and watched the truck's taillights glowing small and smaller all the way down the road. Then she turned back to the diamond-windowed house and went inside to help her sister put the dishes away.

CHAPTER TEN

It was a beautiful Sunday morning in October, and it was her fourteenth birthday. Jory lay in Henry Kleinfelter's old metal-framed bed beneath the wedding quilt and inspected the rays of sunlight filling her bedroom. It was going to be warm and sunny. And she was going to be fourteen! Jory stretched her toes out beneath the quilt luxuriously. She had been born at noon exactly. Her mother had told her this story many times, how Dr. Henry had had to be called out of church, and how everyone knew exactly where he was going since Jory's mother was the only pregnant lady in their church at that particular time, and how Pastor Ron had said, right in the middle of his sermon, "Well, I guess there'll be another Quanbeck joining us for church next Sunday," and how everyone in the congregation had smiled and laughed and then how the moment the service was over they had all (or nearly all) trooped over to the Good Samaritan Hospital, which was right across the block, and peered in at Jory in her incubator bed or whatever it was that the nurses put the newborns in. And then her father was there and he had dragged some of his graduate students over to see Jory too because he was so proud and he really didn't want any sons anyway — they were nothing but trouble — but girls, well, girls were lovely and sweet.

The phone rang downstairs, which meant her father was calling, since no one else knew (or was allowed to know) their number. Although Jory was thinking of giving it to Grip, since he'd already met Grace now and there was no more real harm to be done.

Already in the birthday dress she'd chosen — sleeveless lavender — Jory ran down the stairs and into the kitchen. Grace was sitting at the table with her Bible and book of commentary open in front of her. Jory gazed around the kitchen, looking expectantly at the oven, at the countertops. The kitchen looked the way it always did — slightly old and messy and yellowish. "Hey," said Jory.

"Hey," said Grace, not looking up. She underlined something in her book of commentary.

Jory sat down at the table across from Grace. She watched as Grace wrote a sentence down on a small sheet of paper. "What are you doing?"

"My daily devotions." Grace turned a page in the Bible.

"Nothing else?"

Grace put her pen down and turned toward Jory. "I'm reading about the Parable of the Ten Virgins. Do you remember how it goes?"

"Sure," said Jory. "I think so."

Grace looked down at her Bible. "Matthew 25," she said. She cleared her throat and began reading. *"The kingdom of heaven shall be likened to ten virgins who took their lamps and went out to meet the bridegroom. Now five of them were wise, and five of them were foolish. Those who were foolish took their lamps and took no oil with them, but the wise took oil in their vessels with their lamps. But while the bridegroom was delayed, they all slumbered and slept."* Grace turned the page and began reading again. *"And at midnight a cry was heard: 'Behold, the bridegroom is coming; go out to meet him!' Then all those virgins arose and trimmed their lamps. And the foolish said to the wise, 'Give us some of your oil, for our lamps are going out.' But the wise answered, saying, 'No, lest there should not be enough for us and you; but go rather to those who sell, and buy for yourselves.' And while they went to buy, the bridegroom came, and those who were ready went in with him to the wedding; and the door was shut. Afterward the other virgins came also, saying, 'Lord, Lord, open to us!' But he answered and said, 'Assuredly, I say to you, I do not know you.' Watch therefore, for you know neither the day nor the hour in which the Son of Man is coming."*

Grace put the Bible down on the table. "Now, what do you think that means?"

"Well." Jory examined her own thumbnail. "I guess it means that you should always be doing whatever it is that you're supposed to be doing because you never know when you might be caught not doing it."

Grace sighed. "Seriously, Jory, what does God want us to be doing?"

"Not sharing our oil with foolish virgins?" Jory glanced up at Grace. "I know all about what it means. I went to Sunday School and Junior Church and Bible School, too, you know."

"Okay, then you understand that God wants us to be ever vigilant — to be ever ready for the world that is to come after this one. Which means sometimes not doing the fun, easy thing that everyone else is doing, and instead doing the difficult, self-sacrificing thing that would make Jesus happy. That would make Jesus proud to say that he knows us."

Jory put her hands in her lap. "Are we talking about dancing now?"

Grace shut the Bible and stacked it carefully on top of her commentary. "This passage concerns all kinds of behavior," she said. "Not just dancing."

"Today's my birthday." Jory trained her eyes on Grace.

Grace picked up her books and stood up. "That's right," she said, "which makes it the perfect time to think about how you'd like to live the rest of your life. How you'd like to develop spiritually as a young Christian woman."

Jory cocked her head. "Did you make me a cake?"

"Yes, I did."

Jory hopped up. "Where is it? I didn't smell it baking."

"Mrs. Kleinfelter has it at her house. She helped me make it yesterday. It's supposed to be a surprise, so when she brings it over, look surprised, all right?"

"Is it chocolate with white frosting?"

Grace smiled.

"Ha!" Jory did a tiny dance on the kitchen

floor. "Do I get any presents?"

"Yes, but you have to wait until Mom and Dad get here."

"Is Frances coming?"

"Of course. What's she going to do — stay home by herself?"

"This is going to be weird," said Jory. She walked into the living room and sat down on the couch.

Grace followed her into the room. "It'll be okay," Grace said, but she didn't look entirely convinced.

There was a faint knocking on the front door. "That has to be Hilda," said Grace.

Jory hardly had time to register her surprise at this sudden familiarity since Mrs. Kleinfelter was already opening the door and stepping inside. "Many happy returns," Mrs. Kleinfelter said. She was holding a white-frosted layer cake in one hand and a grocery sack in the other. She seemed slightly frazzled and her large men's cardigan was buttoned wrong.

"A cake?" Jory clasped her hands together. "For me?"

Mrs. Kleinfelter frowned. "I just pray it's any good. I haven't baked a cake in years. Your sister did most of it." She handed the cake to Grace and the grocery sack to Jory. "That's your birthday present," she said. "I hope you're not allergic."

Jory peered inside the large brown bag. A small gray kitten with huge yellow eyes peered back at her. "Oh!" Jory said. "Grace, look!" She reached into the bag. "It's a kitten!" She pulled the little thing out and cradled it against her chest.

Grace and Mrs. Kleinfelter looked on. "I'm going to take care of it when you're at school," Grace said.

"It doesn't know how to pull its claws back in yet," Mrs. Kleinfelter said, reaching out and unhooking one of the kitten's paws from Jory's dress. "My old housecat, Birdie, surprised me with this batch. I thought she was long done with that kind of thing, but no." Mrs. Kleinfelter made a sort of snortling noise. "Oh, well, they pretty much take care of themselves — unlike human babies." Mrs. Kleinfelter's face suddenly flushed a bright pink. She fiddled quickly with her topknot. "I'd probably better be going," she said. "Your folks will be showing up and everything."

"Thank you *so* much." Jory tore her eyes away from her kitten. "I love her. Him?" Jory held her cat up above her head and peered beneath. "He doesn't have a tail!"

"It's a Manx," said Mrs. Kleinfelter. "I saw this old tailless tom skulking about a

312

while ago, and sure enough." She shook her head.

Jory ran over and hugged Mrs. Kleinfelter, who looked more than a little surprised. "Goodness," Mrs. Kleinfelter said, stiffly returning Jory's embrace and patting Jory lightly on the back. "Let's not squish the cat, now."

A car door slammed, and then another. Grace leaned forward and peered out the front window. "It's them," Grace said. She turned and gave Jory a look of fear and happiness.

"Oh, my — I'd really better be going." Mrs. Kleinfelter opened the front door. Jory peeked around her shoulder at the sight of her father and mother and little sister walking up the driveway to Henry's house. Jory felt strangely light-headed at the thought of meeting her mother's eyes for the first time in two months.

"Come on," said Grace. She pulled at Jory's hand. Jory followed Grace out the front door, the kitten still clenched tightly to her chest.

The two groups of Quanbecks met at the bottom of the porch steps.

"Well, hello hello," said Jory's father, smiling and reaching out to shake Mrs. Kleinfelter's hand. "It's nice to see you again . . .

313

Mrs. . . . um — mm —"

"Hilda."

"Mrs. Hilda."

Grace touched her father's shirtsleeve. "Hilda's her first name, Dad."

"Oh, right, of course." Her father ran his hand through his hair. "Hilda, um, this is my wife, Esther, and our youngest daughter, Frances."

Mrs. Kleinfelter stepped forward and shook Jory's mother's hand. "You have two very wonderful girls here," Mrs. Kleinfelter said.

Jory's mother smiled a very small smile and then trained her eyes on the ground near her feet.

"They really are," said Mrs. Kleinfelter. "Wonderful, that is." She nodded, as if to further convince everyone of Grace's and Jory's wonderfulness.

For a moment no one said anything.

"Hey, Franny," said Jory, bending down.

Frances was partially hidden behind the fullness of their mother's Sunday skirt.

"Look what I have," said Jory, holding the kitten out in Frances's direction.

Frances peeped shyly at Jory, while still holding tight to some lace beneath their mother's skirt. "What is it?" she said in a small, croaky voice.

"Don't be silly, Frances." Their mother pulled Frances firmly out from behind her and gave her a push in Jory's direction.

Frances smiled in a dazed fashion, and plucked at her own skirt.

"It doesn't have any tail," said Jory, turning the cat around to verify this information. "See?" The kitten clawed the air and began to mew with urgency.

Frances gazed at the kitten's backside. "Why not? Who cut it off?"

"It was born like that. Look, you can feel just a teeny tiny little bone where its tail should be." Jory took Frances's hand and rubbed it over the kitten's rump.

Frances pulled back her hand and made a funny face. The grown-ups laughed a little more than necessary.

"Well," said Mrs. Kleinfelter, "you folks enjoy your day. I'm off to weed my tomatoes." She waved one hand and walked quickly in the direction of her house.

Jory's father turned back around and clapped his hands together. "What do you say? Shall we all go inside?" Jory's father appealed to one pair of females and then the other. "I believe we have a couple of presents to open, and some cake to eat, right?" He put his arm around Jory's mother. "This is a pretty important day for all of us." He gave his wife's arm a squeeze. "We certainly remember fourteen years ago today, don't we?" Jory's mother said nothing. "And it was even on a Sunday, just like today." He steered his wife ahead of him, up the front steps, and through the open door. Once inside, Jory's mother shook his arm off and walked over to the dead cat couch, where she stood.

"Do you want to sit down?" Grace pointed vaguely at the kitchen. "We can eat in there, or in here — it doesn't really matter."

"Where on earth did you get that dress?" It was the first time Jory's mother had spoken to them.

Grace held out the hem of the long brown paisley dress she was wearing. "Hilda gave it to me. It's an old one of hers that she altered . . . at the waist."

Their mother sat down on the arm of the couch as if the air had suddenly been let out of her.

"She gave me the kitten, too." Jory tried to smile. "The Manx kitten." She glanced at her father, who was running his hand through his hair again. "For my birthday," she finished weakly.

"Well, I'm afraid we didn't bring anything half that interesting." Jory's mother sat up a little straighter and stared directly at Jory.

"Not a single dog or puppy or Shetland pony."

"Afro Cat died," said Frances. "Mr. Garmendia put him in a cupboard out in his lawn mower shed. I got to see him. He's going to get stuffed."

"Stuffed?" Jory made a face.

"Frances, get up off the floor." Their mother frowned. "Oren, why don't you get the things out of the trunk?"

"Good idea, good idea." Jory's father sprang out of the chair he was sitting in. "Come on, Frances, you can help me carry the presents."

"I'll get the cake ready," said Grace, and disappeared into the kitchen.

Jory and her mother were left alone together in the living room. Her mother sat on the edge of the couch, gazing down and rearranging the folds in her skirt. Jory felt herself breathe in and out. Once. Twice. Three times.

Her mother stood up. "Where's the bathroom?" she asked.

"Oh," said Jory, quickly standing up too. "It's down the hall on the left-hand side." She pointed.

Her mother swept past her. Caron's Fleurs de Rocaille, Aqua Net hair spray, and talcum powder: the most powerful scents of

Jory's childhood. She'd almost forgotten.

Her father and Frances banged back in through the front door, carrying several small, brightly wrapped packages. Frances laid her package on the coffee table; she was still holding the kitten in her other arm. "I picked out the cowboy paper," she said.

"I love it," said Jory.

Grace came through the kitchen door carrying the cake. It was now lit by fourteen yellow and white candles.

"Ooh," said Frances. The kitten squirmed wildly in her arms.

"Shall we sing?" said Grace. She glanced around the room. "Where's Mom?"

"In the bathroom," said Jory.

"I'm sure she'll be out in a minute," their father said. "Here, I'll hold the cake." He took the cake from Grace and held it out toward Jory with a certain amount of ceremony. "Do you have a good wish ready?"

Jory gave him a look. "I can think of one or two."

The candles flickered and burned. The four of them stood together in a small circle.

"I guess we could blow them out and relight them if they get down too far." Grace knit her brows together. "I'll go get the matches."

"No," said Frances, hopping up and

down. "That's not how it works — the wish won't count then!"

Their father leaned his head hallward. "Esther!" He raised his voice further. "We have the cake in here!" He smiled apologetically. "She hasn't been feeling very well."

"It's okay," said Jory. "It doesn't matter."

"Well, of course it does." Her father stared at the cake and the rapidly melting candles. He gave a quick glance down the hall. Jory could tell he wanted to run his hand through his hair. "Well, okay, all right," he said, and smiled a crooked smile. "Let's go ahead and sing."

They sat around the kitchen table and ate the cake and the Neapolitan ice cream, which (Grace told Jory) *someone* had anonymously provided. Frances had the kitten in her lap and was surreptitiously allowing it generous licks off her spoon. Their father had two bowls "in honor of the day" and their mother had none. "It's just a little stomach thing," she said, and scooted her chair a ways back from the table.

"So," said their father. He handed Jory a small, flat package covered in bronco-busting, cow-lassoing cowboys.

Inside was a new red leather Bible with her name embossed in gold across the bot-

319

tom right corner. Jory held the Bible in her lap. "Thank you," she said, still looking at its cover. She ran her finger slowly across her name.

"It's the newest version," her father said. "The *Good News for Modern Man.* Evidently the young people think its language is more accessible." He frowned at this. "It was gone over by a lot of genuinely excellent Bible scholars, though, so even if it doesn't have the beauty of the King James language, it still retains the meaning of the original." He crossed one leg over the other. "I feel pretty good about it."

"I'm sure Jory will get lots of use out of it." Grace smiled at their father. And then at Jory.

Jory tried to nod.

"Okay." Her father handed her a slightly larger package.

"This is from me," said Frances.

"Oh, really," said Jory. "Should I be afraid to open it?"

Frances held her spoon in midair. "I can't remember." Frances squinted at their mother. "I can't remember. Should she?"

Their mother sighed and rolled her eyes. "Really, Frances, I don't know why you're acting like this."

Jory tore the paper wrapping off and put

it on the table.

"Now I remember," said Frances, standing up on her chair and letting the sleeping kitten slide scratchily to the floor. "It's a bug house!"

Jory turned the box over. "How wonderful, Fran. Tell me what I do with it."

"It has baby butterflies in there that hatch out when they're ready. And you get to watch them."

"A friend of mine in the biology lab got it for me," her father said. "It has a dozen monarch butterfly chrysali in stasis that will hatch out in a few weeks, if you follow the instructions."

"How cool," said Jory, busily reading about the four stages of the butterfly's life: egg, larva, pupa, adult. "Thank you very much, Frances."

"You're very welcome," said Frances.

"One more," said her father. "This one's from your mother."

"Oren." Her mother clucked her tongue.

Jory unwrapped the largest box and lifted the lid. Inside, underneath a layer of white tissue paper, were three pairs of corduroy bell-bottoms. In her size. One pair was sky blue and another was a beautiful deep rust red. The third was a golden sand shade that matched her moccasins exactly. She turned to look at her mother.

Her mother was busily winding her watch. "Grace mentioned that you didn't have any appropriate school clothes." She quit her winding and gazed out the window.

"Thank you," whispered Jory. Her mother was a riddle that she could never quite solve. Even if her mother was currently incensed or furious or deeply depressed, each Christmas and birthday was a magical event thanks to her ability and willingness to choose and wrap and present the most marvelous and unforeseen gifts. She somehow seemed to know and anticipate exactly what each of her daughters most longed for. Whether she might later retract these presents or even throw them in the trash was another matter entirely. Jory gazed down in wonder at her new and perfect clothes.

Grace held up the serving knife. "Who'd like more cake?"

"Oh, no," said Frances.

They all turned to look as Frances ran over and squatted down next to the kitten. It was making several desperate noises and widening its mouth alarmingly. Suddenly it arched its tiny back and disgorged a large pool of pinky-brown ice cream next to a crumpled sheet of cowboy paper.

"Well," said their father, "now it's a party."

They all stood outside in the dark next to the green Buick. Frances was sound asleep and slung over their father's shoulder. She had had a very bad tantrum of sorts at the end of the night; why wasn't entirely clear.

"Thank you both for coming," Grace said.

"For Pete's sake, Grace — you sound like you're our dinner hostess." Their mother pulled a sweater across her shoulders. "Will we be getting a thank-you card in the mail?"

Jory could see the look on Grace's face.

"Esther," their father said.

"Whatever you are angry about," said Grace, "it probably isn't because I'm acting like a dinner hostess."

"Well, I for one had a wonderful time." Their father smiled brightly in the semidarkness. "Wonderful cake, wonderful company."

"Yes, we're all just wonderful," said their mother, buttoning the buttons on her sweater. "Oh — and, Jory, by the way, I got a call from Rhonda Russell's mother the other day, and she was wondering why exactly you and Rhonda and your grandmother got evicted from Super Thrift Drug. And, well, frankly, I just didn't know what

323

to tell her. So maybe you'd like to explain to your father and me why it is that you and your *grandmother* got evicted from Super Thrift." Her mother crossed her sweatered arms over her chest.

Grace stared at Jory.

"Esther," her father said. "Do we need to talk about this right now?"

"Why not?" Jory's mother turned to him. "What's wrong with right now? I think right now is a perfectly good time to talk about this."

"It was my fault." Grace put her hands in the pockets of her dress.

"Oh, really?" Their mother shook her head at Grace.

Jory closed her eyes and took a breath. "It was *my* fault," she said. "I lied. I lied to Dad about having my period so I could skip PE and Grace talked Mrs. Kleinfelter into taking me to get . . . sanitary stuff and Mrs. Kleinfelter automatically went to Super Thrift because that's where she gets her prescriptions filled and so we had to go in and Rhonda was there and then when they saw me they made us leave because they think I stole the earrings but I didn't — and it doesn't matter what you think because I didn't steal them. I *didn't* steal them. I've done plenty of bad things, but that wasn't one of them."

A light winked on in Mrs. Kleinfelter's house and a lone cricket suddenly ceased its scritching. The night breeze stirred and Jory hugged her own elbows tightly.

Jory's father switched Frances to his other shoulder. "Well, I guess that pretty much answers that." He reached out and patted Jory on the arm.

Jory's mother stood in the dimness, the whites of her eyes glowing bright. "I just don't see how everything we've done for you girls has resulted in *this*."

No one said anything in response, although Jory knew that she or Grace was meant to. That this was the characteristic gambit to which they were expected to provide a soothing and chastened response.

"I think it's the selfishness that hurts me the worst. All your father and I have ever asked is that you not shame us. Or yourselves. And look —" She waved her hand wildly at Jory and Grace. "Just look."

Jory could feel her own sense of guilt weighing heavily in her body, although Grace seemed to be standing up straighter than ever, her abdomen standing out proudly in relief.

Their mother shook her head and walked around to the passenger side of the car and

325

got in. She pulled the door shut after her and sat there staring straight ahead.

Their father took a few deliberate steps away from the car. He leaned forward and gave Grace and then Jory a kiss on the forehead. "Happy birthday, birthday girl," he whispered as he held Jory tight with one of his arms.

Jory hugged him back, and she stroked Frances's dangling foot. "Tell Frances she can come and play with the kitten anytime she wants."

Her father let go of Jory. He ran his free hand through his hair. "You know, I'm not sure that would be such a good idea right now. Maybe she can come see the kitten sometime later, when everything has calmed down some."

"Calmed down?" Jory's voice rose perceptibly. "Why do you always say that, Dad? Seriously — do you think things are ever really going to *calm down*?"

"Frances can't come see us again?" Grace said. "Is that what you're saying?"

"Oh, I don't know," said their father. "But let's not get upset, all right? I think we've all had enough excitement here for one evening." Their father walked over to the car, opened the back door, and laid Frances gently in the backseat. He said something to their mother and then shut the door and walked back toward them.

"That just isn't right," said Jory. "It's not."

Grace stepped closer to their father. "Do you really think it's fair to punish Frances too?"

Their father gazed up at the sky. "This has been a very confusing time for everyone," he said. "Maybe especially for Frances. She's too young to understand what's going on, and we'd like to try to shield her from any real . . ." Here their father's voice trailed off. "Your mother and I don't want to see her permanently hurt or damaged by any of this."

Grace seemed stunned. An idea bloomed across her face and settled. "So you *are* ashamed of us. Of *me.*"

Their father sighed and rubbed the bridge of his nose.

Jory peered at her father. "Why did you let her come today, then?"

"It was your birthday," he said, sounding horribly sad.

"So that means we get to see her again when? Only on holidays? At Thanksgiving? Christmas?"

"Jory, I just don't know."

"Christmas?"

Grace leaned forward and tried to touch

her father's shirt cuff. Whether he didn't realize this in the dark or whether he deliberately pulled back, Jory couldn't tell. "Have you prayed about this, Dad?"

"Grace."

"Have you?"

"Okay. Look, it's late now and I need to get your mother and Frances home, and, Jory, you have school tomorrow. So we will consider this discussion closed for the evening, all right?"

Jory and Grace said nothing.

"And, Jory, if you need any supplies or . . . anything from town, you should call me first and I'll be happy to get whatever you want. So you don't need to bother Mrs. Kleinfelter anymore with that kind of thing, okay?" Their father pulled his car keys out of his pocket. "Okay?"

Grace took a step or two in the direction of the house and suddenly stopped and turned her gaze toward their father. *"The way of a fool is right in his own eyes,"* she said. "Proverbs 12:15." Grace turned around again and then walked all the way across the grass, up the steps onto the porch, and into the house. The front door slammed shut.

Jory and her father stood alone in the yard. He sighed once. Heavily. "You know that I love you two girls," her father said. Something about the dampness of the night air, or the fact that she couldn't see his mouth moving in the dark, made his words seem to be coming from a distance away. For some reason, Jory couldn't think of a response to his statement. She merely watched as he lowered himself into the driver's seat of the Buick and then stared backward the entire time he put the car into reverse and backed the car out of the long dirt driveway.

CHAPTER ELEVEN

The days were getting shorter and cooler now. Albertsons' supply of Jonathan apples was spotty, and the kitten, who was named So Handsome, spent each night curled up on the quilt next to Jory's feet. Next week, Grip was going to take her trick-or-treating in the ice cream truck. Although how she was going to talk Grace into this, Jory wasn't entirely sure. He had come over for Sunday morning "services" twice in a row and had ended up staying till Sunday evening each time. Last Sunday night, he had taught Grace how to crochet with the old box of needles and crochet thread that Grace had found in the basement. Jory found this amazing, the sight of Grip and Grace sitting on the couch, their heads bent together over balls of yarn with a crochet book from 1949 between them. It was both thrilling and slightly troubling to see Grip's long and slightly matted red hair leaning into Grace's smooth, short brunette cap as he taught her about chains and knots and slip stitches.

This morning when she got up, she found Grace sitting on the porch, concentratedly working away at some small unidentifiable square of stuff in her lap. "Look what Hilda brought me," Grace said, pointing to something on the top step. "It's a pattern for a baby cap."

Mrs. Kleinfelter was sitting in the porch swing reading a *National Geographic.* "How was school yesterday?" she asked without looking up.

"Okay, I guess," said Jory, yawning. "We made soufflés in home ec."

"Hm," said Mrs. Kleinfelter. "I don't think I've eaten a soufflé in my life. Nor have I really wanted to." She turned a page in her magazine. "The Incas were more bloodthirsty than the Aztecs. A little-known fact."

"My friend's uncle got eaten by cannibals in Peru."

"Really," said Mrs. Kleinfelter, putting down her magazine.

"He was a missionary and they killed him and ate him."

"My, my," said Mrs. Kleinfelter. "Didn't like his sermons?"

"This is terrible talk," said Grace. "Philip Albright was an obedient servant of God. He was a willing martyr for the cause of Christ."

"He sits next to me in earth science."

"What?" said Grace.

"The guy with the uncle who got eaten," said Jory. "Laird Albright. I already told you." Jory lay down on the wooden floor of the porch and let So Handsome walk on her chest. "Don't I need to get him shots and stuff?"

"I never do with my cats, but I know that's not very modern." Jory had noticed that being and not being modern was often a point of contention for Mrs. Kleinfelter. "If you want to get him shots, I suppose we can take him to that vet clinic in town."

"I don't want him to die or get rabies," Jory said. She lifted each of the kitten's feet and peered at the tiny pink pads on the bottom. "Why did Frances call these 'doughnuts'? They look nothing like doughnuts."

No one answered her.

"I'm thinking of moving into town," Mrs. Kleinfelter said. She gazed peaceably out at the late afternoon sun.

"What?" Jory sat up, feeling an unexpected pang at the thought of this. "When?"

"Oh, in a little while, I guess. It'd probably take me at least a month or two to sell the main house." Mrs. Kleinfelter waved her hand airily, as if moving and selling her house were an everyday affair.

"I don't think you should go," said Jory. "I don't think you'd like it in town. It's really noisy and busy and stuff. And there's tons of traffic."

"Jory," said Grace.

"Well," said Mrs. Kleinfelter. "I read an article in that AARP magazine that said the chief predictor of longevity is the number of people with whom you associate — I'm quoting now — and I realized that I don't *associate* an awful lot. It also said that you're more likely to get sick and go nuts if you don't get out much."

"That's sounds like quite a quote," said Grace, pulling another stitch onto her crochet hook.

"I guess that last part wasn't exactly word for word, but that's pretty much the gist of it."

"You do too get out," said Jory.

Mrs. Kleinfelter stood up and picked up her magazine. "Well, regardless," she said. "It's good old tuna casserole for me again tonight." She paused. "I bet they don't teach you that in home ec, do they?"

Jory picked up So Handsome and let him walk along the porch railing. "Can I come watch *Jeopardy!* later?"

"If you bring your homework." Mrs. Kleinfelter moved down the stairs and then did her strange striding walk across the yard.

"You shouldn't tell her what to do." Grace carefully moved the cat away from her crocheting.

"Why not? You're telling me what to do right now. You're always telling people what to do. And not do."

Grace looked crestfallen. "Really?" She let her crocheting drop into her lap. "Is that how I seem to you? Like I'm always bossing you around?"

Jory said nothing.

"I guess I need to work on that, then," said Grace, her words coming slowly. "Jesus warns against noticing the specks in other people's eyes and ignoring the log in your own. I didn't realize that I was being like that."

Jory smoothed down the nap on her new rust-colored bell-bottoms. "Just forget it."

"No," said Grace. "I don't want to be like that. I don't *mean* to be like that."

The phone began to ring. Jory hopped up and flung open the front door and then dashed into the kitchen to get it. "Hello," she said, somewhat breathlessly.

"Hey there, Miss Q."

"Hi," said Jory, beginning to smile. She had given Rhea her phone number even though she knew her father would have a fit.

"What's going on?"

"Nothing," said Jory. "What're you doing?"

"Going to a party. And so are you. At Dave Roddy's house."

"I'm invited?" Jory couldn't keep the note of surprise out of her voice.

"Unless there's some other Quanbeck chick named Jory. So hey — my sister's driving and we're gonna pick you up around eight thirty. So be ready."

Jory could hardly think. There was absolutely no way she could do this. "Sure, okay," she said.

"Killer. Wear something really sexy, and see if you can bring some booze. Just *kidding*!" Rhea laughed. "See ya in a bit!"

"Bye," said Jory. She hung up the phone and felt her stomach begin to twist. Maybe she could call Rhea back later and tell her she was sick. She gazed faintly around the room.

"Who was that?" Grace came into the kitchen, So Handsome batting at her heels with each step.

"Nobody," said Jory. "Just a girl from school."

"Your new friend? The one from PE?"

"Yeah, I gave her our number so I could get homework assignments." Jory picked up the kitten and buried her face in its fur. "In case I was sick. Or something." Jory put the cat into the wide porcelain sink, where it began lapping at drips from the faucet. "In fact, she wanted to know if I could come over tonight and help her study for our algebra test."

"Where? At her house?"

"Um-hm. Her sister's going to come get me at eight thirty."

"Tonight? Oh." Grace sat down at the kitchen table. "What do you expect me to tell Dad if he comes over?"

"I don't know. That I'm a normal human being and that I might need to go over to my friend's house once every eon?" Jory listened to the escalating sounds of her own supposed self-righteous indignation. "I can't get decent grades if no one ever helps me. I don't know anything at all about math."

"I'm helping you — I can help you."

"No, you can't. You just can't." Jory threw herself around the kitchen with abandon. "I can't learn from you because every time you try to help me, all I can think of is how much smarter you are than I am and how Dad likes you better because you're like him." Jory shook her head. "I can't help it if I'm not mathematically inclined."

Grace looked stunned. "I don't know how you got the idea that I'm smarter than you. It's not true at all."

"Well, that's how I feel." Jory gazed blindly out the window above the kitchen sink, trying to summon up any other possible personal grievances and injustices.

What was she doing? She didn't know what to do at a party. Not at a grown-up public high school party. She barely even knew these kids. Jory brushed past her sister and ran upstairs and sat down on the edge of the bed, breathless. Plus, she needed something really, really cute to wear.

At eight o'clock, Jory descended the stairs to sit carefully in the brown horsehair chair, trying not to wrinkle her shirt. She was wearing her new pale blue corduroy bell-bottoms and a lacy white blouse that she had made a year ago in Pathfinders. And her new moccasins. She had also found a tiny Avon sample lipstick of Pinch-Me-Not that she had rubbed on her cheeks as blusher, and she had brushed and brushed

337

her hair until it was smooth and, hopefully, shiny. She had her algebra I book in her bag even though it wasn't likely that she would be needing it.

"It would be really great if you could talk to your friend about your walk with Christ, at least a little." Grace looked fondly at Jory.

Jory nodded, thinking not-so-kind thoughts about Grace's own distinct and deliberate lack of style, about her impossibly outdated hairdo and completely makeup-free face. Grace was still wearing the dress Mrs. Kleinfelter had altered for her. She had been wearing it for days, even though Jory suggested that it might be time for a change — that she and Grip and even Mrs. Kleinfelter might like to see her in something else once in a while. And Jory still could not get used to seeing her sister's belly protruding so roundly in front of her. For some reason it made Jory feel as if her own stomach were sticking out too. What was that called? Sympathetic something or other. Jory tightened her abdominal muscles and sucked in her stomach.

"Seriously, any chance you get to talk to her about Christianity would be wonderful." Grace smiled.

Jory nodded again and readjusted the lace on her shirt cuff.

"I don't think Episcopalians are very Christ centered; I'm pretty sure it's a ritual-based religion. Lots of communion and incense, but no real faith-based teachings about how to live. So it would be neat if you could ask her a little bit about her own personal feelings about faith, you know?"

Jory stood up and went to the front door. "Did you hear a car?"

"You know I've been surprised lately at how open Grip has been to some of the things I've been teaching him about the Gospel."

Jory peered out the window. "I think I'm just going to wait on the porch."

"He definitely seems hungry for the word of God," said Grace. "Oh, and Jory, don't forget your Bible."

Jory whirled around and stamped her foot on the floor. "Shut up! Just *shut up*!" She blanched then and covered her mouth with her hands. "Oh, no," she said. "I'm so sorry! I didn't mean to say that. I don't know what's wrong with me. I'm sorry, Grace."

Grace sat on the couch looking down at the baby cap pattern. "It's all right," she said.

"No, it's not." Jory shook her head in dismay.

"Yes. I'm probably pushing you too hard.

About witnessing and things." Grace still wouldn't meet Jory's eyes. She smoothed out the pattern against her leg. "Plus, I was telling you what to do again." Her voice was filled with remorse.

Headlights panned across the living room wall and a car horn beeped twice.

"I'm sorry, Grace."

Grace half nodded. "It's my fault," she said sadly.

Jory fled out the door, down the steps, and across the grass. A long blue station wagon waited in the driveway. Its passenger window rolled noisily down and a song by the Guess Who streamed out into the night. "Hey there, party girl," Rhea yelled. "Get your ass in here."

Jory stared back at the house. At the light coming from the living room, and from the diamond-shaped window on the second floor, where she had forgotten, yet again, to turn off her bedroom lamp.

She opened the car door and got in.

Dave Roddy lived in an old farmhouse somewhere on a deserted stretch of road even farther out in the country than Henry Kleinfelter's. Without any other cars or streetlights or stars, it was as if they had driven through a dark, winding tunnel to get there, but once inside the house it was achingly, solidly bright and filled with sound. Jory swore that the record player was playing the same song they had been listening to in the car, but she couldn't be sure because everyone in the house was talking so loud. She recognized no one from school — not anyone that she knew personally, anyway. Rhea's sister Connie said that this was a senior party, strictly upperclassmen, and that the only reason she had let Rhea come was because she would have had to stay home and babysit her if she hadn't. She had lit up a cigarette after she said this, and then didn't say anything else the whole time she was driving them there, except to tell them that if they acted weird or like freaking babies in front of her friends she would never take them anywhere ever again. Ever.

"Here," said Rhea now, handing Jory a Styrofoam cup. "Drink up."

"What is it?" Jory tipped the cup back and forth, inspecting its contents.

"I don't know — it's called Purple Jesus, so I guess it's like taking communion or something," said Rhea. "I already had two." Rhea was wearing a leather headband that she kept having to readjust. "Did you see the guy over by the stereo? That's Randy Asumendi." Rhea took a long drink from her cup. "He's the football captain, or star or whatever." She took another drink. "He evidently thinks he's, like, *it.*" Rhea snorted. "I told him I liked his shirt." She laughed loudly. "Look at that shirt!"

The person named Randy, who could evidently see Rhea laughing at him, began sauntering across the room in their direction. His tight-fitting shirt was made of shiny cream-colored polyester with collar points that veered sharply down toward each pectoral muscle. A wildly rearing orange horse featured prominently across the front.

"Oh, brother," said Rhea, draining the last of her drink.

"Hey," said the Randy person, smiling at Rhea.

"Hey, yourself," said Rhea. "I'm getting a refill." Rhea turned and headed toward the kitchen.

With more than a little effort, Randy redirected his attention to Jory. He gave Jory a sidelong glance. "Are you as big a bitch as your friend over there?"

Jory could think of absolutely nothing to say in response to this. She held her cup up to her lips and took a drink. It tasted like grape cough syrup. Sort of.

"How come I've never seen you before?"

Randy had leaned one of his hands against the wall, so that his bare arm was now next to Jory's head. Jory took another, larger sip of her drink.

"I don't know," she said finally.

"What are you? Sophomore? Freshman?" His eyes seemed to take a sort of vertical inventory of her. "You're too young and skinny for a tenth grader."

"What?" Jory was taking nervous sips from her cup.

Randy shook his head. He snapped his fingers directly in front of Jory's face. "*Hablas inglés?* You speak-uh zee English?" He pulled a flat glass bottle out of his back pocket. "You two are weird — you know that? You and your friend. Weird and crazy." He made a circling motion next to his ear and laughed, then took a drink and coughed. "*Whew*," he said, and laughed some more.

"Whew," said Jory. She had finished her cup of purple juice. She examined the cup's bottom.

"So, who do you go with? Some freshman guy? Somebody on JV?"

"I don't go with anybody," Jory admitted.

"Oh, yeah?" Randy unscrewed the lid on the flat glass bottle again and handed it to Jory. She lifted the bottle to her mouth and took a drink. The liquid was like sweet, sticky fire in her mouth and it burned all the way down her throat like something no one should ever be drinking. She coughed and coughed again, blindly handing the bottle back to him.

"What a lightweight! Haven't you ever had any booze before?" Randy appeared delighted at this development, and his role in it.

Jory shook her head and wiped her mouth with the back of her hand.

"Hey, so what'd you think of that little Mexican runt from Wilder last Friday? Everybody thought he was gonna be such hot shit, but I showed him."

Jory looked blankly at Randy.

"Weren't you there? Didn't you see me play?" Randy now leaned in confidentially toward her, his breath tickling her ear.

"Play what?"

"Play *what*?" Randy leaned back and shook his head in disbelief. "Are you shitting me?"

"The accordion," said Jory suddenly. She snapped her fingers. "For five hundred dollars, Alex, *'What is the accordion?'* "

Randy Asumendi's face registered first shock and then anger and finally disgust. "At least your friend has some tits," he said, and then turned and sauntered off in the opposite direction.

Jory stood holding her empty cup. She tried to remember where the kitchen was. She wended her way down a promising-looking hall, but there were so many bodies in the way that it took forever to get to the end of it. Slowly she squeezed past any number of people standing in groups of various configurations. The kitchen seemed especially filled with people talking and laughing and smoking and scooping purple liquid out of an enormous metal washbasin that was resting on a table. Rhea was sitting in something that looked like a baby's high chair and some boy with shaggy brown hair and a Batman T-shirt was squatting down tying her shoe. Rhea grinned happily at Jory. The boy's shirt read *BIFF! BAM! POW!* in explosive red letters.

"Who's that?" Jory nodded at the shaggy-haired boy.

"Don't know," said Rhea.

"You left me out there with that accordion player," said Jory. She gazed around her. A girl wearing a pink paisley minidress was pressing gold stick-on stars onto the back of a boy's cowboy shirt. The boy with the shaggy hair had disappeared. Jory sat down on the floor next to Rhea's feet and Rhea handed her down another cup of juice. "That guy out there thought we were weird. That Randy person." She took a long drink and peered into the purple depths of her cup. "Plus, he said that you were way cuter than me."

Rhea leaned down and began braiding Jory's hair. "He's nuts," she said, but then she smiled. "Is that really what he said?"

"Pretty much," said Jory, feeling strangely calm about the specific thrust of Randy's comment. Ordinarily she would have felt like crawling beneath the floorboards and living there forever at having a boy — a senior! the football captain! — telling her she was breastless, but right now it was as if she were wearing a large plastic shield that made most everything bounce off her and be deflected elsewhere. Or maybe it was more that things didn't quite stick but passed quickly through her without leaving their usual marks. "Like electrons," she said suddenly. "Or protons."

"What?" said Rhea, leaning forward and trying to hear better.

"Or maybe photons," said Jory. "I forget."

Just then, someone from outside flung the kitchen's back door open and an angry-looking boy came flying in as though pushed from behind. A girl wearing a fringed leather dress shrieked in either dismay or delight. Several people got shoved into and knocked around and then someone — a female someone — said, "You idiot — you *fuck*er!" and someone deliberately pushed someone else. There was some slow-motion sort of swearing and jostling and pushing and hitting. The girl in the fringed dress who had been standing next to the drink table came crashing down onto the floor in a painful way. She fell half onto Jory's lap and Jory suddenly saw this girl close up and magnified: her ink black eyes and her eyebrows like two beautiful bird feathers, and it was as if Jory knew this bird girl and saw her better and more intimately than she'd ever seen anyone. It was as if Jory had an X-ray microscope that could see inside things, inside people. Jory smiled at the girl and, for a second, as if she had the microscope too, the girl smiled back, and then frowned horribly and said, "What are *you* doing here?"

Jory was too stunned to say anything.

"Seriously. Who on earth invited you two?" Jude Mullinix stared up at Rhea and then tried to struggle up off of Jory's lap.

"Your mother," said Rhea from up in her high chair. "Seriously."

Jude stood up and smoothed the fringe on

the bottom of her dress back down. She pushed past someone and disappeared back into a circle of people milling loudly around the kitchen table.

"She's just like an Indian princess," said Jory. "If I were a boy, I would love her forever."

"You're insane," said Rhea. "She's the snobbiest snob who ever lived."

"I know," said Jory in a completely awed voice.

The rest of the night went on pretty much like that. At some point, Jory found herself in Dave Roddy's backyard trying to squeeze into a homemade doghouse while several other people stood by encouraging and giving her occasional proddings with their feet. It was cozy in the doghouse and the sounds of people's voices outside reminded her of being small and listening to her parents as she fell asleep in the backseat of the car on the way home from missionary film night at church. The doghouse smelled of dirt and dog chow and the metal of dog chains and was harder to get out of than to get into. As she was struggling back out through the opening of the doghouse, someone reached down and tugged at her arm. Jory grabbed at this helping hand and pulled herself into a standing position next to Jude Mullinix, who now dropped Jory's arm as if it were dirty or diseased. "You're embarrassing yourself," she said, giving Jory a brief, dismissive glance.

Jory felt relatively unconcerned about this. "How do you get your hair to go like that?" She picked up the end of a piece of Jude's hair and let it slide between her fingers. "It's so straight and slippery, it's like liquid glass." She couldn't believe she was touching Jude Mullinix's hair.

Jude gave Jory a look. "Are you serious?"

Jory laid the piece of hair reverently back against Jude's shoulder.

Jude sighed and pulled a cigarette out of her shoulder bag. "Johnson's No More Tangles. After you wash your hair, you spray it on and voilà." Jude leaned down and lit the cigarette that was now in her mouth.

Jory watched in awe.

Jude held her cigarette pack out to Jory.

"You've come a loong waaay, baby," said Jory. "To get where you've got to today. You've got your own cigarette now, baby," Jory was singing full-on now. "You've come a long, long way."

Jude blew a stream of smoke into the air. "Okay, you can shut up now, you weirdo," she said in a not unfriendly voice. "Why don't you smoke — are you a Mormon or something?"

"I wish," said Jory. "They can dance at least, and wear short skirts."

"You can't dance?"

"Or go to movies or bowling alleys or pool halls."

"But you can get drunk?"

"Nope, no alcohol." Jory shook her head. "Or fermented spirits."

"Oh, brother," said Jude. "What do you think this is?" Jude lifted her cup up from off a wooden picnic table.

Just then, Jory spied a tall dark-haired boy in a mustard yellow jacket tiptoeing exaggeratedly up behind Jude and then covering her eyes with his hands. *"Knock-knock!"* he said loudly into her ear.

"Jesus Christ!" said Jude, trying to peel the boy's hands off.

"No, it's not Jesus," said the boy. "Try again. *Knock-knock.*"

"Who's there?" said Jude, sighing and hanging on to the boy's hands.

"Dewey," said the boy, grinning wildly at Jory.

"Dewey who?" said Jude.

"Dewey really hafta get married? I used a rubber!"

"Nicky, you idiot," said Jude, trying to pull the boy's hands away.

The boy laughed and dropped his hands. He grabbed Jude's cup and drank down its remaining contents. "Okay. Hand over the weed."

"Forget it," said Jude, but Jory could see she didn't mean it.

The boy was now patting Jude down in a way that cops did to criminals on TV. Jude was laughing and protesting at the same time as the boy bent down and ran his hand inside her leather boot. "I knew it," he said, holding up a tiny rolled-up baggie of something as Jude beat futilely on his chest. "You are such a fucking thief!" He held the baggie far above Jude's head as she leaped up trying to grab at it. "Good God," he said, shaking his head in mock disgust. "You just can't trust anyone these days." He leaned down then and planted a kiss right next to Jude's open mouth. "Later, Judith Louise," he said, and sauntered away waving the baggie.

"Who was that?" asked Jory, still staring at the boy in wonderment.

"Nicky," said Jude. "My asshole brother."

"Seriously?"

"Yeah," said Jude, struggling to rearrange her fringed dress.

"Wow," said Jory softly. She could see it now: the long, straight, inky black hair, the pointed chin and winglike brows. The smoothly lanky body that seemed to fit together as if it had been architecturally planned. "He's beautiful."

"Ha." Jude snorted. "Don't let him hear you say that. He's conceited enough."

"I've never seen him at school."

"He lives in LA with my mom, but she's off in London doing some dumb movie, so he had to come stay with us till she gets back."

Jory tried to process all of this information. "A *movie*?" she said.

Jude turned on her heel and started walking up the back steps into Dave Roddy's house. "Hey," Jory yelled, but Jude had now inserted herself into the messy throng of people straggling both in and out.

Sometime later, Jory found Rhea, and then she and Rhea found Rhea's sister and some boy asleep in an upstairs bedroom, and the boy cried when they dragged Rhea's sister away. He was wearing a long puffy blue ski jacket and white socks. "I don't understand why he's crying," said Jory as they walked Rhea's sister down the stairs and out the front door. "He's in *l-o-v-e*," said Rhea. "He's in love with my grody old sister." She rolled her eyes at Jory.

Outside, it was cold, cold, and they piled

in the car, a mass of hair and coats and tangled legs. They spoke little on the way home, their breath sending frosty plumes of air into the car's heaterless interior. Jory stared up through the station wagon's huge windshield at the frozen-looking stars. She could see forever with her new microscope/telescope vision, which allowed her to zoom in and out over and through great distances. It occurred suddenly to her that she knew exactly what it would be like to be up there as a star: cold and icy and dark, but a hot sort of dark that could burn right through time, so that you were forever up there alone and icily burning. "I'm a star," she said to Rhea.

"I know!" said Rhea, leaning against her. "You're Venus and I'm Mars."

"Those are planets, not stars. They're two totally different things."

"Okay, professor," said Rhea, snuffling her cold nose into Jory's hair. "Don't get all huffy."

"Jude's mom is some kind of movie star and her brother is beautiful," said Jory.

Rhea stared at Jory. "You've been seduced," she said. "By the Mullinix cult." She made a cross with her two index fingers. "Unclean, unclean," she chanted. "Don't touch me, you leper-wretch. I refuse to be contaminated."

Jory pinched Rhea's arm and then burrowed into her, tickling her in the ribs, as Rhea shrieked and swatted furiously at her.

"Hey," Rhea's sister yelled. "I'm trying to drive here, you morons. Cut it out or you're both walking home."

"Hitching home, you mean," said Rhea, smiling at Jory and smoothing down her hair while she gazed happily at herself in the rearview mirror.

The front door of the diamond-windowed house was locked. Even so, Jory turned its handle several more times, wishfully. She could see that the living room was dark, although upstairs the light behind the diamond-shaped window still shone faintly on.

Jory peered back at Mrs. Kleinfelter's house and then, with a sigh, crossed the frosty grass between the two houses. At the front door, she knocked softly and tried to decide whom it was worse to awaken, Mrs. Kleinfelter or Grace. When no one answered, she knocked again, this time a little more loudly.

"You're lucky I didn't call the police." Mrs. Kleinfelter rummaged around in her pony express bag. "That car woke me up out of a dead sleep. I couldn't imagine who or what could be making that kind of racket at this hour. Here," she said. She handed Jory a slightly crumpled piece of Doublemint gum. "You're much too young to be drinking."

Jory took the gum. "I didn't know I really was," she said. "Until it was too late."

"Your sister's going to be very disappointed." Mrs. Kleinfelter sighed and folded a piece of the gum into her own mouth. "And it probably won't be the last time."

The two of them sat in Mrs. Kleinfelter's unlit living room. With a clank and a hum, the old house's furnace gave a false start, releasing a brief aromatic elixir of dust and heat. Mrs. Kleinfelter pulled at the neckline of the men's striped pajamas she was wearing. "Well, this is certainly livelier than my usual nighttime activities. Maybe it's almost as good as getting out."

Jory stared at Mrs. Kleinfelter through the darkness. "I don't want you to move away," she said.

"Maybe you can go in very quietly." Mrs. Kleinfelter dug her hand back into her leather bag and then took out a small set of keys. "Maybe Grace is already asleep in bed."

"Maybe," Jory said doubtfully. She stood

up and buttoned her coat.

"Here," said Mrs. Kleinfelter. She handed Jory the key ring. "I'll need them back tomorrow, though."

Jory walked toward the front door and opened it. "Thank you," she said. "For everything."

"Go on now," said Mrs. Kleinfelter, shooing Jory with her hand. "You're letting in all kinds of cold air."

Jory shut the door behind her and made her way across the grass and up the front steps of Henry's house. She glanced back at Mrs. Kleinfelter, who now stood in the kitchen window giving her a reassuring wave. Jory put the key in the door and turned the handle. The front door opened with barely a squeak.

It was dark in the living room, and Jory stood there for a moment trying to see what was what. She began tiptoeing across the floor in the direction of the stairway.

"Jory?" Grace sat up on the couch. A blanket fell away from her and onto the floor. "What time is it?"

"I don't know," Jory tried to whisper. "Go back to sleep."

"What? Why are you getting home so late?"

"It's not so late," said Jory, still whispering. "You just think it is because you've been sleeping."

"You smell like smoke." Grace stood up shakily and picked up the blanket and pulled it around her. "Why didn't you call me and tell me you weren't coming home?"

"Because I was coming home. Come on," Jory said. "Let's go to bed."

"You can't stay out this late," said Grace. She began shuffling toward the stairs with the blanket wrapped around her. "I mean it," she said.

"I know," Jory said. "I won't — I won't. Ever again." Jory climbed the stairs and then suddenly tripped on the next-to-last step and fell sideways onto the hardwood landing. "Oh," she said, feeling her forehead and the side of her cheek. "Oww." She rolled over onto her side. "I just swallowed my gum," she said, and began to laugh. She lay on her back and laughed some more.

Grace stood over her in her blanket. "Good grief, Jory." She bent down and tried to help Jory up off the floor. Suddenly her expression changed. She sat back on her heels, her tone now one of complete amazement. "Have you been *drinking*?" She still hung on to Jory's arm, but her expression was horrified.

Jory shrugged her sister's hand off her arm

and stood up on her own. "What are you talking about?"

"You've been drinking alcohol," said Grace, standing too. She peered closely at Jory. "Did that friend of yours give you something to drink?"

"I don't know." Jory shrugged. "Some pop, maybe." Jory tried to move toward her bedroom, but Grace reached out again and was now holding her by the sleeve.

"Jory. You smell like liquor."

"What? How would you know?" Jory tried to direct a suspicious look at her sister.

"There were plenty of drunk men in Mexico, all right?" Grace dropped her sister's sleeve. "Alcoholism runs in our family. And all it takes is one drink."

"Holy cow." Jory made a face of long-suffering indignation. "You sound just like Mom."

"Grandpa Feiten had his first beer when he was only nine."

"Good for him," said Jory. "I'm going to bed."

"It's just that I don't want anything bad to happen to you." The tone in Grace's voice was one of sincere sadness.

"I know, I know," said Jory, trying hard not to feel utterly guilty.

"Jory?"

"I said, I know!"

Grace stood on the hallway floor clutching the blanket around her and looking silently at Jory.

Jory turned and walked toward her bedroom. "You're not my parent, though. And I don't have to do what you say." Jory felt as if she had just stuck her tongue out at her sister. She opened her bedroom door and went inside. She shut her door and leaned against it. She couldn't hear any sounds from the hall. Grace was apparently still standing unmoving in the hallway.

Jory took a step and fell straight onto her bed. She rolled over onto her back and yanked and pulled the bottom quilt up around her until it covered her up to the eyes. She didn't care that she was still wearing her clothes. She didn't even care that she was still wearing her shoes.

Her bedroom door opened and Grace stood just inside it, her messy hair and cape-like blanket making her look somewhat spectral and strange.

"You look like Mrs. Rochester," said Jory, lowering her quilt somewhat. "All you need is a lit candle."

"Oh, Miss Eyre, you've spilled your tea!" Grace curtseyed and pretend batted her eyelashes.

"That wasn't Mrs. Rochester," said Jory.

"I know, but it's the only line I remember." Grace and her blanket walked over and sat down on the edge of Jory's bed. "I know that you think I'm a real drag," she said.

"A *drag*?" Jory said, moving over farther in bed to make room. "Since when do you use that word?"

"I don't," said Grace, smiling sadly, "but I know that's what you think of me. I know you think I'm an old fussbudget or something. A complete stick-in-the-mud."

"A tosspot and a flibbertigibbet," said Jory, beginning to laugh.

"A grumpity-frumper."

"A strumpet and a strutfurrow."

Grace let herself fall backward onto Jory's pillow and their two heads now leaned against the bars of the iron bedframe. Neither one of them said anything more. Jory listened to her sister's breathing slow and then she pulled the quilt back up to her chin and turned on her side. Presently, she felt Grace burrow beneath the blankets too, and then she heard nothing more.

Grace and Jory sat at the kitchen table eating oatmeal. Morning sunlight poured in warmly from the warped glass of the kitchen window. After a moment, Grace picked up her empty bowl and carried it to the sink. Then she turned around and faced Jory. She took a breath and seemed to be waiting for something, a something that involved a slight, inward-turning smile. "Jory," she said.

Jory glanced up sleepily.

"I felt the baby move this morning."

Jory put her spoon down.

"I was lying in bed — you were still asleep — and then, out of nowhere, I felt this squiggle-like thing, like a little worm wriggling inside me."

"A little *worm*?" Jory tried not to shriek.

Grace laughed. "I can't describe it. It was like a twitch, or a flutter, sort of. But not." She shook her head. "I know it was the baby. Moving."

Jory sat perfectly still in her chair. "You have to tell me when it does it again."

"Okay." Grace smiled shyly. "It's four months old now. I'm four months pregnant."

"When do you go see the doctor again?"

"I don't know. I think Dad said something about Dr. Henry coming out here maybe."

"He won't even let you go to the doctor's office?"

Grace turned away from Jory and put her bowl in the sink.

"What about when you go into labor? Is

he going to let you go to the hospital then?"

Grace faced Jory again. "I don't know. We haven't talked about it."

"And after the baby's born." Jory held her toast in midair as if to emphasize her point. "You think Dad's going to let you walk around town then? With a stroller and stuff?"

Grace picked up a dishtowel and refolded it, but then she merely stood, holding the folded towel against her chest.

"You really think he's going to let us come back home, then? And we'll all live just like before, as if nothing's happened? And meanwhile, where did this baby supposedly come from?" Jory was now on some kind of terrible roll. "Seriously. Did you see Mom on my birthday? She won't even look at us."

For a fleeting moment Grace's mouth seemed to crumple. "I just have to have faith. That's what I'm supposed to do. *Wait on the Lord: be of good courage, and He shall strengthen thine heart: wait, I say, on the Lord.*"

"Just how long are you supposed to wait exactly?" Jory felt a small bitter thrill of power surge through her, exacerbated by the onset of a headache that had been lurking behind her eyes all morning. "And for what? A sign in the heavens? An eclipse or meteor or something?"

"Stop it, Jory!" Grace threw the folded dishtowel at her sister, but it merely fell, impotent and soft as a large feather, onto the linoleum floor. The expression on her face revealed something close to fury. "Don't you dare make jokes about this!" Grace's mouth grew thin and ugly. "You don't know the first thing about me and you never have."

Jory was shocked into silence, and Grace seemed too stunned to say or do anything further.

The morning sunlight continued to stream in through the window next to the table; So Handsome lay directly in a patch of it, avidly and silently licking his upstretched back leg. Several silent minutes went by as Jory determinedly stirred her oatmeal around in its bowl, mentally apologizing and then retracting her apology. Grace stood with her back to Jory. She too made no move toward modifying or denying any part of what she had just said.

The back screen door opened and creaked shut and then Grip strode into the kitchen carrying several books in his arms. "Hey, hey," he said, patting Jory on the head. "Am I too late for church?"

Grace tried to rearrange her face into

something resembling a smile. "Maybe we don't really need to have any services today."

Grip took a mock step backward. "Wait. What's this I'm hearing?"

"It's nothing," said Jory. How could Grace say that Jory didn't know her? Jory stood up and began getting a bowl and glass down from the cupboard. And worst of all — and this was a thing she could barely even stand to consider — what if it were true? Jory's face felt tight from smiling so falsely. "Do you want some toast and oatmeal? There's orange juice too."

"Oatmeal!" Grip rubbed his hands together and sat down and spread his books out on the table. "I have to warn y'all, I come armed with information."

Jory leaned over and picked up one of the books, still not daring to look at her sister. "I don't even know how to pronounce that."

"It's the *Tao Te Ching*. Hey." Grip took Jory's chin in his hand and turned her face this way and that. "What happened to the other guy?"

Jory closed her eyes. "I just bumped my cheek, is all — no big deal."

"That's some bruise." Grip took the bowl of oatmeal that Grace handed him and started stirring in some raisins. "So," he said. "Here's the topic for this morning:

there's more than one way to skin a cat — sorry, So Handsome — and there's more than one path to enlightenment." He poured a little milk into his bowl. "And just to even things out a little, since we've had two Sundays with the Good Book, I thought we might extend our knowledge of all things spiritual to include some ancient Eastern wisdom. What do you say?" He took a large bite of oatmeal and one of toast.

"As long as you don't expect to convert us," said Grace. Jory could still hear a residual shakiness in her voice.

"Heavens, no," Grip said, and put his hand on his heart. "So . . . anyone here know anything about Hinduism, Buddhism, Taoism, Confucianism? Any of those ring a bell? No? Okay, well, I don't think we'll try to cover all of them today. We'll just go through the bare-bones basics and see what we think." Grip handed a small piece of paper to Jory and another one to Grace. "I wrote down some of the main ideas from the Tao. Grace, you wanna read the first few?"

Grace sighed a little as she sat down at the table across from Grip and looked at the square of paper. " 'Ice cream treats are good to eat. *Y-U-M* spells dee-licious.' " Grace put the paper down on the table.

"Actually, *Y-U-M* does not spell *delicious.*"

"Turn it over, turn it over." Grip waved his hand at Grace. He shrugged at Jory. "All I had was napkins."

Grace flipped the napkin over. *"One whose needs are simple can fulfill them easily. Material wealth does not enrich the spirit. Self-absorption and self-importance are vain and self-destructive."* Her reading voice had been toneless, but now it lifted in pitch. "The Bible already said these things. It's all in Proverbs and the Beatitudes."

"Exactly," said Grip. "Their ideas are very, very similar. But the weird thing is that Lao-tzu said this stuff five hundred years before Christ was even born."

Jory picked up her napkin. *"The truly wise make little of their wisdom, for the more they know, the more they realize how little they know."* She chose another napkin from the pile on the table. *"Glorification of wealth, power, and beauty beget crime, envy, and shame. Humility is the highest virtue."* Jory leaned her chin on her hand. "And the meek shall inherit the earth, right?"

Grace leaned over and picked up Jory's napkin and closely examined it. "So what then? You're trying to say that this Lao-tzu person is just as much of a God as Christ?"

"No, no — I'm not trying to make any

366

claims about God at all. I just think it's interesting how many of the Bible's basic concepts are already right here, hundreds of years before the Bible was written."

"So you're saying the Bible is just a copycat version of this Tao thing." Grace frowned and folded up the napkin. "Well, there is only one God, and the Bible is His holy word. And the Scriptures are more than just a collection of wise sayings. It's more than just lists of things you should do and not do. The Bible foretells the coming of Christ. The Old Testament predicts it and the New Testament reveals it. I doubt that any of these books do that, do they?"

"Well, actually . . ." Grip raised his eyebrows and smiled and reached for the jar of raspberry jam.

Grace stood up. "You know, I could be wrong, but it seems like your whole goal here is to try to make me look stupid for believing in Christianity." Jory could see Grace's rib cage moving rapidly up and down.

"Hey, hey." Grip stood up and put his hand on Grace's arm. "I thought it would be cool to share some ideas with you, that's all. You've been teaching me about the Bible and I thought it would be fun to show you some stuff." He kept his hand on her arm even as she tried to shrug it off. "I know you're super smart. Maybe I was just trying to show you that I'm smart too." Grip's voice trailed off.

Jory's eyes darted back and forth between Grip and her sister. For more than a second, she felt completely unobserved.

Grace pulled out of Grip's clasp and moved away from the table. She paused for a moment at the screen door. Then she opened it and went outside.

Grip sat back down and then just as suddenly scooted his chair back from the table. He stood up and walked toward the back door, where he stood looking out. "I think I'd better be taking off."

"No," said Jory. "You always stay on Sundays."

"Not this Sunday." He turned around and walked toward the living room. "Tell Grace I said good-bye, okay, and thanks for breakfast."

"Wait." Jory ran forward and tried desperately to think of some way to forestall his leaving.

Grip turned and gave a brief tug at the untied string on Jory's sweatshirt. "See ya later, alligator." He walked to the front door, pulled it open, and bolted down the front steps two at a time.

Jory slammed the door closed behind him and flopped down in the horsehair chair. So Handsome immediately scaled the side of the chair and jumped delicately onto Jory's lap. He licked one of his front paws and then ran that paw over and over his ear. Jory pulled at the loose skin at the back of So Handsome's neck, and as if in obedience the kitten began purring his funny gravelly purr. She petted his belly and felt its soft roundness and its tiny pinpricks of nipples. The midmorning sun poured into the living room at a sharp angle and filled the room with a false autumnal warmth, while somewhere very far away a harvester or a tractor of some sort started up its one-note drone.

When Jory woke up, her neck was stiff and the side of her cheek was covered in drool. For a strange small second, Jory could not think who she was, or even if this was what it meant to be alive. She stood up and went to the front door, and stumbled outside onto the porch. Her feet couldn't seem to feel much anymore. Outside, it was hazily bright, as if there were a layer of smoke in the air. It smelled faintly of newly fallen leaves and the wild anise and flowering sage that grew by the side of the road. She sat down in the porch swing and tried to push off with her sleep-deadened feet. She yawned and then shivered. There was a flat cardboard box resting on the porch railing that she hadn't seen before. She got up and walked over to the box and folded back the two large flaps on top. Inside was a white crocheted blanket. Jory pulled it out of the box and cradled it in her hands. Intricate crocheted stitches formed a tightly woven pattern of stars and moons and planets. It was a small rectangular blanket, just the right size to wrap a newborn baby in. For one wild moment she considered putting the blanket back in the box and throwing it into the bushes. "Grace," Jory turned and called. "Grace!"

After a minute, Grace walked out through the front door. She saw Jory and what she was holding. "Ohhh," she said. She reached out and touched a corner of the blanket. "It's beautiful."

Jory handed the blanket to her.

"Where did it come from?" Grace held the blanket out in front of her. "It's the night sky. Look, it even has Saturn. And different phases of the moon!"

"It's for you," said Jory.

"Do you think?" Grace's eyes were glowing.

Jory held out the napkin.

Grace took the note and read it in a quiet

voice. "*The heavens declare the glory of God; and the firmament showeth His handiwork. Psalms 19:1.*" She put the napkin down on the porch railing.

"I have homework I need to do." Jory turned around and walked into the house and up the flight of stairs. She shut the door to Henry's bedroom and lay down on the metal-framed bed. She stared up at the pink glass light fixture that hung suspended from the ceiling by three silver chains. There were two dead moths inside the fixture's glass dome. Her father said that moths used the moon as their primary reference point and that any light source drew them toward it, even if this often meant their own demise. Jory thought this wasn't a very smart navigational tool, but her father said that overall it worked fairly well. That the greater good was worth some individual unluckiness.

Grace knocked quietly on Jory's door. "Can I come in?" she said from the other side of the door.

"No," said Jory.

Grace opened the door and came in and sat on the edge of the bed. She took hold of Jory's foot. "I think he was just trying to make up for this morning."

"It took a long time to crochet that. Weeks. Or *months*, maybe."

"It doesn't mean anything. He was just trying to be nice."

"I know that," Jory said. She continued to gaze at the light fixture. "I'm not worried about it," she said.

"Of course not," said Grace. "I'm just talking to myself mainly." She retied Jory's moccasin. "What homework do you have?"

"I don't know," said Jory. "Couldn't you wear a different dress sometime?"

Grace glanced down at the brown dress, her face flushing. "I don't really have anything else."

"Maybe you could crochet something." Jory rolled over onto her side away from Grace. She closed her eyes. "You or Grip."

For a moment it was quiet.

Grace began talking in a small serious voice. "I know you're angry with me. And probably for a whole bunch of reasons . . . but we can't keep having this same argument again and again."

Jory rolled back over. "What same argument?"

"The one in which you act like anything bad that happens to you is in some way my fault."

"That doesn't really qualify as an argument per se."

Grace stood up and put her hands in the

pockets of the brown dress. "I am not your enemy."

"Oh, really?" Jory leaned up on her elbows.

Grace said nothing for a moment. "I'll see if Mrs. Kleinfelter has any more old dresses she'll let me wear."

"He's *my* friend," said Jory.

"I know he is." Grace nodded and averted her eyes from her sister's.

"And I do too know you." Jory said this in a quiet voice.

Grace made no response. "Let me know if you want any help with your homework," she said finally. She walked out of the room and Jory could hear her moving toward the stairway and going down the stairs.

Jory reached down and pulled the wedding quilt up and over her again. She lay back against her pillow and closed her eyes; one tear oozed out from beneath her lashes and made its way steadily into her ear. She turned on her side and pulled the quilt up over her head. It was like they were some old married couple who couldn't live without each other, yet couldn't live without fighting with each other, either.

"Don't be a baby, you stupid baby," Jory said. "Don't, don't, don't."

CHAPTER TWELVE

"Hear you had quite the Saturday night." Laird Albright leaned toward Jory and grinned. It was lunchtime and Jory was sitting on the hood of someone's car. "Tipped back a few with the big kids, huh?" Laird made a drinking motion with his thumb and little finger.

Jory shook her head. "It wasn't like that."

Laird crumpled up his potato chip bag and tossed it free throw–style in the direction of a trash can. The bag fell a few inches short. "Shit," he said. "No wonder I'm still on JV." Laird turned and squinted at Jory and then bumped her in the arm with his elbow. "So Randy says he's asking you to Homecoming."

Jory let out a huge breath and slid off the car hood. She began walking quickly in the direction of the main building.

"Hey," said Laird, jogging to catch up with her. "I'm only kidding." He grabbed her elbow. "Wait up." He glanced behind him and lowered his voice. "It's me that's asking you to Homecoming."

Jory stopped on the sidewalk. She peered up at his face. "Is that some kind of a joke?"

Laird tried to smile. "Only if you want it to be."

"What? What do you mean?"

"*Je*sus." Laird put his hands in his pockets. "Am I a freak or something? Just say no if you don't want to go."

"No, no. I mean, okay." Jory's heart seemed to be rising up into her throat. She felt strangely sick and nervously excited all at the same time. "Sure. That'd be okay." She looked straight ahead without seeing anything.

"Well, um, okay then." Laird veered off the sidewalk slightly. "I'll see you tomorrow. Or whenever." He gave Jory a half wave and jogged crookedly off toward the gym.

Jory stood on the sidewalk, students jostling past her. She turned around and waited for Rhea to catch up. "Guess what?" she said, feeling slightly embarrassed. "Laird asked me to Homecoming." She opened her eyes wide at Rhea. "Can you believe it?"

"Yeah, why not?" Rhea did not seem overly impressed.

"Because I didn't think anyone here

would ask me to Homecoming." Jory lowered her voice a little. "What is Homecoming? Is it a dance?"

"What else would it be — a barn raising?" Rhea made a face. "Sorry," she said. "I couldn't resist. Aren't you guys, like, Amish or something?"

"We might as well be."

"Anyway, Homecoming is capital-L lame."

"Why?"

"You know — balloons and streamers and the stage decorated like a fake sunken ship or the inside of a clam or something and Mr. Stoessel and Mrs. VanManen checking everybody's breath at the door and then standing around trying to look like they're not standing around." Rhea rolled her eyes. "All the guys will be drunk and all the girls will be crying in the bathroom. And some truly horrible human being will get Homecoming Queen."

"Wow," said Jory. "I want to go."

"Me too," said Rhea.

Jory had snuck out of typing I and was now standing in front of the long horizontal mirror in the girls' bathroom, blessedly alone. What could she wear to Homecoming? Laird had asked her to Homecoming! There was no way Grace would let her go to

376

Homecoming. She continued scrutinizing her own face in the mirror. Most girls wore blush and eyeliner and had mysteriously straightened hair that fell into long, shiny sheets. Jory's hair was browny blond and wavy and thick and it went sort of everywhere. She had inherited the curliness of her father's hair, but not the gorgeous darkness. Plus, she had a cowlick right above her eyebrows that meant that her hair stuck up in a way that precluded a perfect middle part. "You frumpity frump," she murmured. She was engaged in smoothing and pulling her hair down tightly on either side of her face when Jude opened the bathroom door. "Oh, hey," whispered Jory, trying to do something casual with her hands that would make it look like she hadn't been doing what she had been doing.

"Hey," said Jude in a voice utterly devoid of emotion. She didn't look at Jory, but instead began digging at the contents of her leather shoulder bag. Jude was wearing a tiny dark red dress that barely fell to the tops of her thighs. Its white floppy collar matched her white windowpane tights and brown leather knee-high boots. She looked like someone who should be in *Seventeen* magazine instead of in Jory's typing I class. Jory turned the faucet on at one of the sinks and set the hall pass key on the porcelain rim as she gave her hands a cursory washing. She dried her hands with the bathroom's hideously scratchy paper towels while making a point of *not* looking at herself in the mirror.

Jude was now sitting on the room's old radiator, smoking a cigarette and swinging her crossed legs. The window above her head was open.

"Did he ask you?"

"What?" Jory turned and looked at Jude, who was busily blowing a stream of smoke toward the open window.

"He asked you, right?"

For some reason, Jory's heart was beating fast. "Yes," she said, but it sounded as if it were a question rather than an answer.

"He asked me who he should take." Jude stubbed her cigarette out on the metal lip of the radiator and stood up. "I said you."

Jory had no idea what to say. "You did?" Her voice sounded like it belonged to a cartoon character. A mouse or small rabbit maybe.

Jude put her pack of cigarettes back into her leather bag and reshouldered it, gathering her raven's wing of hair into a ponytail that she then let fall like a length of black silk down her back. She unleashed a swift and gorgeous smile at Jory.

"I thought *you* liked him." This was out before Jory could think.

"He milks cows," Jude said. "Nice guy, but not quite my type."

"Oh," said Jory. "So who are you going with?"

"My brother," said Jude, grimacing. "My dad said I had to take him since Nicky doesn't know anyone yet."

"Wow," said Jory. "That's . . . kind of weird."

"Kind *of*," said Jude. She peered at herself in the mirror and brushed an imaginary flake of something out from under one long-lashed eye.

"Is your mom really a movie star?"

"No," said Jude, now raking her fingers through her hair. "She's just a stupid actress in even stupider movies."

"That still sounds pretty cool," said Jory. "To have your mom be an actress."

"It's not," said Jude. "She's an idiot."

Jory watched speechlessly as Jude brushed past her and out the restroom door. She stood next to the mirror seeing her own quizzical and foolish face staring back.

After school, Jory met Rhea at the drinking fountain in the courtyard. The courtyard consisted of a large cement square between the main building and the gym that you could stand on while waiting for the bus to come or for class to get over or for the day to end. There were two long cement benches on which you could sit if you had a spine of steel, and in the very center of the cement square was the drinking fountain that hardly ever worked.

"Hola," said Rhea as she flung her book bag onto one of the benches. *"Cómo estás?"*

"Muy bien," said Jory. *"Y tú?"*

This was as far as they ever got in this exchange.

Rhea sat down on the bench next to her bag and looked at her shoes. She moved her feet back and forth as if she were clicking her heels together. "I like your pants," she said to Jory.

"Thanks," said Jory. "My mom got them for me for my birthday."

"How come you only live with your sister?" Rhea squinted up at her, the wind blowing strands of her hair into her eyes.

"I don't know. It's sort of a long story," said Jory.

"Did your parents kick you guys out?"

Jory had never thought of it like this, but she guessed it was true.

"Maybe they're getting a divorce and

380

don't want you to know."

"No," said Jory.

"Mine are."

"Really?"

"Yeah, my dad got mad because he couldn't figure out how to do his taxes last year, so he drove all the way to Boise to have someone do it for him. And so this woman did. Do it for him. And now my mom is saying that we're all going to have to go live with my aunt in Jackpot." Rhea put her hands underneath her head. "My dad is such a complete goober. I can't imagine anyone in the whole world even wanting to kiss him." Rhea shook her head and then sat up. "He leaves little bristly black hairs in the soap next to our bathroom sink and his underwear is all gross and saggy."

"I know," said Jory, although she didn't really know what she meant by this. "Jude said that she told Laird to ask me to Homecoming."

"Huh?"

"We were in the girls' bathroom during typing and she told me he'd asked her who he should take and she said me."

"I don't believe it."

"I know!"

"She's up to something." Rhea picked a stray leaf out of her hair and twirled its stem

381

between her fingers. "And it's probably nothing good."

Jory felt a sting of disappointment at her own naiveté.

"Hey," said Rhea, "there's the bus."

"Oh, yippee," said Jory, hoisting her bag. "Another exciting afternoon in Arco, Idaho."

Jory lugged her book bag up the front steps of the diamond-windowed house and let the screen door fall shut behind her. The air inside smelled spicy and warm like some kind of cinnamon deliciousness. Jory dropped her bag on the couch and peered into the kitchen. Grace was sitting at the kitchen table with several textbooks spread out in front of her. Her dark, semi-unflattering cap of hair was gone and in its place was the merest sort of shadowy stubble. Jory stopped still in the doorway. "What happened to your *hair*?" she squealed.

Grace's hand rose instinctively to the top of her head. Her face flushed a bright shade of pink. "Nothing," she said.

Jory sank down in the chair across from Grace and stared open-mouthed at her sister. Grace's hair, which had always been thick and stubbornly wavy and cut in a sort of strange Peter Pan–style, was now shorn like a man's military crew cut, minus any regularity in length. Entire patches of Grace's pale scalp showed through in several spots and her birthmark was now totally on display. The whole look reminded Jory wrenchingly of the translucent and vulnerable skull of a brand-new baby bird. "You look *terrible*," she said, as if beseeching Grace to contradict her.

"Well, I'm sorry about that," said Grace, whose hand still roamed the back of her neck.

"But what . . . why did you do this?" Jory continued to stare unabashedly, mesmerized by Grace's hideously ravaged scalp. It was like seeing someone for the first time after they'd had surgery or been in a car accident. "I mean, what were you trying to do?" Jory's voice rose further in pitch.

"How was school today? Did you turn in your *Lord of the Flies* essay?" Grace turned a page in her trigonometry book. "I made that gingerbread of Mom's that you like."

Jory stared at her sister. At the bald spots of skin and the short bristly remains of Grace's hair. At her reddening birthmark, which Jory could see now resembled a sort of half-furled and almost lovely rose. "Wait. Wait a minute." Jory put her face in her hands and closed her eyes. "Does this have something to do with yesterday? With the baby blanket and all that?"

Grace said nothing.

Jory opened her eyes and stared at her sister again.

Grace picked up a pencil and wrote down some figures on the margin of her textbook. "Seriously. You should try the gingerbread while it's still warm."

Jory was unable to tear her eyes away from her sister and her nearly naked head. Finally, she stood up and walked in a daze over to the oven. A square pan of the spicy-smelling cake sat on the counter next to it. She picked up a fork and sank it into the gingerbread, gouging out a small piece. It was delicious. At home they would have made whipped cream to go on top, which they each would have taken turns whipping, carefully stirring in the sugar and vanilla until the cream was thick and sweet. Frances would have insisted on licking the bowl. The contrast between the cool creaminess of the whipping cream and the spicy warmth of the gingerbread was a sort of heaven that always tasted like autumn to Jory. She let the cake dissolve slowly on her tongue.

"You should have some," she said thickly to Grace. "It's wonderful."

Grace placed her finger in her textbook

and regarded her sister, her gray eyes made even larger and more serious-looking by the strange absence of hair. "I can't," she said. "I'm fasting." She turned her head and went back to her work.

Jory didn't know exactly how late it was. From the diamond-shaped window, the ground below appeared almost blue in the darkness and a sheer layer of frost glimmered on top of the propane tank. So Handsome twined between her bare ankles and Jory scooped him up and held him to her chest. He yawned his fishy breath at her, displaying a tiny set of needle-sharp teeth. Jory crept down the stairs holding the kitten. The kitchen still smelled faintly of gingerbread. Jory picked up the old phone receiver and dialed the only number that she knew. The phone rang several times and then she heard her father's sleep-laden voice saying hello with a certain amount of hesitation.

"Dad?" Jory said.

"Jory," he said, "what's wrong?"

"I don't know," she said. "Grace cut all her hair off."

Her father cleared his throat. She imagined him sitting up in bed and putting his glasses on.

"Is this something serious?"

"She's bald."

"Jory," he said. She could hear him sigh and then cover the mouthpiece to say something to her mother. "Do you want me to come over there?"

"No," she said. "Yes."

"Right now?" She could hear him trying valiantly to keep the weariness out of his voice.

"I think she did something to her eyebrows too."

Her father said nothing for a moment. "I was planning on coming out that way tomorrow anyway. So I'll see you girls then, all right?"

Jory said nothing.

"All right?"

"Okay."

"Go to sleep, Jory."

"Dad."

"Go to sleep."

"Good night, Dad."

So Handsome had leaped up onto the kitchen counter and was cautiously sniffing the half-empty pan of gingerbread. Jory picked him up by his middle and carried him back upstairs to her bed. The sheets were still faintly warm from where she had been sleeping. She pulled the wedding quilt

386

up to her nose and tried to still her heart. Her father would fix things. He would come out here and talk to Grace and he would fix things. She stared up into the darkness of the bedroom ceiling. She could feel So Handsome kneading his tiny claws over and over into the blanket covering her toes. She reached down and pulled him up to her face so that she could hear the subterranean rumble of his purring.

Their father was in the living room with Grace. He was perched on the brown chair directly facing Grace, who was sitting on the dead cat couch with her arms crossed. Jory had been banished to the front porch, where she had stayed for about two minutes before sneaking around to the side of the house. She was now crouched down among the dead hollyhocks, listening beneath the side window. She could hear what was being said, although it was like listening while having a blanket thrown over her head. "I'm just trying to figure out how much to worry here," her father was saying. Jory imagined him rubbing the bridge of his nose.

"There's no need to worry at all." Jory could picture the type of smile that her sister would be wearing.

"Well, of course I am," said her father.

"But there's still no need," said Grace.

There was a long silence during which Jory tried to rearrange her squatting position. A persistent fly kept landing on her calf and she kept swatting it away.

"I read in my *Merck Manual* about something called trichotillomania. People feel a strong desire to pull their hair out. It's a . . . syndrome of some sort."

"All I did was cut my hair, Dad."

There was another protracted silence.

"Well, it's a rather unusual haircut."

"I couldn't find the scissors."

"Grace."

There was another lengthy moment of silence and then Jory could hear her father clearing his throat and possibly recrossing his legs. "Your sister is worried about you."

Jory crouched farther down in the flowerbed, as if they could suddenly both see her. She closed her eyes.

Her father's voice grew more faint. "Jory also mentioned something about your eyebrows."

Jory sighed and shut her eyes even tighter.

Grace said something brief that Jory couldn't make out.

"She's just concerned," her father said.

"I have to do what God wants me to do, Dad."

"God wants you to be hairless?"

"Is that supposed to be funny?"

"Maybe," said her father. "Maybe I'm having to resort to humor."

"This isn't a joke."

"Oh, I know," her father said sadly.

"It was you who taught me that God sometimes asks us to make sacrifices. And that I had to be willing to do whatever was required, no matter how odd or painful it might be."

"But why did it have to be this . . . this particular sacrifice?"

"I don't know exactly," said Grace. "It just did."

Jory guessed that her father was shaking his head or maybe folding and refolding his hands.

"You know, when we had our Bible studies, you said that Jesus cried in the garden. That he begged his father to let the cup pass from him, and that he was so scared he sweat drops of blood, but that he still didn't turn away from the cross. He still faced his own bodily sacrifice."

"But you're not Jesus. You don't have to be crucified."

"I'm a child of God too."

"You're *my* child."

"I'm both," said Grace.

This seemed to silence their father completely, and the lack of noise from inside the living room continued on so long that Jory began to stand up in anticipation of bolting from her hiding spot. But then her sister made a muffled statement of some kind. Jory squatted back down again, and Grace said something else that Jory couldn't hear.

"Well," said their father. "What if I bought you some special scissors or something so you could sort of . . . even it out?"

"Why? Why does this even matter, Dad?" For a second, Jory couldn't believe this was Grace. She sounded genuinely mystified or perhaps hurt. "Do I look that strange and horrible? Do I really look terrible to you now?" *Bereft* was the word Jory had been searching for. *Forsaken.* "Dad, do you think I look *ugly*?"

"No," her father said. "Of course not. You are beautiful. You're my beautiful girl."

"But you can see my birthmark now." Jory had never heard her sister say the word *birthmark* out loud. Ever. To anyone.

"That's perfectly all right," her father said with firm emphasis.

"But everyone can see it now. Every part of it." Grace's voice still sounded as if it belonged to someone else. A young and pitiful someone whom Jory had never met. Jory could hear her sister making some sort of noise, a crying or sobbing sound deep in her throat. And then she said something else that Jory couldn't decipher. Jory suddenly felt as if she were listening to something she shouldn't.

"It doesn't matter." Her father's voice was pitched soft and low, as if he were speaking to a wild creature he didn't want to alarm. "You'll always be lovely — my very lovely girl."

So Handsome trotted around the corner of the house and leaped, clinging to Jory's bare thigh. Jory gave a muffled shriek and sat solidly down in the dirt. The cat was climbing his way up her shirtfront and she was trying to detach his needlelike claws when Jory spied Mrs. Kleinfelter advancing toward their front door with a shallow cardboard box in her hand. Jory struggled up from the ground just as Mrs. K reached the door. When Jory came around the side of the house, she could hear her father opening the screen door and saying something in greeting.

"Oh, these are just the last of my Brandy-wines," Mrs. Kleinfelter said. "I have way more than I can possibly use."

Her father was holding the screen door

open, and Jory watched as Grace now appeared next to him in the doorway.

"Oh, *my,*" said Mrs. Kleinfelter, taking a small step backward and bumping into Jory.

Grace opened the door wider. She came out onto the porch and took the box from Mrs. Kleinfelter's hands. "Thank you so much," said Grace, her eyes still slightly teary. "These look wonderful."

"My," said Mrs. Kleinfelter again, taking covert glances at Grace's hair and wiping her hands on the front of her housedress. "I just had way too many. So I guess . . . Oh, *Jory.*" Mrs. K turned her alarmed eyes on Jory. "Just look how big that kitten of yours is getting."

Jory gamely held So Handsome up for inspection.

"You know, we've been having some pretty hot days for October," their father said.

"Oh, yes," said Mrs. Kleinfelter. "Cooling down at night, though."

"Yes," said their father, nodding.

"I'll take these and put them on the kitchen counter," said Grace, turning and going back into the house.

"Well, I'll just get back to my packing." Mrs. Kleinfelter gestured toward her house and then began going down the porch stairs. Suddenly she stopped. "Oh, dear," she said.

"She didn't get ringworm, did she? From the cat, I mean?"

Jory glanced at her father, who studiously avoided his daughter's gaze. "Um, no, no ringworm," he said. "But we certainly thank you for the tomatoes." Her father smiled. He lifted his hand as if conveying some sort of benediction.

Mrs. Kleinfelter gave Jory a fleeting look and Jory felt a sudden tug, a strong urge to do or say something, but then the moment passed and Mrs. Kleinfelter turned away and headed back down the dirt pathway between the houses.

"She's a nice woman," said her father to himself. "She reminds me of your grandma Eunice."

"If Grandma Eun hadn't been completely cross and mean and horrible," Jory said.

Her father sighed. "Grandma Eun had a hard life." He sat down on the porch's top step with a slight groan.

"What are you going to do now?"

Her father said nothing. So Handsome tugged happily at one of his shoelaces.

Jory lowered her voice. "She's getting worse," said Jory.

"Oh, I don't know about that," said her father. He plucked a pen out of his pants pocket and took its cap off and then put it back on again.

"She's not eating, either. She says she's fasting."

Her father recapped the pen again. "There's nothing wrong with fasting."

"Not even if you're pregnant? And she never takes a shower or changes her clothes or anything. She's been wearing the same dress for at least a month now."

Her father stuffed the pen back into his pocket. "What exactly do you expect me to do, Jory? Stand over her while she eats and changes her clothes? You know what she's like. She's been this way since she was tiny."

"I know." Jory scooped So Handsome up into her arms and then just as quickly dropped him onto the porch's wood floor. "I know," she said again.

"Her hair will grow back," her father said. "In a while."

The two of them sat on the porch steps saying nothing. Mrs. Kleinfelter came outside and waved once as she headed into her garden. So Handsome lay down by the porch railing in a patch of October shade and began absently batting at a lone fly. The maple tree, which was turning early, dropped its fiery leaves, one at a time, onto the still green grass.

"I spoke to a doctor." Her father said this

394

without looking at her.

Jory felt a knot in her stomach tighten. "You did? What do you mean? What doctor?"

"He's a sort of specialist."

"A specialist?"

Her father paused. "A Christian psychiatrist."

"You mean the one from Blackfoot?" Jory wasn't sure why this suddenly seemed important.

Her father still wouldn't look at her. He plucked a long blade of grass out from a crack in the concrete step. "I spoke to him confidentially, of course."

Jory didn't really know what this meant. "What did he say?"

"Well, it doesn't really matter what he said. I just wanted you to know that I am not unaware of the problems here. And I *am* doing something, or as much of something as I can do."

Jory could feel the knot of tightness in her stomach rising up toward her throat. "But what did he think was wrong with Grace?"

Her father paused. "As I already said, I don't think his analysis is really worthy of discussion."

Jory gave him a pleading look.

Her father stared briefly up at the sky. "He

is under the belief that someone with Grace's type of behavior would benefit from a particular sort of treatment." Her father spread the blade of long grass out flat against his pant leg. "And medication."

The tightness in Jory's throat made it hard for her to speak. "You mean like tranquilizers?"

"Not exactly." Her father brushed the blade of grass off his pant leg. "But this man is not an evangelical Christian, remember. He's a Methodist and all his training was done at a large liberal university, where the empirical is the only thing that matters — so his analysis of things is somewhat shortsighted, to say the least."

Jory's father had gone to Harvard for both undergrad and his PhD, but that was somehow different. "*Mom's* taking tranquilizers," she said.

"Well, yes," he said in a voice that betrayed his surprise, "but that's only temporary. And I've already started cutting her dosage back."

"Dr. Henry gave Grace a shot."

"That was an emergency, Jory."

"But what if it helped her? The treatment, I mean. The one this doctor was talking about."

Jory's father rearranged himself on the

porch step with some difficulty. "I think we've discussed this topic thoroughly now, don't you?" He started to stand.

"But if it *helped* her."

Her father made a sudden grimace, as if he had bitten down on something sharp. "You don't understand, Jory. She would have to be sent to . . . she would have to go to a hospital . . . and be hospitalized."

"At *Blackfoot*?"

The screen door opened and Grace walked out onto the porch. Jory and her father grew quiet. "So," said Grace, looking from one of them to the other. "Who's being sent to Blackfoot?"

"No one," said their father, pulling himself up by the porch railing. "No one is being sent anywhere. It was just a figure of speech."

"Like a metaphor?" Grace cocked her head. She stared at her father.

"Yes," he said. "Sort of. So, you know what? I just remembered that I have some groceries out in the car. Who wants to help me bring them in?" He tried to smile at the two of them. "Any volunteers?"

CHAPTER THIRTEEN

Jory peered at herself in Henry's old rectangular mirror. Mrs. Kleinfelter had loaned her an old eyebrow pencil and Jory had spent half an hour giving herself some very Egyptian-looking eyes. Or what she hoped were Egyptian-looking eyes. She had seen a picture in Rhea's *Seventeen* magazine of this girl with amazing sort of bat-wing eyeliner extending from the corners of her eyes and, well, now Jory looked quite different. A little smudgy and strange, but hopefully exotic and possibly even much older. She was wearing a paisley-flowered drawstring blouse that Rhea had given her along with a headband she had made herself out of a strip of felt and a peacock feather. She also had on her rust-colored bell-bottoms, her moccasins, and a wide brown belt that had belonged to Mrs. Kleinfelter's husband. Plus, she had plaited two little tiny braids in her hair on either side of her face and secured them with crochet thread strung with little beads. She was going for the Egyptian-hippie look. Or maybe the Egyptian-Indian-hippie look.

Grace had given no thought whatsoever to her look, unless you counted looking like a pregnant concentration camp victim. Grace, in fact, was sitting downstairs in the kitchen reading her King James Bible, wearing the same old brown dress she had been wearing for the past five or six weeks.

"What do you think?" Jory said, twirling once around for Grace's benefit.

Grace ran a hand up and over her bristly hair. It had apparently become a habit. "Halloween is a pagan holiday that celebrates evil behavior. And you're wearing an awful lot of eye makeup."

"Oh, don't be a poop," said Jory, and she sat down breathlessly at the kitchen table. She was too excited to be affected by her sister's punctiliousness. Even school had been fun today! They hadn't been allowed to wear real costumes because of what had happened with an Indian tomahawk the year before, but there had been candy in homeroom and the school secretary had played "The Monster Mash" over the intercom and the bus driver had on a long blond wig and devil horns. Even Mrs. Cross had worn skeleton earrings. Everything had been wonderful until someone lit a smoke bomb in the girls' lavatory and someone else smashed a pumpkin through the windshield of Mr. Mullinix's Pontiac. Then sixth period was canceled and school was let out early. Jory tried to give Grace her most winsome look. "Oh, please! You can come too. We used to go trick-or-treating all the time when we were little."

"That was before."

"Mom and Dad always let us go."

"Well, maybe they shouldn't have," said Grace. "It probably sends the wrong message to unbelievers when they see Christians celebrating something associated so closely with Satan."

"Oh — argh!" said Jory, jumping up from the table. "You *are* a complete drag, do you know that?"

"You know what the Tao says," Grace said, putting her finger in her Bible. *"Let the world pass as it may. Act and it is ruined, grab and it is gone."*

"What?"

"The Great Way is very smooth, but the people love the bypaths."

"Cut it out, Grace."

"Seriously, though, Jory. I just don't know if it's a good idea."

"Well, it's not like you can stop me." Jory readjusted her hair band.

Grace appeared unmoved by this statement. "I suppose not," she said. "Unless I called Dad." She seemed to momentarily weigh this possibility.

"You wouldn't do that," said Jory.

"No," said Grace. "Probably not."

Grace had never, ever told on Jory, not even when they were little and Jory had done a variety of supposedly bad things. The one thing Grace wasn't was a tattletale. Jory and Frances had happily told on each other many a time, but not Grace. Not telling was evidently part of her moral code.

"So come with me and be my chaperone. Make sure I stay out of trouble." Jory bounced up and down on the balls of her feet. "Please?"

"I don't know," said Grip. "Are you a Moonie, or someone with cancer?"

"Ha ha. Very funny," said Grace. "I am not in costume."

"Well, you've certainly done something interesting with your hair." Grip's widened eyes took in the ruined landscape of Grace's scalp. He appeared more than a little startled. "What's up with that?"

"How about me?" Jory quickly inserted

herself between them, put her hand on her hip, and turned her face so that it was in profile.

"Wow. Hm. You are . . . I don't know, Penelope Tree?"

Jory's face fell. "Who?"

"A very groovy model person from Great Britain. At least, I think she's from Great Britain. Maybe she's not. Maybe she's American. I forget."

"I'm supposed to be an Egyptian-Indian-hippie-princess."

"That's just what I said." Grip smiled at Jory. "You look perfect." He tilted his head at her. "It's kind of like looking into the future."

Jory had to turn around and pretend to be fixing the tie on her blouse. She could feel a huge smile rising up through her whole body.

"Well, it's obvious what *you* are," said Grace. And it was. Grip was an ice cream man. He was The Ice Cream Man. He had slicked his hair back beneath one of those old white paper army-shaped hats. The kind that could be folded flat and put in your back pocket. And he was wearing spotlessly white creased pants and a white short-sleeved button-down shirt that had *Larry* written on the right breast pocket. Jory felt almost shy around him. He was Grip, but a cleaner and older and maybe richer version, like a Grip who was living an entirely different life.

"All righty," he said. "Ladies — Egyptian and otherwise — your chariot awaits."

Jory sat in the back of the truck next to the freezer. The last time she had sat back there, Frances had been in the front and they had gone swimming with Grip in the canal. Jory blushed in the darkness just thinking about it. She had been so young and naive. She had known nothing about anything! It had been four — no, almost five months ago. A lifetime.

She leaned forward. "Grace has been reading your Tao stuff," she said.

"Really?" said Grip. "I'm surprised." Jory could see him smiling, even from where she was sitting.

"Govern a nation as you would fry a small fish," said Grace. "That's my favorite one."

Grip clucked his tongue. "Ah," he said. "You're making fun. I see how it is."

"I'm not," said Grace. "I think it's actually somewhat profound."

"Right," said Grip. "Okay, well, it's a rule that whoever sits in front has to learn to copilot the craft. Jory knows how, Frances

403

knows how, so now it's your turn."

"Oh, no," said Grace, and put her hands up to her face. "I don't know how to drive anything."

"Not yet, you don't. But the night is young."

"Don't we have lots of things we're supposed to be doing?"

"Yes, and the first one on the agenda is teaching you how to shift."

"*Frances* knows how to drive the truck?"

Jory leaned back and peered out the small oval rear window at the sky. Sure enough, there was the moon, big and fat and glowing, looking down at the world with its sad eyes and sorrowful mouth. She remembered the Childcraft books her father had read to them when she was little. In those stories the moon was less mournful and more scary — a half-sentient being who was slightly evil and often grinning or maliciously winking at the tiny humans below. It seemed to know things that no human would be happy to know, and it seemed to want to tell these things — to eagerly open its mouth and let the secrets spill forth in a bright spray of liquid silver that would turn to solid coins as they fell to earth, but still burned like fire if you tried to pick them up.

And if you went up to the moon, if you

rowed a green-bottomed boat through the sky or straddled a broom (like certain Childcraft creatures: cats and cows and wicked women and spoons), you came back terribly changed, or not at all. The moon exacted a heavy price for its dark knowledge. What it whispered in your ear, you could never unhear. But Jory longed to be told. And she was terrified of being told. And once you were told, well . . . who knew? Who knew?

Owls and bats and all shades of black and midnight blue. The planet Pluto. A wizard's pointy hat. A ball stamped with gold stars rolling into a room all by itself. A girl with one striped sock living all alone in a two-story house on the edge of nowhere. An apple so neon green it glowed, with one bite missing.

"The clutch is the hardest part," Grip was saying. "We'll wait and try that on the way home."

Grace refused to say anything. She was entirely intent on shifting into third.

"Where are we going to go?" Jory peered out the window at each of the darkened houses, hoping to see jack-o'-lanterns and kids in ghoulish costumes running by.

"Well," said Grip, pitching his voice girl-ishly high and pretending to flip his hair behind his back, "I hear there's a really superior spook house out at Dave Van-Manen's. Evidently Dave's dad is letting him use their barn and everything and it's going to be really fun and cool and majorly scary."

Grace turned around and gave Jory a dark look. "Jory, we cannot go to the ACA party."

"Why not?" Jory asked.

Grace said nothing.

Jory leaned forward. "What if we just went for a little bit? Just long enough to say hi to people."

Grace continued saying nothing.

Jory leaned back. "It was just a thought."

"Hey," said Grip. "We could go out to Hope House. You know, that great big old blue house on Chicken Dinner Road."

"The *hippie house*?" Jory leaned forward again. "The one with the painted eye on the front?"

"You know those people?" There was a note of dismay in Grace's voice.

"Sure. A little bit." Grip grinned at Grace. "Hippies like ice cream too." He turned and glanced back at Jory. "What do you say, Miss Penelope — shall we take a little look-see?"

"Are you sure this is the kind of place we should be going?" Jory could almost hear

Grace raising her eyebrows.

"Oh, I think it's pretty safe. Besides, you'll be with me, right?"

"I want to go," said Jory. "Anyway, I think I do. It's Hallo*ween,*" she said.

"That's the spirit." Grip made a wide left-hand turn and headed down a slightly bumpy dirt-packed road. "It's down here on the right somewhere. I remember it being past the old water tower a little ways."

The ice cream truck bounced along down the long dirt road and Jory was forced to hold on to the headband's peacock feather that she had pilfered from a box in Henry's basement. They drove along for maybe a mile or two as the dirt road got progressively narrower and less navigable, with Jory bumping her head on the truck's ceiling every little bit.

"Okay," said Grip. "That's it up there." He pointed out the windshield to the right.

"Oh," said Jory. "Look. They're having a bonfire. Or something." She shivered slightly.

Grip pulled the truck into some kind of a long, weedy driveway that was overhung by several large, drooping willow trees. He stopped the truck next to an old school bus painted a swirling lilac purple. The bus had a small-shingled roof affixed to the top of it, and a large ropy hammock was strung between the bus's bumper and one of the willow trees.

"Whoa," said Jory, getting out of the truck. She wasted only a moment's notice on the purple bus. The hippie house itself was several shades of blue and had a huge kohl-lined eye painted directly above its front door. "Look — it has an eye just like our house," Jory said.

"*Our* house has an eye?" Grace stumbled over something in the grass and Grip grabbed her arm to steady her.

"It's the third eye," Grip said. "A symbol of enlightenment or wisdom."

"More Buddhism, I suppose." Grace readjusted her dress front.

Several large glowing metal stars hung down from the porch's overhang. Jory went up the porch steps and gazed reverently at the stars.

"They're punched tin, I think," said Grip. He lifted one by its bottom point. "See? With lit candles inside."

"Oh," said Jory, pointing at the house's front window. Hanging just inside it was a large metal moon: bronze colored and crescent shaped and holding a large golden candle in its horn. "This is so beautiful!"

"Should we even be here?" said Grace,

glancing back at Grip. "It's not like we were invited or anything."

"Oh, please," Jory begged. "I just want to see what everything looks like."

Just then a man with a long dark braid who was wearing white overalls came out of the semidarkness. "Hey there," he said, looking not at all surprised to see them. "Everybody's around back. Come on through." He walked up the porch steps and opened the front door. Jory noticed that the door had a knocker in the very middle of it shaped like an owl. The owl's eyes moved back and forth when she lifted its perch. Inside, the house smelled like some kind of thickly perfumed smoke and there were several people, all of them long-haired and barefoot, sitting or lying on mattress-like things spread across the floor. "Hey," these people all said to them and nodded in a lazy unconcerned way. Everywhere there were intricately woven red rugs and long draping curtains that seemed to melt down right into the floor. They walked through an entryway of hanging red beads that clicked and clacked together when Jory passed between them. Red and yellow candles burned on every surface, and Jory had a momentary glimpse of the ceiling that seemed to be covered with faintly glowing golden stars. "Oh," Jory said in response to each new sight. "Oh, wow."

The overalls-wearing man held the back door open for them. Grip took hold of Grace's and Jory's hands and walked them around the side of the house and then down a curving path of large flat stones placed in the ground. Sad and soft guitar music drifted toward them, and up ahead a group of people stood around an enormous metal barrel or drum that had a fire burning inside. There were faces carved in the large metal drum like those on a jack-o'-lantern, except here there were different faces making different expressions all around the circumference of the drum. Faces that grimaced and grinned and howled as the flames behind them flickered and danced. A man across from them was strumming a guitar and singing something, but Jory couldn't make out any of the words. Whatever he was saying got caught up with the fire's sparks and drifted up into the sky. Some of the people in the circle were swaying and moving languidly in time to the music, although others seemed to be moving in time with something only they could hear.

Jory watched as a girl across from the burning drum moved slowly around in a circle, her hair and arms swinging out behind her. As she twirled, her long-fringed skirt flared out like the unfurling trumpet of a flower — an Easter lily or a morning glory. The twirling girl swirled and swirled faster and faster and finally fell to the ground as if she had suddenly lost all of her bones. No one in the circle made any move toward the girl or even looked her way.

"This is too strange." Grace tugged on Grip's hand. "These people are doing some kind of heathen worship thing."

"Nah," said Grip. "I think they're just trying to have some fun."

The long-haired man with the guitar walked slowly around the circle singing. He slowed and stopped next to Grip and gave him a long, strange look that Jory couldn't decipher. She could, however, make out the words to his song — it was something about stardust and getting back to the garden. Or a garden. Something like that.

The guitar man had now made his way around to Jory. *"Before the snake,"* he sang, *"before the serpent stung."* He stopped and smiled at her and then began singing again.

"We were animals and birds
As unknowing as the stars
And we lived from day to day

411

In that golden bower called Love
Girl, don't let the forest fool you
Don't let the tree seduce you
That apple will undo you
If you give in to its charms."

The guitar man pressed something into Jory's hand and moved on again, singing another song. Jory opened her hand — it was a small square piece of waxed paper with tiny orange stars all over it. She put the paper in her pocket.

"Let's *go,*" said Grace. "These people are worshipping something other than God."

"I think they think they *are* worshipping God," Grip said. "But sure, okay, all right." He gazed back at the guitar man.

"Come on," Grace said. "I mean it."

Jory was so entranced that she hardly even protested as she was dragged away from the bonfire circle and headed back through the wet grass the way they had come. She gazed around her as they walked on up a little hill and then down. She didn't remember there being a hill before, but it was dark, so maybe there had been one. "Oh, look," said Jory, suddenly pulling on Grace's hand. "It's like the one we had when we were little — only a million times bigger!"

Off to the left was a huge canvas teepee of

sorts, large enough to hold at least a dozen people, and lit up from inside. It rose up into the darkness like a sort of glowing pyramid. "Oh, please, can't we just look?" Jory tugged at Grace's hand. "I just want to see what it's like to sit inside. Please?"

Grace said nothing, but allowed herself to be steered in the direction of the teepee. At the front of the tented structure a small flap of canvas had been folded back and stitched in place. Jory bent down and crept through the entryway and she pulled Grace in after her. Grip had to kneel down in order to squeeze through.

Inside the teepee, Jory felt suddenly horribly shy. Several long-haired girls and bearded, long-haired men wearing a variety of strange and exotic clothing — most of it fringed and beaded and embroidered — were sitting cross-legged on colored woven rugs around a small fire.

"Hi." A girl next to Grace grinned at the three of them. She had on a long white nightgown and her face was painted or tattooed so that she had three black teardrops falling from the corner of one eye. Her hair was long and crinkly and copper colored and hung all the way down her back. "I'm Annelise," she said. "Welcome."

Annelise! thought Jory. What a beautiful

name. If she could change her name, that is what she would change it to.

"I'm Grace. And this is my sister Jory and . . . our friend Grip."

Annelise held out her hand and Jory touched it briefly. It was like holding hands with a moth. Jory realized that in comparison to this girl, she, Jory, looked like she was wearing a costume, which of course she was. But this girl lived like this. All of these people did — they weren't dressed up for a holiday. Their clothes were worn in and dirty, and their hair was too. This was what they looked like every day.

The other people in the teepee nodded and went on staring at the fire and smoking. Grace and Jory and Grip all sat down on the floor. Jory stared up at the top of the teepee. There was a small circular opening where the tent poles converged and Jory could see a few stars in the night sky shining through. The smoke from the fire drifted up toward the opening in an almost straight line. It was somewhat hazy inside the teepee and the air smelled faintly like fresh cow manure or maybe a run-over skunk. Jory could now see that Annelise was wearing a sort of crown. A flat crown of small metal circles linked around her head.

"Where did you get your crown?" said

Jory, trying not to blush.

Annelise put her hand to her head. "Angel made it," she said. "He does all our metal-work. He has a shop out behind the barn." She stared directly at Jory and Jory saw that Annelise's eyes were two different colors: one was brown and the other was some lightish color, like blue or maybe green. "He's making me a crib for the baby too. It's going to have fish carved into it. Beauti-ful fish with silver scales. You know, for Pisces and everything."

Grace turned to Annelise. "You're *pregnant*," she said, her voice catching.

Annelise put her hand on her belly. "Four months to go. Angel says it's going to be a boy." She smiled. "He did the thread-and-needle test three times."

"Angel is the baby's father?" Grace's eyes were bright.

"Maybe," said Annelise, and she laughed. She looked around the circle of people and some of them laughed too. "I don't know who the father is. It could be anyone." She smiled happily at them and shrugged. "That's the way we do things here. We share."

"What do you mean?" Grace looked from Annelise to Grip. "Oh," she said, her voice dropping and falling away.

"Well, um," said Grip, "that's to be admired, I suppose. In principle. How are y'all's crops this year and everything?"

"But aren't you worried?" Grace interrupted. She leaned forward toward Annelise. "Aren't you worried about what God will think?"

"What? Oh," said Annelise. "Are you one of those? Is that why your hair's all shaved off?"

Jory closed her eyes and wished herself somewhere else. Anywhere else.

"We've had Moonies out here before, but someone usually finds them and carts them back, just like that." She snapped her fingers.

Grace's horror was undisguised. "Sun Myung Moon is a false messiah. He created a cult that turns people away from the real truth of God."

"So, what then? Are you a Jesus Freak?"

"Well," said Grace. "Yes, I guess maybe I am. If that means loving Christ with all your heart and soul and mind and body."

Annelise nodded. "My mom was a Holy Roller. She drove everybody around her fucking nuts. Especially my dad. He took off with a woman from the post office the first chance he got." She smiled with complete equanimity. "We don't believe in

416

organized religion here. Every major war since the beginning of time has been caused by religion, you know. It's a terribly divisive force — plus it represses women. Makes them wear habits and veils and denies their sexuality. Totally Dark Ages stuff."

"But Christ loves you." Grace was practically whispering now. "Even if you don't believe. Even if you *are* living in terrible sin, he's still willing to save you."

"Okay," said Grip, tugging at Grace's arm. "C'mon. Let's go. Sorry," he said, looking back at Annelise. "It was really nice meeting you." Grip pulled Grace up to her feet and then pushed Jory and Grace back out of the teepee's opening. Suddenly they were outside again in the bitter night air. They started struggling back up the small hill, walking and bumping along together in the dark.

"She's totally misguided," said Grace. "She doesn't know what she's saying! Christ was a huge advocate of women. He loved the two Marys. And Martha. He wants women to be their own best, true selves. He doesn't want to restrict them or keep them from experiencing true joy."

"Okay, okay," said Grip.

"Yes, he wants obedience, and sometimes that means sacrifice and giving up certain things — not doing everything in the world you might want to do. But that sacrifice leads to perfect peace. And joy. And eternal life." Grace stumbled on something and nearly fell, but Grip caught her by the elbow. "And don't apologize for me." She pulled her arm away from him. "If you don't like what I'm saying, then leave, but don't drag me away like I'm some crazy relative of yours that you're ashamed of."

"We're on their property," Grip said quietly.

"Yes," said Grace, "thanks to you." She stopped still in the grass. "I don't even *know* you," she said.

"Grace," said Jory.

"I don't," said Grace. "And neither do you, Jory." She crossed her arms. "Don't you have any family? Or any friends? Like ones your own age?"

Grip said nothing.

"And where do you even live?"

"Stop it," said Jory. "Just stop it!"

The three of them stood in the dark, breathing heavily.

"Let's go," said Grip. "You can hate me all the way home, all right?"

No one said anything in the truck until they pulled into the driveway in front of Henry's house and Grip had turned off the ignition.

"I'm sorry that I got so angry," said Grace. Her voice was small and quiet even in the enclosed space of the truck. "I don't like being patronized."

"No one does," Grip said.

"My faith is very, very important to me."

"That's fine," said Grip. "That's good and great, but not everyone is going to feel like you do, and believe it or not, not everyone has to."

Jory sat in the back of the truck feeling as small and unnoticed as when she hid in Frances's closet and listened in on her parents' arguments.

"I have a calling," said Grace. "And I can't ignore that responsibility just because it's awkward or someone isn't going to like what I say."

Grip took off his ice cream man hat and folded it in two. "Then I guess you'll have to get used to people saying things back to you. And telling you things you don't want to hear."

"I guess so."

"I guess so."

"Okay, then. Fine," said Grace. She opened the truck's door and got out. "Come on, Jory."

"I'll be in in a minute." They both watched

as Grace climbed the stairs to the house and went inside and shut the door. They watched as she turned on a single light.

Jory slid up and over into the front seat.

"Well, happy Halloween." Grip tugged at the feather in Jory's headband.

Jory snatched the headband off and held it in her lap. "She spoils everything."

"No, she doesn't. It just seems like that right now."

"Right now and always."

Grip laughed. "Her intentions are good." He turned sideways in his seat. "She's a very honorable person."

"You don't think I'm an honorable person?"

"No." He laughed again. "You're more like me."

"Well, thanks a lot, I guess."

"I just mean that you're more human. You do more of what you want to all the time. You don't struggle so much."

"I struggle," said Jory.

"Not like that," he said, gesturing back toward the house. "That's a hard road. That takes a weird form of guts." He shook his head.

"I have guts," said Jory, knowing immediately how untrue this was.

"Sure you do," said Grip. "So time to go

in and face the music. With guts."

Jory pulled the feather out of the head-band and let it fall onto the floor. "Where *do* you live?"

"Well, Missy Miss, if you must insist on knowing every little detail of my life . . . I live at the Bali Hai Trailer Court out on Rim Road. Space number 23. It's very, *very* posh, you know."

"How old are you?"

Grip stared fixedly out the windshield. "How old do you think I am?" His voice sounded deliberately casual.

Jory blinked several times. "Twenty-two," she said finally. "Or twenty-three."

"Good guess," said Grip. "Give or take a few."

"And why don't you have any friends your age?"

Grip turned to her with a mock look of exasperation. "I do," he said. "Good God, woman!"

But for the very first time Jory could hear that he was lying.

"Okay," she said, and leaned over and kissed him on his freshly shaved ice cream man cheek. "Night," she said, and raced to open the door before she could feel the extent of her daring. She clattered up the stairs and flung open the door to Henry's house. Halloween was over.

CHAPTER FOURTEEN

Rhea wasn't grounded anymore. At least not as utterly grounded as she had been, which meant that Jory and Laird were going to go to Homecoming with Rhea and . . . Randy Asumendi. This turn of events was, in Jory's view, Shakespearean in its scope and perfectly unexpected expectedness. They were reading *Romeo and Juliet* in English I, and Jory was trying to write an essay about the idea of the inexorability (she had looked this up) of fate. Fate in quotation marks. Fate, according to William Shakespeare. So far, she had one small paragraph and several extensive doodlings of vines and stars and winking moons.

Fate had also decreed that they would have a quiz in earth science today, and that Jory would not know the answers to questions 4, 17, 24, 28, and 33. And it did not matter how long she might sit contemplating and clicking the lead to her mechanical pencil in and out — she was never going to know the answers to these particular questions. She had not studied. Not nearly enough. She sighed and reread question number 4: "What is the age of the most abundant surface bedrock in the Finger Lakes region of New York State: Cambrian, Devonian, Pennsylvanian, or Permian?" This seemed like a trick question, and did it have anything to do with the fact that Pennsylvania was somewhere close-ish to New York? Jory sighed again. She could feel a trickle of sweat making its way down the inside of her sister's bra.

Laird glanced up from his quiz. *What's wrong?* his eyebrows asked.

Everything, hers answered. She made an even more despairing face.

Laird leaned back in his chair and stretched, moving his quiz paper slightly in Jory's direction. Jory squinted hard at Laird's printing. *Devonian* was the answer to number 4. *Devonian,* she wrote down on her paper.

"Miss Quanbeck and Mr. Albright?" Mr. DeNovia was looking sharply in their direction. "Bring your papers and come up to my desk, please."

Jory picked up her paper. Her heart was pounding and she felt suddenly sick to her stomach. Some tiny perverse part of her was making her face do strange things: the corners of her mouth kept jerking upward as she walked past the other quiz-taking students, who appeared both intrigued and empathetic at this unexpected expectedness.

"You find this amusing?" Mr. DeNovia took Jory's paper and then took Laird's and placed them both facedown on his desk.

"No," whispered Jory. "My face just does that sometimes." She blushed furiously.

"You know I'm going to have to report this." Mr. DeNovia looked genuinely unhappy. "Plus, you'll both get failing grades on the quiz." He sighed and pulled at his eyebrow. "Don't you people ever learn?" He pitched his voice loud enough for the whole class to hear. "Can't you think of something more original?"

"Like what?" said a boy in the back row. "There's only so many ways to cheat."

Muted laughter ran through the room. Mr. DeNovia clapped his hands. "Anyone else want to flunk this quiz?" The classroom was immediately silent.

"Go upstairs to Mr. Mullinix's office. I'll meet you there after class." Mr. DeNovia shook his head. "Go on," he said. "Get."

The school secretary gave them both a

scowlingly sympathetic look. Everyone else had left for the day. The buses had come and gone. The janitors were mopping the floors and emptying the garbage cans. Rhea had walked past the office a long time before and stuck out her tongue at them in a show of solidarity. Jory's father and Laird's mother were now in the inner office with Mr. Mullinix. Jory and Laird were in the reception area sitting on the squeaky orange chairs.

"How mad will he be?" Laird whispered.

"Mad enough not to say anything about it for a while." Jory slumped a little lower in her chair.

"My mom's gonna kill me," said Laird. "And she's not gonna wait till later, either."

"Tell her it was my fault. Seriously. Tell her I forced you to let me look at your paper." Jory sat up. "Or that you didn't even know that I was looking at your paper."

Laird shrugged. "It doesn't matter," he said in a tone of voice that revealed how very much it did.

The office door opened and Dr. Quanbeck and Mrs. Albright stepped out, followed by Mr. Mullinix. None of them was smiling.

"Bye," whispered Laird.

"I'm sorry," whispered Jory.

■ ■ ■ ■

Jory wondered how many silent car trips this made for her. Surely quite a few. Her father stopped the car in Henry Kleinfelter's driveway and ran his hand through his hair and then rubbed his eyes and the bridge of his nose. Finally, he put both his hands back on the top of the steering wheel. Turning his head as if it hurt to do so, he regarded his daughter. "Are you trying to get back at me? To punish me for moving you girls out here?"

"No," said Jory, but it came out as more of a squeak. Or half a squeak.

"Well, of the little I know of psychology, it certainly seems like a possibility." Her father paused and simply sat staring out the windshield.

"Dad," said Jory.

He didn't change expression or move his head.

"I'm sorry," she said.

"I know," he said.

They sat in the car. Neither one of them said anything more.

Mrs. Kleinfelter was standing on their front porch in the waning afternoon light. She

427

had a wriggling So Handsome squeezed in a headlock next to her flatish bosom. She waved at Jory's father as he reversed out of the driveway and then turned as Jory came up the steps. "I was just going to knock. Here," she said, thrusting the kitten at Jory. "You missed all the fun."

Jory let herself look as sad as she felt. "Were the shots bad? Did So Handsome cry?"

"He certainly mewed some." Mrs. Kleinfelter wiped her hands down the front of her dress. "He has to go back in four weeks for a second round. You can come and be a part of the painful process then."

Jory opened the front door and ushered Mrs. Kleinfelter inside.

Grace got up from the couch. "Where have you been? Was that Dad?"

Jory sat down in the horsehair chair. She let her bag drop onto the floor next to her.

Grace lifted her empty tuna salad bowl off the coffee table and set it on the floor. The kitten jumped down after it. "What? Did you miss the bus again?"

"No," said Jory. "I cheated on my earth science quiz."

"Oh, dear," said Mrs. Kleinfelter. She pursed her lips. "Maybe I should be heading home."

"Jory." Grace looked genuinely shocked. "You cheated?"

Jory examined her skirt hem.

"Why did you do that?"

"I don't know," said Jory, shrugging slightly. "I didn't know some of the answers."

"You've never cheated before." Grace was silent for a second. "Have you?"

Jory shook her head.

"I'm so surprised," said Grace. Her face wore an expression quite a bit worse than surprise.

"Oh, I don't *know*," said Mrs. Kleinfelter. "Doesn't everyone cheat sometime? I'm sure I probably did on something or other."

Grace looked at Mrs. Kleinfelter with dismay. "I don't really think that's a good excuse. Simply because it's common behavior doesn't make it good behavior."

"Oh, well," said Mrs. Kleinfelter. "It's probably not the end of the world."

"Would you say that to your own child?" Grace's brows knit together.

Mrs. Kleinfelter thought. "Maybe not," she said.

Grace seemed somewhat mollified. She turned to Jory. "What happened after that? Did you flunk the quiz?"

"Yes," said Jory. "I certainly did. And I

have to miss school for the rest of the week."

"That's their idea of punishment?" Mrs. Kleinfelter pushed a stray bobby pin into her hair. "Interesting."

"Well, I just don't know," said Grace. She smoothed her dress down over her rounding front, then turned and went into the kitchen.

Jory and Mrs. Kleinfelter watched the kitten licking Grace's bowl clean and cleaner.

"You were right," Jory said. "That night after the party when you told me it wouldn't be the last time I'd disappoint her."

"Well," said Mrs. Kleinfelter. "That wasn't very nice of me to say, was it?"

"It was true, though," said Jory.

"She's an easy person to disappoint." Mrs. Kleinfelter bent and picked up So Handsome's peacock feather toy off the floor. "Her standards are fairly high."

"*She* lives by them, though."

"Hm," said Mrs. Kleinfelter. "Well."

So Handsome leaped at the bottom of Mrs. Kleinfelter's dress, snagging his claws in the process. Jory detached the kitten and scooped him up and held him under her arm like a purse. "I don't think Laird will get to take me to Homecoming now."

"Homecoming?"

"A boy actually asked me." Jory smiled

430

into the cat's fur. "But I'm pretty sure they don't let suspended people go."

"Maybe they'll have forgotten about it by then."

"It's three weeks from now."

"Oh."

"It doesn't matter. Grace would never have let me go."

"I suppose not." Mrs. Kleinfelter began rebuttoning her cardigan. "With the dancing and everything. There is dancing, isn't there?"

Jory nodded. "I don't know how to dance anyway."

"Oh, you just move around some." Mrs. Kleinfelter waved her hands back and forth. "Nothing to it."

"That's what you say about everything."

"Well, that's what it looks like on the TV — all they do is jump around and wiggle-waggle their bottoms a little."

"No," said Jory, laughing. "You have to look really cool. Especially me — I'd have to look more than okay because everyone at Schism already thinks I am the weirdest, most uncool person ever."

"Obviously not everyone thinks that." Mrs. Kleinfelter smiled.

"Maybe not entirely everyone." Jory held the kitten up by its front legs and made it take several steps across the floor on its hind legs. "What will I do for the rest of the week?"

"Well, you can help me pack up some of my things. How's that for a fun project?"

"But no one's even come to look at your house yet."

"No, but if I get started now, I'll actually be ready when they do."

"You know," said Jory, "if you pack up and move, you'll just have to unpack, and you know how much you hate that."

Mrs. Kleinfelter shook her head.

"I think maybe you should just avoid unpacking altogether."

"By the by," Mrs. Kleinfelter said, lowering her voice and glancing toward the kitchen, "what on earth did happen to her hair? I know your father said no ringworm, but those patchy spots look kind of, well, diseased maybe?"

Jory briefly considered trying to answer this. "It's not a disease," she said. "It's just Grace."

"That sounds almost motto-ish." Mrs. Kleinfelter waved the peacock feather as she walked to the front door. "All right — whatever you say. See you tomorrow," she said, "bright and early."

"Yes, ma'am," said Jory. She waved the

kitten's paw good-bye.

Mrs. K had a lot of junk. No, *stuff* — she had a lot of *stuff*. Jory still had a hard time thinking without her mother's interfering voice editing her thoughts. She and Mrs. Kleinfelter had packed up at least six boxes of *stuff* from just the basement, and these were big boxes.

Jory looked up from the glass of Tang that she was drinking. She and Mrs. K were taking a momentary break.

Mrs. Kleinfelter pushed herself up from the table and walked over to the refrigerator. "How about some lunch? I have bologna and . . . bologna."

"I'll take bologna," said Jory.

"Do you want mustard?"

"I don't know. Is it good?"

"You've never had mustard?"

"No." Jory pulled the rubber band off the end of one of her braids and began rebraiding her hair. "Once, when we were little, my dad took us to Givens Hot Springs and Frances said, 'Bathtub. Big, big bathtub!' She'd never seen a swimming pool before. But later, when we got older, we couldn't go anymore because it would be considered mixed bathing — you know?"

"Mixed bathing?" said Mrs. Kleinfelter.

She spread some mustard on Jory's sandwich and handed it to her on a plate. "Weren't the people wearing swimming suits?"

"Oh, sure, but in our church you're not supposed to go swimming with men if you're a woman and vice versa. And no dancing or going to pool halls or circuses. But anyway, at Givens we got to have hot dogs, which was exciting, but no mustard because it made my dad's scalp tingle."

Mrs. Kleinfelter made a funny face and then sat down at the table with her own plate. "What's wrong with circuses?"

"Oh, they have sideshows and women wearing revealing costumes. Things like that." Jory took a bite of her sandwich. She chewed. "Hey, that's pretty good." She took another large bite. "Sort of sour and tangy, but good."

"You are a strange child," said Mrs. Kleinfelter. She gazed fondly at Jory and then picked up her plate and carried it over to the sink. "Was that enough packing for today?"

"Yes," said Jory. "But do you think you could teach me to dance?"

Mrs. Kleinfelter's radio got only three stations: All-Country All-Day, Big Jack's Rock-

Around-the-Clock, and Easy Listening 95. Mrs. Kleinfelter and Jory were now slow dancing to "Smoke Gets in Your Eyes." Jory had never realized before that she and Mrs. Kleinfelter were almost exactly the same height. She had also never realized how strange it might be to hold an old woman around the waist and to lean your head against her bony shoulder and smell the strangely familiar scent of boiled potatoes that emanated from her old housedress. It was only Jory's extreme anxiety about not knowing how to dance that had brought her to this point, and if anyone came in Mrs. Kleinfelter's house at this moment, Jory thought she might die of true mortification. Although the fact that Mrs. Kleinfelter was willing to do this for her also made her feel slightly like crying.

"There," Mrs. Kleinfelter said, pulling back from Jory's nervous embrace. "See? Nothing to it." Mrs. Kleinfelter patted Jory on the arm and stepped briskly toward the radio. "Enough of that," she said, and switched off the dial. "Well, I don't know about you," she said, wiping her hands down the front of her dress, "but I've got some weeding to do." And without a backward glance, she walked to the back door and marched down the steps and left Jory

435

alone in the house.

Jory stood in the living room still feeling the imprint of Mrs. Kleinfelter's knobby hand in her own. She put her hands in her pants pocket and pulled out the tiny square of paper she found there. It was the paper the guitar man at Hope House had given her — the one with the orange stars on it. Jory ran her finger across the tiny stars and the orange print came off on her thumb. Jory licked the orange stars off and put the square back in her pocket. She remembered the guitar man pressing the paper into the palm of her hand with a certain firmness and singing that song she was embarrassed to hope was directed at her. Jory blushed in remembrance and sat down on the floor next to the row of boxes that she and Hilda had packed up. She picked up the roll of packing tape that was lying next to the boxes. The tape dispenser was unwieldy, though, and she kept getting the tape stuck to itself instead of to the box. "Poop," she said out loud, picking vainly at the edge of the tape. She finally pulled a length of tape off the roll, but she couldn't seem to manage to hold the box's lid down while also smoothing the tape down onto it. After several more tries, she sighed and stood up. She walked over to the row of porcelain figurines on Mrs. Kleinfelter's bookshelf and examined them all again, one at a time. Who would think that Mrs. Kleinfelter would make such tiny, exquisitely painted things? Jory picked up the glossy black panther. For some reason this one was her favorite. Maybe it was the jeweled green eyes or the panther's tiny pink tongue that seemed so incongruously sweet and candy-like coming from between those long white fangs. Jory touched the panther's tongue to her own. It had an actual taste — almost like chalk or dust — although it seemed like she was really smelling this dusty moldiness rather than tasting it. She pricked her finger on the point of the panther's fang. It was actually sharp. In fact, it felt like the panther was sliding its tiny fang deeply and sweetly into the tip of Jory's finger. It seemed to be deliberately biting her. "Hey, cut it out," she said and laughed, then put the panther down next to the ballerina. "Now behave," she said, and laughed again. Jory slid the tiny rickshaw driver back and forth across the smooth surface of the shelf. The rickshaw's wheels seemed to leave little blue-gold trails behind them. It was as if flames from the oven's gas burner were following behind the wheels. Jory closed her eyes, but the tiny wavering meteor trails were still

there — in fact, they were now sort of loop-
ing and spiraling in the most amazing and
horrifying way. Jory put the rickshaw down
and started heading toward the back door,
her heart in her throat. The kitchen, Mrs.
Kleinfelter's kitchen, was now the most
amazing shade of golden yellow, the warmest, most encompassing yellow Jory had ever
seen. The kitchen's walls were like some
kind of butter, heavenly butter that leaned
warmly toward Jory and breathed in and
out through buttery, fluttery gills. Why
hadn't she ever noticed this before? She put
her hand against the wall and tried to pet it,
to let it know that it was breathing beautifully. *Wait,* she thought. *Wait, this is not right.*
Something was utterly and terribly wrong
with the way her mind was seeing or thinking, and the minute she thought this, a
blank sort of encompassing horror swept
over her. Jory stumbled to the door and
seemingly went out it and maybe down the
steps. The sky outside was green like a 7Up
bottle, exactly like that, like the beautiful
transparent green of some candy that a girl
had brought for birthday treats in fourth
grade once. "It's called glass candy," the
girl had said, and it had tasted like spearmint, only sweeter, like spearmint mixed
with clover. That was the sky now too, and

438

Jory could taste the sky on her tongue like smoothest sweetest greenest glass. Jory sank down into the grass and gazed up at the sky, which was also gazing back at her. She smiled and it was like she could feel the sky filling her mouth, it was filling her mouth in a new sort of kissing, and it was like she had been doing this forever. She had been doing this forever, lying back against the curved surface of the world, or else this was what time actually was: one long moment that expanded out past the horizon, like the green glass sky that went on and up and out and all around. Or else it was all very small — time, that is — but the most concentrated small, like a tiny, dense black hole and the way things became too, too heavy in a black hole. *Too dense,* she thought. Too leaden. Too heavy laden. *Oh, no,* she thought. *Oh.* Her thoughts seemed to be like the words in a first-grade reading book and also the most amazing thoughts she had ever had, although she wasn't sure, absolutely sure, which thoughts she had ever had. There was one lone cloud in the vast green of the sky that separated out into letters, or maybe numbers. Maybe it was Aramaic. Ancient Aramaic. Maybe she should go to Blackfoot since she was obviously crazy. Maybe she and Grace were sisters in everything. More than sisters. *Grace,* she thought, and got up from the grass. The diamond-windowed house wavered into view. She climbed the front steps and it took forever because she kept having to step on the same step over and over. She watched a foot in a shoe stepping onto a stair and then the same foot (maybe) stepped onto a different (or maybe the same) stair. *That's my foot,* she said to herself. *And that's my shoe, my sweet old shoe.* She felt a sudden, overwhelming fondness for her shoe. But really, was it *her* shoe, or did it really just belong to itself, in all its very particular shoeness? And could you truly own a shoe, and if so, what did that mean or entail? Did ownership encompass or involve more than just housing a shoe in your closet and claiming it with your foot? The door to Henry's house opened of its own accord and someone was standing there and saying words. It was probably Grace, but Grace with a face that kept changing into someone else's face just long enough that Jory couldn't tell for sure who it was. Each time she was sure it was Grace, Grace would slyly switch her face. It was like a test that Jory was supposed to pass, but for a class she hadn't taken. "Don't do that anymore," Jory said. "Your nose looks too much like Pastor Ron's and your teeth aren't right either." Jory could tell from the look on Grace/Pastor Ron's face that neither of them was happy with her. She tried to tell them that she was sorry, very sorry, but they didn't seem to understand. "It's in ancient Aramaic," she kept saying. "I only just learned it today."

It took until Friday for Jory to come back to herself all the way. On Thursday night, the emergency room nurse had found the tiny square of paper in her pants pocket and then the doctor had given her a shot of something strong to counteract the effects of the first drug. Mrs. Kleinfelter had driven her home stretched out in the front seat of the truck and Grace had put her to bed, where she slept for the next fourteen hours. On Friday evening, Grip came to see her, but Grace met him at the door and sent him away. On Saturday night, Jory was lying on the dead cat couch trying to read Act IV in *Romeo and Juliet* when the back door opened and Grip walked clear through the kitchen and into the living room before Grace could stop him.

"Grip," said Grace, standing up. "Go away."

"Nope," said Grip. "Not going." He

moved over to the couch, right next to where Jory was lying. "I'm so, so sorry, Jory," he said. He had an old brown hat that he kept twisting around in his hands.

Jory realized with a sudden little jolt that she had never heard him say her name before. Ever.

"It's okay," she said. "It's not your fault." Her voice sounded faint and unconvincing, even to her. She cleared her throat. "It was just an accident. I mean, I didn't know what I was doing or anything."

"I should never have taken you out there. It was a stupid idea. Stupid."

Grace coughed briefly.

Jory sat up on the couch and pulled her knees up to her chest. "It's no one's fault. And I'm okay, so let's just forget about it."

Grip sighed and sat down on the arm of the couch. He glanced at Jory and then at Grace. "I took a little drive back out there last night," he said, "after you kicked me out." He gave the brown hat a toss and it sailed across the room and landed with a skid next to the horsehair chair. The kitten pounced on it and tried to drag it off toward the kitchen, his head held high.

"To the hippie house?" Grace put her crocheting down on the floor. "Why? What for?"

"Just wanted to repay the favor, that's all."

"Oh, no," said Grace. "What did you do?"

"Not much. Not nearly as much as I wanted to."

Jory's eyes widened. "You hit him?"

"Only a couple of times."

Jory let out a whoop of laughter and then covered her mouth with both her hands. "Oh, wow. That's awful," she said, suddenly looking serious. "No, it really is."

"That idiot deserved it." Grip shook his head over and over. "And somebody should have messed me up for taking you out there in the first place." He shook his head again. "I'm sorry," he said again, looking at Jory. "Really sorry."

"Hey," said Jory. She stood carefully up from the couch. "Look — I'm perfectly fine. See?" She shrugged her shoulders and tried to smile. "No more Aramaic."

"Don't, Jory." Grace took a deep breath, and then she too stood up. "This whole thing was just awful. I thought you were *dying,*" she said to Jory. "I thought you had been poisoned or had had a stroke or an aneurysm or something. And the whole ride to the hospital, that whole long, horrible ride, I was thinking desperately about how I was going to explain this to Mom and Dad. How I was going to have to call them up and tell them that you had died."

"I didn't though," Jory said feebly. "I didn't die."

Grace now stood in the kitchen doorway.

"This is all my fault," said Grip. "Every bit of it." He gave Grace a beseeching glance.

"It's all of our faults." Grace stood in the doorway a moment longer looking at Jory, and then she turned and went into the kitchen.

Jory sat on the couch with her head in her hands while Grip stood, shifting from foot to foot. "Oh, hell," he said suddenly. He had moved across the room and was looking out the front window. "Whose car is that?"

"Huh?" said Jory, pushing up behind him and moving the curtain aside. She gave a small gasp. "Oh, no — oh, no. That's my dad. You have to go." She gave him a shove. "Through the kitchen. C'mon . . . *hurry up.*"

"But my truck's out front."

"I know, I know . . . just go out back behind the bushes or the shed or something until he leaves."

"Behind the bushes?" Grip scooped up his hat from the floor and crammed it on his head. "*Je*sus."

Jory continued to push him through the

kitchen. "Dad's here," she hissed at Grace, who was pulling dishes and cups out of the dish drainer.

"I guess you might as well just face the music," Grace said, opening the cupboard and stacking the plates on top of each other.

"I hate that phrase," said Jory in a fierce whisper.

"Knock-knock," their father was calling out from the front door. The front door opened and then closed with a loud squeak and a sigh. "Anybody home in there?"

"Oh, shoot," said Jory, and sank down against the stove.

"It'll be okay," said Grip.

Jory gave Grip an incredulous look.

"Whose truck is that in the driveway?" Their father strolled into the kitchen, smiling quizzically and carrying a bag of groceries. He glanced at Grip. "Oh," he said with a small start.

Grip stepped forward and stretched out his hand. "Pleased to meet you, sir."

Their father shook Grip's hand with the briefest of motions. "And who are you exactly?"

"I'm a friend of your daughters." Grip gestured toward Jory and Grace as if to make clear exactly which daughters he was referring to.

"Thanks so much for bringing us the groceries, Dad." Jory tried to look pleased.

Grace walked directly between the two men and placed a handful of silverware down on the kitchen table. "Grip has been coming to our Sunday morning devotions, Dad. He's very interested in learning more about the Bible and how it relates to Eastern religious thought."

"I see," said their father. "You couldn't find a church of your own?" He cocked his head at Grip. "There are quite a number of good churches all over the city. Probably a half dozen of them."

Jory took the bag of groceries out of her father's arms. "Well, Grip's new to town and didn't know anyone or where to go to church or anything, so we said that until he found a home church of his own, he could come worship with us, like temporarily, because obviously we're not as good as a real church or anything but until he learns his way around Arco and everything, well, we thought it would be better than *nothing* . . ." Jory shifted the bag of groceries from one arm to the other.

"I see," their father said again. "And you girls are conducting services on Saturday nights now, too?"

"Oh, I just stopped by for a moment to

see if Jory was feeling all right, sir," said Grip.

"You've been sick? Grace didn't say anything about it on the phone." He turned his gaze toward Grace.

"I'm fine now," said Jory. "Perfectly fine. It was nothing really."

"Well," said Grip, "I should probably be taking off and leave you folks to your dinner, or whatever. It was nice meeting you." Grip stretched out his hand again and grasped their father's. "You have some very lovely daughters, Mr. Quanbeck — *Dr.* Quanbeck, sir, and, you know, I value their friendship very highly." Grip turned slightly. "Jory, I'm certainly glad you're feeling better." He nodded at the three of them and walked toward the front door.

"I'll walk you out," their father said, and he followed Grip out through the living room.

"Oh no oh no oh no," Jory whispered. As soon as the front door shut, she made a beeline for the front window. From her vantage point behind the curtain, she could see her father and Grip now standing next to Grip's truck. Grip had his hands in his pockets. Her father was doing all the talking. Every once in a while Grip looked up at her father and nodded briefly, his lips

pressed together, not even attempting to speak. After a moment or two, Grip got in his truck and her father turned back toward the house. Jory ran quickly back into the kitchen.

Grace was draining the boiled potatoes. "Mashed?" she said, not looking at Jory. She shrugged disconsolately. Grace handed her the bowl and the red-handled potato masher.

Their father came into the kitchen and sat down at the table. "So what have you girls got going there?" Their father's voice sounded deliberately and overly friendly. He rubbed his hands together. "What delicious thing are you cooking up tonight?" Jory was shocked by her father's tone. His strange lack of anger seemed to indicate something even worse.

"We're having hot dogs and canned corn," said Grace.

"And lumpy potatoes," said Jory.

"Hm," said their father, pulling a chair from the table and sitting down. "Doesn't sound too bad. Say, I wasn't planning on staying long, but I think maybe we should have a little talk. So I think I'll stick around for a bit, if that's okay with you two."

"But you don't eat hot dogs," said Jory weakly.

"Oh, I suppose one probably won't kill me. I've read that rat particles are a fairly good source of protein." He laughed briefly. "So, is there anything I can do to help?"

"You can set the table." Grace pointed to the left kitchen cupboard. "Plates and glasses are in there."

Their father eased his long legs out of his chair and walked over to where Jory was now standing next to the sink. "I talked to Mr. Mullinix yesterday," he said, opening the cupboard above her head, "and he said that the incident in earth science won't become a part of your permanent record. But that if there were a *repeat episode* — these are his words, not mine — you would be immediately expelled from school. And that that information most definitely *would* be placed in your file." Her father got down three dinner plates and stood next to her, holding them. "It made me wonder for a minute whether or not you did this thing simply to get out of going to school there." Her father sounded not just solemn, but sad. "Because if you did, that was certainly not the smartest way to go about it." He held the plates flattened against his chest as if protecting them from harm. "I would hate to see you ruin your high school career merely to prove a point to me."

Jory kept her eyes on her mashing. "I just didn't know the answers," she said, "and I was scared to flunk. You didn't even enter my thinking."

"I see," he said. Grace set two platters down on the table and seated herself next to Jory. Her father stood there a moment more, and then he pulled out a chair and sat down, taking a quick drink of milk and then clearing his throat again. "Actually, part of the reason I came over tonight was to bring you something, Grace." He reached into his jacket pocket and pulled out a slim colored brochure that he then laid on the table next to his plate, although he kept his hand on the bottom of the brochure as if worried that it might escape. Jory could see that there was a young woman on the front of the brochure who looked both serious and peaceful. *The Greatest Gift* was written in gold script right beneath the peaceful girl's face.

"What is that, Dad?" A hint of alarm had entered Grace's voice.

"Well," he said, "I sent for some information in the mail that I thought I would share with you." Their father sounded determined. He still had not moved his hand from the bottom of the brochure. "Your mother and I have been talking lately, and we want to make sure that — well, that you are able to go on with your life. That you are able to go to college and get your degree and be with people your own age. Things that are very important to a young woman." He ran his hand through his hair. "We think that this would be best for everyone — for you, and for . . . everyone."

"What exactly do you mean?"

Jory couldn't tell whether Grace was genuinely ignorant or willfully so.

"Well," said their father, giving the brochure a final pat and then sliding it in Grace's direction, "I'd like you to take a look at this."

"What is it?" said Grace, still refusing to look down at the brochure.

"Well, there are choices that a girl . . . in your position needs to consider. And I think, and your mother thinks — we both think — that this is the all-around best choice for everyone involved." He moved the brochure farther across the table toward Grace, but Grace pulled her hands away as quickly as if a large hairy insect were heading toward them.

"What is this *best choice* you're referring to, Dad? I'd like to hear you say exactly what it is."

"Grace," their father said in a now miserable voice. "This would be for your own good. All I want is for you to have the very best possible future you can have."

"And what about my baby's future? What about that?"

Jory had never heard Grace use that phrase before. *My baby.* Not God's baby. Not an angel's baby. *My* baby.

Their father picked up the brochure and quickly flipped through its glossy pages. "It says that they only place the children — the babies — with financially responsible, loving couples who are unable to become parents on their own. You would be doing them the hugest favor possible." Their father's voice wound down and dwindled. "It's the greatest of gifts," he said finally.

"You want me to give my baby away."

Their father said nothing.

"You want me to give my baby away, is what you're saying." Grace shoved her chair back from the table. Her napkin fell to the floor. "Isn't that what you mean?"

"Oh, honey," their father said. He reached out toward Grace, who evaded his grasp. "Now, I want you to think realistically for a minute. How were you going to raise this child by yourself, with no money, no job, no husband? Have you thought about what that would mean?"

Grace shoved herself farther back from the table and stood halfway up from her chair. She stayed crouched this way, neither standing nor sitting, just breathing rapidly in and out, like an animal that has been hit by a car.

"Think about it, Grace — even now you need me to take care of you. I'm the one who pays your bills and feeds and clothes you. You live here because I bought this house for you. You don't have a job, you don't have any money — you're totally dependent on me and my goodwill."

Their father stood up and started toward Grace, but she stepped deliberately back from him. "Your *goodwill,*" she said, and smiled bitterly. "And then what? After I've given my baby away? We'll all just pretend to the whole world that nothing's changed, and then I'm supposed to go off to college as if none of this has even happened?" Grace's mouth formed a new horrible shape. "How could you even say this to me?" she said. "You need to repent right now, Dad. Right now, before it's too late."

"Grace," said their father. He tried to take her elbow, but she wrenched it roughly out of his grasp. "You're just upset," he said. "Just take some time to think about things. I think you'll come to feel differently about it if you give it some time."

"This is *my* baby." Grace took a step farther back. "God gave this baby to me because I am the person who is supposed to be its mother. I was chosen by God. It is His will. You of all people should know that." Grace put her hand back behind her against the wall. "God has begun a holy work in me that cannot be destroyed. *'My soul doth magnify the Lord, and my spirit hath rejoiced in God my Savior. For he that is mighty hath done to me great things; and holy is his name.'* "

Their father held both of his arms out toward her.

"Don't touch me," Grace said. "I don't want you ever to touch me again."

Their father let out a long sigh that seemed to come from the very bottom of his shoes. "I just don't think that you've thought this through. I don't think you've considered what keeping this baby would really entail. About what other people would say."

"What would other people say, Dad?"

Their father looked suddenly very tired. He seemed to shrink into himself, to become slightly stooped and small. "I think you know."

Jory sat transfixed in her chair.

"I'm not sure I do," said Grace.

Their father's voice was very low. "About what color the baby would be."

"I don't know what you're talking about," said Grace. "I have absolutely no idea what you're saying."

"Grace," said their father. "The Guanajuato police found the man and he's confessed. They're not going to keep him in jail, though, because he has — well, he has some kind of . . . mental impairment."

Grace swayed slightly on her feet. "You're lying," she said.

"It's all right, Grace — everything's all right now." Their father tried to take Grace in his arms. With a sharp cry, Grace gave him a shove and he went stumbling backward into the edge of the stove. Jory could hear the noise her father's back made as it hit the heavy iron corner of the old Wedgewood. He staggered to one side and grimaced horribly. "Oh," he said in a bewildered voice, and his hand went to his back even as he tried to move once again toward Grace.

But Grace was gone. The kitchen's back door was open, and she was gone.

■ ■ ■ ■

PART THREE:
HILDA'S HOUSE

■ ■ ■ ■

Chapter Fifteen

Her father stood on Mrs. Kleinfelter's front porch at midnight and gave sleepy and somewhat flustered Mrs. Kleinfelter the barest of information. Grace had gotten a little upset, he said, but she had probably just wandered down the road somewhere. In fact, she was most likely at that little grocery store at the top of the hill — you know, the one with the broken gas pump. Yes, he said, running his hand through his hair and looking back behind him toward the darkened road, they would certainly all have a laugh about this tomorrow, wouldn't they, and could Jory stay with her just until then? Mrs. Kleinfelter said nothing, just opened the door wider and took Jory in and turned on the radiator in the back bedroom. She gave Jory an extra quilt and then went back into her own bedroom and shut the door.

Jory was now lying in the bed in the spare bedroom. Her father was out somewhere searching for Grace. Jory had begged and pleaded to go out with him, but he had been beyond listening to her. He was going to drive the back roads until he found her, he had said. Why don't we call the police? Jory had asked. Please, can't we just call the police? Her father said to think of what would happen — did she want her sister in the local newspaper, did she want the police to ask her sister questions and to listen closely to her answers? *Think,* he'd said. We're not calling the police.

Jory lay in the bed and listened to the night sounds. A car grew close and then went quickly past. A clock ticked softly somewhere in the house. Jory turned over on her side. Earlier that night, Jory had gone outside with a flashlight and searched through the grape arbor and the tool shed. She had peered down in the basement of Henry's house and behind the boxes of old clothes and the jars of jewel-like peaches and plums. She had even sneaked into Mrs. Kleinfelter's garage. There was nowhere else to hide. Henry's house was clear out in the middle of the country and the nearest farmhouse was a couple of miles away. Jory's father had already been there. No one had seen Grace.

She was supposed to go to school tomorrow. She was supposed to hand in her paper on the inexorability of fate and the expectedness of the unexpected, but which she had been too busy recovering from an LSD trip to complete. Maybe Mrs. Kleinfelter wouldn't remember that Jory was supposed to go to school, or maybe she would call the school and tell them that Jory couldn't come, that there had been a family emergency and that Jory was vitally needed at home. Jory wondered if her father had gone home yet and told her mother that Grace was missing. She tried to imagine her mother lying awake in the dark of her parents' bedroom, worrying. Jory flexed her toes against the bottom of the sheet. There had been no angel — only a Mexican man who was insane or maybe mentally retarded. This revelation should not have been all that surprising, and yet somehow it still was.

Jory couldn't bear to eat any breakfast, even though Mrs. Kleinfelter poured her a big bowl of Malt-O-Meal with the added enticement of maple syrup to put on it. Jory climbed into Hilda's old truck wearing the same clothes she'd had on the day before, her stomach empty and her hair uncombed. As they drove, Jory found herself carefully scanning each field and roadway as if she might see Grace suddenly walking along. She couldn't make herself stop this obsessive looking, so she just gave in and examined every house and farm and empty lot they passed.

"Are you all right?" Mrs. Kleinfelter stared straight ahead.

"Yes," said Jory. "I guess." She watched as a long-legged dog rushed out of a driveway and loped alongside the car, barking furiously. It gave up after half a block and Jory turned around and watched it standing in the middle of the street still barking. "What if she got hit by a car?" Jory turned back around.

Mrs. Kleinfelter flipped on the car's heater and a gust of faintly warm air blew toward Jory's feet. "Your father's a very determined man," Mrs. Kleinfelter said, as if this explained something.

Jory took up her vigil behind the window again. She noticed that today most of the houses had smoke coming from their chimneys. "He won't even call the police," she said.

Mrs. Kleinfelter made a small sound in the back of her throat.

"She won't ever come back," said Jory. "Even if he does find her."

Mrs. Kleinfelter made a left-hand turn

and pulled into the school's parking lot. "I'll be back at three thirty," she said. "Just hang on until then."

Jory stared at the sandwich that Mrs. Kleinfelter had packed for her. She put it back in the little brown bag and folded the top closed. Her stomach still felt strange. More than strange. She gazed around her. It was only noon, but the sky right behind the gym had now turned a dark yellowish gray and the treetops were all starting to bend back and forth. Thunder rumbled from somewhere nearby and Jory felt a fat drop of rain hit her scalp.

"Do you know anyone who has a car?"

Rhea crammed the last of her sandwich into her mouth. "Why — you wanna ditch?"

"I need to go somewhere." Jory patted the hood of the white Ford Falcon they were sitting on. "Whose car is this?"

"I don't know," Rhea said. "Somebody who'd give us a ride if we both gave him hickeys, probably." Rhea stood up and surveyed the school's parking lot. "Why don't you ask your boyfriend over there?"

Jory saw Laird standing in a group with a wildly laughing Jude and Jude's less happy, but equally stunning brother, Nick. "It must be wonderful to be her."

"Who — Jude? Get real," said Rhea. "She's just as messed up as everybody else." Rhea kicked her foot against Jory's. "C'mon, I dare you to go over there and ask him."

"No way," said Jory.

"Seriously," said Rhea, taking Jory by the arm. "Don't be such a pussy." Rhea tightened her grip on Jory's arm and began dragging her across the parking lot.

"Oh, poop. Oh, poop," Jory kept saying under her breath as they approached the group.

"Hey," Rhea said loudly when they came to a stop next to Jude and her brother. "Jory here wants to ask her Homecoming date a favor." Rhea gave Jory a push.

Jory could feel her entire face and neck burning and turning red. "Oh, it's nothing," she said in a small voice. "I was just going to see if someone would give me a ride somewhere."

"What kind of ride do you need?" Nick Mullinix turned and winked at Laird, who was looking down at the pavement of the parking lot and scuffing his boot against an invisible divot in the pavement. "Seriously, where you wanna go?" Nick now made a show of digging his car keys out of his pocket and twirling them around on his finger. "You coming too?" He gave Rhea a look.

"Um, okay," said Rhea.

"Do you know where the Bali Hai Trailer Court is?" Jory tried to steady her voice.

"The *Bali Hai*?" Jude asked.

Laird looked up from the pavement and squinted at Jory. "My brother's got his truck, but I'd have to go find him."

"Forget it, man," said Jude's brother. "I got it covered." He turned to Jory and Rhea. "I doubt we're gonna make it back in time for fifth, you know. If that's, like, a problem."

Jory glanced at Laird and he was already looking at her. "I'll take notes for you in science," he said. "If you don't get back, I mean."

"Thanks," said Jory, trying not to embarrass him further.

Jude squinted her eyes at Jory. Suddenly she reached into the front pocket of her Levis and pulled out a quarter. "Here," she said, handing the coin to Jory. "Bring me back a chocolate Push Up," she said in a strangely quiet voice. "And tell him that I said hi."

Jory stared at Jude.

Nick nodded his head at Jory and Rhea. "Let's book, my beauties," he said, and

465

began heading toward his car. Rhea pulled Jory along behind her. Jory glanced back and saw Jude putting her hand into Laird's shirt pocket and pretending to pull something out. Laird was grabbing at Jude's hand and she was laughing and hiding her hands behind her back.

Jory sat motionless in the backseat of Nick's car, replaying Jude's comment over and over in her head.

"You're a senior, right?" Rhea was saying to Nick. "So who was that I saw you with at Dave Roddy's party?"

He shrugged. "I don't know. Some chick from Arco Christian."

Jory leaned forward. "That's my old school."

"Seriously? I thought it was a reform school." Nick glanced back at Jory. "Jude said that place is seriously fucked up, man. It's supposed to be like a prison. A prison for nuns."

She looked out the side window and rubbed some condensation off with her coat sleeve. The sky was even more gray, purple almost. The trees were swaying, first in one direction and then the other, their branches leaning low. Several drops of rain hit the window, but were quickly whisked away by the wind. Jory tried once again to imagine where Grace might be. But Grace didn't really know anyone besides their family. There wasn't anywhere for her to go.

"Turn left here," said Rhea, "and then it's two more streets, I think." The car bumped over a pothole and Rhea hit her head on the car roof. "*Ow!* Jesus's racehorses!" she said. She rubbed the top of her head. "That hurt."

"Sorry, sorry, sorry," said Nick. He bent Rhea's head down and kissed the top of it.

Rhea looked pleased, even as she massaged her head.

"So what's at the trailer court?" Nick glanced back at Jory with his eyebrows raised.

"Just somebody I know," she said.

"Whatever you say," said Nick. "Anyway, that looks like it up there, right?" He turned into a long rutted driveway. "Bring some back for me, okay?" He grinned at Jory. *"Ass, grass, or cash."*

Jory stared at Nick. "What?"

Nick laughed and shook his head. "You Arco girls. You're hilarious." He stopped the car and Jory leaned forward past Rhea and opened the car door and squeezed out. The rain was starting to come down for real now. She put her hand over her eyes and tried to figure out where to go. There were metal trailers and painted blue ones and some that had little porchlike things hanging over the front doors. One trailer had an empty wading pool next to it that was now slowly filling with water. What number had Grip said? Twenty-three? Twenty-four? Jory walked down one row of trailers after another, the blowing rain plastering her hair down against the sides of her head. At the end of the last row was a trailer with colored Christmas lights strung around it. Space 23. *G. Welker,* it said on the mailbox. Jory stepped up the two wooden stairs and knocked on the trailer's screen door. The rain came down harder. She opened the screen door and knocked on the wooden one inside it. Through the glass window in the door she could see a shirtless Grip as he ambled toward the door yawning and scratching his head. He opened the door and saw Jory. "Whoa," he said, taking a half step backward. "This is a surprise." He opened the door wider and she went in.

Jory turned the drink coaster around and around in her hand. She was sitting at a yellow Formica table that folded out from one of the trailer's walls. Grip was sitting next to her in a pair of brown work pants and no shirt. She tried desperately not to look at his bare chest. Or at the snake tattoo that curled around his upper arm.

"Would she go to that pastor of yours? What's his name?"

"Pastor Ron?" Jory shook her head. "No. Besides, if she did, he'd just call my dad."

Grip yawned once more. He seemed surprisingly unperturbed about Grace's disappearance. "I could drive around and ask some people," he said. "But that's probably what your dad has already done."

Jory put the coaster down on the table. "But he might have missed some places."

"Yeah. Okay," said Grip. "All right." He stood up. "How'd you get out here?"

"A boy from school," said Jory.

Grip gave her a look. "A boy, hm?"

"It's not like that," said Jory. "Can I come with you? Please?"

"Aren't you supposed to be in class?" Grip picked a flannel shirt off the back of a metal-legged chair. He put his arms through the sleeves, buttoned the shirt, and opened a tiny closet next to the trailer's kitchen.

As Jory stood up from the table, she tried to peer as unobtrusively as possible at the rest of the trailer's contents. This was where Grip lived. Where he slept and ate. On a calendar hanging next to the door a girl with white teeth smiled invitingly and held up a bottle of 7Up. Several dirty plates and glasses were piled in the kitchen's small metal sink. Across from where she was standing was an uncomfortable-looking brown couch and a pole lamp with three cone-shaped lights that jutted out at various heights and angles. The door to his bedroom — what must surely be his bedroom — was closed.

Grip zipped up an old wool jacket. He grabbed his keys off a hook next to the door. "Well, come on," he said. "We've got miles to go before we sleep."

"And the *something something* is thick and deep," said Jory.

"Some poet you are." Grip bumped Jory's elbow with his own.

Jory smiled, but her lips felt thin and stretched, her face muscles atrophied. Seeing the inside of Grip's trailer had jostled something loose inside her, revealing just how nebulous her notions about him actually were. What had she thought — that the moment he left her house, he disappeared? He had a whole other life, or lives maybe, in places and with objects and people that she hadn't even considered. She dug her hand in the pocket of her corduroys and felt Jude's quarter still hidden there, smooth and small and warm.

Grip knocked politely on the driver's side window of the Malibu where it was steamed up. With a startled motion Nick pulled his head away from Rhea's. He rolled down the window and rain swept in on his jacket, leaving small darkened spots.

"Sorry," said Grip, "to interrupt. Just wanted to tell you that Jory's coming with me, so you don't need to take her back to school."

"Oh, yeah — sure. Okay." Nick stared at Jory as if he had never seen her before.

"Hey, hi, Jory," said Rhea. Her hair was messy and she was rearranging the neckline of her shirt. She had an odd expression on her face, as if she were both angry and sad.

"Well, see you later," Nick said, and rolled the window back up.

Grip and Jory loped toward the ice cream truck in the rain. "Yeah," said Jory. "Those are my friends from school."

"Go Skullcats," said Grip, climbing up into the driver's seat. He leaned out the passenger side and pulled Jory up into the truck. "Oh, man," he said, rubbing his hands together. "Not exactly ice cream weather."

Jory hugged her arms close to her chest.

"Grace doesn't even have a coat on," she said, and slowly she began to cry.

"Ah," said Grip. "Don't do that — don't do that." He patted her leg and then started the truck engine. He rubbed his hand over his face. "Grace is a very smart girl," he said.

"You said that before, I think," said Jory, wiping her eyes with her coat sleeve. "Or maybe it was my dad."

"Well, she is," said Grip. "She's the smartest girl I know." He peered backward and backed the truck out of the trailer court. "Present company excepted."

"Thanks," said Jory. "I guess."

The rain came down in uneven sheets. Grip turned on the wipers and they slapped ineffectually back and forth, making a strange squeaking sound on each return trip.

Grip turned on the heater and then the radio. Sam Cooke decided he'd been loving her too long to stop now.

"How come some men have such beautiful voices?" said Jory. "My voice sounds like a squawking crow." She pulled the hood on her jacket back and tried to straighten her hair with her hands.

"I love crows," said Grip. "Have you ever seen those bottles of Old Crow whiskey where the crow is smoking a cigar?" He shook his head. "Crows look just like that, like old men who are getting together for a card game . . . and half of them are going to cheat."

Jory tried to smile. "I like the way they talk to each other. And the way they have to hop before they can take off."

"Yeah," said Grip. "They're too heavy to just start flying, so they have to get a running start." He leaned forward and peered out the rain-splattered windshield. "I'm thinking about a crow tattoo." He turned to Jory. "What do you think — a big old crow right on my chest?" He mock flexed his arm. "Very manly, right? Right?" He grinned.

"When did you get the snake one?" Jory tried not to sound shy.

"Oh. Yeah, well, I was living in Texas a while back, in Austin, and a friend and me went to this tattoo parlor on the corner of Twenty-third and Guadalupe, where an old Indian woman said that snakes were good medicine. That this tattoo would bring me luck." He grinned. "I must have been drunk."

"Did it?" Jory looked out at the rain coming down. "Bring you luck?"

Grip adjusted the rearview mirror. "I don't believe in luck."

"Not at all?"

"Nah." Grip wiped his sleeve across the windshield. "People do what they're going to do and then things happen."

"So you don't believe in God, either?"

Grip inspected Jory's face. "Does it matter what I think?"

"Yes," she said, and peered down at her feet. She moved her wet moccasins against the truck's floor mat.

Grip sighed. "Okay," he said. "So why would God, if there is a god, need us to believe in him? What point would that serve?"

"Because it would prove that we were willing to trust in something we couldn't see or touch or anything."

"And why does that matter? Is it some kind of a test that God's giving? Like, hey, here's this really outrageous idea, and if you believe it — even though there's absolutely no proof of any kind — then you get to go to heaven? What kind of weird setup is that?"

Jory watched the rain dripping down the side window and blurring the trees and houses.

"And if God, if there were a god — let's just say there *was* a god — why did he, if he knew everything about everything, why did he not know that Adam and Eve were going to eat the apple? And why did he set it up so that they *would*? And if he was so great and all-powerful and everything, why did he have to fix his mistakes by making himself human and getting himself killed? None of it makes any sense — not from a logical standpoint or even a theological one." Grip shook his head. "I mean, it's a kind of neat story in a sick, messed-up, tortured sort of way, but it doesn't make any sense."

Jory drew a star in the condensation on the window. "My dad says that humans need a god, and that we're lost without one. That we wouldn't know how to live if we weren't afraid of getting punished in the end."

"Your dad says that?"

"Yeah, sometimes he's very practical, but he also thinks that we should live like Christ did. That Christ was the greatest living example of how to behave."

"Well, okay," said Grip. "And that would be great if that's what people did, but no one lives like that, so it really doesn't matter."

"Some people try to." Jory erased the star with her hand. The window was now smudgy and impossible to see out of. "Sometimes."

Grip turned the wipers on high and leaned toward the windshield. "*Shit,* it's raining too hard to see anything out there. I don't think it's even safe to drive. I can't see the other cars anymore." He slowed down and tried to steer them toward the side of the road. "Hang on," he said. "We may end up in the ditch." They bumped and lurched to a stop, and Grip turned on the truck's flashers. "We'll just sit here for a minute until it clears up some." He tried to peer up out of the windshield at the sky. "I don't ever think I've seen it like this here. In Texas, it rained so hard the rainwater ran uphill." He turned around and reached back into the truck's refrigerator and pulled out a bottle of beer. He opened the top and handed it to Jory, and then got another one out for himself. He took a long drink and then leaned forward and fiddled with the radio dial.

"Wait," said Jory, grabbing his hand. "I like that song." Jory tried to hum the tune for a second and then stopped. "What is that?" she said.

"Duke Ellington," said Grip. " 'Prelude to a Kiss.' "

"It sounds like one of the old victrola songs, but there aren't any words."

"There are words. Sarah Vaughan does it best."

"What are they? The words, I mean."

"Be quiet a minute and I'll tell you." He cleared his throat and began singing.

Jory grinned and took another sip of her beer. Since she'd already been drunk, she guessed it didn't matter much that she was drinking now.

Grip's scratchy baritone filled the truck's cab for a moment or two longer and then died away.

Jory clapped her hands and smiled hugely. "You have a really nice voice. How do you know all that stuff? All that old stuff?"

Grip took a drink of his beer. "Because I'm all old and stuff."

"No, you're not," said Jory. She took another hesitant sip of her beer. "My teachers at school are all way older than you."

"Thank God for that," said Grip. He clinked his beer bottle against Jory's. "Maybe you should hook me up with one of those ancient crones."

"There's Ms. Lindbloom, my English teacher — she's actually really pretty. You'd probably like her." Jory drank some more of her beer. It was tasting a little less bad.

"Nah, I never go for the pretty ones. They're too much trouble. I like the ones that nobody else likes. The ones with lots of zits and ugly legs." He drained the last of

477

his beer.

"Well, thanks a lot," said Jory, making a face.

"What?" said Grip, leaning back in his seat. "You thought I liked you or something?" He rolled his eyes. "Definitely not my type."

"What? Why not?" said Jory, kicking at him with her wet moccasin.

"Hey," he said, swiping at his leg. "These are my best pants now, so don't go getting them all messed up."

Jory reached over and brushed at the imaginary dirt on his pant leg. "Do you really think I'm too ugly?" she said, looking serious.

Grip grabbed her forearm. His face was suddenly next to hers. "Yes," he said, tightening his hand around her wrist. He smiled at her and yet he looked angry. "You are one of the very ugliest girls."

Jory could smell the bitter tang of beer on his breath. She breathed it in and leaned toward him and all of a sudden she could see his eyes quickly searching hers for something. His mouth was cooler than she had expected. His lips were softer and his chin scratched hers horribly. Her head was filled with a thrilling sort of buzzing. He was running his tongue over the front and back of her teeth. She breathed in the whole smell of his mouth and his face and then his neck. "Jory," he was saying into her hair, and then he had her by the arms and he pushed her back into her seat. "Hey," he said, and she could see his chest moving in and out, fast.

"Hey what?" she said, trying to read his face. Her body was still singing with new knowledge.

He turned around and put his hands on the steering wheel. "Hey," he said again.

"I'm not a baby," she said.

"I know that," he said. He ran his hand over his face. "I think it's clearing up," he said, and he reached up and wiped wildly with the palm of his hand at the inside of the windshield. "I think it's mostly stopped." He leaned forward and turned on the truck's ignition. It coughed and sputtered and refused to start. "Shouldn't have left the radio on," he said. He turned the key again and the truck's engine groaned once or twice and then finally caught. "Okay," he said, and pulled the truck back roughly onto the roadway.

They rode along in silence for a block or two. Jory tried to look out through the windshield. The rain was still coming down as hard as ever. The wipers could barely keep up. It was like being inside a gigantic car wash that never stopped. "Maybe we should pull over somewhere," said Jory.

"No," said Grip. "We can make it. It has to slow down in a minute or two." He rolled down the window and stuck his head out. "Dammit," he said. He tried to wipe off the side mirror with his coat sleeve. It was no better than before. He cranked the window back up. The rainwater ran off his head and down his coat; he shook his head like a dog. "This is insane," he said, and tried to turn the wipers on high. The wipers whipped back and forth with greater urgency, and then suddenly the wiper blade nearest Jory snapped off and flew away into the wind. "Goddammit!" Grip pounded his fist against the steering wheel. The lone wiper squeaked back and forth. The world in front of Jory was a watery blur.

"Let's just stop," Jory said again.

"Please be quiet." Grip leaned forward, peering intently through the small swath the lone wiper cleared in the windshield. "I think we're not too far from Hope House. Hey, wouldn't that be great? We could stop there — I'm sure they'd like me to pay them another visit." He laughed bitterly once and shook his head. His rain-wet hair was the color of old pennies.

The truck hit a pothole, probably the same one that Nick's car had hit on the way out, and Jory slammed against the truck's passenger door. *"Ow,"* she said as the truck now veered even more sharply to the right and began slowing. "What's going on?" Jory asked. She rubbed her right shoulder.

"Flat tire," said Grip. The truck made a loud *thwap-thwap-thwap*ping sound and they pulled off the road and came to a stop next to some sort of shadowy outbuilding. Jory tried to peer out her window but could see next to nothing through the downpour.

Grip rested his forehead between his hands on the steering wheel. "We don't have a spare," he said. His voice was directed toward the floor. "There's not enough room in the back to carry one." He turned his head and looked sideways at Jory with his head still resting on the wheel.

"Maybe this is inexorable fate," said Jory. "The unexpected expected."

"What?" said Grip.

Jory rolled her window down. "There's a barn," she said. "Or it could be a really weird house." She opened the truck door and jumped down and ran toward the building. She could hear Grip calling her name from inside the truck. She splashed through the mud toward what looked like an over-

481

hang. There was a door underneath it with a curved top and a wooden handle at waist height. *Like a hobbit house,* Jory thought before she could stop herself. She pounded on the door and tried to stamp the rainwater off her shoes. Her moccasins were ruined. The door opened just as Grip came sloshing up beside her. Jory recognized the man in the doorway only after she had said hello, and even then for a second she wasn't sure. It was the black eye and the bandage across his nose that made him look different. Plus the fact that he was no longer holding a guitar.

Inside there was a fire burning in a small stone fireplace and a large dirty brown dog stretched out next to it. "Some guard dog you are," said the guitar man fondly. "We could all be dead by now." The dog thumped its tail lazily against the floor. "Yeah, you know we're talking about you, don'tcha?" The guitar man stared at Grip. "I wouldn't have let you in except for her." He nodded his head at Jory.

Grip said nothing.

"Do you think we could maybe use your phone?" Jory asked.

"Sure," the guitar man said. "If I had one." He squatted next to the fire and placed a small log on top of the one that was already burning brightly. "No phone, no TV, no radio." The guitar man was wearing what looked like buckskin pants — what Jory imagined buckskin pants would look like — and a long-sleeved undershirt with several large holes in it. He had two gold hoops in one of his ears and his hair was in a long dark braid that hung all the way down his back. "You wanna hang your clothes up by the fire? It's the only way you're gonna get dry." The guitar man stood up and gestured at Jory.

Jory looked at Grip.

Grip shrugged.

Jory took off her wet moccasins and her jacket. She handed them to the guitar man.

"Anything else?" he asked, cocking his head and smiling.

Grip gave him a look.

He held up his hands. "Dude, I just meant, like, her socks or something."

Jory peeled off her horribly wet knee-highs. "Ugh," she said, and handed them to him.

The guitar man stretched her clothing out on the hearth. "Toasty in no time," he said.

Jory sat down on an old green velvet couch. Or what used to be a green velvet couch. The velvet was now so thin and worn that there was hardly any velvet nap left at all. There was a coffee table of sorts in front of the couch that appeared to have been hewn out of a middle of a tree. Jory ran her hand over its smooth-ringed top. Everything in the little house — the walls, the floor, the ceiling — all of it was made of thick planks of wood, sanded smooth and varnished a glossy, almost glowing golden brown.

"Weird weather, huh?" the guitar man said. "Doesn't usually rain like this. I saw a double dog around the moon the other night, though, and sure enough —" He snapped his fingers.

"I think that means there's going to be a frost," said Jory. "It's actually just the nearly frozen condensation in the air that makes it look that way. There really isn't anything around the moon at all."

"Her father's an astronomer," said Grip. "There's no arguing with her." He glanced grudgingly at the guitar man as if the two of them suddenly had something in common. "Her sister's the same way."

Jory turned to the guitar man. "You haven't heard anything about a girl wandering around lost, have you? My sister — you maybe saw her on Halloween — she's gone. We can't find her." Jory glanced back at Grip, trying to gauge from his expression just how much to say. Grip, for some reason, wouldn't meet her eyes. Jory continued, "She sort of wandered away from our house a night ago. Last night, I mean."

The guitar man leaned down next to the fire and poked at it with a long stick he had hanging below the mantel. Sparks, like angry insects, flew up out of the burning logs. "Are you sure she's lost?" he said, looking back at Grip. "Maybe she doesn't exactly want to be found."

"Ah, the great philosopher," said Grip, standing up. "Don't get all voodooy with me. If you're just dying to say something, go ahead. If you aren't, then shut up."

The guitar man held up his hands again. He was decidedly smaller and thinner than Grip. "This is my house, man," he said. "You're just standing in it. You asked to come in, remember? All I'm saying is that lots of times people leave places because they want to. You know?"

"Are your clothes dry yet?" Grip frowned at Jory. "There's no point in sitting around here." He marched over to a tiny window and looked out.

"Look," said the guitar man. "Don't get all jumpy. I'm just pointing out something, is all."

Jory walked over to the fireplace and

picked up one of her socks. It was slightly less damp than it was before. She turned to the guitar man again. "You haven't seen her, have you? Or heard anyone say anything about a tall dark-haired girl? Well, she used to be dark haired — now she mostly doesn't have any hair. She's seventeen, and she's . . . pregnant."

"Pregnant," said the guitar man, as if this were a slightly pleasing thought. "Well, well."

"Well, what?" said Grip. "You have something to say about that?" He looked out the window again. "What I really need is a spare tire. Do you or any of your so-called friends have something I could use, even temporarily? I've got about five bucks" — Grip fished around in his pants pocket — "six bucks and change, if you can find me a truck tire."

"You're asking for another favor?" The guitar man smiled and pulled gently on one of his earrings. "Not quite as high and mighty as the last time I saw you. You nearly broke my nose, man."

"Look, do you think you can just find me that tire?" Grip laid a five-dollar bill in the guitar man's hand.

He shrugged. "There's a couple of old ones in the woodshed. You can check it out if you want."

Grip glanced briefly at Jory. "I'll be back in a minute." He struggled into his wet coat and went out the front door.

The guitar man sauntered into the kitchen and began opening some cupboards and setting things on the stove while Jory continued to sit by the fireplace. The brown dog was asleep, its rib cage rising and falling in short, slightly staccato movements. The dog's paws twitched, and it made a softly muffled sort of bark, its dog lips fluttering. It was dreaming. Jory petted its flank and the dog sighed and lifted its head and then drifted back down into sleep again.

The guitar man came into the living room carrying two blue mugs and grinning with his chipped front tooth. He settled onto the green velvet couch, eyeing Jory. "It's tea," he said, smiling. "With nothing added."

Even so, the tea tasted different from any drink she had ever had: slightly bitter and smoky flavored. She lifted the mug to her mouth again and immediately burned her tongue.

"Why'd she run off?" he asked. He meant Grace.

"I don't know," said Jory. She stared into the fire and watched as a small piece of wood burned and shrank and then fell down below the grate.

"I was fifteen." The guitar man put his mug down on the tree ring table. "Best thing I ever did. Freud says the son has to kill off the father in order to become a man, and in my case that meant killing off my mother, too." The guitar man laughed briefly. "She was more of a man than my old man ever was. Jesus" — he shook his head — "she could make a person feel guilty just for breathing too loud."

"How old are you now?" Jory took several more sips of her drink, trying to ignore the burned spot on her tongue.

"Twenty-five — going on sixty-five." He chuckled.

"Have you lived here the whole time?"

"Nah. For a while I hung out in San Diego and then I went down to south Texas, Austin. Me and some of my friends down there, we had a nice little business going, pretty good bucks too, but then, well, things got a little too close for comfort — if you know what I mean — so I came on up here. Hey," the guitar man said, "what exactly are you doing with Grip?"

"Oh," said Jory, looking determinedly down into her mug. "He's just my friend."

"Yeah, I hope so. 'Cuz he's, like, older than me even."

Jory glanced back up in shock. "Wait," she

said. "You know Grip? Was he with you in Texas, too?"

The guitar man itched at his chin again, and then smiled a little knowing smile that made Jory feel about ten years old. "Maybe you should ask him about that."

"He wouldn't tell me."

"Yeah, well, I s'pose that's the best to stay out of trouble." The guitar man set his mug down next to hers on the table. "Look. All I'm saying is that maybe you should be a little careful . . ." He shrugged. " 'Cuz you seem pretty young and straight-edge, and you might not wanna get mixed up in any of that."

"Any of what?" Jory knew she was sounding stupid and naive, but her drive to know now trumped her desire to look any type of cool.

The guitar man leaned forward and searched her face with his eyes. "Seriously?" He blinked and glanced away. "Jesus," he said. He sighed and picked the two mugs off the coffee table and then stood up next to the couch. "What, you think he's just selling ice cream out of that truck of his?" One side of his mouth crimped up in a half smile and he shook his head. "He's hiding out here. We all are. It's the boonies and nobody knows us, okay?" He spread his arms out

489

wide. "It's Idaho, man."

The front door opened and Grip stood stamping his feet in the doorway, rainwater dripping off his jacket. "All right," he said, rubbing his hands together, "we're good to go. Get your stuff back on." After taking a quick scan of the room, he squinted. "Did I miss something here?"

Jory was tying and then retying her left shoe, looking down. "Not really."

The guitar man cleared his throat and looked at Jory. "I wanted to tell you — I didn't know you were so young. I mean, I can definitely see it now, but I didn't know it that night on Halloween. I wouldn't have given you the party favors if I'd known."

"Hey, man," said Grip with a warning note in his voice.

The guitar man put his hands in his pants pockets. He lowered his voice. "Hope you felt something cool, though. The first time can be pretty amazing — sometimes the best time ever."

"Shut *up,*" said Grip, his hand now on the doorknob. "Don't say another word to her."

The guitar man shrugged. "Look, I'm just apologizing, man."

"Fine," said Grip. "C'mon, Jory."

"Well," said the guitar man, "all right,

then. Don't be a stranger." He smiled and fingered the bandage on his nose. "Anytime you feel like beating someone up again, just come on out."

Grip opened the door and he and Jory stepped out into the downpour. They ran through the wet weeds and grass toward the truck.

Grip spent the whole ride back tightly gripping the steering wheel as the rain continued to pour down. Jory said nothing as she watched the lone wiper slap back and forth, back and forth, carving out its little half-moon of clarity on the windshield. At one point Jory turned on the radio and Grip reached over and switched it off again. They continued on their careful, silent way down Chicken Dinner Road and Deer Flat. Grip finally stopped the truck a little ways away from Mrs. Kleinfelter's driveway and let the engine idle.

Jory picked her books up off the floor. Her throat tightened. "That guy back there, that guy at Hope House, he said he knows you."

Grip leaned back in his seat. "Oh, yeah?"

Jory held her books to her chest.

The rain continued to slide down the windshield.

Grip cleared his throat. "I think I better

491

be going now."

Jory tried to keep the note of longing out of her voice. "You don't want to come in until it stops raining?"

"Nope," said Grip, looking out his side window. "I've gotta get a real tire put on." He ran his hand over his jaw. "Besides, I think we've seen enough of each other for one day, don't you?"

Jory felt her stomach turn over. "You're mad at me. Because we kissed?"

"That should never have happened," said Grip. "I should never have let that happen. We just need to forget that, all right?"

"All right," said Jory. "I guess." She swallowed. "What was wrong with it, though?" She asked this last in a very small voice.

"You know perfectly well," said Grip, an angry edge creeping into his voice. "You're way too young. Way too young," he said again.

"I'm not that young," said Jory.

"Yes, you are, and you should only do things . . . things like that with boys your own age."

"I liked it, though." Jory had never felt so embarrassed. Or so compelled to say something.

"It doesn't matter." Grip tightened both hands on the truck's steering wheel. "It does not matter what it feels like. It's not okay, and we're never doing anything like that ever again. All right? Got it?"

Jory nodded. She could feel herself starting to cry. She grabbed the door handle and opened the door.

"Jory." Grip reached out and grabbed her arm. "I'm sorry," he said, and she could see that his eyes were filled with a strange, sad look she'd never seen before. He held her arm more tightly. "You're going to be fine," he said. "Everything's going to be fine."

Jory glanced wildly around the inside of the truck as if she had never seen it before. "He said you were hiding out here. That you needed to hide out."

Grip's face wore a look of surprise that slipped slowly and incrementally into one of resignation. "Jimmy always did have a big mouth."

Jory stared miserably at Grip. A long moment went by. "Jude Mullinix says to tell you hi."

Grip closed his eyes and leaned back in his seat. His head rested on the metal wall of the ice cream freezer behind him. "That's enough, Jory," he said. "None of this is any of your business anyway, is it?" With a sudden motion, he leaned clear across her and opened the truck door. "You need to go," he said. "Right now."

Jory gave Grip a final miserable look and then she stepped down from the truck and ran toward Mrs. Kleinfelter's house, her chest filled with a tightness that hurt worse than anything, anything at all.

Inside, her father was sitting on Mrs. Kleinfelter's couch. Mrs. Kleinfelter was leaning forward in her chair trying not to look alarmed.

"Dad," Jory said, "I didn't see your car."

"Jory, where have you been?" said her father. "Mrs. Kleinfelter tried to pick you up from school, but you weren't there. She finally had to call me at work."

Jory's brain sorted frantically through the list of places she could have possibly been. "We had a field trip for earth science —" She waited desperately for more inspiration. "But then it ended up getting canceled after we were already on the bus and practically there, because of all the rain and stuff, so then we got back to the school late and I just had one of my friends bring me home." Jory paused in her recitation. "But, you know, the whole thing took longer than it was supposed to and, well" — she shrugged — "here I am."

"Well, there you go," Mrs. Kleinfelter said,

eagerly waving the problem away. "I figured it was something like that." She eased herself up from her chair. "So, I was just trying to convince your father to eat some dinner with me. It's only toasted cheese sandwiches, but I might be able to locate some tomato soup somewhere."

"Actually, I was thinking of taking Jory off your hands for a bit. You don't mind, do you?" Jory's father didn't wait for an answer; instead, he took Jory by her elbow and began piloting her toward the back door.

"Well, all right, then, if you're sure. But, Jory, I'll save you something to eat for later, just in case. And — oh, say, Dr. Quanbeck?"

"Oren," he said with a strained smile.

"Um, yes," said Mrs. Kleinfelter. "I'm just wondering if it might not be helpful to talk to the police or the sheriff or someone about this. Isn't it their job to find missing people? I mean, don't they get paid by the county to do just this type of thing?"

Her father was still wearing his earlier smile. "Well, I guess I've just been hoping to avoid involving any outsiders in what seems like a private family matter. But I definitely appreciate your concern and, of course, your taking care of Jory in the way that you have. I'm very grateful for that, Hilda." He held out his hand and Mrs.

Kleinfelter slowly took it. "My wife and I both appreciate everything you're doing."

Jory glanced back at Mrs. Kleinfelter as her father continued to steer her through the kitchen and down the two steps to the back door, which shut behind them with a finality that was distressing.

Outside, it had finally stopped raining, but the dusky air was still damp and heavy with the odor of something her father called geosmin, but which always reminded Jory of the smell of an Indian head nickel collection she kept in a leather coin purse. Her father got behind the wheel of the old green Buick and Jory slipped in beside him. He didn't put the key in the ignition.

"Jory. That was unacceptable."

"I'm sorry, Dad," Jory said. And she was. She shrank down a little in the seat.

Her father placed his hand on her shoulder and left it there. "I mean it. I need you to help me here. I can't have another lost daughter. I won't be able to stand it."

"I know."

"I need you to think very hard and help me come up with a list of people that your sister might have contacted — might have called — or perhaps gone to see." Her father pulled a note card out of his shirt pocket. "What about someone at church? Who were her good friends?"

Jory glanced up at her father to see if he was serious. "She didn't have any friends."

A sharp look passed over her father's face. "That's not true, Jory. Grace had friends. She *has* friends."

Jory shook her head. "Not really. Not like normal people." Jory felt a sudden pang about revealing this fact to her father. And about the fact that he hadn't known this in the first place.

Her father tried to brush this comment off. He uncapped a ballpoint pen. "Who would she have turned to? We need to think here. What about girls from school? Someone in her class at Arco Christian?"

Jory felt like crying.

"And what about that man who was with you girls at Mrs. Kleinfelter's house that one night? The one with the red hair. The strange one."

"Grip?"

"Is that his real name?" Her father was writing again. "*G-r-i-p?* What's his last name?"

"Welker," Jory said, before she could stop herself.

"Where does he live?"

Jory thought for a second. "I don't know," she said finally.

"That's all right," her father said. "Ed will find out."

"Ed?"

"Ed Hewett. You know, from next door. I hired him to try to find Grace. Well, I didn't really hire him, per se; I just spoke to him in confidence, and he decided to do this for free out of the goodness of his heart." Her father's voice softened. "That's not ordinarily a phrase I would have associated with him in the past, but he's a father too, and he's familiar with these kinds of things . . . these types of problems." Her father drew several crooked stars on the note card.

"I thought you didn't want anyone to know about Grace."

"Well, he thinks he can do a certain amount of checking on these people without them even being aware. He can watch and ask questions and see if anything suspicious is going on." Her father put the card back in his pocket, then patted her hand and gave her a brief smile. "Everything's going to be fine. We're all going to be all right."

"I know," she said. It was clear that no one thought this at all. Which was why they all kept saying it. And why she kept agreeing with them. As if repetition alone could keep whatever it was they were all worried about at bay.

CHAPTER SIXTEEN

A day went by. Two days. And then a week. A week in which Jory went to school and slept and ate at Mrs. Kleinfelter's house. A week in which no one heard from Grace and in which Jory did not see Grip. It was as if certain important things had now been erased, or had never existed in the first place. Jory felt as if she had a missing tooth, as if there were a raw and seeping gap somewhere that ached and bled whenever she ran her tongue against the spot. Which she did over and over, as if it were some kind of test. As if her tooth might be back if she checked just once more, just once more, one last time. Everyone else seemed fine: Mrs. Kleinfelter, the people at school — no one but Jory seemed to realize that there was a horrible hole in the world.

"What's your dress like?" Rhea took a bite of yogurt and then licked the spoon clean. "Is it short or long, sexy or sophisticated,

Twiggy or Cher?"

"I don't know," said Jory. She wadded up her lunch sack. She couldn't eat. Her stomach seemed to have shut down completely. She tried to take a sip of milk. It was warm and tasted faintly like metal.

"How can you not know? It's this Friday." Rhea pinched Jory's upper arm. "Mine is dark burgundy red with black lace all around the hem, and it has a slit up to here so I can dance." Rhea wiggled her eyebrows. "Randy's bringing a flask."

"Okay," said Jory. She put her milk carton on the ground. "I'm going inside," she said, and stood up.

"What's wrong with you?" said Rhea. "Lunch isn't even over yet. Hey — where're you going? I wanted to talk to you."

Jory said nothing; she just walked toward the main building and down the stairs to the girls' bathroom. She threw her lunch sack in the garbage can and opened the door to the very last stall. She sat on the closed toilet lid with her head in her hands until the bell for class had rung, and then the tardy bell too. After it had gotten completely quiet, she came out and climbed up onto the bathroom radiator and stared out the window. She could see the girls lined up outside on the baseball field waiting to play softball. She was missing PE. She watched as Rhea hit the ball to some girl she'd never seen before. "Catch it, you retard," Rhea was yelling. "It's right in front of you."

Jory jumped down off the radiator and stood up. She walked out of the bathroom and back up the stairs and out the front door of the school. The parking lot was filled with cars; the sun shone blindingly off their hoods and bumpers. Jory walked between the rows of cars until she came to the sea green '67 Malibu. She opened the driver's door and sat down. The seat was sun warmed and inviting. Jory opened up the jockey box and fished around under the eight-track tapes until she found the key that she had seen Nick leave there the time before. With a small lurch in her stomach, she put the key in the ignition and tried turning it to the right. The car's engine roared to life with a sound that Jory was sure would bring the entire school's administration running. She flinched and lowered her head, but, amazingly, no one seemed to notice or care that she was now driving someone else's car. She had never driven a car before, but she had gotten pretty good at changing gears in the ice cream truck, and this car was an automatic. She studied

501

the gearshift. P, R, N, and D. Carefully, she moved the gearshift into R and stepped slightly on the gas. The car rolled backward as easy as can be, but then it just kept going. Jory put her foot on a pedal and the car jerked suddenly and slammed to a halt. Now she was halfway out in the middle of the parking lot. She looked down at the gearshift again and moved the lever into D. She stepped gingerly on the gas pedal and pulled slowly out of the parking lot. It was as if someone else were doing this. She coasted down the hill and past the Day 'N' Nite grocery store. She tried stepping on the brake again and was still shocked when the car jerked to a squealing halt. She would have to do that even more gently. Jory's head felt clear and empty as a pane of new glass as she steered the car down the country roads. She stayed at one speed and slowed down way in advance of any stop signs. At the gas station, she made a careful turn and pulled in far behind the pumps. She got out of the car and headed toward the man inside, and it was only then that she realized that her legs were shaking. The bell of the station's door dinged when she opened it and the man in the blue coveralls glanced up from his clipboard. "Yeah? What can I do for you?" the man said. Jory tried to smile, to still the uncontrollable shaking of her knees. "Can you tell me how to get to the Bali Hai Trailer Court?"

Her back and sides were now quite slippery with sweat. She made two wrong turns and had to backtrack a few miles before she found it. The fake plastic palm trees at the trailer court's entrance waved familiarly at Jory, and at this, her deadened heart gave a sudden small leap. She parked the car and got out and began walking down the rows of trailers. It all looked just the same, although the empty wading pool was now completely filled with greenish water. Jory walked to the farthest row and saw number 23, its string of colored lights still hanging, but no longer lit. Grip's old black Schwinn was no longer leaning against the side of the trailer, either. She opened the trailer's screen door and took a breath and knocked at the solid wooden one inside it. After a moment, she knocked again, her heart thudding. Jory cupped her hand over her eyes and peered in through the door's window. It was dim inside, but she could see that the Formica table was now folded back up into the wall and there were no coats in the open closet next to the kitchen. She put both hands around her eyes. The cactus sat in its spot above the kitchen sink and there were three clean plates standing in the dish drainer. The calendar girl still smiled out from the wall and held out her bottle of 7Up. Jory stepped down from the door. She backed up and glanced around her. The ice cream truck was parked over next to the left side of the trailer park's lone picnic table. She ran over to the truck, pushed open the door, and leaped up inside it. The green plastic beads were still hanging around the rearview mirror. She crawled into the back of the truck and knelt and lifted up the lid on the ice cream freezer. A waft of stale, warm air rose up to greet her. Inside the freezer was carton after carton of melting ice cream.

She let the freezer lid slam shut. She sat on the floor of the truck and leaned her head against the side of the freezer. Maybe he was just riding his bike somewhere and had forgotten to plug in the freezer. Maybe he was out getting groceries. Or a newspaper. Maybe he was riding by her house this very minute. Jory scrambled up off the floor and scooted between the truck's seats and jumped down onto the ground. She walked across the gravel toward the other side of Grip's trailer. She brushed through a thick patch of weeds and cheatgrass. The back side of the trailer seemed very similar to the front, except that there were two small windows instead of one, and two concrete blocks that served as steps to the back door. Jory stepped up onto the top cement block and turned the door's handle carefully back and forth. This yellow plastic door had no window cut in it and it was locked. Jory stepped down off the cement blocks. She stood back and gazed at the two windows. She gave a sudden impotent leap — a completely stupid and pointless maneuver since they were both too high up for her to see into. She bent down and hoisted the uppermost of the cement blocks and hauled it over to a spot directly beneath one of the windows. Picking up the bottom cinder block, she shuddered. A revelation of worms, now bare and uncovered, writhed whitely in the sun's glare. She quickly carried the second cinder block over to the first and, with a grating sound, set it on top of the first. Stepping gingerly up onto them, she leaned against the trailer window, her hands cupped around her eyes. Inside was Grip's bedroom. She stared intently at his bed, which was covered with a nondescript blue bedspread. A goose-necked lamp sat on the linoleum floor of the trailer, along with some shoes, old tan work boots that

Jory had seen Grip wear before, and something that looked like Mrs. Kleinfelter's old brown dress — the one that had been let out at the waist — crumpled up beneath the bottom of the bed. She stared at the dresslike thing — the smallish portion of it that was poking out from underneath the bed — and at its brown paisley pattern. Jory stared and stared, as if the dress might shift and move or change into something else. As if it contained a message within it that Jory could decipher if she stared just a little longer.

Off in the distance, she could hear a crow cawing mightily, and then another one, farther away, cawing back.

All the way to school, Jory could feel her heart in her chest, its steady, painful throbbing. Her heart beat on and on as she piloted the car back to Schism. Fifth period had just begun when she pulled into the parking lot. She found her seat in earth science and got out her notebook and began taking notes. "The earth is a relative newcomer," Mr. DeNovia was saying. "While the universe is at least thirteen billion years old, the earth has been around for only 4.55 billion years of that. This birth date was determined by C. C. Patterson using uranium-lead isotope dating on several meteorites including the Canyon Diablo meteorite."

"We always called 'em shooting stars," said Laird, leaning toward her and whispering.

Jory knew what she was supposed to say, but she couldn't do it. She stared down at her notebook instead.

"Hey," he said, still whispering.

Jory was appalled to see a teardrop splat onto her writing. The blue ink bled outward and obscured what had been written there. The earth was now a bleary, unknown age, although the universe's age remained clear. Her small world had been wiped out while the rest of the cosmos went on unchanged — a tiny lesser planet washed away in a small, second flood, and barely even noticed in its passing.

Chapter Seventeen

Jory leaned her head against the glass of the diamond-shaped window. The leaves were nearly all gone and the plum tree was a tangle of knotted black branches. Any crows that alighted now were simply doing so to clean their beaks; there were no more plums — green, ripe, or rotten — to be had. The propane tank had a rim of frost on its rounded top, and the clothesline hung empty and vibrating in the wind. Jory had finagled Mrs. Kleinfelter into letting her stay home from school and she was supposed to be folding up her pants and skirts and dresses and putting them in a box to take to Mrs. Kleinfelter's. Jory's father didn't want her staying in the house by herself. Ed Hewett had done a certain amount of investigative work to help find Grace, but so far the detective had had no luck. Which seemed amazing, Jory had heard her father telling Mrs. Kleinfelter, in a town of this size. Jory was leaving all of Grace's clothes in Henry Kleinfelter's bedroom closet. Grace would need them when she got back.

Jory carried the box of clothes down the stairs and out the front door. She crossed the frozen lawn between the two houses and then dropped the box and knocked at the back door.

"You don't need to knock," said Mrs. Kleinfelter, wiping her hands on her house-dress. She opened the door and Jory carried her box in through the kitchen and down the hall to the spare bedroom. Jory dropped the box next to Dix's wardrobe and then lay down on the scratchy brownish red blanket at the bottom of the bed.

Mrs. Kleinfelter came in and stood in the bedroom doorway. "Why don't we drive up to Idaho Falls and go shopping," she said. "I hear they have some very nice dresses at that Mr. Alexander store."

"Thanks," said Jory, staring up at the ceiling through her laced fingers, "but I really don't want to go to Homecoming."

"Well, you could always use another dress, though, right?" Mrs. Kleinfelter leaned against the door frame. "This is the girl that loves clothes."

"I do love clothes," said Jory. "I just don't feel like going to Homecoming anymore."

"Fine," said Mrs. Kleinfelter. "I guess I'll just have to go clothes shopping by myself, then." She turned around and went into the living room. Jory could hear her opening the hall closet and getting out her coat.

Jory got off the bed and walked into the living room. "I'll go," she said.

"Oh, don't do it on my account," said Mrs. Kleinfelter, tying a scarf around her head. "I need a new sweater anyway."

"I know," said Jory. She got her own coat out and put it on. It seemed to weigh several pounds and felt horribly scratchy around her neck. She had a sudden desire to rip all the coats and their hangers off the clothes rod and throw them on the floor. She shuddered once quickly and tried to banish this thought from her head. *Everything's going to be all right,* she told herself. *Everything is going to be all right. Everything is going to be fine.*

"My," said the sales clerk, "she certainly is a thin little thing, isn't she?"

Mrs. Kleinfelter clucked in agreement.

"I don't know if any of these junior-size dresses will even fit her. We may have to drop down to the petites. Or the tween sizes."

"Tween?" Jory peered at herself in the

dressing room's full-length mirror. The dark green dress she had on hung off her shoulders and she kept having to hitch the bosom portion up in vain.

"And, sweetheart, I think you're going to need something a little more darted in the bust," the saleswoman said, pursing her lips.

"Well, what do you have that would fit?" Mrs. Kleinfelter sat in the dressing room chair, fanning herself with her checkbook.

"I'll go see what else I can rustle up." The sales clerk sailed out of the room, leaving the permeating odor of White Shoulders perfume behind.

"I hate that kind of woman," said Mrs. Kleinfelter.

"What kind?" asked Jory, still hitching.

"*That* kind," said Mrs. Kleinfelter.

"I look awful," said Jory, and she sank down onto the floor in a dark green froth. "I look like a hideous scarecrow."

Mrs. Kleinfelter laughed and then tried to change her expression. "It's just the dress," she said. "It's too severe."

The dressing room lady pulled back the curtain and came in with a flourish of perfume and hangers clacking. "Let's just try these on for the style," she said. "We can always size up or down." She smiled, revealing an amazing number of teeth.

"Maybe we could have a little privacy," said Mrs. Kleinfelter.

"Oh, well, of course," said the dressing room lady, "but you'll want to consult with me about the fit, you know."

"Of course," said Mrs. Kleinfelter, opening the curtain so that the saleslady could go out. "We'll call you when we need you."

Jory picked up one of the dresses and held it up against her. "Purple?" she asked, looking dubious.

"No," said Mrs. Kleinfelter. "Especially not in silk."

For someone who routinely wore men's work shoes, Mrs. Kleinfelter had surprisingly strong feelings about fashion. Jory held up another dress. It was knee length and made of black lace.

"Too grown-up. Like Sophia Loren or some foreign person."

Jory held the third dress up against her waist. "Oh," she said. She turned around so Mrs. Kleinfelter could get the full effect.

"Hmmm," said Mrs. Kleinfelter.

Jory slipped the dress on over her underwear while Mrs. Kleinfelter discreetly turned away. The floor-length dress was made of cream-colored velvet with a rose-colored satin sash and tiny cream-colored rosebuds that lined the neck.

As Jory stood and contemplated herself in the mirror, Mrs. Kleinfelter took her time doing up all the buttons in the back. Afterward, she gathered up Jory's hair in her own perpetually cool hands and held all of it there on top of Jory's head. "I can teach you how to do that if you want," she said.

Jory eyed her reflection. With this dress on and her hair up, she looked taller and almost grown up. Like someone quite a bit older and more serious. She looked like Grace, she realized. Grace in her baptismal dress from the year before. A small cry escaped Jory's lips.

Mrs. Kleinfelter let Jory's hair fall back down. "You don't have to wear it like that."

"No," said Jory, turning and holding Mrs. Kleinfelter's hands in her own. "It's not my hair. It's just everything else." She dropped Mrs. Kleinfelter's hands and sank down onto the little dressing room stool.

"You probably haven't had anything to eat today, have you?"

"I don't know," said Jory miserably.

"Come on," said Mrs. Kleinfelter, gathering up the discarded dresses. "Let's pay for this and get out of here," she said. "I'm sure our saleslady is more than ready to make her commission."

■ ■ ■ ■

On the way back home, Mrs. Kleinfelter insisted that they stop at the Me-O-My-O for dinner. "I haven't eaten there in years," was her excuse. "And the lasagna's supposed to be good. Let's live dangerously."

The restaurant was cozy and dimly lit, with red-and-white-checked tablecloths and red-flocked wallpaper featuring flotillas of Venetian gondoliers sailing eternally past. The restaurant's red leatherette booths were filled to capacity with middle-aged couples, some with children. While they waited for their lasagna, Mrs. Kleinfelter grilled Jory about what shoes she could possibly wear to Homecoming.

Jory picked at a lemon slice bobbing in her water. "I don't know," she said. "Maybe Grace has something that I could wear."

"The dance is tomorrow night. Are you sure?"

"I'll look in her closet when we get back." Jory fell silent and pushed her water glass to the edge of the table. The lasagna had arrived, perfect squares on their white plates. "I think Grip went away," she finally said. "He went away somewhere. He's gone."

"What makes you say that?"

"I went to his trailer."

"Oh?" Mrs. Kleinfelter's eyebrows shot up.

At this admission, Jory's heart gave a jolt. She took a drink of water and then another. "What would you do if you knew something bad about someone, or you thought you knew something bad about someone, but you weren't entirely sure how bad it might be, or even if you knew it for sure?" She paused for breath. "Would you tell?"

Mrs. Kleinfelter stopped her chewing. "I've somehow lost the drift of this conversation."

Jory tried to slow her thoughts. "I think I saw Grace's dress," she said, watching Mrs. Kleinfelter's face. "Your old brown dress. It was in Grip's trailer."

Mrs. Kleinfelter put her fork down next to her plate. "Are you sure?"

"Pretty sure. It was half hidden under his bed." *Half hidden.* For some reason, this phrase had been stuck in her head since she had first peered through Grip's trailer window, and the words had obviously been waiting and ready to pop out of her mouth ever since.

Mrs. Kleinfelter looked very solemn. "Jory," she said. "Have you told your father about this?"

Jory shook her head.

"When was this? That you saw my dress, I mean."

"Yesterday. On Wednesday." In fact, it had been Monday. Three days had passed already. Four, if you counted Monday.

Mrs. Kleinfelter frowned. "You have to tell him."

"But maybe it doesn't mean anything," Jory tried.

"How can it not mean anything? It has to mean something."

"But maybe not something bad. If I tell my dad, he'll automatically think it's something bad — that Grip did something bad. I know he will."

"Be that as it may."

Jory felt her shoulders droop. "He wouldn't hurt Grace," she said, but even she could hear the tiny bit of hesitancy that had crept into her voice.

Mrs. Kleinfelter gazed around the restaurant for a moment or two, and then she fixed her eyes on Jory with something like renewed purpose. "I lied to you," she said. "That day when I said that Dix and I had never had any children." Mrs. Kleinfelter rearranged her napkin on her lap and quickly cleared her throat. "We had a baby boy, David Daniel was his name, and he had blue eyes just like his father." She smiled briefly. "I didn't know the first thing about mothering and he was a colicky baby and I was already forty-two — I already had quite a bit of gray hair." She shook her head. "When he was three years old, he got the chicken pox, but then he was fine. He only had a few of the little blisters left on the bottoms of his feet, and the doctor said it had already run its course, and we — that is, David Daniel and I — were lying on my bed. I was tired from all the nursing of him, from all the days and nights of sickroom care, and I wanted to take a nap and he — he just wouldn't be quiet or lie still, and I told him to be quiet, to just shut up and be quiet for one goddamn minute, and then he did get quiet and I was so glad that I drifted off, and a few hours later I woke up and he was dead." Mrs. Kleinfelter looked down at her lap. "That was the last thing I said to him — that was the very last thing he heard me say. The doctor claimed it was something called Reye's syndrome, that it couldn't have been helped, that I couldn't have known." Mrs. Kleinfelter stopped talking and sat silently in her chair.

"I'm so sorry," said Jory. "That's terrible." Mrs. Kleinfelter said nothing.

"But it wasn't your fault." Jory gazed at

Mrs. Kleinfelter's large, almost transparent-lidded eyes, at her long, knobby fingers now interlaced on the tabletop. "You didn't know."

Mrs. Kleinfelter smiled briefly. "It was years and years ago. Talk to your father," she said.

When they got back, Mrs. Kleinfelter went straight inside to watch Ben Casey on TV, but Jory walked down the path between the houses and up the stairs to Henry's house. She opened the door and stood in the darkening room staring about her. There was nothing to see — just the old furniture squatting in the usual spots, accumulating more dust — but it felt strange to be here now that she was staying at Mrs. Kleinfelter's. Now that Grace was gone. Jory climbed the stairs to Grace's bedroom and opened her closet door and peered inside with a growing sense of futility and unease. None of Grace's old tennis shoes or boots would be appropriate for her new Homecoming dress. What had she been thinking?

Jory made her way back downstairs. She went through the kitchen, pointlessly running her hand over the counters and tabletops. She opened cupboards and the pantry door — here were all their boxes of cereal and macaroni and below them cans of tuna and soup still waiting to be eaten. She came back into the living room and sank down on the dead cat couch. She leaned back and looked up at the ceiling. She examined the cracks in the ceiling's plaster. This house was a hundred years old. At least a hundred. The people who had built this house were all dead. And the people who had lived in it. Just like Mrs. Kleinfelter's baby was dead. *David Daniel.* He, too, was dead and buried and no one even gave him much of a thought anymore, even though he had been only three and had had beautiful blue eyes. No one cared about Henry Kleinfelter or the people he loved or his old house and all his old stuff.

Jory stood up. She went over to the victrola and lifted its lid. There was already a record on the player's turntable. A tiny little .45 with one of those yellow plastic things stuck in the middle to make it fit. Jory lifted it cautiously off the spindle. "Prelude to a Kiss." Sarah Vaughan. She held the record closer to her face. *I'm sorry — XOXOXO* was written in blue ink on the record's center label. Jory stared at the record again and then she sat down on the floor, still holding the record. She inspected it again. She ran her fingers over the *X*'s and *O*'s. She gave a cry that she was glad no one was there to hear. She stood up again and shakily placed the record back on the turntable. She cranked the victrola's handle and put the needle in place. The record crackled and hummed and popped and then a woman's voice, sweet and yet deep, began singing. Jory stood next to the victrola with her heart swelling tight and tighter. She thought that surely soon her heart might burst open and spill its contents out into her chest. Even now, a piece of her heart seemed to be stabbing her over and over in a horrible, wonderful spot behind her breastbone. Jory listened to the song three more times before she turned the victrola off.

She sat down on the hardwood floor and leaned her head back against the wall. She held the record in her lap. Her heart was still sweetly, wondrously sore, but there was also something else — a niggling, struggling bit of something that was crawling its way to the forefront of her brain. She had a sudden, momentary flash of uncovering the mess of writhing worms beneath Grip's back step. *I'm sorry — XOXOXO,* the record said. *I'm sorry.* What did he mean? In reference to what? Was he sorry about what he'd last said to her? Sorry about leaving? Sorry about not saying good-bye? Sorry about the brown paisley dress that was crumpled beneath his bed?

Jory continued to sit as the evening light outside dimmed and disappeared completely. When she stood up, one of her feet had fallen asleep and it tingled and buzzed as she hobbled into the kitchen and picked up the heavy phone receiver. She dialed her old phone number and listened to it ring. Her heart, which had been so thick and swollen with feeling, was now back to its painful jerky thrumming. She held the phone tightly to her ear. The phone in her old house on Ninth Avenue rang hollowly on and on. For once, there was no one there to hear the news that she had been finally willing to impart.

CHAPTER EIGHTEEN

Laird was wearing an off-white tuxedo with tan velvet piping and a stiffly ruffled shirt that matched Jory's dress, and Mrs. Kleinfelter was helping him pin Jory's corsage onto the shoulder of her gown. Laird kept fumbling with the long pearly-headed pin, and finally Mrs. Kleinfelter tut-tutted and batted him away with her hand. Jory held completely still as Hilda inserted her long, coolly-knobbed fingers inside the front portion of her dress and fastened the fragrant red rosebuds to her shoulder. "There," Mrs. Kleinfelter said, standing back and assessing her handiwork. "Lovely, if I say so myself. Good choice," she said to Laird. "Both the flowers and the girl." Laird smiled and glanced nervously at Jory. Jory patted her hair. It was in a sleek knot on top of her head, fastened there by about a million bobby pins, but she was not entirely sure of its sturdiness or stability. "Well, I guess we better go," said Laird, looking apologetically at Mrs. Kleinfelter. "Randy and Rhea are waiting in the car."

"Randy and Rhea," said Mrs. Kleinfelter. "Sounds like a comedy team."

"Or a disease," said Jory.

They trooped out to the porch, and Jory held the bottom of her dress up as she made her way down the stairs and into the back-seat of Randy's newly washed Camaro. The driver's door — the only part of the car that was still a primer gray — was open and Laird squeezed carefully in next to her. Jory waved at Mrs. Kleinfelter, who was still standing on the porch.

"Is that your grandmother?" asked Rhea, who was examining herself in the sun visor's mirror.

"Sort of," said Jory.

"She's really old," said Rhea.

"She's not that old," said Jory, feeling at her hair, which was nearly brushing the car's ceiling.

"Okay, kids," said Randy, turning around and backing the car out of the drive. "Who wants peppermint schnapps?"

Jory watched as a pair of headlights behind them slowly lit up the interior of their car, and then her father's green Buick pulled up and into the driveway next to them. She could see her father's face slowly registering Jory's presence in the Camaro.

"Hey, who's that?" said Randy.

"Just go," said Jory. "Go. *Hurry.*"

With a roar of the car's engine, Randy reversed out into the street and Jory sat back and tried not to feel guilty about leaving Mrs. Kleinfelter to deal with this situation. Her head felt both tingly and fuzzy. Or maybe it was that her hair was too tight. Laird handed her Randy's flask and she took a drink. "Urg," she said, wiping her mouth. "That is *horr*ible."

"Only the best for my friends," said Randy. "We're all going first class tonight."

"It's not so bad after the first few," said Rhea. "And besides, it freshens your breath." She turned and grinned at Jory and Laird, the stiffly curled ringlets in front of her ears bobbing with each movement. "Minty fresh, see?" She blew a puff of air at them. "Hey, was that your dad in that car?"

Jory nodded glumly.

"I don't understand your family." Rhea turned back around and adjusted the top portion of her hair, which — she had told Jory on the phone — was now padded with a "wiglet."

"Me either," said Jory. Her father would be so disappointed in her. He already *was* disappointed in her. She bent her head down and smelled her corsage. "How'd you know what color to get?" she asked Laird.

"My mom called your grandma." He put his arm around the back of the seat. It rested there, not touching her shoulder.

Jory noticed that his hair was slicked down. Differently. And he smelled like some kind of green or blue soap. She suddenly felt shy, as if she had never met him before. She folded her hands together in her lap. She was wearing gloves.

"I like your dress." Laird leaned closer toward her. "I like these little things." He touched one of the velvet rosebuds at her neckline.

"Thanks," she said, not looking at him.

"How do your gloves stay up?" He tried to encircle her bicep with his fingers.

"I don't know," said Jory, feeling quite strange. "They just do."

"Hey," said Rhea, leaning back from the front seat, "what do you bet some of the teachers are drunk tonight?"

"Shit," said Randy. He took his hand off the wheel and struggled to find something in his jacket pocket — finally, he pulled his hand out and tossed a package of gum into the backseat. "Chew some of that before you go in. They're gonna try and check your

525

breath." Randy was wearing a bright red crushed velvet tux with a red velvet bow tie, both of which were supposed to match Rhea's burgundy dress, but instead clashed horribly. The tux shop had made a mistake, Rhea had told Jory, but they had gotten a fifteen percent discount and free white patent leather platform shoes for Randy, so it was almost worth it.

"What about me?" said Rhea, turning back toward him and pretending to pout. "Don't you care if my breath reeks of booze?"

Randy grinned. "I'll test it for you ahead of time."

Jory picked up the pack of Doublemint and tried to pull a piece of gum out of its paper slot, but her fingers were all thick inside her gloves.

"Here," said Laird. He took the package and pulled a foiled piece of gum out and unwrapped it. He turned to Jory. "Open up," he said. Jory opened her mouth slightly and Laird laid the piece of gum carefully on her tongue. He smiled at her. She blushed and then smiled back and began to chew, the gum's sweet mintiness filling her mouth. Laird's arm was now resting on the back of her shoulder.

"Okay, boozehounds," said Rhea. She

turned around and narrowed her eyes. "Hand over the schnapps."

Jory sat dazedly in the car's backseat, feeling more sophisticated than she had in her entire life. She was wearing a pair of cream-colored suede pumps that Mrs. Kleinfelter had bought at Nafziger's just this afternoon. She also had on nylons and a garter belt and girdle, plus Mrs. Kleinfelter's very own clip-on pearl earrings. Jory tugged tentatively on her left earlobe. What if one of them fell off and she didn't notice?

They drove past the now familiar houses and farms, and finally climbed the little hill to the Day 'N' Nite grocery. A few minutes later they made a long turn. "Hey, hey," said Randy. "Get a load of this." With a sudden bump and a screeching of tires, he pulled the Camaro into the school parking lot and Jory craned her neck looking to see who was here. Girls in long Gunne Sax dresses and ratted and ringleted hairdos and guys in ruffle-shirted, ill-fitting tuxes and shiny rented shoes stood somewhat awkwardly in the parking lot, smoking and rushing in and out of the brightly lit gym, the girls squealing and hugging as if they hadn't just seen each other at school that very afternoon.

Randy found a parking spot and backed the car carefully into it. He turned off the engine. "Well, now," he said. He took a long drink from the flask, put it into his breast pocket, and leaned over toward Rhea. Jory watched, embarrassed, as Rhea wrapped her arms around his neck and began kissing Randy as if receiving life-sustaining sustenance. Jory felt a pang of nervousness that was only slightly tempered by the thrill of being here in the first place. She smoothed the folds of her dress and tried to figure out what to do with her gum.

"*All* right," said Laird, leaning forward and punching Randy once on the shoulder. "Hey, Asumendi," he said. "C'mon. Let's go. You guys can do that later."

Rhea laughed and unlinked her arms from around Randy's neck. She unscrewed the lid on the flask and took a long drink. "One for the road." She dangled the flask over the backseat, offering it to Jory and Laird.

Jory, for reasons that remained obscure to her, took the flask and tipped it up to her own mouth. The schnapps still tasted terrible, absolutely horrible, like a Christmas candy cane mixed with mentholated fire. Jory took one drink and then another. She swallowed and gasped and then swallowed again. An amazing warmth spread slowly down her throat and into her stomach; it seemed to fill every empty hollow of her, the nervous, anxious, saddened, scooped-out part of her. It was like taking a luxuriously hot bath on a cold night. She lifted the flask up and took another drink. It was considerably less horrid this time. She took a final lengthy sip. "Hey-o," said Laird, looking surprised. He took the flask out of Jory's grip and handed it back to Rhea. "Can we go now?"

Rhea and Jory and Laird clambered out of the car. Jory lifted her hand to her hair for the umpteenth time. She could feel her hair, but it didn't seem to make any sense to her anymore. She couldn't quite remember what it was supposed to be doing. "Do I look okay?" she asked Rhea.

"Simply *loverly,*" said Rhea, linking her arm through Jory's. They stumbled through the graveled parking lot in their strange high-heeled shoes, laughing and grabbing at each other for support. As they got closer to the gym, Jory could hear music pouring forth from the golden-lit doorway. "Is it a band?" she asked Laird, who had caught up to them.

"What else would it be?" Laird put his hand on Jory's arm.

"I don't know," she said. "A record?" Her shoes seemed to be getting increasingly wobbly.

Laird shook his head. "Oh, boy," he said.

"What a lightweight," said Randy, smiling. He socked Laird on the shoulder. "Way to go, my man."

At the gym's doorway, a girl Jory thought she recognized from typing I took their tickets. And then they were inside. The music issuing from the stage was *loud.* Jory felt as if her whole body, from her feet up, was vibrating like a big pulsing heart. She liked this new heart beating; it was so much more friendly than the thing her heart had been doing lately. She smiled and couldn't seem to stop.

The gym was now, as Rhea had told her it would be, "A Whiter Shade of Pale." What this meant was that the ceiling of the gym was now covered with white and silver crepe paper streamers and many, many helium-filled balloons, and on the stage was a backdrop of silver stars and planets and an enormous lopsided crescent-shaped moon that tilted precipitously to one side. Toilet paper and tinfoil had obviously been utilized to full effect.

"Saturn is in the wrong spot," said Jory, standing on her tiptoes and yelling into Laird's ear.

"What?" he said, leaning down and hanging on to her arm.

"Nothing," said Jory, gaping about her. The band! On the stage there was an actual band! Jory had never seen a band before. She had glimpsed one once on *American Bandstand* right before her mother made her turn off the TV, but she had never seen a musical group in real life before, and not one up close like this. There was a guitar player and a guy playing the drums and some other guy and they all had long hair — much longer than the guys at school — and they looked like maybe they were in college. The guy playing the guitar was wearing striped pants and a silver shirt. They reminded Jory of the people at Hope House; in fact, the guitar player had a long dark braid just like the guitar player who lived in the cabin behind Hope House. Jory squinted up at the stage.

"Nice dress." Jude Mullinix had walked up with her brother in tow and now stood staring about the gym with a slightly bored look. "Very Laura Ashley. It suits you." Jory couldn't detect a single note of sarcasm in Jude's voice.

Jude was wearing a long sleeveless dress made of some kind of slinky navy blue formfitting satin. Beautiful blue sequins fell randomly down its length like dark glistening raindrops. Jude's hair was one long

531

sheath of shining blackness, like the back of a radiant, shower-wet crow. "You look beautiful," Jory said. She hadn't meant to say this at all, but it was so true that it had come out regardless.

Jude looked momentarily nonplussed. "Thanks," she said finally.

"What about me?" said Nick, pivoting on one heel. "How gorgeous am I?"

Jory laughed. "Very," she said, and he was. He looked unlike any other boy here, with his smooth chin-length black hair and navy pants and silk dress shirt. He had on no bow tie or suit jacket, but instead wore black suspenders and expensive, complicated-looking shoes.

Jude smoothed down the sequined portion of her dress. "Where's your date?"

"Off getting punch, I think," said Jory.

"Well," said Nick, "if that's the manly thing . . ." He gave his sister's elbow a squeeze and sauntered off in the direction of the punch bowl.

Jory took a deep breath. "So, how do you know Grip?" She felt as if she had been waiting forever to ask this.

Jude's expression didn't shift and her dark eyes remained as blank and inscrutable as ever. "How do *you* know him?"

"Oh," said Jory. She shrugged. "I don't

know. He's my friend," she said finally, lamely.

"What a coincidence," said Jude.

Jory's stomach felt a pinch of residual tightness. She hadn't envisioned the conversation going like this at all. In her obsessive nighttime thoughts she had foolishly pictured Jude providing an explanation that would soften or even remove the hateful sting of her earlier implication. Jory glanced around her in desperation. "I just don't understand," she said, miserably.

"Really?" said Jude. She gave Jory a long, and perhaps genuinely empathetic, look. "I think you probably do."

Laird came up beside them now, holding a triangle of punch cups. "Here you go," he said, handing Jude and Jory small cups of some pinkish liquid. *"Salud,"* he said, and, grinning, lifted his own cup in the air. He downed his quickly. "Okay," he said, "let the festivities begin!"

Laird pulled her out into the middle of the gym floor, where Jory put her arms lightly around his neck the way Mrs. Kleinfelter had shown her, although Laird was much taller than Mrs. Kleinfelter and he felt nothing like her either. She could feel herself smiling into the shoulder portion of Laird's

533

tuxedo. Over his shoulder, on the stage, the guitar-playing guy held the last note of the song that she recognized from her transistor radio, and then he caught sight of Jory and winked and she saw that he *was* the guitar man from Hope House. She stopped still on the dance floor, but everyone else stopped too. They were clapping while Jory was still looking up at the guitar-playing man, until Laird took her arm and steered her across the gym floor through one of the open side doors.

They stepped out into the dark, freezing air of the parking lot. Here and there students could be seen furtively lighting cigarettes and embracing in the darkness. Laird took Jory's hand and walked her over to the nearest car. They sat on its hood. Jory carefully rearranged her dress's folds and Laird pulled the flask out of his jacket pocket. He unscrewed the lid and offered it to Jory and she took a long drink of the horrible stuff. "I know the guitar player," she said, handing him back the flask.

"Who? The guy in the band?" Laird took a drink, then passed the flask to Jory again.

She nodded.

"How'd you meet him?"

"It's hard to explain," Jory said. "Do you think Mr. DeNovia and Mrs. Cross are, like, friends or something?" Jory took another sip of the schnapps.

Laird laughed. "Something like that."

Jory watched her breath condense in the frigid air. "Where do you think Rhea and Randy are?"

"I don't know. Down in the ditch maybe."

"No," said Jory. "Not in her new dress." The ditch was actually a canal that ran along the length of the football field. It was where the kids went during school to do things they didn't want to be seen doing. For some reason the canal was hardly ever filled with water. Jory had never been down in the ditch, although a boy had once thrown her knit hat into its murky depths.

Laird held the flask between his legs. "How come when it's colder you can see so many more stars?"

"No cloud cover," said Jory. She shivered and Laird put his arm carefully around her. She gazed up at the sky and the dotted pattern of constellations. "Pythagoras thought that the stars were singing."

"Who?"

"An old Greek guy. He thought that the spinning of the planets and stars made music only the gods could hear."

"Wow," said Laird. "How do you know all this stuff?"

"My dad's an astronomer."

"Yeah, well, I'm an Aquarius."

"That's not the same thing at all," said Jory, sighing.

"It was just a joke," said Laird. "Jeez, how dumb do you think I am?"

"So dumb I have to cheat off your earth science paper." Jory squeezed Laird's arm and he grabbed her hand and brought it to his chest.

"You're cute," he said, and he kissed her hand through its glove.

Jory blushed and then laughed. "I'm not beautiful, though," she said, looking up at him. "Like Jude."

Laird rolled his eyes and then leaned toward Jory. She could smell his pepperminty breath coming closer to her. She closed her eyes and then felt his mouth, soft and surprisingly small, lighting on hers for a second. He pulled away and they sat on the hood of the car in the dark, their warm breath leaving cloudlike traces in the evening air.

"Singing stars, huh?" said Laird.

Jory grinned shyly. She had a sudden, unexpected thought. "Did Jude really tell you to ask me to Homecoming?"

"What? Huh? No, I just told her I was going to. I wanted to know if she thought you'd turn me down."

"How weird," said Jory. She tried to remember the exact wording of that conversation in the bathroom. Maybe, just maybe, if Jude had lied about Homecoming, that meant that she might be lying about Grip as well.

Or maybe that wasn't it at all.

With Jude, it was somehow completely impossible to know.

Jory craned her head up at the sky again, at the stars sprinkled across its velvet darkness like an enormous spangled sash. Did anyone ever really know anyone else? Really, truly know them, so much so that you never even had to doubt their thoughts or intentions? Maybe this was a rhetorical question. Her father once told her that most people who ask questions aren't looking for information, but affirmation. Jory guessed this was true now in her case as well.

The dance was ending. Jory and Rhea stood under the gym's overhang and fanned themselves with their hands. "Randy's a drip," Rhea said. "He makes out like he thinks someone's watching."

"What do you mean?" Jory peered back at the doors, looking for Laird.

"You know. Like he's practicing posing

for the camera or something." Rhea held her hair up off her neck. "I caught him looking in the rearview mirror while we were kissing."

"Uck," said Jory. "Don't make out with him anymore."

"I have to," said Rhea. "I came with him."

Jory paused. "You could get Jude's brother to take you home. He likes you."

"Nick?" Rhea gave Jory an incredulous look. "The only girl he likes is Jude. Which is weird enough, but he also just tried to off himself." Rhea lowered her voice. "That's what he's doing here in Arco — recovering. He showed me his wrists that day out at the trailer court." Rhea made a face.

What? said Jory.

The side doors opened and the four band members sauntered out and began immediately lighting cigarettes. They stood underneath the overhang a few feet away from Jory and Rhea. "Hey there, girls," said one of them. *The drummer,* Jory thought.

"Hey, yourself," said Rhea.

"You two go to school here?" The drummer blew a stream of cigarette smoke up into the air.

"No, we teach here," said Rhea. "Spanish and biology."

"Ha," said the drummer, and looked back

to his bandmates. "The young comedian."

The guitar player walked over closer to them and stared at Jory. "Well, hello there," he said, grinning. "Long time no see."

"Hi," Jory said shyly.

Rhea looked at Jory.

The guitar player leaned his back against the gym's doorway. "Where's your date? Gawky young guy in the white tux?"

"He's still in the gym, I guess."

"Glad to see you wised up about the other guy."

Jory blushed fiercely.

"I'm totally lost," said Rhea, looking from one of them to the other.

The guitar player shook his head and took another drag on his cigarette. "Grip's trouble with a capital fuckin' *T.*"

Jory tried to distract him from this topic. "I didn't know you played in a band." She eyed his silver shirt and his well-worn boots, which looked almost red in the darkness.

"Whenever I can get a gig. Times are hard when you're on the straight and narrow — got to make money somehow." He winked or blinked — it was hard to tell which. "Hey, what's your name, anyway? Didn't Grip call you something like Johnny?"

"Jory."

"And my name's Rhea," said Rhea, leaning forward. "In case you were wondering."

"Nice to meet you," said the guitar man. "I'm Jimmy, and that's Jack and Marcus and over there's our drummer, Stryder." He pointed at the other band members, who nodded at the girls and moved a little closer.

"Stryder?" said Rhea.

"Yeah, yeah, *The Hobbit,* blah blah blah, whatever." The drummer pulled a small brown bottle out of his jacket pocket and unscrewed the lid. "For God and country," he said, and took a drink.

More people poured noisily out of the gym and headed toward the parking lot, but even though Jory stood on her tiptoes, she didn't see Laird anywhere.

"Want some?" The drummer held the bottle out toward Rhea and she took it happily, but then made a face after she took a drink. "Urg," she said, and wiped her mouth with the back of her hand. "I thought that schnapps was bad."

"Hey," said Jimmy, the guitar player, suddenly taking hold of Jory's upper arm and leaning in toward her face. "You still looking for your sister?"

"What" said Jory. "Why?"

"Well," he said. He scratched at his cheek for a long moment. "I just might know where she is."

"Wait a minute," said Jory. "What do you mean?"

The guitar man glanced off into the distance and then seemed to make a sudden decision. He now had an almost gloating look in his eye. "She's out at Hope House with your old buddy Grip. You know . . . my old business partner who tried to beat me up. *That* guy. They're staying in the main house with Angel and Sam and Nadia."

"I don't believe it," said Jory. Her heart lurched against her ribs. She felt suddenly as if she might fall down right on the parking lot pavement. "Are you sure it's her?"

Rhea looked from one of them to the other.

The guitar man stared at Jory, almost guiltily now, as if he hadn't entirely anticipated the effect his words were having. "Shaved head and out to here?" He held his hands out in front of his abdomen and then nodded and lit another cigarette. "Yeah — it's her."

Jory stood in the darkness and stared at the guitar man. Her heart was beating as if she had just run several miles. "You mean they're living together?"

"The two of 'em showed up at Hope House trying to scrape up some road trip money for Mexico or something." He shook his head. "As if I owe him a fucking penny! It's definitely the other way around, man, if you ask me."

"Mexico?" Jory said this so quietly she wasn't sure who she thought she was asking.

The guitar man was looking off toward the gym and didn't seem to hear her. "Ah, shit," he said. "Duty calls." He took a long last drag on his cigarette and dropped it onto the pavement and then ground it out with the toe of his boot. "See you inside," he said, and walked back toward the doors of the gym.

Jory stood in the darkness. She felt sick. There had been a dense spot of poison in her heart, but it had burst and was spreading quick as mercury through all her veins. She felt her heart continue to thud. Grip knew where Grace was, and always had, and that's why her dress had been under his bed. She had been with him all along. Which meant that he had been lying to Jory from the very start. Or maybe — maybe Grip was just helping Grace because of the way he felt about Jory. Maybe he had found Grace somewhere and was taking care of her for Jory's sake. He probably thought Jory would want him to do that. Wouldn't she want him to do that?

"What in the hell was that guy talking about?" Rhea had grabbed her hand and was squeezing it hard as she led Jory back into the gym. "Your sister is a hippie now?" She shook her ringleted head. "This has been the weirdest night ever."

Inside it was noisy and unbelievably warm and the band was now gearing up for its final go-round. Jimmy stood in front of the microphone. He tapped on it experimentally and slung his guitar strap around his shoulder. "The next song is dedicated to a girl named Jory," he said, "who's learning about life the way we all do — the hard way." He stepped back and began to play a few chords. The drummer started in and Jory stood next to Rhea aware that most of the people in the gym were now staring at her. She had no idea where to look, what to do with her face. "You're famous," Rhea whispered. "Did you go out with him or make out with him or what?" Jory suddenly spied Laird standing a ways across the gym looking at her, and next to him, Jude, who had a particularly interesting look on her face. A self-satisfied look that seemed to have nothing to do with the guitar man's dedication. People were still looking at her and murmuring even as the song began, and out of the corner of her eye Jory could see Mrs. Cross heading in her direction, and behind Mrs. Cross was Jory's father. Jory took an involuntary step backward. "Ouch!" said Rhea. "Jesus, watch my shoes." Mrs. Cross and Jory's father reached Jory just as the band got to the part about starting out walking and learning to run since we've only just begun. Jory stood looking at her father, at his baggy brown suit and windblown hair, at his nose that was slightly red from driving all this way in the cold. "Hi, Dad," she said. Her father took her arm and they made their way out of the gym together. She cast a backward glance at Rhea, who was staring openmouthed after her and at Laird, whose tuxedoed arm was now being held firmly by Jude Mullinix. The gym's twin doors opened and then shut behind them with a bang.

It was freezing in the car. Jory sat huddled in the front seat, staring out through the windshield as her father tried vainly to adjust the heater. He finally gave up and sat back with a sigh. They passed the Day 'N' Nite grocery store and crested and then rolled down the little hill. "Jory, do you have anything you want to say to me?" Her father stared straight ahead.

Jory was silent.

"No apologies? No excuses for why I find you at some sort of a dance you definitely don't have permission to attend, with a boy I've never met before?" Her father shook his head and kept shaking it. "Right now, of all times, you choose to do something like this — knowing what your mother and I are going through? How worried sick we are?" His voice dwindled away, but his head shaking continued.

Jory noticed that there were single lights on in most of the farmhouses they passed. Solitary lights left on for someone's comfort and security in the night. Left on so someone wouldn't be scared of the darkness.

"You have nothing to say for yourself?" Her father gripped the steering wheel.

"I know where Grace is," Jory said. And the moment she said it, it couldn't be unsaid.

At Hope House, her father wanted to go up to the door by himself — in fact, he'd insisted upon it — but once he stepped out of the car and started walking toward the porch's large kohl-painted eye, Jory leaped out of the car and ran up the steps behind him. He began pounding on the front door until finally the girl with the long red hair and teardrop tattoo opened it. She was now even more pregnant than before and she seemed to be wearing the same long white dress that she had been wearing on Halloween.

"Hey," she said rather tentatively, and looked from Jory to Jory's father.

"I'm here to get my daughter." Jory's father's voice sounded horrible and strangled even to Jory. He took one step into the house, and the copper-haired girl couldn't shut the door against him in time. "I'm not sure she wants to see you," said the girl, still holding the edge of the door.

Jory's father stepped around the girl and into the room. "Where is she?" he said.

"I could call the police," the girl said, lifting her chin up.

"Go ahead," said Jory's father. "That might be a good idea all around."

The girl stepped away from the door a little, but she didn't move any farther into the room.

"I'll just search until I've found her," Jory's father said. "So you might as well tell me where she is."

The girl said nothing, but she turned and started walking through the living room and into the kitchen. Jory and her father followed close behind. They passed through the clacking red bead curtain and out through the kitchen and down a long hallway painted blue and silver with all the signs of the zodiac. The girl stopped in front of a closed green door. She knocked once and then again. The door opened and Grip stood in the doorway, looking tired, but happy. He saw Jory and her father and his face changed shape and he stepped back from the doorway. Jory's father gave him a shove that sent him sprawling even farther into the room. Jory could hear her sister gasp and she saw Grace get up from a bed she had been lying on. "Dad," Grace said. Grace's head was now completely bald and she had a red dot in the middle of her forehead and her hands and arms were covered with interwoven and intricate drawings. Her father strode into the room and gripped Grace by both of her elbows. He began shaking her, hard, and Jory watched amazed as Grace's head flopped back and forth. Grip tried to insinuate himself between Grace and her father with no success. Jory put her hands over her mouth. Her father slowly stopped his shaking, but he still held Grace's arms. "Get your things," he said. "We're going home." Grace said nothing, but simply gazed at her father in awe. She was wearing a long flowered nightgown Jory had never seen before. It was unbuttoned part of the way down the front and Grace didn't seem to be wearing any underwear.

"She's not leaving," said Grip. "Not if she doesn't want to."

Their father pointed his finger at Grip. "You," he said, "have nothing to say about this." He turned to Grace. "Go get in the car," he said. "Now."

"Grace," said Grip.

"Shut up," their father said. Jory had never heard him use this phrase with anyone ever before. Their father still had Grace by the arms and he now began pushing her out of the bedroom. Grip tried to touch Grace as she passed by, but their father elbowed him out of the way. The girl with the tear tattoo was nowhere to be seen. Jory looked at Grip looking at Grace and saw for the first time what had been there all along. She didn't think she would be able to stand this, she had been sure she would never be able to stand this, and yet here it was. She followed her sister and her father out of the room and down the hall and through the living room and down the front steps and into the car, and the whole time Grip was calling after them in a voice Jory had never heard him use before. *No.* He wasn't calling after

them, he was calling after her sister. He was calling after Grace.

Jory now sat in the backseat of the car. She watched Grace's completely shorn head from behind as they drove ever onward, back toward the house they had lived in all their lives. For all the years of their lives except this one.

In silence, they drove down one road after another. They passed Mrs. Kleinfelter's house, where a lone light still burned. Jory realized with a sinking sensation that Mrs. Kleinfelter was probably still up waiting to hear how Homecoming had gone.

Grace turned toward their father. "You can't do this," she said, in a voice that was as full of radiant bitterness as anything Jory had ever heard. Their father reached over and across Grace and pressed down the lock key on the passenger door. "I can do this," their father said, "and I am." He seemed utterly unperturbed by Grace's brand-new voice.

Of all the silent car trips Jory had ever taken, this one was the worst. Grace was alive. She wasn't hurt or dead or run over or lying in a ditch somewhere — but some part of Jory, the most selfish, horrible, and the very truest part, wished that she were.

Jory stared out the window in a wide, unblinking, heart-pounding fury. She had previously wished Grace gone in a sort of halfhearted, abstract way, but this was different. If she had the power to do so now, she would wish Grace utterly out of existence. The toxic substance that had zinged through Jory's veins back at the Homecoming dance had filled her head completely now — even her fingertips felt buzzy and electric with the full extent of her hatred for her sister. She sank down in the car seat and allowed herself to imagine Grace unlocking the car door and tumbling onto the unforgiving concrete of the roadway. Or floating down the Elijah drain ditch, her fingers catching in the reeds and cattails, her mouth and nose stopped with brackish water. Grace's funeral was a dramatic affair that, as it grew, featured Jory in the starring and pivotal role. There were carpets of white flowers and weeping and the illicit thrill of seeing the now diminished and vastly lessened Grace laid out in her coffin — a sight that Jory lingered over and stared at unabashedly. It was a scene of strangely sensual proportions.

Jory bent her head down into the tightly knotted buds of her corsage and took a deep breath. The cluster of roses smelled as fresh and sweet as if they had just been picked or were still happily growing in someone's garden. Jory felt her throat fill with tears. She swallowed and swallowed again. She hated Grace. She hated everyone in this car. The car's heater, however, hummed steadfastly and her father kept his hands safely at the ten and two positions on the steering wheel. And the people in the front seat, Grace and her father, continued staring straight ahead, oblivious to Jory's hatred, as the Buick's headlights illuminated the familiar stretch of road leading back to the house on Ninth Avenue. Back to their old house. Back to their home.

■ ■ ■ ■

Part Four:
The House on
Ninth Avenue
(Again)

■ ■ ■ ■

CHAPTER NINETEEN

Even before she woke up, Jory knew exactly where she was. Somewhere in her sleep, she had heard the familiar sound of the basement furnace coming on, roaring dustily to life in its warm, reassuring way, and her father clearing his throat in the bathroom as he did each morning after he brushed his teeth. She could smell the burned toast and her mother's baked oatmeal that Frances insisted on having every day of the week. Jory opened her eyes and there was the wallpaper with the blue swans floating serenely down the unknown river and her sock monkey that seemed dirtier and slightly sadder than she remembered. Everything and nothing was the same.

Jory scrambled out of her bed and stood in her bare feet on the hardwood floor. Her Homecoming dress was in a heap next to the closet, the corsage Laird had given her still pinned firmly to its shoulder portion.

One cream-colored suede pump lay on its side under her desk. Jory moved over to her dresser and pulled open a drawer and surveyed its contents. There were her cutoffs from last summer and her sailor top and two stretched-out T-shirts. She shut the drawer and pulled open another one. Her old blue sweater lay on top. She pulled the sweater over her head and then on the floor of the closet she found a pair of gray pants that almost still fit.

Her father was sitting at the dining room table in his teaching clothes, even though it was Saturday. He was writing something on a yellow legal pad that he had in front of him. Jory's mother was scraping the burned portions off a slice of toast and not looking at Grace, who was sitting at the table with her hands folded. The red dot that had been on the center of Grace's forehead had faded somewhat, but Jory could still see the swirled brown drawings on the backs of Grace's hands.

"Good morning, Jory," her father said. "Have a seat."

"Where's Frances?" asked Jory.

"She's next door at the Hewetts'," said her father. "We didn't think she needed to be here for this."

"This?" Jory stood by her chair for a

second and then finally sat down.

Her father cleared his throat. Her mother put her butter knife on her plate, but still didn't look up. Grace said nothing. Jory felt as if she had entered the stage with the action already in progress.

"There's no point in beating around the bush here; this past month has been something of a revelation to me," her father said. He picked up his pencil and traced a straight line back and forth on the pad of paper. "Over the course of the past three weeks I was forced to consider the terrible possibility that my oldest daughter might be injured or dead." He cleared his throat again. "And then I discovered that all my worrying was for naught since she was alive and happily living with a strange man in a house full of hippies and unemployed drug users." Grace made a noise, but her father held up his hand. "I also discovered that my middle daughter was attending dances and parties that I had never sanctioned, with boys whom I had never met." Their father continued to trace the same line with his pencil, making an ever-deepening groove in the yellow sheet of paper. "And what I realized, among other things, was that I was partly to blame for these events because I had naively or foolishly put my two daughters in a situation where it was possible for things like this to occur." Their father put his pencil down. "A mistake I'm not going to make again."

"Dad," said Jory.

"So I stayed up all of last night thinking, and I decided that it would be best if Jory skips these last few months of school." Her father picked up his pencil and moved it an inch or two to the left on the table. "She can do correspondence work here at home just like Grace did."

"Me?" said Jory. "Wait. You want *me* to quit school?"

"It wouldn't be permanently," said her father. "You can always go back next year, or maybe even later on in the spring sometime."

"No," said Jory, shaking her head. "Nope."

Their mother glanced up, her head vibrating slightly the way it did when she was furious but didn't want to show it. "Let's be frank, Jory. You haven't exactly had a stellar year. Between the shoplifting and the cheating and the dancing and who knows what else." She closed her eyes briefly.

"This is nuts!" Jory turned from her mother to her father, trying to appeal to whoever might be most amenable. "Everyone goes to school! And I didn't shoplift

558

anything — how many times do I have to tell you? I didn't steal anything!"

"That's really beside the point, though — isn't it? — since all the rest of it is true." Their mother's head and hair continued to quaver. "I can hardly believe that you are the same girl who used to live in this house."

"Okay, okay," said their father. "All right, now. What we're trying to do here is to make a plan for the future — one that will ensure you girls' safety and well-being. And as your parents, we both have a responsibility to do just that. Do you understand?" He nodded, as if for all of them. "Of course you do," he said. "So we're all agreed, Jory will stay home just for the remainder of this school year, and then next year she can go back to Arco Christian."

"I'm not going back to ACA," said Jory. "You can't make me."

"Don't you dare tell us what we can and cannot do, Jory." Her mother put her napkin on the table. "This isn't a debate. And it isn't open to discussion." Her mother's face seemed more pointed and narrow than it had been just a month earlier. And she looked vastly more tired, as if the skin around her cheeks and eye sockets had had something vital and life-affirming sucked out from underneath. Jory felt suddenly shamed for her part in her mother's exhaustion. Her depletion.

"Also," their father said, as if he hadn't even heard this last interchange, "and perhaps somewhat more importantly, I talked to some people on the phone and I found a place that is willing to take Grace in for the next few months and provide her with the type of care that she obviously needs." Their father flipped over a new page on the pad of paper. "This is going to set us back a bit money-wise, but I think I can sell the house on Deer Flat back to Mrs. Kleinfelter, and if we just tighten our belts a little with the weekly groceries we'll be fine." Their father crossed something off the piece of paper with his pencil, an expression of grim accomplishment on his face.

Jory noticed that Grace was now sitting up very straight in her chair. She stared at their father, apparently incapable of speech.

"The care that she needs?" said Jory, her voice rising. "You mean you're sending her to Blackfoot?"

There was a moment's silence.

Grace finally spoke, her voice utterly composed. "I am not crazy," she said. "In fact, I've never seen things more clearly. It's you and your particular way of thinking that are insane."

"What?" said their mother, her words spilling out like a sudden dam burst. "Just *look* at you, Grace. You're bald! And you have some sort of absurd drawing or painting or something all over you. Not to mention that you've been living in sin with a disgusting long-haired *man* who's probably twice your age." Their mother was now twisting her napkin around and around in her fingers. "I still don't believe any of this." She shook her head. "I really don't."

"All right, now," said their father. "Let's try to stay focused on the positive."

"But you're sending her to the insane asylum!" Jory reached out and latched on to her father's shirtsleeve. She suddenly remembered that it was just last night that she had wanted her sister dead. She dropped her father's sleeve.

Their mother frowned. "Good grief, Jory."

"It's an unwed mothers' home," her father said. He flipped over a new page on the pad of paper. "The St. Agnes Home for Girls. It's in Wichita, Kansas, and even though it is a Catholic institution, the woman I spoke to assured me that the Sunday services are quite Christ centered."

"*Kan*sas?" Jory squeaked. "But that's, like, a million miles from here."

"It's only for a while," their father said.

561

"And then Grace can come home and start her life as a college student. As a young adult woman with her whole life in front of her." He tried unsuccessfully to smile.

"I'm not going," said Grace. She had her hands folded calmly in her lap and was speaking in a voice that she seemed to have borrowed from someone royal or presidential. "Not to an unwed mothers' home or to the loony bin or to anywhere else you try to send me. I'm nearly eighteen and I can decide for myself where I'm going to live. My life is my own to do with as I please."

A sort of hush fell over the table. Jory could see her father mentally regrouping, his forehead tightening. He pursed his lips and then visibly tried to relax his face. "You're still seventeen, Grace. And a minor."

"I turn eighteen in exactly one month."

"Well, during that month you are still my charge and I will be deciding where you are going to stay."

"I have rights," said Grace. "About what happens to me." She lifted her chin and smiled grimly at her father. "And about what happens to my baby."

"Where are you getting these ideas?" Their mother shot a look at Grace. "Or do I even need to ask?"

"Grace," said their father. "The law dictates that you are my child and my responsibility until you are old enough to take care of yourself. And even if you were eighteen, what would you do for money? How would you support yourself — much less a baby?" Their father gazed at his oldest daughter with infinite sadness.

Grace's equanimity seemed to falter for only the briefest second. "I've thought of that."

"And?" their father asked.

Grace paused. "I have my resources."

Their mother made a brief expulsive sound through her nose.

"You just can't count on someone like that, Grace." Their father rubbed his hand across his forehead. He wore a sad and almost defeated look. "You don't understand how the world works yet." He lowered his voice. "How some men can be."

Grace looked steadily at her father. "Oh, really?" she said.

"Don't be disgusting," their mother said.

"And even if you made me go, what makes you think I wouldn't just run away again?"

Jory was amazed at Grace's continued tone of defiance.

"Well, Grace," said their father with a certain resignation in his voice, "you'll be

563

watched and essentially guarded every moment when you're there." He shifted in his chair. "That's partly what I'm paying for."

"Why not just send me to jail, then?"

"If I could, I just might," said their father.

"Oren," said their mother.

Grace leaned back in her chair. "I'm getting married," she said. The note of triumph in her voice was unmistakable.

This idea seemed to take a minute to sink in across the table.

"You most certainly are not," said their mother. "Not to that . . . that person."

"Grip is not just a person," said Grace.

"You're not marrying him," said Jory, staring at her sister. "I don't believe you."

"Girls," said their father. "We will not be talking about that person anymore."

"Would everyone quit calling him 'that person'?" Jory could hear how childishly high her own voice had risen.

" 'That *person*,' " said their father deliberately, "is not to be discussed or mentioned in this house ever again."

"He's my best friend," said Jory.

"And mine," said Grace.

"He's no one's *friend,*" said their father. "Least of all, either of yours. And I am saying this one more time — we will not be speaking of him ever again. Is that under-stood?"

Jory and Grace said nothing.

Their father lowered his voice. "And if I ever find out that he has tried to contact either one of you, I will call the police. Immediately." Their father leaned forward intently and smacked both of his hands flat down on the tabletop. "I do not want to involve the authorities in our personal family business, but I will if I have to. If you force me to. Do you understand? Is that clear?"

Jory felt a shock run down her spine. Her father never spoke like this. He never threatened anyone with anything. And he never slapped the table.

Their mother's face had now taken on a look of dismayed fury that had finally reached its boiling point. "And, Grace, what on earth makes you think that a grown man . . . an adult male . . . would do a completely absurd thing like that with a seventeen-year-old girl?"

Grace stared at her mother. "You mean, why would he want to marry me? Is that it? Is that what you mean — a seventeen-year-old girl like me? A girl as ugly and unattractive and unfeminine as me?"

"As *I*," said their mother.

Grace gasped as if she'd been hit.

"Esther," said their father. "That's *enough.*"

Their mother suddenly seemed to deflate, to lose the fiery air that had kept her fury afloat. She rubbed her fingers against her temples. "I think I feel a migraine coming on."

"Vengeance is mine," said Grace.

Jory stared at her sister.

"Grace," said their father, a note of shame in his voice. "Don't." Their father pushed his chair back and stood up from the table. "All right. I think we've talked about this enough for now. Grace, I'll be taking you to the airport tomorrow morning. The woman I talked to said it's still fairly warm in Kansas, so you'll want to think about that when you're choosing what to pack."

Grace shook her head. "Oh, *Dad,*" she said. "Is that really what you want to say to me right now?"

"Don't talk to your father like that." Their mother gave Grace a look of saddened reproach. "He's doing all of this for you — sacrificing everything so that your entire life won't be ruined. So that everyone won't know what you've done." She shook her head and couldn't seem to say anything more.

"What *I've* done?" Grace stared at her mother. "It's like you think this is all my fault — that I somehow did this to myself just to humiliate you. Just to make your life miserable."

"Didn't you?" Their mother picked up her napkin and folded it carefully in half. She stood up and placed her napkin down on the table next to her plate. "I'm not feeling well," she said. "I think I need to lie down." She moved past the three of them and walked down the hall to her bedroom.

Jory and Grace and their father now sat at the table not looking at each other. Finally, their father glanced at his watch and sighed. "I'd better be getting to the credit union before they close for the day. You're going to need a certain amount of money." He nodded at Grace. "For clothes and food and necessities and things."

"Dad," said Grace, her voice shaking.

"Yes," he said. He fumbled around in his jacket and pants pocket and finally pulled out his keys.

"You don't know what you're doing."

"Possibly not," said their father.

"You can't send me away like this," said Grace. "I won't go."

"Grace," said their father. "You don't have any choice."

"I do," said Grace. "You just don't realize it yet."

Their father stood up and jingled his car keys in his palm. He wore a look of sheer determination.

"Someday," Grace said, "I may forgive you for what you're doing. For what you already did and for what you're doing now, but I don't think that will happen anytime soon."

"Well, Grace," said their father in his calmest voice, "I guess I'll just have to look forward to that eventuality."

Jory stared out the living room window at the first few flakes of snow that were coming down. The sky was gray and sunless, even though it was only midafternoon. Jory's head felt strange, as if a small group of bees or ants had taken up residence in her skull and was busily rearranging its contents. She made her way through the kitchen and into the garage and sat carefully down on the piano bench. She looked at the sheets of music sitting on the piano's lid. "Jesu, Joy of Man's Desiring" was open to its second page. Grace had played this song at their last Christmas piano recital and then the three of them, Grace, Jory, and Frances, had played a six-handed rendition of "Silent Night" that had ended the program and had made everyone clap and then sigh with contentment. The three of them had worn matching red velvet dresses that their mother had found for them in the Sears catalog. Jory put her index finger on middle C and pressed the key so softly that no sound was made. She tried to play the first notes of her part in "Silent Night," but she couldn't remember how it started. She couldn't remember any of it. They had worn white lacy tights and had cameos pinned to the collar portion of their velvet dresses. Frances had cried at the end of the recital, though, because she had to finally relinquish the book of Life Savers that she had brought as a Secret Santa present. Their father had scooped Frances up onto his hip and let her touch the spun-haired angel on the very top of the tree. Then they had driven slowly down Arco's icy streets singing Christmas carols. That had been a year ago. Not quite a year.

Grace came down the garage steps and sat down on the piano bench next to Jory. "Scoot over," she said. Jory was so surprised that she moved to the right without even thinking. "Six-eighths time," Grace said. "You start first and then I come in." She played the first few chords of Jory's part. "Remember?" She played the first four chords again. Grace seemed intent on what she was doing, but also happy. Something else about Grace looked different. Besides the faded outlines of the strange swirly tattoo things on her hands and arms. Jory peered at her sister. Two tiny silver stars hung from Grace's earlobes. "You got your ears pierced," Jory said. She stared at Grace in amazement. Grace's hand went up to one of her earlobes. She turned and looked at Jory, her face now slightly pink. "Annelise did it for me," Grace said.

"What? That red-haired girl from Hope House? The one with the teardrop tattoos? Did she do the weird stuff on your hands?"

"It's *mehndi.*" Grace held out her hands and turned them palms up. "It's on my feet too."

"You thought she was a terrible sinner," said Jory. "On Halloween, you told her she needed to be saved."

Grace put her hands back in her lap. "Did I?"

"Yes," said Jory, "you most definitely did."

"Well," said Grace. Her smile was slightly lopsided. "I guess I've had some time to rethink things since then."

"I guess," said Jory.

Grace's smile grew even more wobbly. "You know, it's become more apparent to me lately that I haven't always been very understanding of other people's points of view. As understanding as Jesus might have been."

"He was *mine*," said Jory. "You didn't even like him. You thought he was way too old and too sinful. Isn't that what you said? Too 'scruffy' and 'dirty'?" She stood up from the piano bench. "He smokes, you know, and he drinks beer too. He has a tattoo on his shoulder and he's going to get another one." Jory took a deep breath. "He was in *jail*." This last bit she said with a certain amount of triumph.

"Just juvenile detention," said Grace. "And it was a long time ago."

The buzzing in Jory's head made her feel as if everything — the floor, the piano bench, her sister — were all stretching out long and then narrow like taffy being pulled on one of those machines at the state fair. "He's *friends* with a girl from my school. An incredibly beautiful, absolutely gorgeous freshman girl with long black hair who smokes and who's going to be a model or an actress. He's probably in love with her." She stared defiantly down at Grace. "He sells drugs," she said, even though she wasn't sure any of these last pieces of information were entirely true.

571

"Jory," said Grace. She reached out and touched Jory's sweater.

Jory pulled her arm away. "Don't feel sorry for me," she said. "It's me that feels sorry for you. You're the one getting shipped off to Kansas."

The front door of the house opened and closed with a bang, and Frances ran through the kitchen, paused for a moment, and then came sprinting out into the garage. Frances stopped still at the sight of Grace and Jory next to the piano, and stood unsmiling in her brown jumper with the gray felt mouse on the pocket. Her hair was in two slightly messy braids and she leaned shyly against the garage doorway.

Grace turned toward Frances. "Hey, Franny, do you want to play your old recital piece with Jory and me?" She patted the spot on the piano bench next to her.

Frances shook her head wordlessly. She made a funny scowling face and looked down at the garage floor. Just as suddenly, she looked back up at her eldest sister. "Where's all your hair, Grace?"

For a second, Grace said nothing. "Oh," she said, blushing slightly and running her hand up over her scalp. "My friend shaved it all off for me." She smiled at Frances. "Do you want to feel?"

Frances took a step or two nearer to Grace, and then Grace took her small hand and placed it on top of her bent head. "It's prickly," said Frances, quickly withdrawing her hand. "Like porcupine whiskers."

"Quills," said Jory.

"It does feel sort of strange, doesn't it?" said Grace. "But it's a sign of my willingness to sacrifice my own selfish desires. To rid myself of my own ego."

"Oh, *Grace,*" said Jory.

"But why are your hands all brown and dirty?"

Grace smiled at Frances. "It was part of a ceremony. See?" She held her palms out for Frances to examine. "The women get their hands and feet painted in preparation for an important bodily change, like marriage, or even burial."

Jory stared at Grace. "What's that supposed to mean? You're really getting married? Did he actually ask you?"

Grace stood up from the piano bench without acknowledging this comment and knelt down next to Frances. She touched the felt mouse on Frances's pocket. "How's school?" she asked.

"I like Miss Boosinger," said Frances. "She lets me grade the papers sometimes. After the other kids are gone."

"That's good," said Grace. "You shouldn't tell the other kids how they did, though."

"I don't," said Frances. "It's a secret between me and Miss Boosinger. I only grade the quizzes. And only sometimes." Frances put her hand on Grace's knee. "I was going to be a big sister," she said.

Grace leaned closer to Frances. She ran her hands down both of Frances's small braids. "Yes," she said. "You are."

"She was going to sleep in my old crib," said Frances. "And use my green blanket, but now she's going to live with some people who can't have their own baby and get to have this one instead."

Grace's mouth fell. She stood up and stared out the garage window.

"And we get to have pot roast for dinner," said Frances. "And baked potatoes and cooked carrots. I hate cooked carrots — they're like rubber fingers," she added.

Jory moved over and sat down in one of the old-school desks. Instead of looking at Grace, she picked up an empty carton of milk that was lying on the desktop. *"La leche,"* the carton said, its black-and-white printed label still safely adhered. Jory set the carton upright on the desk. It wobbled and tipped back over on its side.

"I get to be a horn of plenty in the Thanksgiving play." Frances held out the bottom of her jumper. "I wanted to be an Indian, but Miss Boosinger said my hair's not dark enough."

"That's absurd," said Grace in a dazed voice. "You shouldn't believe everything people tell you. Not even authority figures."

Jory gave Grace a scornful look. "Did you read that in the Tao?"

Grace glanced at Jory. "No," she said. "I've always thought that."

"Right," said Jory. "Like you've always had pierced ears."

Grace made a sound that wasn't quite a sigh. "Please don't be like this, Jory. Not now." She glanced at Frances, who was taking all of this in without saying anything. "I didn't mean to hurt you. And I wouldn't ever, if I could help it."

Jory pulled herself out from behind the desk and stood up. "I was the one who told Dad where to find you," she said.

Grace now wore a look of disbelief.

"I did, and I'm glad, too."

"I don't believe you — you're just upset right now," said Grace, her voice shaking again. "But if you did tell him, I forgive you."

"Don't try to sound holy," said Jory. "Not anymore."

575

Grace didn't respond to this. She was peering at the school desk where Jory had been sitting. *"Oh,"* she said.

Jory turned to see what Grace was looking at. The school desk now had a spot of brownish liquid pooled in the middle of the wooden seat. "What is that?" said Jory. Her hand went automatically to the back of her pants. It came away wet.

"Oh, *Jory,*" said Grace again. She gave her sister a look of knowing concern.

Jory had a moment's confusion and then she stood upright and motionless, holding her wet hand out slightly in front of her.

Jory turned and walked up the garage steps and past her mother, who was now in the kitchen stirring a small flatish pan of something on the stove. She walked through the dining room and down the hallway and into the bathroom, where she closed the door and locked it. She could hear Grace following after her and then trying to turn the handle on the bathroom door. Grace knocked softly. "Go away," said Jory. Grace said nothing, but Jory could hear her just outside the door breathing quietly. "I mean it," said Jory. "Leave me alone." After a minute or two, she heard Grace sigh deeply and then walk back toward the kitchen.

Jory stood next to the sink and ran hot

water over her hands. She glanced up at the mirror and saw herself staring blankly back, her hair slightly messy and her face as pale and uninteresting as usual. She was no different than before, no more mature or grown up or womanly. She felt a dull heaviness beginning to lodge itself in her gut as if she had the beginnings of a mild stomachache. She sat down on the edge of the tub. She didn't even know what day it was. Wasn't she supposed to keep track so she would know to expect this again a month from now? And where was the blood? She stood up and unbuttoned her pants and pulled down her underwear. It was just a brownish, gooey stain. It looked more like a small spot of spilled gravy than something powerful and mysterious.

She made a face and sat back down on the tub's edge. She didn't want to do this — this thing was doing whatever it was doing all on its own. It was stronger than she was, or was separate from her and didn't give a crap what she thought about anything. She felt oddly betrayed. The buzzing in her head hummed on unrelentingly. She pulled a long length of toilet paper off the roll. She folded the paper up into a thick square and lined her underwear with it and then she stood on top of the closed toilet seat lid and pushed open the bathroom window.

The ground was shockingly hard when she jumped down, and outside it was getting colder. She began to walk, hugging her arms to her chest as she marched across the backyard and into the silent street. The air was quiet and thickly still, the way it got right before it was going to snow. It was a soft sort of cold that made Jory feel strangely calm. She had no idea where she was going. Maybe this was how Grace had felt the night she ran away from the diamond-windowed house, and maybe Jory was now simply repeating everything that Grace had done. Maybe she was still merely imitating Grace in some weird, juvenile way. Jory walked faster. The clouds were now so thick and heavy that they had caused the street-lights to come on even though it was only late afternoon, and in the conical glow cast by the one on her corner she could see tiny particles of something in the air, fine partic-ulates of frost or snow or ice just beginning to form and swirl lazily down. Jory blew on her hands and rubbed them together and kept walking.

There was a pay phone next to the Texaco gas station on the corner, but Jory didn't

578

have any money. She stood across the street from the gas station and stomped her feet. There were no cars at the pump, but she could see that the station was lit up and there was someone inside. Jory walked across the street and with a pounding heart opened the glass door. A tiny bell dinged and the man behind the counter looked up from the notebook he had been writing in. "Hey there," he said. It was warm and bright inside the station and it smelled marvelously of gasoline and new tires. Jory felt suddenly euphoric as if she had reached a place she had been searching for all her life. This sensation was just as quickly replaced with another, equally strong one. "I need to make a phone call," she said, blushing furiously. The man in the blue overalls gestured toward the pay phone with his pen. "Except that I don't have any change." Jory could feel how hot her face was becoming. "I didn't bring any with me," she said, "and I really need to contact some-one."

"Contact," the man said, as if he had never heard the word before. He scratched at his cheek, and Jory noticed that he had a tattoo between his fingers much like Grip's. The man's fingertips were all stained a greasy gray-black. He was probably only in his twenties, but his blond hair was thin enough that the light from overhead shone through it and revealed his rounded pink scalp.

"Well, I guess you can use this. But it can't be long distance." He picked a red rotary dial phone off the counter and moved it closer to Jory. "Gotta dial nine to get out first." He also pulled a dog-eared phone book up onto the counter and pushed it toward Jory. "Phone book," he said.

She began thumbing through the tissue-thin pages. Arco didn't have that many residents. The yellow pages section was thicker than the white. Jory turned another page and then ran her finger down the list of names until she came to the one she wanted.

"Yeah?" Grip said, his voice sounding as if he had been asleep and wished he still were.

Jory's heart lurched. "It's me," she said.

There was a moment of silence on the other end. "Jory?" Grip sounded suddenly much more awake. "What's going on? Did something happen?"

"Can you come get me?" Jory could feel her eyes starting to fill. She scrubbed the back of her hand across her eyes. The gas station man peered up from his notebook at her. She turned slightly sideways. "I'm at the Texaco station on Sixteenth Avenue."

Grip said nothing for a second. Then she heard him sigh. "Your dad is going to kill me," he said. "He'll probably call the cops."

"No, he won't," said Jory. "I don't think."

"Oh, yeah," Grip said. "He most definitely will."

Jory listened to him breathing into the phone. "Okay, then," she said finally. "Never mind."

Grip sighed again. She could hear him doing something, pulling coins or keys out of his pocket. "Stay inside till I get there," he said, and hung up.

Jory put the receiver in the cradle and pushed the phone back toward the gas station man. "Thank you," she said.

"Supposed to get real snow tonight," the man said. "First one of the season." He turned a page in his notebook and leaned his elbows on the counter. "Need some snow tires?"

"I guess not," said Jory.

"You never know," said the man. "Here," he said, and handed Jory a nickel. He pointed over to the two candy machines that stood next to the wall. "The Boston Baked Beans are good."

Jory took the nickel and walked over and inserted it into the candy machine's slot.

She twisted the silver handle. A handful of brownish red pellets filled her hand. She spilled them into her mouth and began to chew.

Outside, the snow was coming down in earnest. The flakes were fat and slow and drifted through the air like duck feathers, swirling sideways as much as down. The gas pumps each wore a small rounded hat of snow.

"And it isn't even Thanksgiving," said the gas station man. He shook his head happily.

Grip had the ice cream truck's heater going and the windshield wipers on. He didn't come inside the gas station, so Jory ran out to the truck and hoisted herself up into the leather passenger seat. "Hi," she said breathlessly, glancing at him and then away. The last time she had seen Grip he had been shirtless and struggling with her father. He was now wearing a heavy wool jacket buttoned up to his chin. It was orange and brown plaid with a fur collar. Jory had never seen it before.

Grip pulled the truck out of the parking lot. They drove down Sixteenth Avenue, the wipers making a protesting sound against the mostly dry windshield. Jory slid her hands beneath her thighs. She watched the

582

snowflakes hitting the windshield and melting instantly against the glass. After they had gone a block or two, Grip turned. "How 'bout I take you home," he asked.

She shook her head. "I'm not going back."

"I think you'd better," he said, and glanced in the rearview mirror.

"Why?" Jory noticed that he had red and gold whiskers sprouting all over his face and his hair sprung in unwashed spirals from beneath a faded blue watch cap. He looked tired and not particularly glad to see her. "Are you still worried that my dad will call the police on you?"

"It's crossed my mind."

Jory could feel her throat constricting, as if she had tried to swallow something a little too large. "So you would help Grace run away, but not me?"

"Is that what you think you're doing?"

Jory said nothing. They drove on in silence past Arco's downtown area, past Rol's Car Bath and Tic Tac Towing and Super Thrift Drug. Jory watched a man wearing only a windbreaker slip on the icy sidewalk and catch himself by grabbing on to a lightpost. She tried to swallow past the lump in her throat. "She's really horribly annoying, you know. When she was little, she wouldn't let my mom and dad undress her for bed, so they just had to let her sleep in her clothes every night. And if she didn't get her way, she would cry until she passed out. They thought about sending her to a psychiatrist when she was ten. I heard them talking about it."

"Stop it," Grip said.

"She's half insane."

"I mean it, Jory."

"You just don't know yet because you haven't lived with her. Oh, wait," she said, turning and looking at him. "I guess you have lived with her, haven't you? So now you've seen her complete and utter freakiness in action."

Grip turned the truck's wipers on high. "She's your sister," he said. "And you love her."

"Just like you do, right?" Jory could feel the lump in her throat becoming something solid, a burning densely packed lump of heat that was scalding her from inside.

"I'll take you out to Mrs. Kleinfelter's," said Grip. "You can call your father from there and tell him where you are."

Jory stared out the passenger window at the snow. At the way it was covering everything with white, making the houses and buildings and fields so much cleaner and prettier than they actually were. "She's having someone else's baby," Jory said. "What do you think about that?"

"I think that's old news," Grip said, but he pressed on the gas pedal and the truck swerved slightly across the middle of the road. He spun the steering wheel to the left and the back end of the truck swung around in a wide arc. Jory grabbed the door handle. The truck drifted sideways toward the edge of the road and then slid slowly to a halt with a muffled thump. They sat in stunned silence as the truck engine idled and the wipers continued to squeak back and forth.

Grip rested his head against the top of the steering wheel. "God*dammit,*" he said.

"She's only seventeen," said Jory. Her voice cracked. "That's not so much older than me. Than *I.*"

"Jory," said Grip. "You're just a kid. A fucking little kid."

"No," said Jory. She put both her hands up to her face and shook her head. Then she let her hands fall back into her lap. "You kissed me," she said. "And you meant it. And that was after you knew Grace."

"That was a mistake," said Grip. "I should never, ever have let that happen."

"You left me the record!" said Jory, her voice rising further still. "All the *X*'s and *O*'s."

"Oh, God." Grip shook his head. "I was just trying to say good-bye. And to let you know I still cared about you."

"Are you going to marry her?" Jory asked. She pressed at her eyes with the heels of both hands. "Is that what's going to happen?"

Grip looked down at the floor of the truck for a moment. "I don't know," he said. His voice was very sad. "I'd like to."

Jory gazed at him openmouthed. "You'd be my brother-in-law." She laughed once then, a strange laugh that seemed to rip and tear as it left her throat.

"Look, I'm so sorry if I hurt you," Grip said. "I didn't mean to. I didn't know anything was going to turn out like this."

"You don't think of me like your sister," said Jory. "Not even close."

"No," said Grip. "I don't. But I think I could learn to."

Jory shoved the truck's door open and got out. Her feet slid in the snow on the road and she almost fell.

"Hey," Grip called. He leaned out toward the open door. "Get back *in* here."

Jory slammed the truck door shut and balanced herself against its side. Snow was coming down against her face and hair and the back of her neck. She could feel its icy wetness seeping into the collar of her sweater. She slid sideways down the shoulder of the road and into some snowy grass. She had no idea where she was, but she started marching blindly across what looked like a farmer's field, its brittle weeds whipping wetly against her pant legs. She was stumbling up and down a snowy hillock when she heard the truck door slam and Grip yelling her name. She crossed her arms and tried to walk faster. She could hear him running behind her now, trying to catch up, and then she could hear him breathing and panting, his boots pounding heavily against the ground. At this, she too began to run, and she had a sudden memory of playing Fox and Geese with her father at Christmastime and of the joy-filled terror in knowing that there was no escape. Knowing that the person chasing you, the large male person chasing you, would soon be on you and there was nothing, absolutely nothing, you could do. Jory was running full out now, her arms flailing and her feet sliding beneath her, but Grip grabbed her from behind and she tried to twist out of his grasp and they both fell to the ground. For a second she smelled snow-covered dirt and the wet wool of his coat and felt the sensation of his full weight moving on top of her, something thick and pleasurable rising in her even though her arm was pinned painfully beneath her. Grip breathed heavily in her ear and she felt the sensation again, more strongly this time, and she squirmed wondrously against the whole length of his solid bulk, but then Grip was thrusting himself off her, pulling her up with him. "Get up," he said sharply, even though she was already standing. They stood in the field breathing plumes of smoke out into the snowy air. "I *hate* you," she said, and he dragged her back to the truck by the arm.

They drove on past the water tower and the sugar beet factory and the alfalfa fields now covered in snow. The Birds Eye plant was shut for the winter, but the farmhouses on Chicken Dinner Road each had at least one light burning steadily, and several of their chimneys were now curling with smoke. Grip turned the truck onto Deer Flat Road and made his way down to the end to Mrs. Kleinfelter's house. He pulled into the driveway and then stopped the truck and turned off the ignition. He turned in his seat and took one of Jory's hands in his. She jerked her hand away as hard as she could, but he was stronger and wouldn't let go. He turned her hand over in his and traced the lines in her palm with his finger. "You're going to be fine," he said. "And everything that's happening now will only be a funny memory later on." He frowned at her and folded all her fingers down one at a time until they were wrapped around his. "You'll look back on this and you won't be able to imagine that you ever felt this way. No really." He shushed her head shaking. "You'll be embarrassed to think you ever cared about a weird old guy like me." He nodded. "You'll grow up and meet a hundred more guys and you'll probably break all their hearts and you'll never give me a second thought, except to laugh and wonder what in the hell you were thinking."

Jory tried again to pull her hand away. "You don't know anything," she said. And embarrassingly, she began to cry.

"You're a wonderful person, Jory," he said. "You're smart and beautiful and very brave."

Jory snatched her hand out from under his and held it awkwardly to her chest as if it were burned. Outside the snow kept falling, silent and thick. A layer of it had now completely covered the truck's windshield in a way that made the truck as dark and close as a small enclosed cave.

Grip took his arm off the back of Jory's

seat and sat up. "When you get inside, you should call and tell your father where you are," he said. "He'll be getting worried by now."

Jory reached out and took hold of the truck's door handle. She could suddenly feel that the toilet paper in her underwear was soaked through with blood. "Don't tell me what to do," she said, and she opened the truck's door and stepped out. A large clump of snow fell off the truck's roof and onto the ground, and the blowing snow stung Jory's face and sent icy wet sparks down her hair and neck. She glanced at Grip and then up at Mrs. Kleinfelter's house. The porch light was on and it sent a small beacon of light out through the swirling snow. Behind was Henry's house, deserted and empty. Even the diamond-shaped window was dark now.

Grip leaned out toward her through the open door. "Jory," he said, and there was a small question in his voice. A seeming bit of hesitation. One moment's worth of uncertainty.

Jory looked at his face, at the way his eyes seemed to look into her, but also past her, as if there was something important just over her head, something vital just beyond her profile that he was attempting to see.

She swallowed. "They're sending her away tomorrow," Jory said. "To some unwed mothers' home in Kansas."

"What?" said Grip, but it was obvious that he understood. "What do you mean? When tomorrow?" He leaned forward and clutched at the door handle. His fingers were so close to hers that she could feel the slight human heat that they gave off.

"I don't know," said Jory. "Why does it matter? She's just going."

Grip had turned completely sideways in his seat, so that he now faced Jory. "Listen. I need you to do something for me," he said. He leaned farther out of the truck and was trying to take hold of her wrist. "I need you to call Grace and tell her — tell her to meet me somewhere. Down the block from your house or somewhere." His eyes darted across Jory's face.

"You can't come there."

"Tell her to meet me down the block from your house, all right? At the other end of the block — no, down the street by God's Park or God's Lot or whatever it's called. In — I don't know" — Grip glanced at his watch — "one hour. Exactly one hour from now. Okay?" Grip eased himself out from under the steering wheel, moving over into the passenger seat. His knees were now directly in front of Jory's chest. He was so close that she could smell the tang of beer and something that smelled like canned plums on his breath. He reached out and clamped his hands down on top of both of hers and squeezed them tightly. "I need you to do this for me, Jory. Please?"

Jory tried to pull away from him, to move out of his reach, but he only gripped her wrists more firmly.

"I know you'll do this for me," he said. He peered carefully into her eyes, scanning them for a particular response, an unspoken agreement. His fingers tightened around hers and she had a sudden impulse to scratch and slap at him, to leave marks that would last for at least a day or two. "I *know* you'll do this," he said again. "I know I can count on you."

"You don't know anything," said Jory, and she realized that this was the second time she had said this tonight. With a sudden wrench of her arms, she twisted out of his hold, the momentum sending her a step sideways in the snow. She glanced back at Grip once more, at his fearful and agonized expression that had absolutely nothing to do with her. Then she shut the truck's door and ran through the snow and up the stairs to Mrs. Kleinfelter's house, where she opened the door without knocking, as if someone inside had already invited her in.

Inside, the house was warm and smelled faintly of dust and oil, like a furnace that has just been turned on. Mrs. Kleinfelter was sitting in her favorite chair reading some sort of magazine, but she stood up when Jory came in. "Well, look who's here," she said, smiling.

Jory stood unmoving on the living room rug, as if on a small island that now separated her from the rest of the world. "Oh, Hilda," she said, and then she couldn't say anything more.

Mrs. Kleinfelter took a step toward Jory, but Jory had suddenly found the ability to move, and she walked quickly and with purpose past Mrs. Kleinfelter and into the kitchen, where she picked up the heavy black phone receiver and dialed. The phone rang only once.

"Hello?" her father said, the note of panic in his voice apparent even to her.

"Dad," she said.

"Jory, where are you?" She could hear a note of anger now expanding to fill the space his fear had previously occupied.

"Dad," she said again, as her heart beat fast and faster. "Is Grace there?"

"Just tell me where you are and I'll come pick you up."

Jory took a shaky breath. She suddenly saw that this moment weighed as much as all the previous ones combined. That all the other mental skirmishes had been small change, child's play. Here, now, was her very own unexpected expected. For one small suspended second in time, she still had the ability to do or not do something, that once done she would then never be able to undo.

She let out her long-held breath with a quavering sigh. "Grip is coming for Grace," she said.

And then it was done.

Mrs. Kleinfelter drove the car cautiously down the snowy streets. Jory sat huddled on her side of the car, gazing reflexively out the passenger window, watching but not seeing the houses and countryside sliding past. The snow had stopped falling and the early evening sky was suddenly clear; an almost rosy-colored blue shown through the scattered clouds that remained. And even though the sky was now nearly empty, the snow that had blanketed the landscape remained, covering the fields and roads and houses with a beautifying, cleansing layer of crystalline white that rounded and softened all of Arco's sharp angles and edges.

With some remote part of herself, Jory continued to register the car's silent and ineluctable movement down these most familiar streets. They glided past her old elementary school, the Strike It Rich Bowling Lanes, Vanny's Line-a-Diner, and Wretha's Beauty Salon, where her mother went once a year to have her hair permed — her one concession to beauty. Next came each of the neighborhood houses she knew as well as her own, and the front yards she had ridden her bike past and taken shortcuts through and stolen flowers from. Finally, they turned the corner onto Ninth Avenue and Jory could see, even from the end of the block, the police cruiser's red revolving lights casting a silent searchlight's glow through the evening air. She sat up with a start, her stomach giving a horrible squeeze.

"Oh, dear," said Mrs. Kleinfelter, peering concentratedly out the windshield. "What on earth is going on?"

Mrs. Kleinfelter's car continued its stately path to the house on Ninth Avenue, and Jory watched, wide-eyed now, as the police car in front of her house reversed and then backed out of their driveway, slowly passing directly next to Mrs. Kleinfelter's car, going the opposite direction. Jory held perfectly still, watching the black-and-white car pass within two feet of the car she was in. She had only one glance at Grip's face as he gazed at her in amazement from the back-seat of the police car. And then he was gone.

"Oh, no," said Mrs. Kleinfelter. She turned and stared backward at the police car and then caught herself and veered awkwardly across the road, finally pulling the car to a crooked halt a little way in front of Jory's house.

"I have to go," Jory said, already bolting out of the car. She didn't even wait to hear what Mrs. Kleinfelter was saying in response, but ran through the melting snow across the driveway and into the front yard.

Her father stood on the sidewalk, coatless, holding Grace by the arms. Grace seemed to be barefoot, but when she caught sight of Jory, she wrenched herself out of her father's grasp and strode across the snowy lawn toward her younger sister. Jory saw the look on her sister's face and tried to take a backward step, but Grace was on her in a moment, slapping and scratching furiously at Jory's chest and neck. "What did you do?" Grace cried, flailing wildly at Jory with both of her hands. "What did you *do*?" Jory tried to fend Grace off, but Grace was shockingly strong and landed several blows solidly on the side of Jory's head. Jory's ear rang with a sensation that was oddly enlivening; in fact, even as Jory could feel the skin on her face stinging and burning, she wondered at the marvel of being this physically close to her sister again, of breathing in Grace's slightly bitter breath and feeling the jarring solidity of her bones and the active tension in her sister's hands and arms. Jory had a sudden vivid long-buried memory of the times from their childhood in which it was *she* who had flown at Grace, biting and clawing, while Grace had merely stood — smiling and imperturbable — as Jory's fury raged higher, provoked onward by Grace's apparent joy in her own martyrdom. And now, finally, here was Grace — righteous, implacable Grace — furiously hitting her sister with complete abandon. The joy that surged through Jory was unaccountable. She could hear their father shouting their names and trying to pry them apart, but Jory hung desperately on, gripping Grace by the wrists and then the hands, both of them clutching at each other as if they were drowning, as their father continued to drag Grace backward until, with a sudden ripping tug, their hold on each other was broken.

Their father took Grace completely in his

arms, holding her tightly around the waist as if in an embrace. "Grace," he was saying, and his voice sounded infinitely tender, as if he were speaking to a much younger child. "Come on," he said, "come on inside, Grace," and then he turned her away from Jory and began shepherding her back toward the house, both of his arms still around Grace's now suddenly slumping shoulders. Jory watched, and as they were walking she saw Grace slip once and almost fall in the snowy grass, but her father lifted her up, righted her, and continued to gently pull her toward the porch. Then her father opened the front door and the two of them disappeared inside and the door was shut behind them.

Jory stood panting on the lawn, her hands on her knees. The Reisensteins' dog barked twice and then there was no other sound to be heard. It was now as if nothing had ever happened to disturb this silent, wintry night — as if all the actors and players and all their little ecstasies and anguishes had been mysteriously whisked offstage in an instant. As if they had never even been. In a daze, Jory walked up to the porch and sank down on one of the snow-dusted steps. She could feel the shock of the cement's freezing wetness seeping instantly through her pants and her underwear, past the bloody toilet paper, clear to her skin. Jory heard the front door open behind her and her father came out onto the stoop. He was now wearing his winter coat and carrying an old brown woolen one of her mother's. "Put this on," he said.

Jory didn't move.

He leaned down and draped the wool coat over her shoulders. Then he sat down next to her on the step and then leaned over and carefully forced each of her arms through the coat sleeves, pulling the coat tightly around her and buttoning it to the collar.

"You promised you wouldn't call the police." Jory's words came out in a strangled choke. "You *promised*."

Her father stared straight ahead. He said nothing and he didn't even try to smile.

"He doesn't need to go to jail!" Jory felt as if she were pleading with someone far more important than her father — with God, or a judge, someone who could repeal judgments or commute sentences.

This statement seemed to reanimate her father. "Jory, I don't even know where to begin." He stared at her as if trying to decide what to say. Finally, he held up his index finger. "Number one, he has a record. Ed Hewett says he was involved in some kind of bad drug-dealing business down in Texas. And number two, this is *in addition* to the fact that he was keeping your sister — who is a minor — at that house full of reprobates and runaways."

Jory looked down at the cement step. "She went there herself."

"We have no idea how she got there, Jory. And no matter what happened, no matter what went on, she is only seventeen years old. He is a grown-up male who knew exactly what he was doing."

Jory had no response to this. She watched her own breath crystallizing in the air between them. "What will happen to him now?"

"I don't know. They're taking him to the county jail for the time being."

Jory put her arms around her knees and then leaned her head down onto them.

"Jory," he said firmly. "We did the right thing."

"You don't know anything," she said into her knees.

"What?"

Jory raised her head and spoke more clearly. "Maybe we should have just let her go. Let *them* go."

Her father breathed heavily in and out through his nose. "Sometimes in life we have to do things we don't like to do. Hard things that don't please everyone."

"*You're* pleased," said Jory, deliberately turning her full gaze on him. "You're glad the police came and took him away. You're glad Grace is going."

Her father did his best to look unperturbed by this comment. He rubbed his hands together and then blew into them to warm them. After a moment he folded his hands and clasped them between his knees, and then he turned his head and looked Jory in the eye. "You're the one who told me he was coming here."

Jory gave a tiny gasp. It felt oddly as if he, too, had slapped her. She bit the inside of her cheek with a swift deliberateness that surprised even her. A swirl of salty blood flooded her tongue.

Her father carefully reached out his arm and pulled her in close to him. She could feel the scratchy collar of her mother's coat against her face and could smell the hint of Fleurs de Rocaille perfume that permeated it. Her eyes and throat began to fill. Her father hugged her even closer, as if trying to comfort her and restrain her at the same time. He patted and stroked her arm through the thickness of the coat and Jory buried her head in the hollow of his shoulder. She could hear his heart beating quiet and steady beneath her ear. It thumped on and on, never changing or slackening in its pace as she leaned into him.

After a minute or two, her father lifted his head and stared deliberately up at the evening sky. "Look at that," he said. "Venus is clear over next to Mars." He pointed so that Jory could see. "I'd forgotten they were going to line up this month. You know that's what they think was going on the year Christ was born. That the star of Bethlehem was actually Venus, Jupiter, and Mars all in alignment."

Jory righted herself on the step. She tried to wipe her nose on the scratchy nap of her mother's coat sleeve. She gazed up briefly into the plummy violet of the darkening winter sky. "I don't really care, Dad."

She saw in the light that he looked infinitely sad. And then furious. And then finally sad again.

"I love him," she said.

Her father made a noise somewhere deep in his throat and closed his eyes. He sounded not angry, but disgusted. Perhaps even embarrassed.

Jory sat silently on the step looking anywhere but at her father.

"Jory, look. I cannot stress this strongly

enough." Her father reached out and took her hand. He gripped her fingers between his own. "Listen to me, Jory." He seemed suddenly determined to say her name as many times as possible. "This man is a criminal. He preys on young, inexperienced girls. And he tries to act like some kind of guru or Svengali or something, because his own life is so miserable that he has to find teenagers who'll worship him to make himself feel better." Her father had obviously given this subject some thought.

He was crushing her hand between both of his. "Do you understand this? Do you? Tell me you do."

Jory tried to pull her hand out from between his, but he was stronger and held on.

He sighed audibly. "Someday, when you're quite a bit older than you are now, this will all look different. This man will look very different to you. But for now, Jory, you're just going to have to take my word for it — this man is *no good.* And his intentions — for you and your sister — are and were *no good.* They were *worse* than no good." He blinked several times and then ran his hand through his hair. "And that," he said, unfolding his long legs and standing wearily up from the step, "is the end of this discussion."

Jory continued to sit on the step long after her father had gone inside. Her head felt empty and shaken, as if its contents — the ants or bees that had taken up residence there — were still humming, but at a lower-level frequency, a nighttime stupor. Too much had happened for her to even take in, and now, somewhere across town, Grip was in jail. And inside her house Grace was waiting for the morning, when their father would drive her and her old blue suitcase to the airport. Jory could not believe any of it, even though she had had a large hand in all of its unfolding. It was Saturday, November 21, she suddenly remembered, and she had started her first period. She was grown up now, with the heavy aching in her gut and the bloodstains on her pants to prove it.

CHAPTER TWENTY

They didn't find her right way.

In fact, the next morning, their father's first thought was that Grace had taken off again, even though her suitcase and purse were still in her room, and so he had gone next door to the Hewetts' to talk to the detective, to see what legal or investigative steps he should take now.

The hour for Sunday School and church came and went, but no one in the house mentioned this or made a move toward going. As the long afternoon wore on, her father had had to call the airline and cancel the plane ticket, but then that evening, after their mother had discovered that her pill bottle was missing, he finally gave in to their mother's pleas and called the Arco police. Two men in tightly fitting navy blue uniforms, smelling like coffee and cigarette smoke, came and sat in their living room and talked to her parents, as Jory read book after book to Frances, who was sitting up very excitedly in her bed. The men searched the backyard and alley with flashlights and went through Grace's dresser drawers and closet, but, still, it wasn't until they looked in the garage and asked her father to lift the heavy door on the bomb shelter that they realized what had happened. Right before-hand, her father had said over and over that he didn't see how Grace could have lifted the door by herself, that he had built it deliberately so that none of them but he could do it. He had made it that way on purpose, he'd said. He had made careful calculations in advance. Very careful, specific calculations that were scientifically accurate and sound.

Later, after the ambulance had left, Jory overheard one of the policemen remark to the other that perhaps Grace had grown some since her father had made those calculations. Either that, he said, or she had been very determined. Or maybe both, said the other policeman, who was younger and seemed bent on having the final word.

At the hospital, in the emergency room, Jory and Frances were made to wait out in the hallway while their mother and father met with the doctors. A few hours later, when

Grace was moved into the critical care unit, Jory and Frances sat in a small beige-colored waiting room because only their parents were allowed to stay next to Grace's bedside. Frances was too young — the rules said you had to be fourteen or older — so Jory was forced to stay in the family waiting room with her younger sister. Periodically, their father would come briefly out into the waiting room and sit on one of the green vinyl couches next to Jory. Frances would clamber onto his lap and the three of them would sit silently, as if waiting for a church service to begin. There were magazines in the waiting room and occasionally a few other very silently waiting, woebegone-looking people, and quite a bit more frequently nurses, whose white shoes squeaked across the waxed squares in the linoleum floor.

Without meaning to, Jory had now memorized the watermarks in the acoustic tile ceiling and the three paintings of pastel-colored boating scenes on the waiting room's walls, and she had repeatedly and blankly observed the view from the waiting room's one small window. The view was of the parking lot below, filled with only a few shiny-hooded cars and a lone flagpole that supported a periodically flapping American flag. Their mother refused to come back into the waiting room at all. She was sitting next to Grace's bed, their father said, holding Grace's hand and singing "Catch a Falling Star" and "Lollipops and Roses" and "When Your Hair Has Turned to Silver." These, for inexplicable reasons, were Grace's favorite childhood songs. "But why won't she wake up?" Frances kept saying. "She's slept all night long already."

The next afternoon sometime, when a faint, nauseating smell of roast beef drifted up from the hospital cafeteria, Frances began very quietly to cry. She was sitting across from Jory on the other green vinyl couch and her head was down, but Jory could see Frances's shoulders shaking. "What's wrong?" Jory whispered across the room at her. Frances looked up.

"Nothing," she said, sobbing a little.

Jory walked over to the couch and peered down at her. After a moment, Frances lifted up her car coat's hem. Underneath, a large pool of liquid was spreading quickly across the shiny green of the couch. "I didn't know where the bathroom was," said Frances, gulping. "And I didn't want Grace to wake up while I was gone." She stared down at the couch as if it were partly to blame. Jory took her hand and tugged her off the couch and they walked down the tiled hall, with Frances taking wary peeks at the lone nurse sitting in the nurses' station.

Inside the restroom, Jory locked the door and tugged off Frances's coat and her corduroy pants and her underwear and rolled them hastily up into a ball, and after glancing around the room she stuffed the sodden mass into a metal garbage can with a swinging lid.

"That's my Christmas coat," Frances wailed, "and now I don't have any underwear on."

"It doesn't matter," said Jory. She took off her own short jacket and pulled it firmly around Frances, buttoning it and rolling up the sleeves. "See?" said Jory. The navy peacoat hung down considerably past Frances's bare knees. Jory smoothed down the hem of the wool coat. "You're all covered up now."

Frances looked tearfully unconvinced. "But underneath my bottom is all bare," she whispered. She shrank back against the bathroom wall and began breathing haphazardly in and out, in the way she did in times of great personal distress. "And you threw my red coat away."

Jory took Frances by the shoulder and guided her into one of the stalls. She toed off her own mary janes and unsnapped and unzipped her own corduroy pants and shrugged out of both them and her day-of-the-week underwear. Frances stared with great fascination at the sanitary napkin and belt Jory was wearing. "What is that? That diaper . . . strap thing?" she asked. For a moment she seemed to have forgotten her perturbation at her own clothing situation.

"It's nothing," said Jory.

Frances looked stricken. "But what is it? Do you pee into it?"

"No, said Jory, "of course not. It's just something girls have to wear sometimes when they get big."

"Why?" said Frances.

"Just because," said Jory. "Now be quiet." She sat on the closed toilet lid and stood Frances in front of her, pulling her own panties up over Frances's bare feet and legs and up to her rounded little belly.

"Put your hand on my shoulder," she said, and Frances circled her small arm around Jory's neck while Jory put Frances's socks and shoes back on. "But if it's just like sleeping, why doesn't Dad just wake her up and put her in the car?" said Frances.

"Don't start that again," said Jory. She tied a tight bow in each of Frances's shoes. She stood up and pulled her own pants back on, feeling vulnerable and naked without her underwear.

"But why did Grace go down into the bomb shelter to get into her coma?"

Jory gazed back into Frances's brown eyes, which looked so much like their mother's.

"Because she wanted to be alone," Jory said. "She was feeling sad, and she wanted to change things — to make things different." This was a thought that had come to Jory sometime late the night before when she had been sitting in the waiting room. That Grace had just been trying to change things. To fix things. To make things better. This rationalization was obviously easier to consider than its opposite: that Grace had wanted to strike back, to make things far worse, to make things forever and ever unfixable.

She and her sisters were all born in this same hospital. Rumor had it that when Frances was born, Jory had been too young to be allowed into the maternity ward, so she and Grace stood outside on that blustery March evening and gazed up at their mother, who was on the second floor and leaning out the window. This next event was something that their mother loved to retell, how Jory had yelled upward to her, "Are you still fat?" and how her mother had yelled back down, "Yes, but I'm not pregnant anymore, if that's what you mean." Jory had no memory of this: neither of the event nor of her participation in it.

They returned to the family waiting room. When the elevator at the end of the hall pinged sharply, Jory's heart lurched and she hoped it was her father. But it was only a man in a suit and large gray overcoat who walked past them and down the long tiled hallway, his unbuttoned coat billowing slightly behind him. Surely someone would come and tell them something sometime soon. Surely there would be some kind of news, some new information that the doctors would give them. Where was their father and why hadn't he come back?

That night, much later, after the waiting room window had grown dark and Frances had fallen asleep on the floor, still wearing her big sister's coat, Jory lay on her side on the green plastic couch and rubbed her feet together, back and forth, back and forth, making endless bargainings with God. She would never go to another dance or listen to her transistor radio or worry about what her clothes looked like ever again. She would happily drop out of high school and never touch a drop of alcohol. She would cut off her hair, she would shave her head bald too, she would never make out with or even kiss a single boy or man. She would be the maid of honor at Grip and Grace's wedding and she would never think of him as anything other than her brother-in-law — her sister's husband. And she would do these things happily and without question, no matter how humiliating or hard, no matter how disgusting or unappealing or embarrassing. She would do all this and more. In fact, she would do anything, give up anything, anything at all, if only God would keep His part of the bargain. If only He would save Grace. *Save her. Save her. Save her.* The waiting room seemed to have a sort of humming noise coming from somewhere in its walls or ceiling. The elevator had quit pinging and the only noise now was the room's strange low-pitched humming and the night nurse coughing quietly once in a while. The rest of the world, the part that was outside this building, made no sound at all.

Sometime in the very early morning, Jory woke up with a start to find her father sitting next to her and holding her sock foot. He was rubbing her foot and looking out into the empty waiting room, not making a sound. Jory leaned up on her elbows. "Where're my shoes?" she said. Jory tried to sit up, but her father hung grimly on to her foot. "What is it?" she said. "What's happened? Is she awake?" Her father kept rubbing the bottom of her foot, massaging the same small spot over and over through her sock, while still not looking at her. Jory wrenched her foot out of his hand. "Dad?" she said, beginning to cry. She held her hands up to her mouth and made a terrible gagging, retching sound. *"Dad?"* she said again, pleading now. He lifted his head finally and forced his eyes to meet hers.

And in that instant, she saw. She saw that everything she had once known or thought she had known had been lifted up and away, as lightly and easily as if it had never even been at all. "No," she said, *"NoNoNoNo."* and she clutched at his shirtfront, pulling at his pocket and ripping out its stitches, and then she was standing and a noise was rising up out of her and a nurse was hurrying toward them, her white rubber-bottomed shoes shrieking against the spotless tile. Jory thrashed and struggled against the stricture of her father's arms and cried out in a voice that was new to her and in sounds unmusical, while her father told her softly that the wedding had come to pass while Jory had

614

been dreaming, all unwatchful — the bride-groom had come for the wedding feast and had chosen his bride, but Jory had been asleep and had been caught unawares, Jory had foolishly let her lamp go out, her father said. She had slept, and the world had blinked its eye and all in a twinkling instant the door had been forever shut. Jory was now on the floor, clutching the knee por-tion of her father's pant leg, but she could still hear his voice from up above, *Then spake the Lord saying, Verily I say unto you, watch therefore, for no one knows the hour nor the day when the Son of Man cometh.* No, Jory cried now, no, no! Lord, Lord, she begged, open unto me! *But the Lord said, the door is shut tight against you, for you have been foolish, and I know you not.*

I know you not.

CHAPTER TWENTY-ONE

The Good Shepherd Funeral Home was a white-stuccoed building partially covered with ivy. Outside in the parking lot it was cold and windy, the sky brilliantly over-exposed and combed free of clouds. Jory wasn't sure which day of the week it was, Wednesday maybe, or Thursday.

She remembers a side door and a faceless young man wearing a dark, slightly too small suit who led them down an arched hallway that smelled of antiseptic and carnations overlaid with a faint cedar odor. They were made to sit behind a thickly gauzed red curtain in something called the "private family alcove," a tiny room to one side of the chapel where everything on the outside could be seen only hazily and at a red remove. It was silent and dim in the alcove and the close smell of the flower arrangements on either side of them made Jory feel that something was expected of her, something that she would not be able to deliver. When she had imagined this moment, last night, at home, in her bed, she had thought that something might occur here today that would make all of this seem vitally, indisputably real. That seeing the looks on other people's faces would cause her own to adopt a similar expression, that her face and feelings would then mirror theirs, and that Grace being gone — this was how she thought of it, as *Grace being gone* — would become, through imitation or symbiosis, something acknowledged, accepted, and possibly even almost borne. She could see now how laughable, how absurdly idiotic that idea had been.

Faint minor-key organ music played from somewhere, although from where Jory was unsure, since there was no organ to be seen. A small group of people filed silently past the red curtain and sat, hushed or occasionally coughing and gazing toward the front of the chapel in the short rows of hardwood pews: Rhonda Russell and her parents, Ms. Lindbloom, the guitar man from Hope House, Detective Hewett and his wife, and Mrs. Kleinfelter. Laird was there, along with Rhea and her sister Connie, as well as Jude Mullinix, who sat straight-backed and all alone in the last pew. Jory had watched as these people made their silent way past the alcove's red-filtering curtain, and she had seen their faces, even though they apparently could not see hers.

Grip was not there. Neither were nine-tenths of the people from their church. The Quanbecks had not been allowed to hold the service in their own church, for reasons — Pastor Ron had said, clearing his throat — that should be obvious. Jory's mother had slapped his arm hard when he said this, even though Pastor Ron was standing in her hospital room holding a cup of coffee. The burning coffee had then sloshed out of the cup and down his pant leg, but no one, including her father, had apologized or volunteered to clean it up. And so it wasn't Pastor Ron who now read the eulogy or even Brother Elmore; it was a smiling white-haired man with scrubbed ruddy skin whose neck bulged out over his starched shirt collar. Jory would remember the man's reddened and practically nonporous skin as if she had examined it every day, as if she had looked upon his beaming, rubberized face her whole life long. The man claimed that Grace's middle name was Marie, not Mary. He liked using Grace's full name, as if that were what people had called her, and each time he did, Jory's mother took a small intake of breath that sounded almost like a hiss. "Grace *Mary,*" her mother would whisper loudly, her voice surely penetrating past the mesh curtain. Jory's father did nothing to stop her, but sat with his head down, not even looking at what was going on. He would occasionally stretch his hand out toward Jory's mother, as if he were going to touch her, but then he would apparently change his mind and instead let his hand hang there in the air for a minute before slowly drawing it back.

The white-haired man spoke on: "As Paul said in Philippians 1:21, *'For me to live is Christ, and to die is gain.'* And indeed, fellow mourners, though our hearts are very heavy today and filled with sorrowing, it is a joyful occasion for the one who has passed over into God's abundance. For she has gone to be with her Lord, and will live forever in a place where there's no pain or grief. No disease or death. Only joy everlasting with her bridegroom, Christ Jesus."

The white-haired man leaned forward and beamed at his small audience. "The angels in heaven are celebrating today at the addition of Grace Marie, Heaven's newest bright and beautiful star." Jory's mother seethed. She was sitting on one of the padded folding chairs to the left of Jory and was wearing a dark oxblood-colored dress that almost matched the curtain they were sitting behind. Jory had never seen the dark red dress before today. It had buttons in the front, but they were done up incorrectly. Her mother had been let out of the hospital only this morning. The doctor had said that she could come to the funeral, but that she should probably return to the fifth floor of Good Samaritan tonight. The fifth floor of the hospital was where they kept people who "just needed a little time to recuperate." This was what her father had told Jory three days ago. Her mother was now busily ripping the funeral program into tiny pieces. Jory peered down at her own program. It was engraved in gold letters with her sister's name across the top and several lines of writing below:

GRACE M. QUANBECK
December 7, 1953–November 22, 1970

~A ROSEBUD~

When a teen is lifted to her heavenly father
  up above
Those left behind might ponder the depth of
  His great love,
The sadness that we feel is so immense

That we are tempted to question God's
   good sense.
Why not take just those whose time has
   run,
Whose days have been long beneath our
   sun?
But you see — God needs most the bud
   that has yet to bloom
To fill heaven's air with youth's sweet
   perfume,
So today as a new young angel sings on
   high
Those of us left below must learn to say
   good-bye.

Jory placed her program under her leg.
Her mother's was now a drifted pile of
white confetti on the floor. Frances was
leaning forward and avidly watching the
proceedings going on outside of the red
curtain and kicking her feet, in their black
Sunday shoes, against the metal rung of the
folding chair. Jory had a sudden impulse to
turn to Grace, to nudge her with her elbow
and point out the terrible rhymes in the
program, but with a sensation as swift and
terrible as an elevator's sickening, disorient-
ing drop, she realized that Grace was not
here. She was the only person with whom
Jory needed to speak or be next to or even

621

look at and she was the only person with whom Jory could do none of those things. She wanted Grace to explain what was going on and what all of this meant and how best to live through this experience — which was what Grace had always done for her — but her sister was gone. She had gone somewhere that Jory could not follow and she had thoughtlessly left no instructions or help to show the way.

Jory's mother now began silently shaking her head back and forth and then she stood up and teetered on her high heels through the torn pieces of her program, stepping past Jory and Frances and their father and stumbling slightly in her rush to get out of the private family alcove. Frances stood up too and tried to start after her mother, but Jory grabbed her by the coat sleeve and held her sister fast. Their father seemed incapable of noticing any of this and merely sat, his head hanging down in a way that was completely unfamiliar to Jory. He looked like someone else's father. Like any other father in the world, but not hers.

The same young man in the ill-fitting suit who had ushered them into the Good Shepherd Funeral Home now led them back down the arched and antiseptic-smelling hallway. As they walked, he murmured something about "greeting the other mourners in the reception area," but her father had shaken his head so vigorously that the young man had said nothing further and allowed them to escape unaided through the chapel's outer door. Jory squinted in the brilliant glare of the parking lot, looking blankly at the scattered cars lined up and waiting for reanimation. Her mother was already sitting in the front seat of the green Buick and Frances now dropped their father's hand and ran toward the car. Behind Jory, the chapel's door opened and shut with a sound like a nail being pulled out of wood and Jory turned and saw Mrs. Kleinfelter buttoning up her gray wool coat and stepping out onto the pavement. The two of them stood looking at each other. Suddenly Jory crossed the space between them and was pinned firmly to the scratchy front of Mrs. Kleinfelter's coat. She breathed in the faint odor of naphthalene, boiled potatoes, and waxy dust even as she simultaneously registered the fragility of Mrs. Kleinfelter's shoulder bones, her soft arm flesh, and the cobwebbed nature of her hair. Mrs. Kleinfelter held Jory close and stroked her head as if it were made of something breakable, and then she pulled back from Jory and took her by the arms. "I'll take care of So Handsome until you're ready to come get him," she said. "But just until then." Jory shook her head and gazed blindly at Mrs. Kleinfelter's face. At the small pearl earrings clipped haphazardly on her earlobes. "I can't," Jory whispered desperately, her voice caught somewhere far back in her throat. "I can't do this." Mrs. Kleinfelter grasped Jory's upper arms so tightly it hurt. "You can," she said. "And you're going to." Jory could feel her own mouth falling, crumpling into something terrible. "Please," she whispered, "please help me." Mrs. Kleinfelter gave Jory's arms a final squeeze and took a step backward. "The worst part's already over," she said in the firmest voice Jory had ever heard her use, "and you'll live through the rest." Her face took on the look of most impartial truth telling. "You're the kind that can," she said. Jory tried to swallow. "Let me stay with you," she begged. Mrs. Kleinfelter glanced over at the green Buick. She shook her head, but Jory could see that this thought was not new to her. Mrs. Kleinfelter took a further step backward and then she turned and, without looking back once, walked with stiff purpose toward her truck. A fierce wind now gusted and blew. Jory could hear her father starting the Buick's engine, but she continued to stand watching as Mrs. Kleinfelter climbed up into her old truck and then closed the door behind her.

At the cemetery, her mother absolutely refused to get out of the car, and Jory and Frances and their father had had to hold hands and walk, leaning into the glaring brightness of the November wind. They picked their way through the cemetery's slightly frozen grass, moving carefully past the blocky squares of granite headstones, as Jory tried to keep a tight purchase on the hem of her skirt. The white-haired man had gotten there ahead of them. He now stood waiting beneath a pagoda-like structure that had been erected over a small dark hole that had been dug in the ground. The hole was next to a double headstone inscribed with the names of Jory's grandparents: *Gilbert Clayton and Eunice Opal Quanbeck — Faithful Servants of the Lord — Now Gone to Their Glory.* The white-haired man was holding a large black Bible down against his thigh and his tie kept blowing up and over his shoulder. Jory watched as he finally gave up and set the Bible on the ground next to the hole in order to capture his tie and pin it beneath his suit jacket. He held out his hand as they approached and her father had to drop Jory's hand to shake his.

The white-haired man smiled and said something, but his words were blown away in the wind. Jory had no clear memory of what happened while he spoke, except that the wind made whipping sounds on the open pages of his Bible and the bottom of her dress would not stay down no matter how she grasped at it. She could feel a terrible need to laugh rising up in her throat — a tearing, tickling sensation that made sweat suddenly break out on her forehead.

The man stopped speaking then. He closed his Bible and tried to plaster his hair back into place across his scalp. Then he bent over, and as Jory watched, he opened a large tan-colored rectangular box and picked out the delicate pale blue urn that held her sister's ashes. He held it out toward her father.

Frances tugged fiercely on Jory's hand. "Is the angel baby in there, too?" Her bright peeping voice rang out and then was just as quickly whisked away. No one answered her.

Her father took the urn and cupped it in his hands. He held it just slightly out from his body and examined it, smoothing his large hand down one side as if it were a beautiful but skittish horse he was trying to bridle. The white-haired man nodded, indicating that their father should kneel and place the pale blue urn into the hole, but her father seemed unable to believe what was being required of him. He faltered and stepped backward with the urn instead, holding it tight to his chest. "No," her father said, and he took another step backward, away from the small dark square cut in the earth. *"No,"* he said, and then he turned toward the car, carrying the urn half beneath the flap of his suit jacket, as if someone might try to steal it from him.

Jory could hear the white-haired man calling after her father, but she, too, had turned and taken Frances's hand and was pulling her along after their father, who was now heading back toward the car, striding ahead of his daughters and not even waiting for them to catch up. The wind snatched and tore at Jory's dress and at her eyes and they filled so that she could barely make out her father's outline as he continued to march ahead of them, never even turning around once as Jory tried to call out to him. She could feel Frances trip and lose her balance and then begin to cry as Jory continued to drag her across the lumpy and frozen ground of the cemetery; she no longer cared what happened to any of them and hadn't since that moment in the hospital. The universe had opened up and revealed its own perfectly blank face to her own, returning her gaze with a flattened emptiness that stretched on and on and on — a world so wide and featureless and open, so dark and formless, that light never pierced it: no sun, no moon, no stars. And it now seemed entirely possible that two girls and a stooped man carrying a pale blue urn could stumble mutely on across the face of it forever, seeking a home, or at least a resting place, and finding none.

■ ■ ■ ■

PART FIVE:
SUNNY SAN DIEGO

■ ■ ■ ■

Chapter Twenty-Two

The stars are not wanted now; put out
   every one,
Pack up the moon and dismantle the sun,
Pour away the ocean and sweep up the
   wood;
For nothing now can ever come to any
   good.
                    W. H. Auden, "Funeral Blues"

It was the end of March and unseasonably warm the day that Jory's father told her that her mother was going to go stay in California for a while. She would be staying at their aunt Annette's in San Diego, and she would be taking Frances with her. Jory and her father were sitting in the front yard in two of the lawn chairs, which she had set up with a certain amount of hopefulness. The sky overhead was becoming a deep and shadowy blue, and at her father's announcement Jory felt a wave of heavy torpor washing over and through her.

"What if Mom doesn't come back?"

"Oh," her father said, "I think she will."

"How can you be sure?"

Her father turned his head toward her. "She can only tolerate Aunt Annette in very small doses. Plus, she hates California." He smiled weakly.

"Maybe she'll like it more this time."

"Maybe."

"There will only be two of us." Jory could hear the catch in her own voice.

"Only for a little while." Her father gazed up at the sky. After a moment he raised his hand and pointed at a tiny pinpoint of light that had just appeared.

"Please don't tell me about the stars, Dad."

Her father lowered his hand and then held it in his lap. He wore a small look of hurt and dismay.

"I don't care about the grandeur of the universe anymore, and neither should you."

Her father said nothing. He made no objection, even to this blasphemy.

Jory felt a band of something tight inside her give a twinge and then break and snap free. "There are ants that are alive. Ants! And stray dogs and murderers and insane people and psychopaths and people who only have brain stems and can't even think. And retarded people and crazy people. People who shoot other people and kill them and torture them. They're all alive. They get to be alive." Jory stopped as if finally choking on her own vehemence. She shook her head. She shook her head again and looked her father full in the face.

The night was settling in now — the sky was shifting from light to dark with a disconcerting urgency. Her father's eyes looked abnormally bright, but that could have been because of how dark everything else now was. He continued to stare at her without speaking.

"Mom's never going to come back," she said.

She could hear her father's sudden intake of breath.

"I want to go live with Mrs. Kleinfelter." Jory felt as if she had reached out and pinched her father, hard and with complete deliberation.

"What?" Her father held perfectly still in his chair.

Jory couldn't seem to say any more. It was as if she had held these things in for so long that now there was nothing more to be said. There was no more explanation needed.

"No," her father said. As she had known

he would.

"We made her do what she did," Jory said. "It was our fault. Yours and mine."

There was a moment of shocked silence before her father spoke. "What are you talking about?"

"You know what I'm talking about."

"Jory," her father said in a tone that was sad but also held a note of sternest warning. "I already told you that I don't ever want to discuss this."

"It's true, though," she said. "And I don't care what you say. We should have just let her stay with Grip. We should have just let her do whatever she wanted."

"She *did* do whatever she wanted." Her father's voice grew suddenly sharp and so pointed that it seemed to be hurting him to speak. "She got her way completely."

Jory sat in her chair. She thought about what her father had just said.

"She always did just exactly what she pleased. No one ever controlled her for even a minute." He laughed suddenly, a strange barking laugh that softened just a little toward the end. He was silent for a moment and Jory thought maybe he was done, that that was all they were ever going to say on the subject, but then he started again. "When Grace was just tiny," he said, "before you were even born, a man came by our house leading a Shetland pony and Grace got so excited that I asked the man if she could sit on the horse for a minute and he said sure and so I lifted her onto this pony's back and she was so thrilled and entranced that she started to shiver. I had to stand there and hold her on that horse's back for about ten minutes while I tried to engage this old farmer in conversation so that he wouldn't want to take off. But finally he had to move on, so I lifted Grace off the pony and she screamed so loudly and kicked me so furiously that even the old farmer looked genuinely worried. I took her into the house, but it didn't do any good, she screamed and flailed wildly enough that she scratched up her own face and your mother's too. She even took out a small patch of her own hair. This went on for about an hour or two before we finally had to call Dr. Henry and he came out to the house and gave her a shot. Dr. Henry tried to laugh it off, asking Esther if she had any tiger blood in the family, but I knew then and there that things were not going to go easily with Grace."

Jory had never heard this story before.

"When she was little she hated taking off her clothes at night. Hated it. She threw such fits that Esther and I finally gave in and simply let her sleep in whatever she'd been wearing that day, shoes and all." Her father laughed softly. "One night I got the idea that this had gone on long enough, so I literally held her down on the floor and stripped off her clothes and tried to stuff her into her pajamas." Her father shook his head. "She kicked me so hard I was bruised for weeks. And the most amazing part was what she said afterward. She looked at me with those eyes of hers — those eyes that saw right through to whatever was most weak and false in you — and said, 'If you knew how much I hated you, you'd hate me, too.' "

Jory stared at her father.

"And she was only four years old."

"Grip said that she was more brave than the rest of us. That her life was harder than ours."

Jory could tell that her father had already reached the end of his willingness to hear about Grip's thoughts, but she hazarded one more comment. "He said that I was more like him — that we were more weak and selfish."

Her father leaned forward and put his hands on his knees. "There are different kinds of bravery. And selfishness."

The streetlight on the corner winked on with a small, almost imperceptible hum. Almost immediately several moths swirled upward, as if drawn magnetically into its cone of light. Jory watched their futile flutterings.

"Jory," her father said in a voice so quiet she could barely hear it. "I need you to stay with me." She could hear him making some sound now in his throat. Perhaps he was merely swallowing. "Please."

Jory felt something close to shock. She held perfectly still, and it was as if her heart and breath and blood had stopped. In the silence, Jory thought she could hear a moth's wings battening against the searing heat of the streetlight bulb. It would be like flying into the sun, she thought. Like turning your face into the brightest, whitest, most brilliant light. Like deliberately diving into a beautiful, self-obliterating pool of fire.

Would that be such a terrible and foolish trade: a moment's pure and incandescent joy in exchange for an eternity of darkest nothingness? She closed her eyes tight and tighter, and for almost a second allowed herself to imagine that she still knew how to pray.

CHAPTER TWENTY-THREE

On the drive home from the Greyhound bus station, Jory's father said nothing, but when he parked the Buick in the driveway he braked too late and ran into the front of the garage, completely splintering one panel of the wooden door. For a second afterward, he and Jory merely sat in the car, the two of them silently registering the slight concussive feeling of having smacked into something so solid. Then her father got out of the car and trudged toward the front door without even looking at the damage. Jory, too, simply followed her father inside the house. She watched as he walked through the kitchen and into the interior of the garage, where he took a pair of bolt cutters and cut the two locks on the bomb shelter's door that he had placed there back in November, as if to symbolically undo what had already occurred there. Then he went down below.

■ ■ ■ ■

In the past — the distant past — her father had gone down to the bomb shelter only on weekend evenings, or maybe when he was bored or needed to escape momentarily from the sheer number of females in the household, but now he seemed to want to live there, enclosed by the windowless walls and his headphones, his vision and hearing narrowed and focused to a manageable limit. Now he spent most evenings shut down there, listening to his ham radio and speaking softly to people in faraway countries, leaning forward and carefully turning one of the dials on his ham radio receiver, his head cocked as if listening for some vital signals from a distant planet.

All of April had gone by in pretty much this fashion, her father finding out each day how the weather was in Heidelberg and Hamburg and Tlaquepaque. And now May was beginning to creep past without her mother returning or her father going back to his teaching job at the college. Back in November, he had asked for two months bereavement leave, but now, Jory knew, it had been more than five.

Plus, for reasons that made no sense at

all, he wouldn't let her go back to school. He needed her here at home, he said. Which was somewhat absurd since he spent all his time entombed in the bomb shelter, while Jory sat on the couch and read and reread every book from the several bookcases in their house. Each evening she tried to make something that resembled a dinner, tuna salad on toast or spaghetti from a can, and each evening the two of them would sit at the dining table and try to eat this food and try to find something to talk about. Then her father would slink back to the garage and to his friends from foreign lands, and Jory would be left alone, staring at the blue princess phone sitting silently in its little cutout alcove in the wall.

One night, Jory pulled the phone book up onto the table again and opened it to the inside of the front cover. A note was taped here with *Important Phone #s* inscribed in blue ink in her father's firm printing. The numbers that followed were to be used only in emergency situations. With only a moment's hesitation, she dialed the numeral 1 and the long number that followed it. After several rings during which Jory's heart continued to thud, her aunt Annette said hello in a voice that sounded both cheery and unbothered until she realized who it was on the other end. "JoryAnne," her aunt said then, her voice sounding like Jory's mother's, but without the same undertone of sadness and disapproval. "Your mom is taking a little nap out by the pool. Do you want me to wake her up?"

Jory thought about this. "No," she said. "I guess not. Is Frances around?"

"Well, sure, honey. I'll get her." Her aunt's voice took on a note of concern. "How're you doing there? With your dad and all?"

"Oh, just fine," said Jory. "Dad and I were actually getting ready to go running in a few minutes. We just bought some new jogging shoes and now we're going to go try them out." This was a lie. Jory had tried and failed yet again today to get her father to even leave the house.

"That's wonderful! What else have you been up to? Has Oren gone back to teaching yet?"

"He starts tomorrow," said Jory. This was also untrue.

"That's terrific! Well, tell him hello from me — and, Jory, if you ever need anything, you know you can just call, right?" Her aunt cleared her throat and lowered her voice slightly. "Your mom is finally getting the rest she needs — thank goodness. And you should see her tan! You'd hardly recognize her. She was just a ghost when she got off that bus. I mean it — she looked like one of those pictures of women from the TB camps. I took her straight to my doctor and he gave her a shot of vitamin B12 and he said plenty of sun and plenty of rest, and absolutely no stress, so that's what we're doing — just following doctor's orders." Her aunt seemed to have suddenly run out of steam. "Oh, and here's your little sister," she said, a trifle breathlessly.

There was a moment or two of silence, and then Frances's voice peeped up and into Jory's ear. "Hello?" her sister said, and Jory could feel tears immediately gathering where there had been none only a moment before.

"Hey, Franny," said Jory, trying to steady her voice. "What're you doing?"

"I'm blowing up my swimming tube. It's a sea monster like Beany and Cecil, Aunt Annette bought it for me, and the pool has a heater in it so you can swim anytime, even after dinner." Frances sounded very excited. "I got some sandals too, they're called huaraches, and I'm even going to wear them to school."

"To school?"

"I'm going to go to Parkview Elementary. It's only one block away and they have palm trees and a tire swing and some of the girls are Japanese."

"What do you mean? You're going to school there?"

"Not till next week. We have to get my school supplies first. I have young Mrs. Moto for my teacher."

"What?" Jory could now hear her aunt saying something in the distance. Something corrective sounding. Jory could hear Frances having a quick consultation with her aunt.

"Mrs. *Ya-ma-moto.* Mrs. Yamamoto is my teacher."

"Frances," said Jory. "How is Mom — is she okay?"

"She's all right." There was a moment's silence. "She still sleeps a lot. But she swims in the pool sometimes and we're looking for apartments that are close to the beach and take pets, 'cause we're going to get a canary. Remember Mr. Sunny?"

"Frances, you need to come back. Dad and I need you and Mom to come back."

There was another silence.

"Did you hear what I said?"

"But I'm learning to swim," said Frances.

Jory could hear her aunt saying something in the background.

"And I get to wear shorts to school and

643

there's a tire swing that everyone takes turns on."

Jory could hear Frances's voice growing suddenly fainter and then her aunt was on the phone. "Jory, doll, I'll have your mom call you back in a little bit, okay? Just as soon as she wakes up and eats some dinner, all right? We're having taco salad tonight and it's your mom's favorite, so I've got to run right now and get some avocados down at Vons, but we'll talk to you later, okay?"

"Yes," said Jory. "Okay, sure. Good-bye." And then she hung up the phone.

She sat in the chair next to the dining room table with her hand still on the telephone's receiver. She held her hand there on the phone's smooth pale blue plastic, feeling its unblemished smoothness. It was such a terrible and unimportant thing. She put her hands in her lap and tried to make her mind be filled with nothing. She closed her eyes and leaned back in her chair and then plugged both of her ears with her fingers. She squeezed her eyes shut as hard as she could. It was sort of like being underwater — the slightly shifting light source and the softly muffled sound of her own blood beating in her veins.

She took her fingers out of her ears and that was when she heard it — the sound of a tinkling kind of carnival music. Without hesitating or bothering to think, she stood up and raced toward the front door, shoved it open, and then stood in the front yard for a moment, listening. The music seemed to be coming from a few blocks down the street, its familiar tune winding into her heart as seamlessly as a snake coiling up a smooth young tree.

She began striding awkwardly down the block in the direction of the music, her heart keeping time with her strides. She was half jogging as she passed the Newmans' and the Lockeys' and the Reisensteins' and then the houses on the next block that belonged to people whose last names she didn't know. The neighborhood seemed to shimmer in the early evening air and a car in a driveway glinted in the low-slanting sunlight, as did someone's metal mailbox and the waxy leaves on a low hedge of holly bushes. The tiny edges of each plant and the bark on tree trunks — all of it was as specific and individual as if she were seeing it all through a type of magnifying, illuminating, beautifying glass. The cracks in the sidewalk, the amazing bits of multifaceted gravel! Her heart and blood and vision and everything that made up her body was operating at a new, higher, more perfect level. It was as if she had been sick, very sick, and now suddenly, at a moment's notice, she was well.

At the corner right before the little grassy parcel of land called God's Park, she stopped and tried to catch her breath. The ice cream truck was parked next to the curb, its music still going. Grip was sitting in the grass, just as he had been that night he had held her hand and they had first talked about Grace. Jory could feel her features rearranging themselves into one anxious configuration after another as the many things inside her collided and spread outward across her face. With a bravery born out of pure need, she took the final steps forward, then sat down in the grass and gazed at him.

"Hey," he said.

He looked exactly the same, even though his hair had been cut conventionally short. How could she have thought that she'd forgotten a single aspect of his face, his dog-colored eyes, the slight dimple in his chin where no hair grew? She tried to slow her breathing and look away casually as he stood up, brushed off his pants, and then stepped up into the truck and turned its loudspeaker off. The music wound down and died away. Grip jumped back out of the truck and sat down on the ground a few inches closer to her than before.

"How are you?" he asked. He looked at her and she couldn't believe how long she had gone without being looked at in this very specific, particular way. By him.

She shrugged helplessly. She couldn't possibly explain anything from the last six months, plus the corners of her mouth kept tugging upward in a way that was beyond her control. She had thought she would never see him again. "When did you get out?" she said.

"A few days ago."

"You still have your truck." She realized that this made no sense and that she was just saying anything that came to her. She examined him while trying not to look like that was what she was doing. He was thinner maybe, and his hair looked so strange cut short — just like anyone else's. He was wearing an orange T-shirt that she remembered from before and a pair of baggy corduroy pants that she didn't. She couldn't believe that even after everything that had happened, she still felt the exact same wondrous airy weightlessness in her head that she always did whenever he was next to her. Of all the many things that had changed, this was the one that hadn't.

"Your hair's longer," he said to her, picking up a strand of it and rubbing the ends of it between his fingers.

"Yours isn't."

"Regulation standards, ma'am," he said. "County jail rules. No longer than the shirt collar."

"Are you all right?"

"Are you?" He seemed reluctant to let go of her strand of hair.

Jory still couldn't decide how to answer this. "I'm alive," she said. "I guess."

"Where is she?"

Jory squinted up at him. For a second she wasn't quite sure what he meant. She looked down at the blades of grass between her feet. At her still moccasined feet. "She's nowhere. She's in a blue vase — an urn. She was supposed to be buried next to my grandparents, but my dad wouldn't do it. He put her in our bomb shelter, I think. He hid her away somewhere. Hid *it*, I mean."

Grip wore a sudden pained expression. "He had her cremated?"

Jory looked confused. "I don't think it was just his idea."

"Whose was it?"

"I don't know — does it even matter?" Jory felt a small pang of annoyance and was also hurt for reasons she didn't want to examine.

"I guess it doesn't."

Jory smoothed down the nap on one of her moccasins. The suede was darker in color than when he'd given them to her and even stained in some spots. Grip's feet were bare. She surreptitiously examined the curly red hairs that fanned delicately across the tops of his naked toes.

"I was sitting there in my cell drinking coffee out of my no-handled cup and I saw this little article on page three of the *Arcade*. I almost didn't read it." He paused. "They didn't use her name, but I knew in my gut it was her."

Jory pulled her knees up to her chest. Her heart was still beating at a rapid rate. She felt sick almost, thrilled and nervous and wonderful and sick just from looking at him and hearing him speak.

"What happened?"

Jory knew what he was asking. "She took my mom's pills," she said. This was the first time she had ever talked about this with anyone and the words felt odd in her mouth. Illicit almost. "And then she shut herself in the bomb shelter. My dad found her."

Grip was watching her as she spoke. She could see him picturing these events in his head. "Oh, Jesus," he said, and put his face in his hands. Jory could barely hear what he was muttering, but she knew it was bad. He lifted his head. "Did she leave a note? Did she say anything to you beforehand?"

"She beat me up pretty bad for telling my dad you were coming." Jory could feel herself starting to smile. "She hit me hard." For some reason this fact still pleased her. "I don't know if she wrote a note or anything. My dad wouldn't let anyone go down there afterward. Maybe he hid it." She shrugged.

"I still can't believe this," he said. "While I was in there it didn't quite seem real, you know? I kept thinking that there was still a chance it was all a mistake."

Jory didn't respond to this. She felt oddly envious of even his temporary disbelief.

"Where's your sister? The little one, I mean?" Grip glanced down the block. A trifle cautiously, Jory thought.

"In California. With my mom."

"What for? Vacation?"

"Sort of."

"Why didn't you go?

Jory shrugged. It was strange how few real answers there were to his questions.

"You mean it's just you and your dad? For how long? When's your mom coming back?"

Jory stared across the lot at the ice cream

650

truck, at the several spots on its side where the blue-painted lettering was starting to fade. "I don't know. I don't think they are coming back."

Grip was now plucking pieces of grass out of the ground. He pulled up a blade of grass and began tearing it into small bits. "Maybe you should go to California too."

"What? Why?"

Grip ran a hand through his shortened hair. A gesture that reminded Jory of her father. "I just mean that maybe it'd be good for you to live somewhere else . . . with someone else."

Jory felt stunned by the unexpectedness of this conversation. "My dad needs me," she said. "He's not the same anymore."

"I hope not," said Grip.

Jory made an exasperated sound in the back of her throat. "There's no point in still being mad at him now. He probably hates you too, you know, but it doesn't matter anymore."

Grip shook his head again. "You don't get it. I don't hate him, or maybe I do, but it's not for the reasons you think." He reached out and put a hand on her bare arm. "I'm telling you, this is not a good situation for you." Grip turned her arm over so that her hand lay palm up. He lightly touched the

651

tendons that ran up her wrist. "I'm thinking of taking off for Phoenix in a day or two. My mom's there and she said I could stay for a while. Until I find a job or something." He glanced at Jory. "You could come visit."

"I'm not going anywhere." Jory's own surety surprised her. She pulled her arm away, even though his fingers had felt wonderful. "My dad doesn't have anybody else now."

"Yeah? Why do you think that is?"

Jory was beyond amazed at the turns this conversation was taking. "Because my mom is . . . my *mom*. This is what she does when things get too hard. She goes into her bedroom and shuts the door or she goes to Blackfoot and gets shock treatments. Now she's in San Diego sitting by a pool and letting her sister take care of her."

For a moment neither one of them said anything.

"I should never have let her go that night. That night at Hope House." Grip sounded almost as if he were talking to himself. He smacked himself in the forehead with his fist. "I've thought about it a million times since then. I should never have let him take her."

Jory gazed at him in silence. Absolutely none of this was how she had imagined it.

No one was saying or doing any of the right things. Not even close.

"I could have stopped him and I didn't. But I knew the cops wouldn't believe me over him — why would they? And I was scared to go to jail." He hung his head slightly. "She told me she didn't know what she'd do if he made her go back, and look what happened. I should have had the fucking balls." He pushed himself up to his feet and then stood over her. "I was a stupid miserable coward."

"No, you weren't."

"Oh, yeah — I sure as hell was. I could have told the cops that she was scared of him, or at least threatened to. She'd still be here now, right now, if I'd had the nerve."

"What are you *talking* about?" Jory stood up and brushed the dirt off the back of her pants. She stared down at Grip. "Grace wasn't scared of my dad — she adored him."

Grip seemed to be debating something and he gave Jory a long evaluative look, one that seemed to contain both anger and sorrow. At last he sighed, letting out a long, almost quavering breath. "He killed her, Jory."

Jory stood there blinking as if trying to slow or clear her vision. For a second, she felt absolutely nothing, the expression on her face one of flat incomprehensibility.

"She would never have killed herself. Not voluntarily." Grip shook his head. "Not with the baby." His head shaking continued. "He pushed her into it."

Jory was dumbstruck. Both by what he was saying and the strange assurance with which he was saying it.

"He backed her into a corner." Grip stood up and began pacing in the grass now as if he'd been storing these words up for months. "Just like she was some kind of dog. Like he owned her and *he* was going to decide what would happen to her."

"That's not true," said Jory, her voice rising in pitch. "He was trying to protect her."

"From what?" Grip turned away from her and threw an invisible something — a blade of grass or a thread from his shirt maybe — across the grassy lot. "It was completely his fault. He might as well've handed her those pills and a glass of water."

Jory could feel herself breathing much too fast. "Grace chose to do what she did all by herself. She *chose* to kill herself. And her baby." Jory felt sick for saying these words. Sick and traitorous.

Grip stared at her, a sad, almost pitying look on his face. "Your father is a megalomaniac or something. He's like an egotistical freak who has to control everything in his own little world. He thinks he's a so-called god and that his word is law and that everyone should do exactly as he says. Or else."

Jory could hear herself scrambling for words. "He said the exact same thing about you!" She gave a sort of hollow-sounding laugh. "That you needed to have other people admire you to feed your own ego, that you tried to manipulate people, like Grace and me. That you needed attention." She could no longer remember the exact specifics of her father's admonishment. "He said you were bad — that you were no good." It had come back to her. "That you were a *criminal.*"

"That's bullshit." Grip reached out one hand and took her elbow. "I know it hurts to hear these things, Jory, but you needed to find out what he was like sooner or later. For your own good."

"You're wrong, completely and totally wrong," she said, stepping back from him and out of his grasp. "And if you only knew my father even the littlest, tiniest bit, you'd know how utterly wrong you are. Grace was crazy. She had . . . problems." Jory turned away from him and realized that her knee-caps were shaking. "My dad had to take her to a psychiatrist and the psychiatrist thought she was so nuts that she should be put in the hospital, that she should be *institutionalized,* but my dad wouldn't let them because that's how much he loved her. And he's sick now because of what happened to her. He can't even leave our house. He's skinny and he can't go to work or run or sleep or do anything because of how terrible he feels — because this has ruined his life — because of what she did to *him.* Because she killed herself to get back at him." Jory suddenly gasped and put her hands over her mouth.

"That's right," said Grip. "That's why she did it — to get back at him. For all the really *rotten* things he did to her."

Jory could not seem to stop her kneecaps from doing this utterly strange movement. She turned and then began to walk and then to run haphazardly, blindly, across the grass and over the curb.

"Jory! Hey! Wait — *wait!*"

She could hear Grip calling her, but she didn't stop. She ran down the sidewalk, her breath catching and her eyes blurred with tears. She could hear herself making noise as she ran, some kind of strange and ragged talking she was doing to herself, garbled words or cries that made no sense.

She ran and she didn't stop until she was

inside the house and had locked the door behind her. For a moment or two she leaned there against the door frame, gasping. And then, as if helpless to resist, she rushed to the front window.

He was gone.

Jory stumbled down the hall, her hands held against her mouth.

At Grace's closed bedroom door she stopped. She opened the door and stood looking at her older sister's small white metal bed and her white-painted dresser, her nightstand and the milk glass lamp that sat on the dresser, and the hooked oval rug placed directly in front of the tall wooden rocking chair. This was exactly how her sister's room had always looked. The only thing out of place was the old blue suitcase that was perched at the end of the bed, opened wide and still waiting to be packed. Jory turned away from this last sight, but it was too late, much too late to unsee anything. A large leather Bible sat on the dresser top with an unused bottle of Wind Song perfume next to it and next to that stood a little photo in a gold frame: a picture of the three Quanbeck sisters on a sandbar in Banks, Idaho. They were all smiling and wearing identical red bandannas to keep the wind and sand out of their hair. Their father had taken the picture and because the sun was behind him his shadow cast a large dark blob across a portion of their bare legs. Jory remembered that day. Their mother had discovered their Siamese cat in the process of giving birth and so she hustled them all into the car and insisted that their father drive them all the way to Banks. Their mother made them stay at the river's shore until the sun went down and she was quite sure that the bloody and most likely obscene event back home was over and done with. Her mother's caution — which Jory learned about only later — was ironically short-sighted since the very next day Frances discovered the mother cat in a corner of the laundry room in the process of calmly eating her one remaining kitten.

Jory picked up the photo and carried it with her over to her sister's wooden desk, where she sat down in the desk chair and opened the desk's lone drawer. Inside the drawer was a copy of *Discipline: The Glad Surrender* by Elisabeth Elliot and a red leather Spanish New Testament. There was also a white silk bookmark with the Beatitudes printed on it and a handful of gold cross pins that were given out for perfect attendance at Sunday School. Next to the pins was a dried carnation with a hat pin stuck through its stem, an empty beaded coin purse from Yellowstone, a tiny white tube of Avon Kiss Me Quick lipstick, a small plastic giraffe wearing a halo, an instruction booklet for a Timex watch, and a green spiral notepad. Jory pulled the notepad out of the drawer and put it on top of the desk. She flipped open the notebook's cover and felt a terrible wrenching deep in her chest as she was confronted with her sister's childish straight up-and-down writing, its modest loops and careful curls as familiar to her as her own. *The Keys to a Happy Life: (1) Live only to please Jesus. (2) Do not concern yourself with what others think of you. (3) Keep your eyes firmly on the heavenly prize. (4) Make certain that your outward adornment is befitting of a child of God. (5) Give of your time, your money, and your possessions to the poor, and to the poor in spirit. (6) Spread the good news of Christ to everyone you meet. (7) Be humble and patient. (8) Forgive those who harm you, just as Jesus has forgiven you.* There were checkmarks next to each of these numbers; some items had more checks than others. Jory turned to the next page. *Seven and eight are the hardest. At least for me they are. This means that I need to rededicate myself each day to being more Christlike and less like the selfish and petty human being that I am.* Jory turned to the next page. *Weaknesses,* it read. *Eating more than my share. Fighting with Jory. Thinking bad thoughts about Mom. Wishing I were prettier. Being jealous of Charlene Doremus.* Charlene Doremus! Jory's mouth dropped open involuntarily. She reread the list. But we didn't fight *that* much, she thought. Did we? *Did we?* Her heart felt pinched and small. Bruised, almost. She turned another page in the notebook, but it was blank, as were all the rest of the pages in the notepad. She flipped through the pages again and again, but there was nothing else to see.

At her sister's closet her throat closed tight at the sight of the limply hanging skirts and blouses, the somewhat worn and scuffed size 8.5 leather shoes that still held the impressions of Grace's very particular feet. Jory turned away with a quick movement and slid the closet door closed behind her.

She stood in front of Grace's white-painted dresser and pulled out each drawer in turn, running her hands blindly through her sister's other belongings while barely daring to look at them: socks and underwear and bras, pajamas and slips and T-shirts and pedal pushers, wool sweaters, an old button-down shirt of their father's that she must have begun wearing after she'd gotten back from Mexico. The material and the slight weight of each worn item seemed to hold within it some essence or magic transferred there by its wearer. They were just clothes, Jory tried to tell herself, just random pieces of fabric that could have belonged to any-one. But it was the belonging that was the thing. The possessing, the owning, the wear-ing. Each of these items surely still had cells of her sister clinging to them. Little bits of her. Jory had the sudden wish to climb inside the drawer and live there, to sleep and rest there as if in a cottony cocoon, swaddled in the same clothes her sister had worn next to her very own body. With a feel-ing of bold inevitability, Jory pulled a faded green T-shirt out of the middle drawer and looked at it. *Only Visiting This Planet,* the shirt read in round, bubbly script. She held the shirt up to her face and breathed in as deeply as she could. She let its slightly salty, slightly detergent-scented folds fall across her face and neck and she held the shirt there across her eyes and nose and mouth, rocking herself back and forth on her knees. She put her hands deep inside the shirt and pulled its neckline over her head, tugging it down and over her own. In the back of the bottom drawer was an old pair of blue bedroom slippers that Jory found herself hugging unaccountably to her chest. She had still found nothing revealing here, no notes or photos, no clues about anything, no new hints about what had happened that might tell her how to feel or what to think. There were only the lived-in and left-behind belongings of her sister, her strange, wonderful, hideously frustrating sister who would never write in her notepad or wear her pajamas or fight with Jory or strive for holiness or hide her truest thoughts from her family ever, ever again.

Jory held the slippers tightly to her T-shirt-covered chest and moved over to the bed and pulled back the bedspread and crawled beneath. The sheets smelled of nothing but laundry detergent, as did the pillow. She turned the pillow over and breathed in deeply. It, too, smelled only of Tide. She wasn't sure if she was relieved or heartbroken, or if it was even possible to be both. It wasn't dark outside — there was still some softly warm light slanting through the window blinds, but Jory put her hands inside each of the slippers as if they were mittens and held them up next to her face and lay there listening to the sounds of the house: the soft ticking of the clock on the dresser and the even quieter sound of the few cars shushing by on the street outside. There was no carnival music to be heard, not a single bewitching, tinkling note. Jory guessed that she would probably never hear that peculiarly magical tune again. She could feel the babylike softness of one of the terry cloth slippers against her cheek as she drifted toward sleep, and for a second she even thought she could smell a hint of something very Grace-like in the room, something ineffable but close, mysterious, and utterly singular. The scent of her older sister, who would live on only inside the people who had loved and perhaps harmed her the very most.

The next morning Jory took a scalding hot shower that felt wonderful as it beat on the back of her neck. She couldn't remember how long it had been since she had done this, showered and used lotion all over her skin. She examined herself in the steamy mirror. Her breasts were actually slightly bigger now, although this realization didn't quite thrill her in the way that she had expected it to. Nothing was the way she had expected it to be.

Jory pulled her pants back on and then carefully eased Grace's faded green T-shirt on. She brushed her wet hair until the tangles were completely gone.

Her father was at the dining room table. The *Arco Arcade* was spread out in front of him, but he didn't seem to be reading any of it. Jory sat down across from him and for an extended moment she examined him.

His hair was slightly messy and a mechanical pencil was clipped haphazardly to his pants belt loop. The shoestrings in his long, worn oxfords were two quite different shades of brown. He was much sloppier than he used to be, more wrinkled and shopworn and quite a bit skinnier, and sometimes he didn't seem to know that she was talking to him, but he was her father. He would never be anything other than that. Even if he had done the worst possible things for dubious reasons, even if he had ended up destroying the very things he was trying to protect, he had loved her and cared for her and excused her flaws and faults since the moment she was born. And he continued to watch over her with the kind of firm devotion any real god should show, but rarely does. In return, she gave him this: immunity from accusation and a firm pedestal on which to stand, above and immortal. Was that too much to ask? But it didn't really matter, this question or its answer, because she knew that as much as she might want to, much as she might try to, she would never really be able to see him any differently — or feel any differently about him, either — no matter what.

Their new shoes were blue with bright orange stripes and her father looked dubious even as he tied them snuggly around his feet. They had each gotten a pair of the exact same type, her father's in size 11 and hers in size 7.5. He glanced down at his shoes again, as if they were a foreign appendage he wasn't quite sure about. "Can we wait for the sun to go down a bit more? I only really like to do this once it gets good and dark." Her father sat gingerly down in the broken lawn chair and Jory sat down in the grass next to him. The ground felt cool and solidly lumpy beneath her.

For a while neither of them said anything. They just sat and gazed ahead of them at the sky. The evening air was soft and quiet, no lawn mowers or crickets or carnival music. There was the faint sound of a screen door opening and then slamming shut somewhere down the block.

"When I try to think about space going on forever," Jory said, clearing her throat, "I can't really even picture it in my head. I can't really believe it. I always imagine that there's an edge or a stopping point some-where."

"No one can picture anything infinite." Her father reached down and put his hand on her knee and gave it a squeeze. "All we know are things with edges and ends. I think that's why people get bothered by looking at the ocean sometimes, because they can't really see the end of it. It's too huge. That's why the moon shots made such a difference — you know, the pictures Armstrong and Aldrin took of earth from out in space. All of a sudden we got to see the edges of our world, and I think it made everything seem both smaller and bigger all at the same time."

"Is that why you believe in God? Because it gives things edges?"

"No," said her father. "I believe in God because it dissolves the edges." He removed his hand from her leg and Jory shivered slightly, the evening's cool air seeming almost autumnlike. "If there's a god, then there doesn't have to be an end to things," he said, "to space, to time, to life. Things can be bigger than whatever it is we're merely able to see or measure."

"But they already are," said Jory. "Mole-cules and atoms and black holes and quarks.

Everything is plenty huge even without God."

"Well," her father said, "yes, so to speak."

"You always told me that space went on forever," said Jory. "And that there were more stars than anyone could ever count no matter how long they went on counting."

"That's true," her father said. "Pretty much."

"And everything that's dark is actually full of light, and all things that seem to be holding still are really moving, right?" The night sky was coming on in earnest now, its purpling dye flattening and darkening the enormous bowl that was upended over the earth.

"I've always believed that science and religion don't have to be mutually exclusive."

"Grace says . . . Grace said . . . that science is just there to uncover the watermark of God. That all of nature is merely the outward sign of an omnipotent being."

"Yes," he said. "Grace would be certain to correct us if we'd gone astray in our theological reasoning."

This statement seemed to put a temporary end to their conversation.

The sky was now an almost midnight blue, and so dark that she had to strain to

667

see her father's face or even read his expression. Was this what faith was? Just a believing and hoping and trusting in something, regardless of the evidence to the contrary? And if so, what kind of idiotic belief system was that? The sky suddenly seemed to bend or slip, revealing a radiant white slice of moon where before there had been only darkness. It reminded Jory of a lily's trumpet just beginning to unfurl.

"Jory — do you think I've done wrong by you girls?"

Her father was looking at her in a new, oddly fearful way, and waiting hopefully for her response.

How was it possible to care deeply about people and not hurt them? To touch them and not leave terrible marks? Her father said that even meteors left fingerprints: imprints as distinct and specific as those produced by human hands, little rills or valleys that revealed the meteor's size and weight and velocity. And that sometimes if a falling star was large enough, its impact could change a planet's course forever — that simply by touching the planet's surface it could eternally alter its course through space.

"I love you, Dad," she said, and as she said it she realized that this was suddenly, utterly, and inviolably true. She hoped that this one small truth might be answer enough to make up for the scars that his loving, and hers, had already left behind.

Her father's shy smile bloomed at her through the dusk. "Well," he said, giving his lawn chair's armrest a gentle tap, "we might as well give these fancy new shoes of ours a trial run." He stood up and swung his arms above his head. "Okay," he said. "Let's start out slow and just see how it goes."

The two of them now, father and daughter, began jogging around the perimeter of the backyard, next to each other in the nighttime air. Nothing seemed important enough to say. Jory listened to her father's breathing and felt an awkward sense of intimacy with this human body running so close beside her, deliberately matching its strides to hers. She could hear, but no longer see, his footsteps, so she had to trust that he knew the way, and that any of the ground's rough spots or upheavals had already been worn away by years and years of her father tracing his careful, deliberate orbit through the darkness.

ACKNOWLEDGMENTS

I am deeply indebted to my phenomenal agent, PJ Mark, whose sharp-eyed vision for this book enhanced its scope and meaning in ways both great and small, and to Marya Spence for her excellent revision suggestions. Endless thanks are due my editor, the extraordinary Allison Lorentzen; her wisdom and encouragement made the editorial process surprisingly pain free. I am also grateful to Diego Nuñez and to my copyeditors and proofreaders at Viking for their tireless attention. And an enormous thank you goes to Paul Buckley for his amazing design work, which, along with Alessandro Gottardo's evocative illustration, made the book's cover a thing of genuine beauty.

I am forever grateful to the Wallace Stegner Program at Stanford University, to Elizabeth Tallent, my beloved John L'Heureux, and particularly Tobias Wolff, who helped me immeasurably with the first draft of this story. Thanks go, too, to the University of Virginia and its excellent instructors: John Casey, Ann Beattie, and the wondrous Deborah Eisenberg.

I also want to thank Bill Clegg and Michelle Velasco, two early readers of my manuscript, for their many insightful comments. I am ever beholden to Andrew Altschul, Scott Hutchins, and Josh Weil, whose continued friendship, generosity, and aid I treasure highly.

To my sisters, Constance Ford and Gail Roberts, who shared with me many of the experiences portrayed on these pages, I owe a deep debt of gratitude and love that cannot be adequately expressed here. This is equally true of my obligation to Tim Brelinski, whose assistance has been wise, unfailing, and inexhaustible. And to Max Boyd, my child and chief adviser, my son and fundamental support system, goes all my love and more besides.

ABOUT THE AUTHOR

Val Brelinski was born and raised in Nampa, Idaho, the daughter of devout evangelical Christians. She was a recent Wallace Stegner Fellow at Stanford, where she was also a Jones Lecturer in fiction writing. She received an MFA from the University of Virginia, and her writing has been published in *VQR* and *The Rumpus.* She lives in Northern California.